CHOOSING

GUILT

Also by Frances Aylor:

Novels:
Money Grab

Anthologies:
Deadly Southern Charm
Malice Domestic: Mystery Most Theatrical
Murder by the Glass
Virginia is for Mysteries, volume iii

CHOOSING

GUILT

A Novel of Suspense

Frances Aylor

Hastings Bay Press

ISBN 978-0-9987959-2-8

Hastings Bay Press

Cover by Vince Robertson

Acknowledgments

This book was inspired by a Rhine River cruise I took several years ago. While in Interlaken, just like my character Corinne, I watched the colorful rectangular wings of the paragliders swoop over my head. Fascinated, I signed up to try it out for myself.

While I was up in the air, I asked my tandem pilot if anyone ever jumped off the mountain and panicked. He said it sometimes happened when there was a reluctant member of a group who only participated because of peer pressure. That comment inspired Luke's paragliding misadventures at the beginning of the book.

Many thanks to everyone who helped in the writing and publishing of *Choosing Guilt*, including:

- my husband, children, family, and friends who always offer encouragement and suggestions.
- our friends Ed and Susan who organized the Rhine River cruise and invited us to join them.
- Sisters in Crime and Sisters in Crime–Central Virginia, for educating me in the craft and business of writing.

Chapter 1

LOOKING DOWN was a big mistake.

My pilot Edgar, strapped tightly to my back, pointed out the sites as casually as if we were on a tour bus rolling slowly down a city street, instead of paragliding 4,000 feet in the air. "The Swiss Alps are in front of us. That's Eiger to the left, and Monch beside it. Jungfrau is to their right. It's over 13,000 feet, one of the tallest mountains in Europe."

"Eiger, Monch, Jungfrau," I repeated. The snow-coated jagged peaks were magnificent, stupendous, unforgettable—all those overwrought adjectives that travel writers tossed out like fairy dust to lure tourists to Switzerland—but all I could think about was the churning sensation in my stomach. I concentrated on staring straight ahead. As long as I didn't look down, I would be all right.

I'd been stupid to let Corinne pressure me into this. But she was my biggest client. Kesbolt Consulting, my public relations firm, would have folded a year ago without her. Lilly and I still weren't making a lot of money, but at least we could now cover the outrageous rent on our tiny New York office.

Corinne, mesmerized by the colorful fabric rectangles that swooped all day across the cloudless Interlaken sky, had roped us in last night at dinner. "Tomorrow we've got to go paragliding. Who's with me?"

"Count me in." Corinne's son Kyle flashed the charismatic smile that went viral a few years ago in one of those *Forty under Forty* media articles about up-and-coming entrepreneurs. His enthusiasm was tough to resist, and his good looks didn't hurt—he had inherited his mother's blue eyes, high cheekbones and golden hair. I'd felt a few sparks of possibility between us yesterday when we first met. After all, he was divorced, and I'd split with my boyfriend over a year ago.

But Emily, Kyle's twenty-something fiancée, had quickly warned me off. Now she threw her arms around his neck, her dark hair cascading possessively over his shoulder. "Can't wait to try it."

"Great." Kyle grinned. "What about you, Sis?"

Bronwyn, also blond and blue-eyed, was a pale reflection of her older brother, like a faded copy spit out by a printer low on ink. She compensated with heavy applications of eye shadow and light dustings of blush. "Wouldn't miss it." Bronwyn glanced at her husband. "Luke, can I talk you into this?"

"You do remember that I have a thing about heights, right?" Luke was a big guy, a former first-string tight end who had packed on pounds since his college football days. "Remember the Grand Canyon? Bright Angel Trail?"

Bronwyn crinkled her nose at the memory. "Oh, yeah. Not our best vacation."

Corinne bounced her fists on the table. "Let's all do it." Always eager for a new adventure, she reminded me of a high-flying circus performer, all glitz and glam and glitter, performing impossible maneuvers on a quivering tight wire. "Madeline, are you up for some fun?"

I shivered under the fur throw the waitress had given me—the beer garden's plastic-sheeted patio was colder than I expected for early May, with tall heat lamps spitting out inadequate waves of warmth—as I struggled to come up with an acceptable excuse to bow out. To me, paragliding seemed too much like skydiving, both of them perfect for crazies with a secret death wish.

But the underlying steeliness in Corinne's voice convinced me I'd better say yes. She planned to announce her candidacy to her family tomorrow night, and she'd brought me along on this trip—a riverboat cruise from Basel to Amsterdam—to get to know them and figure out how best to include them in her social media strategy. "Of course." I tucked loose strands of blond hair back under my cap. "Sounds great."

Corinne leaned toward her husband. "Fred, can we sign you up?"

"Not me. Someone has to be the adult in this group." Fred dug a fork into his rosti, a traditional Swiss dish of potatoes, bacon, cheese and onions, with a fried egg on top. "At least promise you'll leave your jewelry behind. I don't want to pick all those diamonds out of your mangled remains."

She sniffed. "There won't be any mangled remains. It's tandem paragliding, Fred. You've got an experienced pilot strapped to your back. He does all the work. All you do is sit back and enjoy the view."

"Sorry, not for me." Fred turned toward his youngest child, who looked nothing like her older siblings. She had her father's strong jawline, dark hair and thick eyebrows, which she plucked into high arches that gave her an odd, startled appearance, as though someone had just whispered into her ear the most astounding secret. "Holliss, you're not crazy enough to join them, are you? I don't think my unborn grandchild is quite ready for this much adventure."

Holliss and I had been buddies since college, when the shy freshman genius wandered into my senior-year advanced statistics class, a gawky sixteen-year-old so lost and alone that I was convinced she was a high-school student searching for her older sibling. But it didn't take my study group long to figure out she was the smartest person in the room. We never would have passed without her.

Now the thirty-year-old rubbed the gentle mound of her baby bump and smiled at her husband. "Randall and I will stay on the ground and take pictures of you guys."

Corinne turned back to Bronwyn's husband. "Luke, are you with us?"

His shoulders stiffened. It was one thing for him to hesitate when his wife encouraged him to go paragliding. But there was no way he could let his sixty-year-old mother-in-law do this while he stood on the sidelines. "Sure," he mumbled.

The next afternoon we navigated the steep, winding road up the mountain, the gears of our tour bus grinding as it labored to pull the grade.

"Let's go, let's go, let's go," Kyle chanted as the bus finally rolled to a stop.

The pilots unloaded the equipment, laying out the rectangular fabric wings one behind the other on a wide slope cleared of trees, stretching the white cords out to the sides.

Bronwyn hugged Luke. "Honey, I know this isn't your thing, but I'm glad you came with us."

"Listen, Bronwyn," Luke said, chewing his lower lip, "I don't think that …"

"I told her you'd never do it," Kyle said. "But here you are. Proud of you, bro."

"Yeah," Luke muttered.

A thin man in his forties, his complexion splotched with sunspots, approached me. "I'm Edgar, your pilot." He held up a black harness. "Put this on. It's loose around your legs so you can run."

"Run where?"

"Down that slope." He pointed. "Fast. As we get close to the edge of the cliff, the wind will catch the wing and pull us up. I'll be strapped right behind you, so we'll both go up together."

I watched the rest of them as I threaded my arms into the harness. Corinne was first in line. She and her pilot ran down the slope and were soon floating effortlessly in the blue sky. Kyle, Emily, Bronwyn and Luke followed behind and were quickly airborne.

"Our turn." Edgar checked my harness to make sure everything was fastened properly. We walked to the take-off point and he tapped my shoulder. "Off we go. Run."

I ran as fast as I could down the slope, trying not to think about what would happen if the wind didn't inflate the rectangular wing. And trying not to think about what would happen if it did. We floated up a foot and then came back down. I stumbled as my feet touched the ground.

"Keep running," Edgar yelled. "Don't stop."

I took off again, straining forward. At the edge of the cliff, as I stepped on nothing but air, the wind jerked us upward. Suddenly we were floating out over the valley.

"Put your feet up and sit back," Edgar said.

A thin seat popped out beneath me. The ride was easier than I expected. No noisy wind whipping into my face, only the caw of birds gliding effortlessly at eye level. No bouncing off air currents like an airplane hitting turbulence. I felt as steady as if I'd been curled up on my sofa at home, binge-watching all my favorite TV shows.

The ride was quiet. And smooth. And I was still terrified. Only a bit of fabric and a few lengths of rope separated me from certain death.

"Check out the lakes," Edgar said, nodding downward. "Brienz is to the east. Thun to the west. See the sun sparkling on the water? Isn't it beautiful?"

And then I did what I had promised myself I wouldn't do. I looked down. Everything below was tiny. The lakes. The buildings. The trees. Like the miniature model villages my nephews loved to set up beneath the Christmas tree each year. My heart pounded and my lungs strained for air.

"Want to do some tricks?" Edgar asked.

Before I had a chance to answer, he dipped the wing sideways. I felt weightless, all gravity suspended, as we swooshed through the air, rotating to the left and to the right, moving from side to side like a cork bobbing on water. The wind roared in my ears. I clamped my eyes shut as we slid parallel to the horizon.

"That's enough," I squealed. "Stop."

Edgar chuckled as he stabilized us, putting the pieces of the world back into their proper places, with the sky above us and the earth below. I relaxed as gravity pulled my ankles below my head. "You did great," he said. "One more circle and we're coming in for a landing."

A sudden scream made me jerk my head up. A paraglider high above me was doing the same side-to-side rotations that had almost caused me to lose my lunch. "Something's wrong with Luke," I said, recognizing his olive jacket. One hand tugged at the lines, while the other flailed wildly behind him, grabbing for the pilot. His sunglasses flew off and spiraled downward.

"Oh, he's fine," Edgar said, his voice calm. "Smitty's giving him one last thrill before they land."

"That's no thrill. His legs are thrashing around. He's in full panic." Forgetting my own fears, I stretched out toward him, kicking my feet like a swimmer surging through the ocean. "Get closer. We've got to help them."

"Stop that before you put us in a tailspin." Edgar rotated sideways for a better view. "The best thing we can do for them is stay out of their way. Give Smitty plenty of room to maneuver. He's a good pilot. He'll get your man down."

They bobbled as Smitty fought to maintain altitude. A crowd gathered in the landing field below us, people shouting as they pointed up at Luke. A few held up their phones, shooting videos.

I twisted back toward Edgar. "We've got to do something. They're coming down too fast."

"Stay calm. Smitty's got this under control."

"No, he hasn't. They need our help."

The nervous twitch of Edgar's mouth showed he knew Smitty was in trouble. "There's one thing we can try."

"What's that?"

"Bump them from underneath, to help them catch an air current. If we do it right, they'll pop up like a golf ball floating down the fairway."

"Bump into them? Have you ever done that before?"

"Not me. I've seen someone else do it. Saved a guy's life. But it's high risk. If our wings get tangled up, we'll all die."

I stared upward toward Luke and Smitty, my eyes squinting against the sun. In a few seconds they would be beyond help.

"Do it," I croaked, the syllables sticking to my tonsils.

I wanted to pull my words back as soon as I'd said them. What was I thinking? I wasn't one of those brave first responders who rushed into burning buildings to save little old ladies from crackling flames. I would never dive into a raging river to pull someone from a submerged car. Did I really think I could rescue Luke by slamming into him in mid-air? "Wait," I shrieked.

But Edgar was already manipulating the lines, rotating to the right and to the left, as we moved closer to the doomed men. "Hold on," he said.

My muscles tensed as I braced for impact, the painful crack of bone on bone. This was crazy. It would never work. In a few seconds, all four of us would plummet toward the ground.

I let out a desperate, ear-splitting screech of terror.

Chapter 2

AS WE SWOOPED toward them, Smitty frantically waved his arms. "Back off, back off. We can handle this."

Luke realized we were going to crash. He panted, struggling to scream, but only desperate gurgles spilled from his throat.

Edgar grunted and jerked hard on the lines, determined to put more distance between us. My feet flew out and my shoulders dropped as the wing shifted to the side. The move had been scary when he was doing it just for tricks. This time, when I knew we were fighting for our lives, it was terrifying. The harness straps dug into my shoulders. We were dropping much too fast, the tiny buildings and trees growing bigger as we lost altitude. As my world spun, I squeezed my eyes shut and promised God and Mother Nature and any other powers that might be listening that if I survived this, I would never go paragliding again.

Suddenly the wing lurched upward. "It's okay," Edgar said, his voice gruff. "We caught some air."

I opened my eyes as we stabilized, mentally checking my arms, my legs, my torso, to make sure I still had all my body parts. Everything seemed in order. "Is Luke all right? Did they make it?"

"They're fine. I knew Smitty could do it." He cleared his throat. "They're going back around, getting ready to land. Let's get down there."

Edgar and I circled lower until my feet finally touched the landing field. He helped me unsnap the harness, steering me clear of the lines attached to the wing. A few minutes later Smitty and Luke drifted by. As they landed, Luke stumbled and collapsed to his knees.

"Oh, my God, Luke," Bronwyn cried out, slicing through the onlookers that had gathered around him, "are you all right?"

Luke pulled off his gloves and dug his nails into the ground, anchoring himself to the earth. Spiky grass poked between his fingers.

"You scared me." Bronwyn knelt beside him. "I thought you were going to die. What happened up there?" She reached under his chin and unhooked his helmet. "Here, let's get this off you."

"So dizzy," he mumbled, his cheeks chalky white as she helped him to his feet.

"Give these folks some space." Kyle waved his arms, forcing the onlookers back. He poked Luke in the shoulder. "You were screaming like a girl during that last part. Emily got the whole thing on video. You're gonna die laughing when you see it."

Luke swatted at Kyle. "Don't touch me. I feel sick."

"Don't be such a drama queen." Kyle slapped Luke playfully on the back. "You got down okay. It's all good."

Luke pressed his fist hard against his mouth. "No. Not so good." He clutched his stomach and bent over. I pinched my nose to shut out the acrid smell as he hurled slimy bits of partially digested hamburger onto his olive jacket, Bronwyn's jeans and Kyle's favorite boots.

***

"Maybe we should cancel dinner?" Corinne said. She, Fred and I had gathered in the hotel lobby. "I'm afraid Luke and Bronwyn won't want to come."

I tried to listen to what she was saying. My body felt like it was still swooshing through the air to rescue Luke, my muscles tensing as I waited for impact. The paintings on the wall swayed in a queasy rhythm. I pressed my fingertips hard on the concierge's desk to steady myself.

"Are you all right, Madeline?" Fred asked.

"A bit of vertigo. Maybe we could sit?"

He herded us toward a seating area by the window. "You can't cancel dinner, Corinne," Fred said. "It's your big moment."

"But Luke …" she began.

"Luke's a tough guy. Humiliated, sure. Embarrassed as hell. But it's not like he broke any bones or anything. You need to stick to your plan."

"Madeline, what do you think?" Corinne asked.

The chartreuse-striped leaves of the nearby dracaena plant danced in the dappled light. Fighting nausea, I focused on holding my head steady. "We've scheduled your social media blitz to start first thing tomorrow. Unless you want to postpone that, you need to tell your family tonight. Of course, we could do it right here, in the hotel dining room."

Corinne sighed. With a flair for the dramatic, she had booked an ancient stone chateau for her announcement dinner, complete with crenelated walls, towering turrets and sweeping staircases. "I really had my heart set on dinner in a medieval castle."

"Then that's what we'll do," Fred said. "Let me talk to Bronwyn. She'll make sure Luke's there."

***

Thankfully, my dizziness had gone away by the time we headed out for dinner. At the castle entrance we were met by a smiling guide who led us on a tour of the sprawling rooms. Our last stop was the kitchen, where a huge cauldron hung in the massive, blackened fireplace. A dead rabbit, still bearing his fur, hung by his foot from a wooden ceiling beam, staring at me with a glassy eye. Beside him hung two red-bellied ducks, wings outstretched, their beaks dangling limply toward the floor.

Emily shivered. "Yuck. I'm glad my meat comes skinned, gutted and shrink-wrapped."

Luke snorted. "I'm surprised you have time to cook, what with all your impressive camera work." He roughly jostled past Emily as he left the kitchen.

"What was that about?" I asked Holliss, hanging back as everyone else followed the guide out of the room.

She kept her voice low. "Emily posted her video of Luke's paragliding fiasco on the internet. Now it's gone viral. Super embarrassing. Luke's furious."

I remembered Luke struggling with Smitty, his flailing arms, his garbled screams. Not the kind of thing you'd want to share with the world. "Why would she do that? She had to know he wouldn't be happy."

"Like she would care," Holliss said. "That girl is focused on no one but herself. I don't know what Kyle sees in her."

"Other than a gorgeous face and a hot body, you mean? That's not enough?"

She laughed. "Well, there's that." She pressed her hands against the small of her back and leaned against the door frame.

"Do you feel all right?" I asked.

"The baby's bouncing around a lot."

"Let's find someplace to sit down." We walked toward the great hall, outfitted with intricately carved woodwork and enormous oil paintings of long-deceased nobility. The rest of the family had already gathered near the large banquet table, which was set up near a white marble fireplace embellished with fat-legged cherubs.

Holliss lowered herself onto a bench near the doorway. "I can't believe I have three more months until this baby gets here. I feel like I'm going to explode at any minute."

"But your doctor says everything is okay?" I asked.

"Yes. He cleared me for this trip. I'm just tired. And fat. Swollen ankles. Swollen boobs. And a very unattractive double chin." She patted the bench beside her. "Sit here with me a minute. There's something you need to know. About that paragliding thing today."

"That was crazy, wasn't it? Luke and Bronwyn couldn't stop thanking me for trying to save him. Corinne and Fred, too."

"It wasn't Luke's fault." She angled toward me. "Randall and I stayed in the park after you guys all headed back to the hotel. Kyle got into a big argument with Luke's pilot. Smitty wanted a bigger tip."

"I'm surprised Smitty got any tip at all after that performance. Luke almost died."

"It wasn't an accident. Kyle set up the whole thing."

"What do you mean?"

She swiveled around to make sure no one else was listening. "Kyle said, 'I paid you to scare him, not kill him.'"

It took me a minute to process what she'd just said. "You mean Kyle paid Smitty to give Luke a rough ride? He did it on purpose?"

"Yes. Then Luke panicked and almost killed them both."

"Why would Kyle do that? He knew Luke was afraid of heights."

"I don't know. But the two of them have picked at each other this whole trip. There's something weird going on between them."

"Does Luke know? Have you said anything to him?"

"No. And I don't plan to. No way I'm getting in the middle of this." Her determination spoke of someone buffeted by family disagreements too many times in the past. "I wanted to give you a heads up, to be on your guard around Kyle. After all, you almost died out there, too."

"But if …" I began.

"Here you are," Randall called out as he strode toward us. "I turned around and you had disappeared. I've been searching everywhere for you."

"Just needed to sit a minute. Help me up, will you?" She turned to me as he put a hand under her elbow. "Kyle's trouble," she whispered, rising awkwardly to her feet. "You be careful."

***

Dinner was a blur of bustling waiters and fragments of conversation as the nine of us gathered around the banquet table. Kyle kept us laughing with stories of his travels, so entertaining that I wondered if somehow Hollis had gotten her story wrong. Surely someone who had tried to terrorize his brother-in-law a few hours ago couldn't be this relaxed and charming.

As we finished dessert, Corinne stood and waited for the waiters to pour champagne. "We have some news to share with you," she said, as excited as a little kid with a new puppy. "Fred, if you would do the honors?"

Fred walked toward Corinne. "Please raise your glass," he said with a dramatic pause, putting his arm affectionately around his wife, "to toast the next U.S. senator from the state of New York, Corinne Peerland."

I think Corinne expected applause. Or at least hearty words of congratulations. Or even some tough questions. Anything but the shocked silence that greeted her. Her expression slowly morphed from excitement to disappointment to heartbreaking despair as her children stared at her, their mouths hanging open.

"Is this some kind of joke?" Kyle pushed back from the table, waving off the waiter who reached to clear his plate. "U.S. senator? What do you know about politics?"

Corinne bristled, her back stiff. "I've been very active in political issues for quite some time."

Her irritation made me nervous. Tonight she was sharing her plans with her family. Tomorrow we were going public. Things would get a lot tougher once her opponents started to hound her. If she couldn't handle the pressure, if she crashed and burned, Kesbolt Consulting would also.

"Mom, come on," Bronwyn said, brushing back her pale hair. "You've dabbled a bit in politics, made some contributions, but nothing serious."

"I've done a lot more than dabble. I've been very involved in the party."

Kyle sprawled back in his chair. "Mom, it's one thing to be on a bunch of committees. But running for office … that's a huge commitment."

"Getting elected takes connections," Bronwyn said. "You can't just step up one day and decide to run."

"I *have* connections. Senator Twisdale is retiring at the end of his term. He personally asked me to run for his seat. He's pledged his support."

Kyle shook his head. "But you don't know anything about campaigning."

"Of course I do. I've been in advertising for almost forty years. I've spent my whole life running marketing campaigns. Persuading people to buy things they didn't even know they wanted." Corinne's eyes gleamed. "Now I'll convince them that they want me. I'm confident that my team can put this together."

"You already have a *team*?" Bronwyn's voice shot up on the last word.

"You didn't think I would run a Senate campaign all by myself, did you?" She pointed toward me. "Madeline is my public relations consultant. I've been working with her for months to hone my message. She'll be talking to each of you, to figure out how to work you into the campaign."

Holliss's green eyes widened in surprise. I wasn't good at reading lips, but even I could make out the words as she whispered, "Why didn't you tell me?"

"I'll explain later," I mouthed back at her.

Bronwyn's jaw tightened. She and Kyle had been openly suspicious of me ever since we arrived in Switzerland, asking why their mother had included a stranger on a family European river cruise. Corinne had waved off their questions with vague comments about market research.

Kyle tented his fingers together, his eyebrows raised. "What *is* your message?"

"Managing climate change," she said. "Every day more carbon and methane are gushing into the atmosphere. It's making our weather more volatile, causing tornadoes, hurricanes, and floods. Last summer, temperatures hit 100 degrees all over the world. We have to do something about it."

"Climate change?" Kyle stared curiously at his mother. "Where did that come from? You've never been a tree hugger."

"I've always been interested in the environment. It's time to take a more active role. I'm attending an energy conference in Basel tomorrow. Madeline and Senator Twisdale have lined up fact-finding interviews for me with industry leaders."

"An energy conference?" Kyle said. "How can you possibly squeeze that in? We start the riverboat cruise tomorrow."

"My meetings won't take long," Corinne reassured him. "I'll have plenty of time to catch the riverboat."

Bronwyn impatiently tapped her fork on her plate. "This is about Natalie, isn't it?"

I looked quizzically at Corinne. Over the past months, Lilly and I had gotten close to her, the three of us spending late nights talking in a tiny restaurant not far from our office. Corinne laid out her plans for her Senate career. Lilly and I described our ideas for growing Kesbolt Consulting. The third glass of merlot was generally the trigger to loosen our tongues and pierce the filters that protected our public personas. We told each other fears and dreams that we would never have discussed over lunches of crisp salads and sparkling water.

None of us shared everything, of course. Some secrets stayed locked up, defying even the power of that third glass. We never told her the details of that horrible night that ended our careers at our former firm. And Corinne never mentioned Natalie.

"This won't bring her back, Mom," Bronwyn said. "You know that."

Corinne's nose flared. "What I know is that we're facing devastating droughts and wildfires. Scorching summers and bitterly cold winters. We have to develop alternative sources of energy—wind, solar, biofuels—and reduce our use of fossil fuels before we destroy the planet."

Luke balled up his napkin and tossed it on the table. "You do remember, Corinne, that I work for an energy company? That I sell equipment and services to all those fossil fuel companies that you're trying to put out of business?"

"Alternative energy companies will need equipment also. You can sell to them."

He gave a wry grin. "Unless those solar guys start digging sunshine out of the ground, I can't imagine they'll have much need for drill bits. Or fracking equipment."

Bronwyn upset her water glass as she slapped the table. "I can't believe you're doing this to your own family. You know Harrison is starting Princeton next year. How are we supposed to pay for that if Luke loses his job?"

Corinne slowly shook her head. "Luke's job won't be at risk anytime soon. Traditional fuels provide eighty percent of the world's energy. The transition to alternative energy will be a slow process."

Bronwyn turned to her brother. "You've got to stop her."

"Mom, let's be reasonable," Kyle said. "This Senate thing may be a big waste of time and money."

Corinne watched her children whisper among themselves. "It pains me that you don't have any confidence that I can get elected."

"That's not it, Mom," Holliss said. "We're surprised, that's all. We thought you brought us on this trip to announce your retirement."

She grasped the back of her chair. "I don't think I would like retirement. When it doesn't matter if you do something today, or next week, or a month from now, or maybe not at all."

Luke laughed as he reached for his champagne glass. "Are you kidding? To have the freedom to do what you want, when you want? Isn't that what we work for all our lives?"

"That may be fine for some people, but not for me. I need structure. I need purpose. I need something to give my life meaning."

"Your life has meaning, Mom," Holliss said. "You're going to have another grandchild soon. You can help me with the baby."

"Of course, Holliss. But this campaign is important to me, too. And I was counting on my family for support."

Everyone was silent, glancing down at their plates to avoid Corinne's determined stare. Finally, Randall stood and raised his glass, the champagne a pale gold in the candlelight. "Congratulations, Corinne. We wish you the very best."

The others reluctantly rose to their feet. "Congratulations," they mumbled.

Corinne sniffed at their muted response. "Come on, Fred," she said, grabbing her husband's arm. "Let's head back to the hotel. I've got lots to do before we catch the train tomorrow for Basel."

***

"Dinner was a disaster." I put my cellphone on speaker as I paced the floor of my hotel room. "Kyle and Bronwyn gave Corinne a lot of pushback on her Senate plans. Even Holliss seemed lukewarm on the idea."

"Are you kidding me?" Lilly's voice crackled as it traveled across the ocean. With the six-hour time difference between Switzerland and New York, I'd caught her right before she closed the office for the day. "Corinne convinced us she'd have her family's support. It was her idea to feature them in the campaign."

"I know. But that might not work."

"You don't think she'll drop out, do you?" Anxiety made Lilly's voice brittle. "We can't afford to lose her as a client."

Lilly Turnbolt and I had maxed out our credit cards, pledged all our worldly goods as collateral, and funneled every penny of our life savings into funding our new public relations company. I wanted to call it TBW Consulting, for *Two Broke Women*, but a quick internet search showed that name was already taken. So were the next twenty names we researched. Finally, we combined syllables from our last names of Keswick and Turnbolt to create *Kesbolt Consulting*.

"No chance of her dropping out," I assured Lilly. "Go ahead and activate her website. Be sure you include that endorsement from Senator Twisdale. I'll post pictures and commentary tomorrow after the energy conference."

"What about her blogs? Can we schedule those?"

"Absolutely. You already have the first five. They're ready to publish. She's pulling ideas from her journal for the next ones." Corinne carried her journal everywhere, recording notes on everything from climate change to new advertising campaigns to birthday gifts for the grandchildren. "She should finish them in a couple of days."

"Sounds good." I could almost hear Lilly checking items off her to-do list.

"I'm really excited about this, Lilly." After months of work, we were finally going live. "It's our chance to show potential clients what we can do. I think it's a game-changer."

"Speaking of game-changers …" Lilly's voice took on a teasing drawl. "Travis stopped by today. He's writing a new series on start-up companies for his online magazine, and he wants to include Kesbolt Consulting. But he says you're not returning his messages."

For years Travis Lawson and I had been bar buddies, part of a millennial crowd that hung out at Sheila's, a trendy after-hours spot in Manhattan. Gradually our relationship developed well beyond buddy status. We'd even kept toothbrushes at each other's apartments.

Then Travis got involved in the fiasco that cost me my job. I was so angry that I broke off all contact. "He's sent me some emails. But it's too soon for an article like that. We need more of a track record."

"Are you kidding? This is exactly what we need to raise our profile."

"We're not ready for all that publicity," I said.

"You mean you're not ready to spend that much time with Travis." Her tone was disapproving. "It's an article, Madeline. Not a lifetime commitment."

"Travis has already done enough to screw up my life. I don't want to give him any more chances."

She sighed. "You know he was only trying to help."

"Didn't exactly work out that way, did it?"

"Keep an open mind, Madeline. Publicity like that could bring in a lot of new business."

"I'll think about it. Meanwhile, let's stay focused on Corinne's campaign."

Chapter 3

WHEN I WALKED into the train station the next morning, I could tell Corinne was still upset about her announcement dinner. She usually was at the center of the action, making plans and coordinating schedules. Today she and Fred stood at the far end of the station, studying a collection of faded wall maps, their backs to the room. The rest of the family huddled by the entrance, lining up roller bags, pulling out tickets, glancing at watches.

I quickly passed them and headed toward Corinne. "Did you check out your website? We went live last night. The news release announcing your candidacy is getting a lot of traction."

"Yes, I saw it. It's really happening, isn't it? Too late to turn back, I guess."

"Turn back?" My eyebrows shot up. "What are you talking about?"

"Madeline, I've thought about this all night. I need my family to be behind me on this. And if they're not …"

I wanted to grab her shoulders and shake sense into her. Was she seriously considering throwing away everything we'd worked for, because of one disappointing dinner? "It's normal to feel nervous at the beginning," I said, quick to reassure her. "But we're off to a great start. And your meetings at the energy conference today will show the world you're a global player. Over the next few weeks, everyone will learn who you are and what you stand for."

"I'm not sure …" Her words trailed off.

I gave Fred a worried glance. Was her candidacy going to fall apart before we'd barely started? Corinne had Senator Twisdale's support, but beyond that, little name recognition. If she didn't fight hard for every vote, she would never win.

"This is what you've wanted, Corinne," Fred said, putting his arm around her. "What you've worked so hard for. You caught the kids off guard, that's all. Once they've gotten used to the idea, they'll be right there with you, campaigning. You'll see."

"I'd like to believe that."

"Let's get through the energy conference." I tried to stay calm, to keep my voice neutral. "We'll focus on getting your name out there. Start to build a strong base of followers. When you see those numbers come in, you'll feel much more confident."

Fred put a finger under her chin, gently lifting so that his eyes stared directly into hers. "I'm proud of you, Corinne. *She* would be proud of you. You can do this."

I wondered which *she* he meant. Certainly not Bronwyn, who had been so critical of her mother last night. Probably not Holliss, who'd barely said anything at dinner. Perhaps the mysterious Natalie?

Corinne's eyes flitted across his face, an unspoken dialogue flowing between them. "You're right. It's just nerves, I guess."

A low rumble made us all startle. "Sounds like the train is here," Fred said.

Corinne gripped the handle of her roller bag. "Let's go."

***

We pulled into Basel a few hours later. Fred took charge of getting the family and luggage headed toward the riverboat, while Corinne and I hailed a taxi to take us to the conference.

"These meetings are mainly a meet and greet," I reminded her. "You can follow up with these CEOs later if you want to dig deeper into what they're doing." I pulled out my phone to send a quick text to my local contact. "I've arranged for someone to take pictures and coordinate our European coverage. I told him we were on our way."

"That's great." She flipped through her notes for a final review. "Thanks for setting all this up."

"By the way," I asked, tucking my phone into my purse, "who is Natalie?"

She kept her eyes down on her notebook. "What's that?"

"Natalie," I repeated. "Bronwyn mentioned her at dinner last night. Said she might have something to do with your run for the Senate."

Corinne concentrated on the material in front of her, underlining sentences and scribbling in the margins. Just when I'd decided she wasn't going to answer me, she mumbled, "Natalie was my niece."

I noticed the past tense. "Was?" I repeated. "What happened to her?"

She flipped her notebook closed. "We don't talk about it. It's been very painful."

My curiosity demanded more. "But why did Bronwyn ..."

The taxi driver cut me off as he pulled to the curb. "Sorry, this is as close as I can get." He pointed to a tall building in the next block. "Your conference is up there. At the hotel."

Metal barricades blocked car traffic while throngs of protestors crowded the streets, shouting slogans and brandishing homemade signs, primarily in German and French. I spotted a few in English that said *Stop Killing Our Planet* and *Climate Justice Now.*

I fumbled in my purse for cab fare. "We have to walk through that to get to the energy conference?"

"You'll be fine," he said. "We've had protests all over Switzerland the past few months, but they've all been peaceful."

Next time I would arrange security for Corinne, a couple of big burly guys who could move us safely through traffic. But for now, we were on our own. "Corinne, are you okay with this? Maybe the driver can drop us off on another street."

"I'm fine." She reached for the door. "I'm on their side. I want to save the planet, too."

We exited the taxi and started for the hotel, me in the lead and Corinne a few steps behind, slowly angling our way through an unruly group that became more agitated the closer we came to the conference. "We're going to be late," I said, turning toward Corinne. Only she wasn't behind me. After an initial moment of panic, I finally spotted her several yards back, chatting and nodding. I made my way toward her. "Let's go, Corinne. Only ten minutes until your meeting with Liam Schmidt."

We entered the hotel and took the escalator to the second level, a sprawling maze of vendor displays, breakout rooms, and coffee stations. I pointed out Schmidt near a back table, recognizing him from his website photos. "Introduce yourself," I said to Corinne. "I'm going to find our media contact."

I roamed the room until I spotted a young man dressed in jeans and a snug sweater, rapidly snapping pictures. A familiar news logo was on the camera bag slung over his shoulder. "You're Lucius, right?" I said, extending my hand. "I'm Madeline Keswick, here with Corinne Peerland. You're taking pictures for us?"

"Yes. Welcome to Switzerland."

I pointed to a far corner. "Corinne is over there, with Liam Schmidt. You know him?"

"Of course. Everyone knows the king of solar energy."

We walked together toward Corinne and Schmidt. "Can we get a shot of you two?" Lucius asked. "Turn this way a bit?"

Corinne smoothed her skirt, raised her chin and smiled. We had spent a lot of time on that smile, transitioning her typical stern expression into something softer and more voter friendly. She had practiced in her mirror, over and over. I gave her a thumbs up as Schmidt moved beside her.

Lucius kept taking pictures as Corinne met with a manufacturer of wind turbines, a developer of hydroelectric batteries, and an operator of geothermal electrical plants. "We have one more meeting," I told him. "In conference room C. With Nils Kiener of Gurtmeyer Industries."

"Oh, yes, the oil and gas production company. One of the good ones. They've been getting a lot of publicity for innovative technology to reduce their carbon footprint."

Kiener was in a small conference room at the end of the hall, pacing the floor as he talked on his phone. He waved us over as he finished his call. "Mrs. Peerland?" His expression was apologetic. "I am sorry to cut our meeting short, but my office has called with an urgent problem. Perhaps you can ride back with me? We can talk in the car."

I knew Corinne well enough to realize she was frustrated—the slight lifting of her left eyebrow, a barely perceptible tightening at the corner of her mouth— but she hid her irritation well as the three of us rode the escalator down to the ground level. Through the hotel's front wall of floor-to-ceiling windows, I could see the protestors circling outside, more frenzied than before, all pumping their fists and hoisting signs. A young man with curly blond hair and dark-framed glasses shouted into a bullhorn, leading the crowd in chants.

"Corinne, this isn't safe," I said. "Let's find another exit."

"Don't be ridiculous. Kiener's car is right here. We only have to walk six feet." She gestured toward a black limo parked at the curb. "Besides, I've talked with these folks. They're reasonable people with legitimate concerns."

Those angry mouths spouting heated chants didn't seem all that reasonable to me, but Corinne had already started out the door, following closely behind Kiener. There was little choice but to join them.

Arms and hands and shoulders pressed against me as I stepped onto the sidewalk, lifting me off my feet, propelling me back toward the building. I tried to move toward Corinne, desperate to pull her to safety, but I was helpless in this tangle of pulsating bodies.

The man with the bullhorn kept shouting, revving up the crowd. Suddenly there was a loud crash, and the wall of windows behind me began to crack. I tucked my head as shards of glass rained down. A woman howled as rivulets of blood ran down her cheek.

A dark-suited man jumped out of the limo and strong-armed his way through the crush until he reached Kiener. Guiding him into the back seat, he slammed the door shut. The limo slowly edged away from the curb.

Corinne, left behind on the sidewalk, stepped back. The frantic mob surrounded her, reaching out, only inches away.

"Stop. Get away from her," I screamed, my voice lost in the escalating chants. Terror gave me super-human strength as I wrestled my way through the human barricade. She spotted me and yelled out my name. I stretched toward her just as a man latched onto her shoulders. She tried to pull away but he hung on, spinning her around in an awkward dance. When he finally let go, she stumbled for a few steps, off balance. Then she fell, disappearing from view.

Chapter 4

KIENER'S SECURITY MAN reached her first. He pulled her to her feet and then grasped my wrist, moving us both through the revolving door and back into the hotel.

"Corinne, are you all right?" I asked as we spilled into the lobby. "Are you hurt?"

"I'm fine." She brushed her sleeves and smoothed her skirt. "Except for my pride."

"You're bleeding." I pulled a tissue from my pocket and pressed it against an oozing slash above her eye. "That glass must have cut you."

"It's nothing. I don't feel it."

The security man pressed a finger to his ear, listening to a message only he could hear. "Please, this way." We followed him as he walked rapidly through a hallway. "My apologies. The police should have been here to manage this." He opened a rear exit and led us to a side street, where a dark blue car was waiting. "The driver will take you wherever you want to go. I am sorry for the inconvenience."

"We need to go to Kiener's office," Corinne asked. "We didn't get a chance to talk."

He shook his head. "Today is not good. You will have to reschedule."

"But we're leaving Basel tonight," Corinne said. "There's no more time."

"I'm sorry. He cannot see you today."

She was still grumbling as we climbed into the back seat of the waiting car. "Please take us to the dock," I told the driver. "We're catching a riverboat. The *Rhinelinder*."

Police sirens, faint at first, grew louder as we pulled into traffic and left the hotel behind.

***

The *Rhinelinder* was narrow and flat, low-slung to fit under the many bridges that spanned the river, reminding me more of a child's rectangular crayon box than the towering ocean liners I had cruised on previously.

Corinne and I, still shaken up by our confrontation, went immediately to our cabins, agreeing to meet later for dinner. I stepped out onto my balcony, filling my lungs with river air. The Rhine was narrower than I expected, a calm strip of gray water flowing between two riverbanks crammed with apartment buildings and office towers.

As I pulled out my phone to post on Corinne's website, a headline in the newsfeed caught my eye: *U.S. Senate Candidate Accosted in Street Brawl.* A video showed Corinne leaving the conference with Kiener and then going nose-to-nose with the protestors before stumbling to the sidewalk, her legs askew and her skirt riding up almost to her waist. She would be furious once she saw it.

Doing quick damage control, I posted my own version of events. Then I sent an email to Lilly requesting that she stay on top of this and do whatever she could to bury the bad news.

After changing for dinner, I headed downstairs. The dining room pulsed with the laughter and boisterous conversations of excited travelers celebrating the first night of their cruise, but the joyous sounds quieted as the maître d' led me toward the far corner and our own table of gloom. Corinne and her family had the haggard air of exhausted travelers who had just missed their last connecting flight of the evening.

Corinne confronted me immediately. "You saw that video of me on the internet? Sprawled on my ass? The whole world got a great shot of my crotch."

"That was embarrassing," I admitted, "but I'm controlling the narrative. We're getting a lot of hits on articles and pictures I've posted about the conference."

"But not nearly as many as that crotch video, I'll bet," Corinne said. "Which was taken when I was talking with the CEO of an oil production company. Now everyone thinks I'm in league with big energy."

I kept my voice calm, trying to defuse her anger. "You've interacted with the media all your life. You know that sometimes coverage isn't flattering. But we have well over a year to build your image and get your message out there to the voters. This incident will be quickly forgotten."

"I'm not sure you can fix this."

Our campaign had just started, and she was already second-guessing me. Was this what the next eighteen months would be like?

Her family quickly piled on. "This whole thing is stupid," Bronwyn said. "Mom needs to drop out of this race. It's too dangerous. She could have been killed."

"It was a little frightening," I agreed. "Next time we'll beef up security."

"There shouldn't be a next time," Kyle insisted. "Mom, you need to stop this nonsense, right now."

Bronwyn was winding up for another caustic comment when Fred jumped in. He was Corinne's faithful safety net, always at the edges of her spotlight, ready to smooth over any rough spots. "Is everyone's room all right?" he asked, his deep voice a comforting rumble. "Madeline, you good?"

"Yes," I said. "The room is great. And I love my balcony."

Emily sighed as she reached for a breadstick. "There's nothing to do on this boat. The gym is a joke—two treadmills in an oversized closet. And the hot tub up on deck is tiny. I'm not sure Kyle and I can both fit in there at the same time."

Corinne's mouth puckered. "I'm so sorry you're disappointed."

"She's not disappointed, Mom," Kyle said quickly, holding up a warning hand as Emily started to speak. "But her last cruise was on one of those huge ocean liners. You know, with rock climbing walls and ice-skating rinks. This is quite a bit smaller."

Fred tried to make peace. "We won't be on the boat that much anyway. Each day we'll stop at a new city. You can tour castles, wineries, perhaps go bike riding? There's a famous spa at Baden-Baden."

"That sounds good," Emily agreed, crunching on her breadstick. "But what about at night? Are there Broadway shows? Chinese acrobats? Magicians?"

"There's a piano bar," Bronwyn said. "Tonight's theme is Frank Sinatra."

Emily looked puzzled. "Sinatra?"

Bronwyn snickered. "Kyle, just how young *is* your fiancée, anyway?"

A dark stain spread up Emily's neck.

Our waiter Sergey provided a welcome diversion as he took food and drink orders, but conversation stalled after he left. Corinne, still fuming over the internet video, sent back not one steak but two, claiming they were both overcooked, and demanded to see the manager. Sergey sulked, his eyes burning with anger, as Corinne loudly complained to his boss about the food, the wine and the service.

"You keep this up and they'll be spitting in your mashed potatoes," Fred cautioned her. "Eat your steak and stop complaining."

Corinne stood up. "I've lost my appetite."

Kyle pushed back his chair. "Hey, Mom, why don't we go up on deck? You and me. Get some fresh air. A change of scenery?"

"That sounds like a great idea," Fred said. "The rest of us can head to the piano bar. I'd like to introduce Emily to Frank Sinatra."

***

The pianist had worked through his entire repertoire by the time Kyle finally joined us in the lounge. He was accompanied by a tall man, maybe in his mid-forties, with deep-set brown eyes and a sharp jawline.

"Hey, folks, this is Wyatt Carlton. Wyatt, my family," Kyle said, introducing each of us. "Wyatt had a killer poker game going on upstairs, and was kind enough to let Mom and me join in. You know how competitive she is. She cleaned everybody out and is now in a much better mood. She'll join us after she locks up her winnings."

Fred raised his glass toward Emily. "We've made great progress here, too. I'm happy to report that your fiancée is now a Sinatra aficionado."

Emily fingered her necklace, a chunky arrangement of silver beads and colorful, flower-shaped crystals. "I've heard worse."

"A rousing recommendation, don't you think?" Fred said, laughing.

"Glad to see that everyone is getting along." Kyle turned to Emily. "A dance, my dear?"

"Sure." She held out a well-toned arm. Emily had the body of a gymnast, compact and wiry, with a tight butt and robust biceps that could easily have hoisted a small car. Her white sleeveless dress was a dramatic counterpoint to her dark hair and tanned skin, hitting her mid-thigh, barely containing the rippling muscles that hinted at her strength. Men at surrounding tables took notice as she stood up.

It seemed unfair that she could have both a great body and a gorgeous face. I exercised, jogged a couple of times a week, and spent an ungodly amount of my paycheck on salon visits, but my girl-next-door wholesomeness was no challenge for her exotic beauty. It was easy to see why Kyle was besotted with her.

My envy ratcheted down a bit as Wyatt moved toward me. "How about you, Madeline? Would you like to dance?"

He was an easy partner to follow. Soon we were swirling, coming together, backing apart, hips swaying in rhythm, both of us as lithe and limber as a pair of Argentinian tango dancers.

"Pretty impressive, guys," Kyle said, as we returned to our seats. He waved as his mother entered the lounge. "Here's the lucky winner now."

"We need to get you a drink," Fred said as Corinne sat down with us. "Do you see our waitress?"

"It will be quicker if I go to the bar and order," Kyle said. "Your usual, Mom?"

"Yes, a bloody mary." She reached for the peanuts.

"I'll go with you," Wyatt said. "I could use a refill."

Corinne chatted happily as Sinatra songs played in the background. For the moment, at least, she seemed to have gotten over the video snafu. I relaxed, thinking that perhaps my job of directing her social media campaign wouldn't be so impossible after all.

"Here you go, Mom," Kyle said as he and Wyatt returned. He set her beverage in front of her, then lifted his glass. "Cheers, folks. To a happy cruise."

"Cheers," the rest of us responded, raising our glasses.

Corinne took several swallows, then coughed. "Whoa, that's spicy. I need some water."

Fred caught the eye of the waitress. "Some water over here?"

Corinne coughed again. "My throat," she gasped. "It's closing up. I'm choking." Two large lumps puffed out under her eyes.

Fred jumped up. "She's having an allergic reaction. Corinne, where's your EpiPen?"

"In the room," she said in a hoarse whisper. "My makeup bag."

"Give me your room key, Fred," I volunteered. "I'll go get it."

"I'll go with you," Bronwyn said.

As we rushed out of the lounge, I could hear Kyle shouting, "We need a doctor here. A doctor!"

Chapter 5

BY THE TIME Bronwyn and I returned to the lounge, Corinne was stretched out on a couch, her head propped up on pillows. A man in a white uniform knelt on the floor beside her, his fingers on her wrist.

Bronwyn thrust the EpiPen toward Fred. "Dad, quick. Take it."

"It's okay," Fred said. "Dr. Maynard has already given her a shot. Her breathing is much calmer."

"Her blood pressure has normalized, which is good." Dr. Maynard twisted toward the family. "Do you know what triggered this?"

"She was fine up on deck during the poker game," Kyle said. "And then we came down here for drinks, and suddenly she puffed up."

"Peanuts, perhaps?" the doctor said, glancing at the bowl on the table.

"She's never had a reaction to peanuts before," Fred said. "She's allergic to shellfish, but she had steak for dinner. No reason for her to swell up like that."

"Sometimes allergies come on suddenly," Maynard replied. "She should check with her doctor once she gets home." He stood up. "Can you walk now?" he asked Corinne. "I want you to come down to the clinic, so we can keep you under observation for a while. Make sure you don't have a relapse."

"I'm fine," she said, sitting up. "I want to go to my room. My husband can keep an eye on me."

"Come on, Corinne, do what the doctor says. I'll go to the clinic with you," Fred said. "Better to get this checked out now than wake up in the middle of the night, gasping for breath."

She reluctantly agreed and made her way to the elevator, with Fred and Dr. Maynard walking slowly beside her.

"That was terrifying," Bronwyn said. "I can't remember the last time Mom had an attack like that. She's always so careful to stay away from shellfish."

"She was turning purple by the time the doctor got here," Kyle said. "I thought she was going to die."

"So now what?" Luke asked. "Should we call it a night? Doesn't seem right to hang out here at the bar after something like that."

"Let's pack it up," Holliss said as she took Randall's arm. "It's been a long day, and we have an early start tomorrow for the Lucerne tour. We'll see you guys at breakfast."

***

Back in my cabin, I punched Lilly's number into my phone and went out on the balcony, watching the lights of Basel fade into the distance as we moved down the river.

The door to Kyle and Emily's cabin, which was next door to mine, slid open. The sound of their arguing voices drifted out. "You should have told me sooner," Emily said.

Kyle's voice was heavy with sarcasm. "What would you have done about it?"

"I don't know, but we can't let this deal fall apart."

Emily had told me that Kyle was lining up investors for his new company. I wondered if that was what they were fighting about. Before I could hear more, however, Lilly answered her phone. I stepped back into my room and slid the balcony door closed. "Corinne almost died tonight," I blurted out, filling her in on what had happened in the lounge.

"Oh, my God, that's horrible. Is she all right now?"

"She's down in the clinic with the doctor, to make sure she doesn't have a relapse." I slipped off my shoes and flopped on the bed. "I think stress could have contributed to this. She was really upset about that video at the energy conference. Did you see it?"

"The whole world has seen it. Exactly how did you let *that* happen?" I could envision her perched on the corner of her desk, legs crossed, bouncing a Manolo-shod foot. Her teasing tone almost covered her annoyance.

"Total incompetence, I guess. I never expected those folks to get so physical." I put the phone on speaker and fished my hot-pink stress ball from my briefcase, flattening it with my palms. "I feel like I'm losing Corinne's confidence."

"Come on, Madeline, we've just started her social media blitz. Once we get rolling, she'll see what a genius you are. That conference video was a minor hiccup."

"I hope you're right." Her pep talk was reassuring, but we both knew how important this account was. I had left Lilly behind in New York to do all the heavy lifting for our firm, while I was off on a junket that sounded a lot more like a vacation than a business trip. If I screwed this up, if Corinne decided I was the wrong person for the job, I'd never forgive myself. And I wasn't sure Lilly would, either. "How is everything back home?" I asked. "What about the product launch party for Renley Cosmetics?"

"It's taken care of," Lilly said. "The displays have been delivered to the hotel. Gift bags are stuffed with product samples. Everybody's buzzing online. We're good to go."

At least something was going right for Kesbolt Consulting. "And that new client?" I asked. "The upscale vacation resort in South Carolina?"

"I've finished the brand awareness proposal. I'll email it to you, and we can go over it whenever you're ready."

"You're the best. I feel better about all this. Even if Corinne drops us, it won't be the end of the world."

"Yes, it will. Don't you dare let that happen." Her voice was serious. "Corinne's potential commissions are larger than our next three biggest clients combined." She paused, then said lightly, "But hey, no pressure."

"Got it." I needed to fix this.

There was a frantic pounding on my door. "I've got to go, Lilly. I'll check with you tomorrow." Tossing the phone on the bed, I called out, "Who is it?"

"Madeline, it's Fred."

Worry lines were deeply etched in his forehead. "Corinne wants you to come to our room. Right now."

I followed Fred down the hall to their cabin, where the family had already gathered. Kyle and Bronwyn each had an arm around their mother.

"Corinne, what's wrong?" I asked, crossing over to her. "Is it your allergies?"

"Worse." She pointed to the shiny black door of the safe, now hanging open. "I've been robbed. All my poker winnings. They're gone."

***

Fred introduced me to two men dressed in crisp white uniforms. Werner Smithson, head of security, had the rounded shoulders of a tall man who had spent his whole life stooping down to get through doorways. His assistant Jonas Lundgren, blond and pale, was thick and stocky like a bulldog.

Smithson peered into the empty safe. "We need a bit more room to work. Could these people wait outside until we're done?"

"Kyle, could you take everyone to your cabin?" Fred said. "We'll let you know as soon as these security folks are finished."

"Of course. Come on, guys."

I started to follow them, but Corinne said, "Madeline, wait. I want you here with me."

After the room cleared, Smithson asked, "Mrs. Peerland, can you tell me what is missing?"

"My poker winnings from tonight. Two thousand dollars. And all my notes from the energy conference today. My contacts. Referrals to other experts. It's all gone." She stared intensely into that yawning black hole, as though by sheer concentration she could make the missing items reappear. "Madeline, what am I going to do? I needed all that."

Our plan had been to strategize after dinner, to go over what she'd learned and decide how to work the ideas into her campaign, but the allergy attack had derailed all that. "I still have my notes," I reassured her, "and we can get back in touch with everyone if you need to follow up."

"But they'll think I'm an idiot. What kind of senator will I be if I can't hold on to confidential information?"

Werner eyed her with increased interest as he pulled a small notepad from his shirt pocket. "You are an American senator?"

"A Senate candidate," she clarified. "I announced today."

"And these documents are valuable?" Suddenly he was eager to investigate, as though he had stumbled onto an international spy ring stealing classified data about U.S. security forces.

"They're valuable to me. Not sure what good they would do for anyone else."

His lips wrinkled in disappointment. "Then let us focus on the money. What time did you put it in the safe?"

"It was about 10 p.m., wouldn't you say, Fred?"

"Something like that."

"Are you sure you locked it before you left the cabin?" His condescending tone indicated that Corinne had been demoted from a headline-grabbing senator to just another careless tourist who couldn't keep up with her belongings.

She picked up on the insult. "Of course, I did. I always tug on the handle once I've shut the door, to make sure it's locked."

"Who knew the combination?"

"All my family did. I've always used the same combination, whenever we travel. It's easier to remember that way. It's the four numbers of our home address."

"So any of them could have opened it? Any of those people who were here a few minutes ago?" Smithson closed his notebook, signaling there was no need to mount an intensive investigation.

"Well, technically yes," Corinne said, "but of course they didn't. My children have no reason to steal from me."

Lundgren, perched on the edge of the credenza, piped up. "It's often the family that's involved in a situation like this."

"That's a horrible thing to say," Corinne began. "To accuse my family of …" She paused, stopping in mid-sentence, her voice catching.

"Corinne, are you all right?" I asked. "Is it your allergies again?"

"No, I'm fine." She ran a hand through her hair. "I just … I remembered something."

"Concerning the robbery?" Smithson asked.

"No." She hesitated. "It's … something else."

Smithson was skeptical. After a few more questions, he turned to his assistant. "Lundgren, can you take a few photos of the safe?"

"Of course." Lundgren snapped several shots of the interior and then stepped back to get a better angle, closing the black door.

"Hey, don't touch that," Fred blurted. "Aren't you going to check for fingerprints?"

Lundgren seemed vaguely apologetic as he slid his phone into his shirt pocket.

"There will be many fingerprints on the safe," Smithson said. "Yours. Your wife's. The cleaning staff."

"And now Mr. Lundgren's," Fred said. "Are you folks going to ignore the evidence?"

"Of course not. We will check the footage on the hallway security cameras. Interview your family, the staff, anyone with access to your room. And contact the local police in Lucerne tomorrow for their assistance with the investigation." Smithson pocketed the notepad as he and Lundgren walked out into the hallway. "Now I suggest you get some sleep."

Fred closed the door behind them and put his arm around his wife. "He's right. We should get some sleep. They'll get fingerprints tomorrow, and then we'll find out who did this."

"Maybe, but I'm not sure those two know what they're doing." Corinne stared at the metal door of the safe. "Madeline, you know how to take fingerprints, don't you?"

I shook my head. "Not me."

"But you're such a fan of those crime shows on TV. Surely you've seen it done a thousand times."

Fred shook his head. "You need to let security deal with this, Corinne."

"Oh, come on, Fred. Once Smithson realized I wasn't storing nuclear missile launch codes in the safe, he lost all interest. You saw them putting their hands on everything. They figure somebody on their staff did this, and they want to protect them. They'll probably send housekeeping in tomorrow to wipe everything down before the Lucerne police get anywhere near this room."

"I doubt that," Fred said.

"Can you get the fingerprints, Madeline?" Corinne asked, ignoring him.

"Don't do this, Corinne," Fred said. "You're interfering with a police investigation."

"It's my money that was stolen. My documents. And I'd much rather take a chance with Madeline than with Smithson."

Fred struggled to convince her. "Once she's tampered with the evidence, it'll ruin any chance the police might have to get some good prints and catch this guy."

"I understand. But if we wait, we probably won't get any prints at all. I'm not going to be able to sleep tonight worrying about this." Her eyes were pleading. "Madeline, can you help me out here?"

It was hard to say no to a client, but I knew Fred was right. "Corinne, I've never done anything with fingerprints before."

Fred took off his jacket and tossed it on the bed. "What's going on here, Corinne? Are you still wound up from that allergy attack?"

"What do you mean?"

"You're not thinking clearly. Somebody might think you didn't really want to get any good fingerprints off that safe."

"Is that so?" Corinne fished her journal out of the nightstand drawer. "Well," she said, reaching for a pen, "somebody would be wrong."

Chapter 6

I WENT BACK to my cabin but was too restless to sleep. Changing into workout clothes, I headed upstairs. The top deck was dark and deserted. The only sound was the swoosh of gentle waves as we moved along the river. I stood for a moment, stretching, and then began a slow jog.

I hadn't done any serious running since we'd been in Switzerland, and tonight I felt like a flabby weekend warrior, my leg muscles squishy and my arms flapping awkwardly by my sides. I slowed to a walk as I passed the hot tub, pressing the stitch in my side.

At the far end, a lone crew member packed away glasses at the bar, illuminated by twisted strands of twinkling fairy lights. He nodded to me as I got closer. Embarrassed to be so sluggish in front of an audience, I picked up my pace. Trying to fall into my normal rhythm, I did a second lap and then a third. My lungs burned. My heart felt ready to burst out of my chest and skitter across the deck. I stopped and sucked in great scoops of damp river air.

"Couldn't sleep?"

I whirled around. Kyle stood several feet behind me. Small spotlights rimming the deck cast a distorted shadow behind him. "Oh, you startled me."

"Sorry. Didn't mean to make you jump like that." He stepped closer. "You okay with some company?"

"Sure." What I really wanted was a hot shower, but Corinne had charged me with getting to get to know her family, and this was my first chance for a one-on-one with Kyle. I exhaled, deep and slow, struggling to slow my pulse to a more normal level. "What are you doing out here so late?"

He held up a cell phone. "Needed to take care of some business." Resting his forearms on the railing, he leaned out over the water to stare at the murky depths below. "This thing about mom. Her campaign." He turned toward me. "It's a bad idea. She could get hurt."

I moved up beside him. "I know today was rough, but nothing like that will happen again. Next time we'll have security in place."

"I'm not convinced you can handle it." His face was mostly in shadow, but I caught the suggestion of a smirk. "This is your first political campaign, right? I hear you talked her into running."

A wide swath of moonlight shimmered on the black water. "Corinne told you that?"

"Doesn't matter who told me. I know your firm's barely scraping by. You think her commissions will bail you out."

Corinne's stamp of approval was already generating new business for us, but I wouldn't admit that to him. "As if anyone could talk Corinne into doing anything she didn't want to do. She approached me about handling her campaign. Not the other way around."

"Seriously?" he snorted. "You want to tell me why someone in her position, a wealthy advertising executive who could get the best firms in New York, would instead pick a no-name firm like yours?"

I struggled to keep my temper in check. "This isn't the first project Corinne and I have collaborated on. We have a good track record together. She's been pleased with my work."

"She's thrown you a few crumbs because you're a friend of Holliss." Tiny lines of irritation were etched at the corners of Kyle's eyes. "Tell Mom to drop the campaign."

I shivered as a cool breeze sliced sweat off my body. "I'm sorry, Kyle. I won't do that."

"Wrong choice." He stepped closer and pinned me against the railing. "This will destroy our family. I won't let that happen."

I knew Luke was worried about his job, but Kyle's passion frightened me, totally out of proportion with any challenges Luke might face. I took a quick glimpse at the bar, but the fairy lights had been turned off, the bartender gone, everything packed up for the night. I was alone with Kyle, the man who had paid a paragliding pilot to terrorize his brother-in-law. "We can discuss this tomorrow. With Corinne."

"It's too late for that." The dim light obscured his expression, but there was no mistaking the anger in his voice. "You've got to go."

What was he going to do? Toss me overboard? I grasped the metal railing, slick with evening dew. "Getting rid of me won't solve anything. Corinne will hire someone else to take my place."

"It will slow her down. Give us more time to convince her that this is the wrong move."

No one else knew where I was. It would be hours before dawn began to peel away the layers of darkness. Hours before anyone searched for me. I wrestled against him, trying to slip free, but his rigid arms held me in place.

Then I heard whistling. "Hey, folks." A crew member hoisted a bucket in front of him as he stepped onto the deck. "Beautiful night, eh?"

Kyle relaxed his grip. I scooted away from him and rushed for the stairwell, glancing back to see if he was following. He stayed behind, calmly chatting with the crew member, watching him splash soapy water onto the deck. My heart pounding, I ran into my cabin and threw the deadbolt, pressing my ear against the door as I listened for footsteps.

Kyle's cabin was next to mine. He could easily sidle over to my balcony and crouch in the dark while he waited for me to fall asleep. It wouldn't be difficult for him to pry open the glass doors, slide me from my bed, and toss me into the Rhine.

Dreaming of drowning, I slept fitfully, jerking awake several times with frantic coughs, desperate to clear river water from my lungs.

Chapter 7

RAIN SPATTERED against the windshield the next morning as we boarded the tour bus for our excursion to Lucerne and Pilatus. Kyle and I very purposefully ignored each other as I moved down the aisle and tossed my tote behind Corinne and Fred. "Corinne, how are you feeling this morning? Any after-effects from your allergy attack?"

She shook her head. "No. I'm fine. The EpiPen took care of it."

The other passengers filed past me as I settled into my seat. "Did you hear any more from Smithson about the robbery?"

"Not a word. I knew he wasn't serious about investigating this."

Wyatt, my dancing partner from last night, was one of the last to board. "Looks like we're on the same tour." He spotted the empty seat beside me. "Mind if I join you?"

"Please," I said, sliding my tote to the floor to give him room.

The tour guide stood up, holding a clipboard. "Morning, folks. We're headed to Lucerne, followed by a trip up Mt. Pilatus. There's a little rain this morning, but it should clear off shortly."

His weather forecast was too optimistic. By the time we reached Lucerne, the rain had become a steady downpour, pounding the streets, pooling along the curbs. Our shoes tossed up miniature geysers as we splashed along the wet pavement, following the guide as he pointed out covered medieval bridges, ancient churches, and the narrow streets of Old Town.

Eager to escape the unrelenting rain, we piled back on the bus for the trip to Pilatus. The rain had stopped by the time we reached the mountain, but thick dark clouds still hovered above us. Ticketholders waited to board cable cars to the top. "Hey, Sergey," I called out, recognizing our waiter from last night. "Sergey," I called again, waving at him. "He must not have heard me," I said to Holliss.

She laughed. "He probably heard you, all right. I'll bet he's trying to stay as far from us as possible. I'd want to forget that dinner, too, if I were him. Mom gave him a rough time."

I remembered his sullen look as Corinne complained about him last night to the dining room manager. "Guess we're not at the top of his buddy list."

We climbed onto the cable car. Through wide windows, we could see bell-tagged cows grazing on the green mountainside. A few hikers attacked the narrow trails winding through the woods. As we moved higher, the landscape changed to a rocky, snow-covered terrain.

Holliss groaned as we reached the top. "You're supposed to be able to see for miles. What a disappointment."

Impenetrable gray mist surrounded us as we stepped out onto the viewing platform, limiting visibility to a few feet. I felt like I was in a post-apocalyptic scene from a sci-fi movie, everything monochromatic and menacing. Cold vapor knifed through my jacket and clung to my hair.

Bronwyn stretched out her fingers to feel the gauzy haze. "We're inside a cloud. How cool is this?"

Kyle and Emily disappeared into the fog as they headed across the ice-crusted concrete. "There's nothing but snow and rocks below us," Kyle called out. "I bet you could drop something down there and it would disappear. You wouldn't find it until the middle of summer. Maybe not even then."

"This is miserable," Holliss said. "You guys can stay out here and freeze all you want. I'm going inside."

Wyatt and I remained on the platform after everyone else had left, hoping the mist would clear. "You know, legend has it that dragons lived on this mountain," he said. "They supposedly had healing powers."

I looked down at my feet. "Do you think they could fix frostbite? A few more minutes out here and I'm going to lose a few toes."

He laughed. "Why don't we go inside with the rest? Warm up a bit?"

We entered the café and ordered lattes. As we walked toward Corinne's table, Bronwyn's angry voice blasted across the café. "You promised you'd help."

I checked to see if anyone was recording this, determined to avoid another damaging video of Corinne. Sitting with a group near the window was a man with dark framed glasses, wearing a baseball cap. The man beside him, with a striped knitted cap pulled down low, stared intently at Corinne. I'd seen him before, but I couldn't place him. He turned away when he realized I was watching.

The harsh fluorescent light made Corinne look older, hollowing her cheeks, sketching extra lines around her lips. "I'll help, Bronwyn, of course I will. But I can't give you as much as you want. I'm kicking in a lot of money toward my campaign."

"Corinne, you don't understand how tough things are right now," Luke said. "With more people clamoring for green energy, companies are cutting back on drilling. My company's stock price is in the toilet, and all my options are worthless. We had counted on them to fund Harrison's tuition." His voice deepened in frustration. "Now you're trying to eliminate my job."

"Luke, could you be a little less melodramatic?" Holliss said. "Mom doesn't have anything to do with your company's stock price. Or the value of your options, for that matter." She picked up her coffee. "The problem is that you two spend every penny that comes in the door, what with your big house and country club memberships and private schools. If you saved a little more money, you wouldn't be in this fix."

"You little …" Bronwyn jumped up and started toward her sister.

Luke held his wife's wrist. "Back off, Bronwyn. She's not worth it."

"Thank you for your sage financial advice, Holliss," Corinne said, "but as I recall, all of my children have hit me up for money in the past. Including you."

Holliss shook her head. "Randall and I don't want your money, Mom. We just want you to spend time with the baby."

"Really? Then it must have been someone else who called last year and asked for help with that condo down payment." Corinne's voice was icy. "I could have sworn that whiny little voice was yours."

Holliss's face colored. More than once in college, I'd seen Holliss hurl her phone across the room after a particularly bitter conversation with her mother.

She'd worked hard in recent years to reconcile, but their relationship was still rocky.

"That's enough, Corinne," Randall said, his voice sharp. "There's no need to talk to my wife like that."

"Come on, Mom," Bronwyn said, "you've had your chance in the spotlight. Just because you didn't get that big promotion you were gunning for, that's no reason to mess up everything for the rest of us."

Corinne reeled at Bronwyn's words. I knew she had expected to take over the CEO spot at her advertising firm, but had been usurped by a man who didn't have her many awards or experience but who did have the support of the company's largest client. The Senate campaign gave her cover to take a much-needed sabbatical. "Don't you realize how dangerous climate change is? What about the wildfires in California and Texas? And that last flood in Venice? The damage to artwork, to priceless documents, even to the structural integrity of the buildings themselves, was catastrophic."

Kyle downed the last of his coffee. "Venice has been flooding forever, Mom. It's nothing new."

"This has been the warmest decade on record," Corinne insisted. "Ocean levels are rising. We have to do something."

"The numbers don't work," Luke insisted. "A natural gas-fired power plant the size of a house can supply over 65,000 homes. A wind farm producing that much power would need about twenty turbines covering ten square miles of land. Plus, you'd need tons of batteries to store the power."

"He's right, Mom," Kyle said. "Without government subsidies and tax credits, none of your green energy makes financial sense."

Luke put his arm around Bronwyn. "Besides, taking care of my family right now is more important to me than how high the ocean level might be a hundred years from now."

"At this rate, the ocean will be lapping at your door in a lot less than a hundred years. I can't believe you are all so short-sighted." Corinne bounced to her feet. "I think I've had quite enough family time for one day. I need to be by myself." She snatched up her coat and stomped out of the café.

***

Back at the boat that evening, I changed for dinner and headed toward the lounge. A crowd in the atrium blocked my way. "What's going on?" I asked a woman beside me.

"All the passengers aren't on board yet," she said. "They won't open the dining room until we cast off."

I spotted Fred down on the dock arguing with Smithson and Lundgren, the security officers from last night. Lundgren grabbed Fred's arm, but Fred pulled free and stormed up the gangplank.

"Fred, what's wrong?" I asked.

"They won't wait." His anger was palpable, enveloping him in an indignant haze.

"Wait for who? What's going on?"

"For Corinne," he said. "She's missing."

Chapter 8

"GET THE FAMILY together, will you?" Fred rushed past me and headed for his cabin. "We need to talk about this."

The atrium was busy, with several large groups waiting to get into the dining room and others lined up at the concierge's desk to register for upcoming excursions. I moved out of the chaos and then sent texts to Corinne's children, telling them she wasn't back, and Fred needed to see them right away. Through the large glass windows, I could see Smithson and Lundgren still at the foot of the gangplank, talking on their cell phones.

Kyle was the first to show up, dressed for dinner in a sport coat and knit shirt. His layered blond hair was fluffed up with product. There was a bit of designer stubble along his chin, not much more yet than a five o'clock shadow, but enough to give him a sexy, adventurous demeanor. A group of ladies in their sixties, gathered near the huge flower arrangement on the center table, smiled and sucked in their tummies as he walked by.

I had avoided him all day, still shaky from our argument on the deck last night, but he walked up as though nothing had happened. "What's up with Mom?" he asked.

"Not sure," I said. "She's not back at the boat yet. Your dad asked me to get all of you together. He went back to his cabin. Should be here in a few minutes."

Kyle rolled his eyes. "Don't tell me we're in for another lecture. I heard enough of that while I was still up on the mountain."

"I don't know," I said. "You'll have to wait for your dad."

Holliss joined us a few minutes later. Wearing jeans and a snug maternity top, she carefully held the railing as she walked down the steps from her cabin. "What's going on, guys?" she asked, wet hair hanging in her eyes. "I just got out of the shower. What's the emergency?"

"It's Mom," Kyle said. "She's not here."

"Where is she?" Holliss asked. "And where's Dad?"

Before I could answer, Bronwyn and Luke stepped off the elevator. The middle finger of Bronwyn's right hand was enclosed in a metal splint covered with strips of navy Velcro, propping up her finger like an enormous claw.

Kyle walked over toward her. "What happened to you? Someone get mad when you flicked them off?"

"Very funny, Kyle," Bronwyn said, leaning against her husband. "I caught my hand in the cable car coming down the mountain. Broke my finger. Really stupid move."

"How the heck did you do that?" Kyle asked.

She spoke with a general air of vagueness. "There was a big crowd. Everybody pushing. Somehow, my finger got stuck in the door."

"Looks painful. Does it hurt?"

"Of course, it hurts. A lot." She winced as she carefully held out her wounded hand. "We were just down with Dr. Maynard. He gave me something for the pain, but it's not working yet. And he says I have to wear this stupid thing for the rest of the cruise." She turned to me. "What's this about Mom?"

"All I know is that she's not back on the boat yet," I said. "Your dad wants to talk to all of you. He should be here soon."

They milled around, talking among themselves while they waited. Fred finally joined us, carrying a bulging duffel bag. "What happened to you?" he asked Bronwyn as he noticed the splint on her hand.

"Broke my finger in the cable car. I'll be fine."

"What's going on, Dad?" Kyle asked. "Where's Mom?"

"That's what I'd like to know." He set the duffel on the floor. "I haven't seen her since she marched out of the café, and she hasn't checked in on the boat. How about the rest of you? Anyone ride down the mountain with her?"

We all shook our heads. "Nope. Haven't seen her," Kyle said.

"It's not like your mom to be late." Fred checked his watch. "She knew when the boat was leaving."

Kyle shoved his hands in his pockets. "You don't think she hiked down, do you, to blow off some steam? She said she wanted to be alone."

Bronwyn shook her head. "Surely Mom's not crazy enough to do something like that."

"She seemed mad enough to do most anything."

"She wouldn't hike down without telling anybody," Bronwyn insisted. "Plus, she's not dressed for it. No heavy coat. Wrong shoes."

"But what if she did?" Holliss said, pointing out the window toward the distant mountains. "She could get lost. Stumble into a ravine somewhere. It's cold out there. She could get hypothermia."

"Hey, cut it out, guys," Fred said. "Let's stop imagining the worst."

"But to come down the mountain by herself," Holliss protested.

"We don't know that she did that," Fred said, zipping up his jacket. "It's much more likely that she was in a shop somewhere, lost track of time, and missed the bus. The captain has already sent out a search team. They'll find her soon." He hoisted the duffel bag up on his shoulder. "Unfortunately, the riverboat won't wait, and I'm not leaving without her."

Holliss reached for his arm. "We'll come, too. Give me a minute to pack."

"There's no need for that," Fred said. "I'll call you as soon as I locate your mom. We'll spend the night in Lucerne, and then catch up with you guys tomorrow in Strasbourg."

Bronwyn hugged her father. "Tell Mom we're sorry we gave her such a hard time about the campaign."

"I will. It's time to stop whining about it," he said. "She's made up her mind. She needs our support."

"But …" Kyle began.

"Not a word." Fred glared at him. "We'll work all this out, somehow. Right now, the most important thing is to find your mother."

He walked down the gangplank and stepped ashore. The crew threw off the lines, and Fred waved as the *Rhinelinder* slowly moved away from the dock.

***

As the atrium crowd thinned, I headed to the lounge. Wyatt, sitting at the bar, beckoned me over. I eased onto a bar stool and ordered a chardonnay.

"Something wrong?" he asked. "You look worried."

"Corinne never returned to the boat this afternoon. Fred's staying overnight in Lucerne to search for her."

He picked up his beer. "What do you think happened? She got distracted? Lost track of time?"

"That's possible, I guess."

He studied my face. "You think she did it on purpose? Because she was angry?"

"Maybe." The bartender set my wine in front of me. "I've never seen her quite that upset."

"I'm sure Fred will find her." Wyatt said. "Once she's had a chance to cool off a bit, everything will be fine."

"I hope so." I should have done more to support Corinne—pushed back harder against her family, given her more encouragement, convinced her that the campaign was on solid footing. But I didn't do that, and now she was missing. "Did you see her after she left the café?"

"Nope. The two of us went to the gift shop, remember?"

"Yes, but you left before I finished shopping. Maybe you …"

"Hey, over here," Wyatt called out, raising a hand as Kyle entered the lounge. He started toward Wyatt but hesitated as he saw me. He had seemed so nonchalant around me all day, to the point that I began to wonder if I had misread him last night on the deck … if I had completely overblown what had happened between us, if I had let the darkness and the silence and the isolation create a threatening scene where there wasn't one. But now his eyes narrowed as he stared at me, his expression heavy and accusing.

"Come join us." Wyatt gestured to the seat beside him.

Kyle settled in and signaled to the bartender. "A Perrier and lime, please."

"Madeline told me Corinne didn't make it back to the boat," Wyatt said. "I hope everything is okay."

"I think she probably realized that this campaign idea was a lot of nonsense." His eyes shifted defiantly my way, as if daring me to disagree. "And she went off somewhere to lick her wounds. Dad will find her and get her settled down. They'll meet us in Strasbourg tomorrow."

"That's good news," Wyatt said.

"Yeah."

I wanted to speak up in Corinne's defense, to tell them that her campaign wasn't nonsense, that she had a lot of good ideas about managing climate change, but there was no point. Kyle would be quick to shoot down my arguments.

Wyatt steered the conversation to sports as he fished pretzels from the bowl in front of him. "Hey, what do you think about the Lakers this year?"

Kyle flicked his wrist in indifference. "I live in Boston. I'm more of a Celtics fan."

"But you like pro basketball?"

The bartender set Kyle's beverage in front of him. "Sure."

"You interested in seeing the playoffs? I think I can get my hands on some tickets."

Kyle's eyes lit up. "Seriously?"

"I work in sports marketing. Let me check with my office and I'll let you know."

"Thanks. That would be fantastic."

For the next half hour, the two men ignored me as they talked about basketball. Then Kyle finished his drink and stood up. "Let's head to dinner. Emily's probably already there. She won't be happy if I'm late."

We entered the dining room and walked to our usual corner table, where Bronwyn, Luke and Emily were already seated. "Hey, guys, Wyatt's joining us for dinner," Kyle said, sitting down beside Emily.

I sat on Emily's other side. Wyatt pulled out a chair across from me. "What happened to you?" he asked, noticing Bronwyn's finger splint.

"Stupidity, mainly. And a close encounter with the door of the cable car. Not my finest moment."

Luke reached for his wine. "But even with a broken finger, Bronwyn had to get her nails done. Women. I'll never understand them."

"The manicurist was very gentle," Bronwyn said, showing nails painted a creamy beige. "She helped me calm down. Deal with the stress."

Emily wiggled her fingers. "I agree." Her nails were painted a glowing flamingo pink. "She was great. Glad she could squeeze me in."

Bronwyn's upper lip quivered. "Great color for you. Suits your personality."

Emily's eyes flickered as she debated her response. It wasn't the first time Bronwyn had taken a snide jab at her future sister-in-law, and I tensed, waiting for fireworks. But Emily just sniffed, raised an eyebrow, and then pulled out her cell phone.

I felt bad for Emily. Except for Fred, who tried to include her in conversations, the rest of the family mostly ignored her. I wondered how she had gotten engaged to someone over fifteen years older. "So, Emily," I asked, sipping from my water glass, "how did you and Kyle meet?"

"Graduate school." Her thumbs flew over the keyboard of her phone. "I had to interview a business executive for my entrepreneurship class, and I got matched up with Kyle."

"He gave you some good ideas?"

"Absolutely." She lowered the phone. "He walked me through the whole process. How he came up with the idea for his company. Developed his business plan. Got investors."

I could imagine Kyle—handsome, successful, and rich—sharing his secrets with the eager acolyte. Emily, sitting at the foot of the master, probably hung on his every word. As the saying went, power was the ultimate aphrodisiac. No wonder they had gotten engaged.

"He sold his first company for hundreds of millions," she said. "Now we're starting another one." Her engagement ring flashed as she pocketed her phone. "We did a lot of brainstorming and came up with a killer business plan."

"That's impressive," I said. "Starting your own company is a lot of work."

"Kyle makes it seem easy. I'm learning so much from him. Lining up investors. Making sure we have enough capital." She shook out her napkin. "Of course, he's learning a lot from me, too. Social media, search engine optimization, that kind of thing."

"My public relations firm is very involved in all that. We should talk. Maybe we can pick up a few pointers from each other."

"Sure. That would be great."

We paused our conversation as Sergey, our waiter, came to the table to take drink orders. "How did you like Pilatus today?" I asked him.

"Pilatus?" he said.

"Yes. We saw you up there, with some other folks from the boat. Too bad it was so cloudy, right?"

He shook his head. "You must have confused me with someone else."

"No, I'm sure it was you," I insisted. "In line, waiting for the cable cars."

"Sorry."

I had gotten a clear look at Sergey and his buddies. Why would he deny that he'd been there? I was ready to press him further when Bronwyn said in a loud voice, "Good lord, Randall, what happened to you?"

Randall stood beside our table, pulling out a chair for Holliss. The left side of his chin was swathed in white gauze. Below the bandage, swollen red lines streaked down his neck. "I cut myself shaving."

"Shaving?" Luke asked, his voice skeptical. "What were you using? A machete? That looks nasty."

Randall sat across from his wife. "What can I say? I wasn't paying attention."

"I bet you were paying attention, all right, but not to your shaving. Those look like claw marks to me." Kyle snickered. "I thought you and Holliss would be taking a break from the kinky stuff, what with the baby and all."

"Shut up, Kyle," Holliss said, blushing. "That's disgusting."

Kyle shook out his napkin. "I'm just saying …"

Bronwyn frowned at her brother. "Would you lay off Randall? We've got more important things to think about than his personal fetishes. Let's focus on Mom. I'm afraid something terrible happened to her."

"Not a chance." Kyle reached for the breadbasket. "Mom disappeared because she wanted to."

"You think she's doing this to scare us?" Bronwyn asked. "So we'll be more supportive of her Senate race?"

"Yep. Remember that time when we were kids, and Mom got that big promotion? Told us we were moving to Connecticut? I thought you would never stop crying."

"That was a tough year. Mom was determined to move, but I didn't want to leave all my school friends."

Kyle scooped butter onto his plate. "Remember Mom and Dad had that huge fight? Then Mom took off? Disappeared for days? Nobody knew where she was."

"I do remember," Bronwyn said, her voice rising. "Dad went looking for her. Grandma came to take care of us."

"Then when she finally came back, there was no more discussion about it. We all moved to Connecticut, like she wanted." He broke off a bit of roll. "That's what she does when things aren't going her way. She disappears, lets everybody stew about where she is and what she's doing. Then by the time we're frantic and willing to agree to whatever she wants, she comes back all calm and collected."

"Why don't I remember any of this?" Holliss asked. "I've never heard this story."

"It was before your time," Kyle said. "But you were born the next year. Make-up sex, you know?"

Holliss sighed. "Is sex all you ever think about?"

He grinned. "Pretty much." He ran a slow finger down Emily's arm. "One of the few things in life that never fails to bring me joy."

Sergey returned to distribute the menus, but I knew I couldn't enjoy a long, leisurely dinner while I was worried about Corinne. "Excuse me," I said, sliding back my chair. "I want to check with Smithson, the security guy, before he goes off duty. See if he's figured out who broke into Corinne's cabin last night."

"Good idea," Bronwyn said. "Let us know what you find out."

Chapter 9

THE SECURITY OFFICE was two levels below the dining room. I walked quickly down the steps and through a heavy door. It was like transitioning from the glittering casinos of Las Vegas to the barren wastelands of the Sahara. There were no chandeliers on this level. No glowing wall sconces. No flamboyantly patterned carpets. Only a nondescript tiled floor anchoring a narrow hallway painted utilitarian beige. A small rectangular plaque pointed me toward the security office. I knocked on the door and a muffled voice said, "Come in."

I entered a small windowless office, dominated by a large desk and a tall filing cabinet. Smithson, wearing round wire-rim glasses, looked up from his computer screen. "Yes?"

I smiled, extending my hand. "I'm Madeline Keswick. We met last night in the Peerland's cabin. After their safe was broken into."

He pulled off his glasses and raised halfway up from his chair to shake my hand. "Yes, I remember you. What can I do for you?"

"Did you have a chance to check your security cameras from last night? To see who entered their cabin?"

I sat in the visitor chair wedged between his desk and the wall, angling my knees to fit into the small space. Smithson absently ran a pen back and forth between his palms, clicking it against the heavy ring he wore on his right hand. "Mrs. Peerland did not return to the boat from her excursion today. This was a big inconvenience for everyone." He tossed down the pen. "Made us late leaving Lucerne. Held up the other boats traveling behind us, waiting to dock. And we had to send out a search team."

He seemed much more concerned about the disruption to his travel schedule than he was about Corinne. "I'm sorry for your inconvenience, but I'm worried about her. Whoever broke into her safe may have attacked her today. Kidnapped her. Or even worse."

Smithson rocked back in his chair. "Perhaps she figured out that someone in her family robbed the safe. Argued with them and then decided to stay away from the boat until everyone had calmed down."

I could understand why he was eager to blame the family. If a passenger or staff member had robbed Corinne, that would lead to an extensive investigation, generating bad publicity for the riverboat and maybe a drop in future bookings. But if a family member did it, he could keep the incident quiet. No big investigation. No big scandal. No black marks for his security team.

"It couldn't have been the family," I said. "We were all with her in the lounge when she had that allergic reaction. That's when the money was stolen."

"Dr. Maynard said the Peerlands were in his clinic for almost an hour after her allergy attack, while he monitored her condition. Plenty of time for someone to get into that safe."

I shook my head. "This is an affluent family. Her poker winnings weren't nearly enough to tempt them." My voice was determined. "Now about that security feed …"

He pulled the keyboard closer. "Unfortunately, there was some type of malfunction with the cameras. All we got was this." He angled the screen toward me.

There was a blurred image that might have been someone's head. I couldn't pick out any details, not even enough to tell if it was a man or a woman. "That's not very helpful." I stared at the fuzzy screen. "What happened? Did somebody tamper with the camera?"

"We've had problems with the cameras before."

"And you didn't bother to fix them?"

"They were working at our routine security check last month."

A month gave someone plenty of time to tamper with the cameras. Was this a temporary blip in the system? Or did someone deliberately sabotage the recording? "What about the Lucerne police?" I asked. "Did they find any evidence in the Peerlands' cabin?"

"They did check out the cabin. Got a few fingerprints."

"That's great news. What happens now?"

"We are interviewing the staff. Someone may have seen something."

"You'll let me know what you find out?"

"I will discuss it with the Peerlands, when they rejoin the boat tomorrow in Strasbourg." He stood up. "Now, if there is nothing else?"

I was frustrated as I headed up to my cabin. The security recordings were useless. Smithson didn't seem eager to pursue suspects other than the family. Our best shot was that the Lucerne police would get a hit on the fingerprints.

But maybe I was getting all wound up over nothing. Maybe Kyle was right, and Corinne was cooling off somewhere. She would meet us tomorrow in Strasbourg with some crazy story about why she didn't make it back to the boat in time—she'd been haggling over the price of an expensive piece of jewelry, or she'd met some new friends and stopped for coffee, or she'd decided to hike down the mountain and hadn't realized how long it would take. She would apologize to the family. There would be hugs and tears and promises to be more careful next time.

It was possible. But as hours passed without any word from Fred, it didn't seem likely.

Chapter 10

WHEN I WOKE UP the next morning, the riverboat was docked in Strasbourg. I immediately grabbed my phone. There was a brief text from Fred: *No news yet. Will call later.*

I cringed at his message. If Corinne had been shopping or sightseeing, Fred would have found her by now. But if she was lost or hurt …. Overnight temperatures in the mountains would have dropped to well below freezing. I tried to remember what she had been wearing. A lightweight hooded jacket. Her favorite blue silk scarf. Flat-soled casual shoes good for city walking, but not much help in getting traction on rocky slopes. How long could she survive?

I took a quick shower, trying to chase away my morning-after fuzzies, the result of one-too-many gin and tonics last night. I had run into Wyatt at the bar after a contentious call with Lilly. She blamed me for Corinne's disappearance, saying I should have stuck with her when she left the café. Wyatt cheered me up, distracting me with funny stories about sports celebrities he'd met on the job.

I guzzled down a quick coffee to clear my cottony head and then headed to the atrium. Emily, wearing a long-sleeved beige sweater and a short turquoise skirt, was perched on a leather banquette, legs crossed, top foot bouncing. She was inspecting her flamingo-pink manicure, first spreading her fingers wide, then rotating her wrists and curving her fingers inward to her palms.

Bronwyn and Kyle were at the customer service desk. "No, this afternoon won't do," Bronwyn burst out, her voice forceful. She leaned over the counter to peer at the attendant's computer screen. "Surely you can arrange something now?"

I walked over to Luke, who stood by the expansive windows studying the shoreline. "Bronwyn wants to leave," he said. "To go back to Lucerne. She's pretty wound up this morning. Worried about her mom."

"I'm sure she is. We all are." I had thought the biggest challenge on this trip would be working her family into her campaign. I never expected her to go missing. "Any news from Fred?"

He shook his head. "A text. Saying he'd call later."

"That's the same message he sent me." I didn't want to say what we probably were both thinking—that no news wasn't a good sign.

Bronwyn turned toward us. Usually stylishly dressed and runway-ready, today she wore faded jeans and a baggy T-shirt. Without makeup, her skin tone was uneven and blotchy. Her hair was pulled back into a loose ponytail, with a few wispy blond tendrils escaping at her hairline. "She can't find a driver," Bronwyn said, gesturing at the customer service rep. "Which is ridiculous. There must be somebody available to take us."

Kyle touched her shoulder. "Would you settle down and wait to hear from Dad? He promised he'd call."

She shook him off and stepped back from the counter. The streaming light from the windows emphasized the dark smudges under her eyes. "I don't see how you can be so calm about this. Mom's been out on that mountain all night. She's probably frozen to death by now."

"You know Mom does this sort of thing," Kyle said. "Takes off on these little adventures. She'll turn up this morning, full of some funny story about what she's been doing."

"Kyle, what in the world are you talking about? Mom disappeared one time, thirty years ago. It hasn't happened since. Why are you so convinced that's what she's doing now?"

"I don't think …"

"You're right, you're not thinking," she said, cutting him off. "Because if you were, you'd be as worried as I am. I've called Dad several times this morning, but he's not picking up. That can't be good."

"Can't you talk some sense into your wife?" Kyle said. "Dad could already be on his way here. We shouldn't make plans until we hear from him."

Luke shook his head. "Whatever Bronwyn wants to do …"

Kyle frowned and turned to me. "Madeline, what do you think?"

I was surprised that he would ask for my opinion. "I'm concerned about Corinne. I don't think she would disappear like this without letting someone know where she was going."

"See there," Bronwyn said, "Madeline agrees with me. Something's very wrong."

I could understand her anxiety. She wanted to take quick action to fix everything, to find her mother and end this unbearable limbo. "But I do think it's best to talk to Fred before we make any plans. I got a text from him this morning. He said he'd call later. I'm sure we'll hear from him soon."

"Way to play both sides of the fence there, Madeline," Bronwyn said. "Thanks for your help." She conferred with Kyle and Luke. "What now? Should we stay on the boat and wait for his call?"

Kyle shook his head. "Are you kidding? Sit around on this boat for hours with nothing to do? That would drive us all nuts. I think we should go on our tour of Strasbourg as planned. We all have our phones."

"We can't just wander around playing tourist while our mother is missing," Bronwyn said.

"I think it's a great idea," Emily said, walking toward us, her tote bag slung over one shoulder. "I really want to get off this boat. Get some exercise."

Bronwyn glared at her. "You're not family. We're not interested in your opinion."

Kyle took a step toward Bronwyn. "Take it easy. I know you're upset, but there's no reason to take it out on Emily."

My phone chirped with an incoming message.

"Is that Dad?" Bronwyn said, peering over my shoulder. "What did he say?"

"It's Holliss," I said, reading the text. "Randall's not feeling well. They're skipping the Strasbourg tour. Said for the rest of us to go without them."

"That machete cut on his neck get infected?" Luke asked.

I shook my head. "Holliss says it's his stomach. He ate something that didn't agree with him. Has been up most of the night. They're both exhausted and are sleeping in."

"That woman is full of surprises," Kyle said, laughing. "Who knew she and Randall would come up with any excuse to hang around together all day in bed?"

"Kyle, can you focus?" Bronwyn said. "The question is, what do *we* do? Stay here or take the tour?"

"Let's do the tour," Luke said. "It will be easier on all of us if we keep busy until we hear from Fred. Hopefully, he'll have some good news."

"And if not?" Bronwyn asked.

Luke put his arm around her. "If not, we won't be that far from the boat. It will only take a few minutes to get back here and make plans for Lucerne."

Passengers milled around us in the atrium, ready to head out for the day's excursions. "Come on, let's get in line," Kyle said. "Some sunshine will do us all good."

"Hey, guys, wait up," a voice behind us called.

I turned to see Wyatt advancing through the crowd. "Any word on Corinne?" he asked.

"Nothing yet," Kyle said. "We're waiting for Dad to call us. Meanwhile, we're touring Strasbourg. Getting some exercise."

"Good idea," Wyatt said. "I'll join you."

***

Our tour guide was a cheerful, slightly overweight middle-aged woman who introduced herself as Gretchen. Wearing a dark skirt, white blouse and heavy-soled walking shoes, she pointed out the sites as she led us into the medieval city.

The bright sunshine of Strasbourg was a welcome contrast to the soggy Lucerne of yesterday, although there were still scattered puddles along the curb. I jumped over one, nimbly touching down on the sidewalk. Wyatt tried to imitate me, but instead stumbled and splashed into the water.

"Careful." I reached out a steadying hand.

"That was embarrassing." He stepped out of the puddle and onto the curb. "Old football injury. All that dancing the other night must have aggravated my back. Threw off my balance."

"You all right?"

He limped for the first few steps. "Need to walk it off. I'll be fine."

I slowed to his pace. Gretchen had almost finished her presentation when we caught up with her. "This section is called Tanners' Quarter," she said, gesturing toward the Tudor-style half-timbered buildings with their white-washed wattle-and-daub walls. "Fishermen, millers and tanners lived and worked here, right on the river."

The multi-story structures, their windows trimmed with colorful flower boxes, were reflected in the dark water of the canal. The scene reminded me of Venice, with buildings crowded right to the edge of the water and tourist boats gliding slowly under the bridges. Moving away from the crowd, I wandered along the river's edge, snapping pictures.

"It's beautiful now," Wyatt said, strolling beside me. "Probably not so much back when all those tanners were dumping their leftover chemicals into the canal. I'll bet at one time this river was a toxic waste dump. If you'd tossed in a match, the whole thing would have lit up."

I grimaced. "Are you trying to ruin this for me?"

"Not at all. Just trying to mix in a little reality."

"Reality is overrated." I pointed toward a side street. "Our group went that way. Let's go."

We caught up with Gretchen at a large plaza. "This is Johannes Gutenberg." She pointed to a large statue, green with age, of a man wearing a cape and braided hat. "The inventor of movable type. He lived in Strasbourg from 1430 to 1440. Around the base of the statue, you can see bas reliefs of people using his printing press."

"Wonder what he would have thought about ebooks?" Wyatt asked me.

"He'd probably be okay with that," I said. "After all, he was a forward thinker. Not afraid to try something new."

Gretchen pointed to the steeple of a cathedral a block or so behind us. "Now we'll visit Notre Dame cathedral, which is almost as famous as Notre Dame in Paris. Our Strasbourg cathedral took over 200 years to build and was completed in 1439. It is the sixth-tallest church in the world and is a marvelous example of Gothic architecture. Notice the pointed arches and flying buttresses."

Emily caught Kyle's elbow as we shuffled off behind Gretchen. "Let's ride the carousel first," she said, gesturing toward the old-fashioned merry-go-round situated near the Gutenberg statue. It was a colorful menagerie of giraffes, elephants and lions, surrounded by brightly painted prancing horses which moved slowly up and down on their brass poles.

Kyle studied the line of small children waiting their turn, scuffing their shoes in the dirt, pulling impatiently at their parents' jackets. "Don't you think we're a little old for that?"

"Come on," she said, tugging at his arm. "Embrace your inner child. It'll be fun. Much more fun than some stuffy old cathedral."

The rest of us followed behind Gretchen. "Emily's ridiculous," Bronwyn muttered as she left Kyle and Emily behind.

Luke chuckled at the sight of Kyle waiting in line behind children a third of his size. "Give her a break. She makes him happy."

Bronwyn sniffed. "She makes him act like a stupid teenager. He did enough of that after Janice left him."

Luke wrapped his arm around Bronwyn's shoulders. "It's a carousel ride, Bronwyn. Not a bar, or a strip club, or some back-room poker game. He's not slipping back into all those bad habits."

"I don't trust her," Bronwyn said. "She's a leech. Sticking with him because she thinks he'll make her rich."

Luke playfully swatted at her ponytail. "You're being too tough on her. She's keeping him focused on his company. I think she's working as hard as he is."

Bronwyn knocked his hand away. "Trust me, if Kyle's company falls apart, Emily will disappear faster than cockroaches at midnight when the kitchen lights come on."

Luke grimaced. "If his company falls apart, I'll be searching for a second and third job. And you may need to polish your resume, too. We have a lot of money invested with him." He tugged at his baseball cap. "Kyle could do a lot worse. Let him have a little fun."

Gretchen was waiting for us at the entrance to the cathedral. "Near the altar, there's a famous astronomical clock you won't want to miss," she said. "It dates back to 1843 and shows the planets, solar and lunar eclipses, and a procession of Christ and the apostles, including a life-size cock that crows three times."

"No home should be without one," Wyatt whispered, bending low so only I could hear him. "I hear Walmart is running a special next week."

"It's the perfect Christmas gift," I joked. "I've been waiting for a sale."

Gretchen moved briskly through the cathedral, gesturing toward the pointed arches, fluted columns and stained-glass windows. Under the towering ceiling I felt tiny and insignificant, which was probably the plan when the medieval architects designed it—to make people feel humble in the majestic presence of God. When the tour was finished, we stepped outside. Bronwyn paced in a circle as she talked on her phone, her coloring even more uneven than it had been this morning.

"What's going on?" I moved toward Luke. "Is she talking to Fred?"

"Yes. But I don't think it's good news."

Bronwyn finished the call. "There's been no sign of Mom." She sniffed and brushed away tears. "It snowed on the mountain last night, which is making the search more difficult. They've sent out helicopters and dogs." She reached out for Luke. "You should have heard Dad's voice. He sounded so lost. So alone. I don't know what he'll do if we can't find her."

Luke hugged her, stroking her back. "We'll find her, Bronwyn. Everyone is out there searching for her. Don't give up."

She broke free. "We've got to go back to Lucerne. Right now. I'll text Kyle."

"I'll go, too," I said. "Corinne means a lot to me. I'm really concerned about her."

"I'd rather you didn't," Bronwyn said, gripping her phone. "You've done quite enough damage already, talking our mother into doing this Senate thing."

Why did her family think I had so much control over Corinne? Did they not realize what a strong-willed woman their mother was? "You think her Senate run was my idea?"

"Why else would she think of it?" Bronwyn's chin trembled. "She was devastated when she didn't get the top job at her company. Hated the thought of retirement. And then she started talking about you. How you had lost your job but bounced back. She told us how much she admired you. If you could start over, she could, too."

I shook my head. "This campaign was her idea. I didn't have anything to do with it."

"Yeah, right." Bronwyn's tears caught in her throat. "If you hadn't been there, goading her along, she wouldn't have done anything so stupid. Our family wouldn't have had that horrible fight. And she'd still be alive."

I could understand why Bronwyn would lash out, eager to put the blame on someone else, but I didn't relish the role of scapegoat. "As far as we know, Bronwyn, she *is* still alive. I'd like to help."

Luke mumbled something into Bronwyn's ear as she started to object. Then they walked away, Luke's arm wrapped around her waist, leaving Wyatt and me standing by the cathedral.

Wyatt put a hand on my shoulder. "You know she didn't mean all that. She's all twisted up inside, worrying about her mother."

"I guess." I was pretty twisted up myself. Corinne had brought me on this trip to work with her family. So far, I wasn't doing a very good job of it. "I'm worried, too. And I'm going back to Lucerne. Corinne isn't only my client. She's my friend."

Chapter 11

WYATT AND I stopped at an outdoor café for coffee, watching the crowds go by, giving Bronwyn time to pack and head out for Lucerne so we could avoid another confrontation. We should have lingered a bit longer, because they were still at the dock when we walked up. Bronwyn stood beside an idling van talking to the driver, while Kyle and Luke helped load up their numerous suitcases.

Emily grabbed her travel tote as Kyle reached for it. "No, I'm keeping that one with me," she said. "There's a lot of breakable stuff in there. I don't want it shoved in the back."

"Suit yourself," Kyle said.

"Where's Holliss?" I asked, walking up to them. "Isn't she going with you?"

Bronwyn exuded a studied air of unconcern. "I texted her. Told her we were heading to Lucerne. Haven't heard anything."

"So you're going to leave her?"

"Holliss can make her own arrangements. Besides, there's not room for anyone else in this van. Not with all our luggage." She wound her ponytail into a knot on the top of her head. "Hey, guys, let's go."

Luke turned to give Wyatt and me a half-hearted wave as they climbed into the van and pulled into traffic.

"That was cold," I said. "I can't believe Bronwyn left her sister behind."

"Families do crazy things. Especially when they're as upset as Bronwyn." Wyatt turned to me. "What about you? You still going to Lucerne?"

"Yes, as soon as I can arrange transportation. But first I need to find Holliss, to tell her what's going on. See if she wants to come with me."

I hustled up the gangplank, flashing my room key at the security guard. Holliss didn't answer her door, so I took a quick spin through the main level, checking the gift shop and lounge, before I moved up to the sundeck. Holliss and Randall were stretched out in lounge chairs, reading paperbacks.

"Hi, Madeline," Holliss said, lifting the brim of her hat as I walked up. "Is your tour over already?"

"We cut it a little short." I tried to think of a gentle way to tell her she'd been deserted. "Have you checked your phone? Bronwyn's sent you a couple of messages."

"We left our phones in the room. Wanted some peace and quiet. Randall was up all night with his stomach."

"You feeling better, Randall?" I asked.

"Some. I'm not ready to chow down on a twelve-ounce filet and a loaded baked potato," he said, "but my stomach has stopped rumbling, so that's good."

Holliss pulled off her sunglasses. "What's up? What did Bronwyn want?"

I sat on the lounge chair beside her. "She talked to your dad."

She shoved the book in her tote. "What's the news? Did they find Mom?"

"Not yet. But there's a full court press, with helicopters and dogs and everything."

"Thank God," Holliss said, with a relieved sigh. "They'll find her soon. This has been a nightmare."

She was assuming a happy ending, which I thought less and less likely as time passed. "There's been more snow," I said, trying to lower her expectations. "That's slowing down the search."

Holliss stood up. "Where's Bronwyn? I want to talk to her."

"She's gone."

"What do you mean, gone? Gone where?"

"Back to Lucerne. To be with your dad."

Anger bubbled up. "She didn't tell me?"

I hesitated. "She said she texted you."

"Luke went, too? And Kyle and Emily?" Holliss let out a long, slow hiss. "So once again, I get left behind. Did they really think I'd want to stay here and finish the cruise? While the rest of them go searching for our mother?"

My heart ached for her. Neither her brother nor sister had given much thought to what Holliss might want. "I'm getting a driver to take me back to Lucerne," I said. "Do you guys want to ride with me?"

Holliss turned to Randall. "Do you feel well enough for that? Can your stomach take it?"

"Let's do it."

"Thanks, Madeline," she said. "That would be helpful. Let me know when you're ready to leave."

Wyatt was standing at customer service when I got back to the atrium. "I've got a driver," he said. "For the four of us."

"The four of us?" I said in surprise. "You're going to Lucerne, too?"

He put his credit card back in his wallet. "I know I haven't known this family very long, but Kyle and I are poker buddies. Corinne, too. I feel like I have to help."

"That's very kind of you, but I'm sure the family doesn't expect you to cut your vacation short."

"You guys are the only people I know on this cruise. I wouldn't be able to enjoy it, not knowing what was happening. Besides, the next couple of days may be tough. You may need someone to run interference in case Bronwyn goes ballistic."

"She might," I agreed, "considering the mood she was in when she left here."

"It's settled then." He thanked the attendant as she handed him the vouchers for the van. "I'll see you down here in an hour."

***

I called Lilly while I packed. Since I didn't know how long we'd be away from the boat, or whether we'd be coming back at all, I stuffed everything into my suitcase. Her phone rang several times before she finally answered, her voice heavy with sleep. "Hello?"

"Lilly, we're heading back to Lucerne, to look for Corinne. I wanted to let you know."

"What?" she mumbled.

"It's Madeline. Did I wake you?"

"Yeah." She groaned. "It's still dark outside. What time is it?"

"I'm sorry, Lilly. I wasn't paying attention to the time difference. Go back to sleep. I'll call you later."

"No. I'm awake now," she said, yawning. "What's going on?"

"We're in Strasbourg, getting ready to go back to Lucerne. Bronwyn talked to her dad this morning. They haven't found Corinne."

"She's been missing all night?"

"Afraid so. And there was new snow on the mountain overnight. It's making the search tougher."

I could hear things rattle in the background. Now that Lilly was awake, she needed coffee. "This is terrible. You've got to find her. You know how important she is to us."

"I know, Lilly. And I'm doing everything I can. Wyatt's lined up a van for us. I'll call you later from Lucerne, when I know more."

"Who's Wyatt?"

"Someone from the cruise. He and Kyle are buddies. Met our first night at a poker game. Wyatt's going back to Lucerne with us."

"He's cutting short his cruise? For a bunch of strangers? Why would he do that?"

"He's traveling by himself. Guess he figures he's part of our group. Wants to help."

Her coffee grinder whirred. "Have you and this Wyatt guy got something going on? Is that why he's headed to Lucerne?"

Trust Lilly to read romance into every relationship. "Come on, Lilly, I hardly know the guy. He's certainly not going back on my account."

"Is he cute?"

"Sort of. Dark hair. Olive skin. Maybe a Mediterranean background. Not handsome enough to be the star in those rom coms you like so much, but definitely cute enough to play the good buddy."

"Travis is not going to like this one bit."

"What's Travis got to do with this?"

"He's been calling every day. About that article he's doing."

"I've already told him I'm not interested." Travis was an uncomfortable reminder of a difficult time in my life.

"Give the guy a break, Madeline. You know it's his way of apologizing for everything that happened."

"Too late for that now. Travis needs to move on."

Chapter 12

WYATT WAS ALREADY at the dock when I rolled my suitcase down the gangplank. "Here, let me help you with that," he said, lifting it into the waiting van. Randall and Holliss joined us a few minutes later.

"I've texted Dad to tell him we're coming," Holliss said. "He's going to make hotel reservations for us."

"Good idea," I said.

Randall helped Holliss up into the van. "You don't mind if I sit up front, do you? I don't think my queasy stomach can deal with a back seat."

"Sure. You guys take the front. That will give you more legroom, anyway. Madeline can sit in the back with me."

As we started off, I pulled out my phone to catch up on emails, but I was too unsettled to concentrate. Corinne's disappearance was my fault. I knew how vulnerable she was. If I had followed her when she left the café, if I'd given her the reassurance she needed, we'd all be together right now. Hopefully, I'd get another chance. I had to believe that Corinne was still alive, that we'd get her campaign back on track. She had worked too hard—Lilly and I had worked too hard—to lose everything now.

Holliss stirred beside me and lifted her arms in a long, leisurely stretch, displaying the five-inch black-and-gold tarantula that was tattooed above her left wrist. She had gotten it when she was fifteen and said it had been well worth the painful hours of needle pricks, even though her livid parents sentenced her to a month of no phone, no video games and no television once they saw it. It was high-quality work, with perfect proportions, crisp lines and subtle shading, three-dimensional and incredibly life-like. When she angled her arm a certain way and the light hit just right, that fat arachnid appeared to be climbing down to wrap its hairy legs around her fingers.

"I'm sorry you didn't get to ride back with Bronwyn," I said, turning toward her. "She should have tried harder to get in touch."

"It's fine." Holliss slowly lowered her arms, dropping them in her lap. "She and Kyle need to be together right now. They're worried about Mom."

"They still should have waited for you," I insisted. "She's your mother, too."

"I've never been part of their team." Her green eyes held a look of studied resignation. "Mom and Kyle and Bronwyn … they've always been like bright suns at the center of the universe, sticking together, doing whatever they want." Her face was layered with regret. "Dad and I, on the other hand, are the outliers, frozen chunks of rock that spin in the shadows around them."

"I'm sure that's not true."

"Of course it is. Take this thing about Natalie. I never heard anything about her until the accident a few years back. Why did I never meet my own cousin?"

"That does seem strange." Corinne had been cryptic with me, saying only that Natalie's death had been very painful for the family. "Do you know what happened to her?"

"Not really. Bronwyn and Kyle were tight-lipped. Said she drowned when her car ran off a bridge into a river."

"That's terrible. And they never mentioned her before the accident?"

"Nope. The two of them operate in their own little world. Not much room for me." Holliss pulled a sweater from her tote. "You've heard the story of how Kyle saved Bronwyn's life when we were kids?"

I shook my head.

"I thought Mom might have told you. It's a famous piece of family folklore."

"Corinne and I mostly talked about work."

Holliss stuck an arm into the sweater. "It's a good story. We were at the river cottage. I was a baby, and the nanny had put me down for a nap. Mom and Dad were visiting friends. Bronwyn and Kyle were outside playing on this old tree that our parents had warned them to stay away from. Bronwyn grabbed the rope and swung way out over the water. The branch broke and she slammed down hard. Came up screaming and then started to sink."

"She couldn't swim?"

"She could, but it turns out she'd dislocated her shoulder, so she floundered there, gulping in water. Kyle dove in after her. He got her to shore, performed CPR, and then drove her to the nearest hospital. He was twelve, maybe thirteen.

It's a wonder they didn't end up in a ditch somewhere." She reached behind her back, searching for the second sleeve. "By the time our parents got home, Kyle had attacked that tree with a chain saw. All that was left was a rotten stump."

"A young kid like that could handle a chain saw?" I asked.

"Are you kidding? The way I heard it, he was so pumped on adrenaline that he probably could have pulled that tree up with his fingernails."

"Sounds like a pretty determined guy."

She smoothed the sweater into place and tugged her hair free, letting the dark curls cascade down her back. "He is. He'd do anything for Bronwyn."

Did that include tossing me off the riverboat? I wasn't sure if I should share that incident with Holliss, but I wanted to get her read on it. "He threatened me, Holliss. Our first night on the *Rhinelinder*. Told me I had to stop your mom's campaign before it destroyed the family."

"A bit melodramatic, but not a surprise. Bronwyn had been after him all night to talk Mom out of running. She was worried about Luke's job."

"You don't understand. He had me pinned to the railing. If a crew member hadn't come up on deck, I think he would have thrown me overboard."

"Now *you're* being melodramatic. Kyle's always pushing the envelope. He was constantly in trouble when we were kids. And he still does dumb stuff, like that paragliding thing with Luke, which is why I warned you about him. But he's not crazy enough to throw you overboard."

"You sure about that?"

"Positive."

"Not even if Bronwyn asked him to?"

She pulled the sweater around her. "Now that's a tough one. If she really wanted him to get rid of somebody, I'm not sure he'd turn her down."

"So he could have done it?" A cold chill ran down my back. "Thrown me overboard?"

"You should see your face. Like you've had a close encounter with a vampire." She laughed as she picked up her phone. "No, I don't think he would throw you overboard. Although I'm sure he wanted to."

"That's not very reassuring."

"Just keep your head down. And maybe stay away from the river. Or tall buildings. Or deserted alleyways. Anyplace, really, where he could cut you off from the herd." She gave me an enigmatic smile. "If that happens, you're on your own."

***

For the rest of the trip, I mentally replayed the riverboat scene, trying to decide how far Kyle would have gone to get rid of me. He had said it would destroy the family if Corinne went through with her campaign. Holliss thought he'd been talking about Luke's job, but there had to be more to it than that. Luke was a talented salesman who would always land on his feet. Even if he did have to eventually switch out of oil drilling and into another industry, that wouldn't destroy the family, would it? What was Kyle hiding from me?

Finally, we reached the outskirts of Lucerne. Holliss texted her dad as our driver skillfully maneuvered through the city traffic. As we pulled into the cobblestone courtyard of Des Balances Hotel, Fred came out to greet us.

"Dad," Holliss said, throwing her arms around him. I was struck again by how much she resembled her dad—the same strong chin, the same coloring. "What's going on? Have you found Mom?"

"Not yet." His clothes were rumpled as though he'd been up all night, his chin dotted with whiskers. "Bronwyn and Kyle are out canvassing the shops with a picture of Corinne, to check if anyone has seen her." He followed the driver to the back of the van, to help unload the luggage. "We've already done that, of course, but who knows? Maybe they'll turn up something that the police and I have missed."

"Fred, you remember Wyatt, from the riverboat," I said, as the driver set my roller bag down on the cobblestones. "He was kind enough to arrange our transportation from Strasbourg."

The two men shook hands and then wrestled our luggage up the steep steps to reception. "Let's get you guys checked in," Fred said. "Go up to your rooms and freshen up. I'll be waiting down here, to update you on what's happened."

The elevator was barely large enough for the four of us. We left the luggage downstairs for the bellman to deliver later. Hollis, Randall and I got off on the third floor. "I'm one floor up," Wyatt said, as the elevator door slowly closed. "I'll see you guys later. Right now, I want to touch base with Kyle."

My room was comfortable, with a double bed, a desk and a small chair. I wanted nothing more than to collapse on the bed and pretend that none of this had happened, but I needed to hear Fred's update. I splashed water on my face and fluffed my hair before I headed downstairs.

Fred and Holliss were waiting for me in the lobby. "Where's Randall?" I asked.

"He's napping," Holliss said. "The medicine that the doctor gave him made him sleepy. He'll join us later."

Fred led us through the main dining room to the long balcony overlooking the river. We had been here yesterday, but my memories were gray and sodden, everything glimpsed through the blurry lens of rain. Today the sun put everything in sharp focus—the painted bridges leading across the river, the magnificent Baroque cathedral with its towering steeples, the swans clamoring onto the sidewalks to scoop up tourist-tossed bread.

"There's no trace of Mom?" Holliss asked after the waiter took our beverage orders. "Nothing at all?"

Fred shook his head. "We've checked everywhere. All the shops in Lucerne and Pilatus and everywhere in between. Hotels. Private homes. Anywhere we think she might have been."

"She's gone?" Holliss's fingernails dug into the tablecloth. "Disappeared without a trace? How is that possible?"

The waiter returned, setting down a bottle of beer in front of Fred and porcelain teapots and cups for Hollis and me. Holliss dunked a teabag in the hot water. "I don't understand how this happened. We were all together in that café. Nobody saw her leave? Nobody saw anything?"

"It's a tourist site," Fred said. "By the time we realized Corinne was missing, a lot of people who might have seen her were long gone. The police are questioning all the employees in the area—the waiters, cable car operators, hotel staff—but so far no one remembers her."

I poured steaming liquid into my cup. "What about security cameras? Did they show anything?"

"They have pictures of us getting off the cable car and going out on the viewing platform, and then later leaving the mountain. Except for Corinne. There's no shot of her getting on the cable car to come down."

Holliss slowly stirred sugar into her tea. "So she's still up there somewhere."

Not wanting to think that Corinne was buried in the snow, I tried to come up with another scenario. "Kyle told us that Corinne has done this before. Gone off without telling anyone. Do you think maybe she did that again?"

A deep groove formed between Fred's eyebrows. "What was he talking about? Corinne's never done anything like this."

"He said it was before I was born," Holliss said. "That she disappeared for a few days. And you left Bronwyn and Kyle with Grandma and took off after her."

"Oh, that." Fred picked at his beer label. "It was nothing. Kyle was a child when that happened. He's gotten the story confused."

Something in his expression hinted that there was more to Kyle's story than Fred was willing to share. He kept his eyes down, sliding the bottle back and forth, leaving a wet channel in the tablecloth. "I feel like I have to do something. It's the waiting … not knowing … that's killing me." He shifted in his chair. "I'm thinking of posting a reward. Maybe putting something on TV. Someone must have seen her."

I'd seen that strategy before, the strained faces of parents or spouses squinting at the bright lights of television cameras, pleading with the public to help them find their loved ones: the teenage jogger who'd disappeared during her nightly run; the college student who vanished after getting separated from friends at a bar; the young mother gone missing after dropping her children off at soccer practice. Families struggling to hold on to hope, even as days passed with no news, and the probability of a happy resolution seemed less and less likely.

But Corinne hadn't gone out at night by herself. She'd been with her family in the middle of the day, in a tourist area crowded with people.

"You think she was kidnapped?" I asked.

"It's possible," Fred said. "A wealthy woman. A prominent U.S. citizen. After all, she had just gone public with her campaign. Her picture was all over the internet."

I sipped my tea. "But you haven't gotten a ransom demand."

"Not yet. But I don't think we can rule it out."

A loud chirping noise startled me.

"It's my phone," Fred said, digging into his pocket. He squinted at the screen. "A message from the policeman who's been working this case. Captain Mueller. He wants to see me."

"He has news about Corinne?" I asked.

"I hope so." Fred frowned as he concentrated on typing a reply, his fingers awkward on the tiny keys. "I told him we were all here at the hotel. That my family had come back to Lucerne." He clutched the phone in his palm, waiting for a response. "Some vacation, huh? Corinne had such high hopes for this trip. And now this, sitting around waiting for the police. Not exactly what she had in mind."

The phone chirped again. "He wants me to meet him at the station." Fred shoved the phone back in his pocket.

"Do you want us to go with you?" I asked, glancing at Holliss. "To talk to him?"

He shook his head. "No. I'll go. See what he's found out. Then we'll get everyone together and share the news."

Holliss and I headed back to our rooms. My luggage had been delivered. I hung a few things in the closet and then stretched out on the bed, fighting off a headache, hoping for a few minutes of uninterrupted oblivion. I was almost asleep when my phone buzzed. Fred's name popped up on my screen. "Did you talk to the police?"

"Yes. I'm with Captain Mueller now. At the station." He paused. "He wants to meet with all of us, Madeline. Right now, at the hotel. I'll call Kyle and Bronwyn. Could you get in touch with Holliss?"

"Of course. We'll be waiting for you."

***

The family had already gathered in the lobby by the time I got downstairs. Holliss and Randall were huddled at one end of a tweed sofa. Bronwyn sat in a wing chair across from them, back straight, feet flat on the floor, as rigid as an anxious candidate at a job interview. Her broken finger in its metal sheath extended upward like the antenna of a giant insect.

Kyle sprawled in a nearby chair, one ankle hooked casually over his knee, thumbing through text messages. Emily perched on an ottoman beside him, her head tilted to the side, methodically braiding her long dark hair. "Are they in or not?" she asked him.

"Give me a break," he said. "I'm trying to put out a fire here."

"There wouldn't be a fire if you had listened to me. If I'd known earlier what was going on …"

"Seriously?" He glared at her. "You really think you could have fixed this?"

She shook out her hair, unwinding the braid. "I would have done something. You let this go on way too long."

"Relax, Emily. I'm taking care of it," Kyle said. "Nothing for you to worry about."

She crossed her legs, nervously bouncing her foot. "I don't think it's right for that detective to keep us waiting like this." She picked at her fingernails. "Fred said he was coming right over, and it's been like half an hour already."

Bronwyn slowly lifted her chin. "You have something better to do? Something more important than finding out what happened to my mother? Maybe get your hair done? Another manicure?" She pointed at Emily's chipped polish.

Emily shook her hair back behind her shoulders. "You don't have to take that tone with me, Bronwyn. It's just that, you know, I'm tired of sitting here."

"You've been here ten minutes," Bronwyn said. "I think my mother is worth a little more time than that."

Kyle put down the phone. "Lighten up, Bronwyn," he said. "We're all a little stressed over this."

Luke, standing by the window, pulled the drapery back as a car pulled up onto the cobblestones outside. "They're here."

Chapter 13

I COULD TELL right away it was bad news.

Fred and three other people got out of the car. Fred started up the steep steps to the lobby, hunched over, his head down. He grabbed at the rail, pulling himself up step by step, as though his legs alone were not strong enough to get him to the top.

The man who walked beside him was stocky and middle-aged, with buzz-cut dark hair graying at the temples. His broad shoulders and straight back were in sharp contrast to Fred's defeated crumple. His hand floated in mid-air below Fred's elbow, ready to grab him if he wobbled.

The other two followed Fred up the steps, younger than the first man, probably in their mid-thirties. One of them was a woman, a slim blond with her hair pulled into a smooth bun at the nape of her neck. The man beside her had the stringy physique of a cross-country runner.

Fred pushed through the revolving glass doors and led them toward us, introducing everyone. "Dad, what's going on?" Bronwyn asked, rushing up to clutch his arm. "Have they found Mom?"

Fred hesitated, struggling to swallow. "Captain Mueller will explain everything."

"Oh, my God," Bronwyn said, her voice rising. "Dad, is she dead?"

Before Fred could answer, Mueller gestured toward the back of the lobby. "There is a conference room, where we can talk privately. If you will follow me?"

"I don't care about your conference room," she said. "I want to know right now. Where is my mother?"

Luke put his arm around his wife. "Please, honey, we don't want to do this here. Let's follow these folks. I'm sure they'll tell us everything."

Bronwyn reluctantly joined the rest of us as we headed down the hallway to a windowless conference room. The detritus of an earlier meeting had not yet been cleared away. A side credenza held several empty pots of coffee as well as a platter bearing a few dried-out croissants. A white board at the end of the room had the title "Future Challenges" written in large letters, with several bullet points beneath.

The two younger detectives herded us into the room and closed the door. We pulled out the heavy chairs and arranged ourselves along the sides of the conference table. Mueller moved in front of the white board, arms hanging stiffly by his sides. He was serious and professional, like an academic ready to lecture on history or economics or tax reform. But we all knew what he was about to say. And we didn't want to hear it.

Mueller cleared his throat. "I am afraid I have some very bad news." He spoke with a slight British accent, which I'd found typical of English-speaking Europeans, each word carefully articulated, using formal sentence structure devoid of contractions. "Our search teams have found the body of Mrs. Peerland."

Bronwyn gripped the arms of her chair. "No. Not my mother. You're wrong."

Luke put his arm around her. "Bronwyn, I'm so sorry."

"What happened?" Holliss's chin trembled as she grabbed Randall's hand. "Where was she?"

Mueller stepped closer to the table. "The teams worked hard to find her. It was difficult because the mountain drops off steeply there. The snow is very deep." He paused. "Mrs. Peerland was found in a ravine below the viewing platform."

"Below the viewing platform?" Kyle said. "Wouldn't that be the first place you'd check? Why did it take almost twenty-four hours to find her?"

I remembered the platform had been slick with ice. And the cloud cover so thick we could barely see from one side of the railing to the other. What had Kyle said that day? That if someone fell off, they wouldn't be found until summer? At least it hadn't taken that long to find Corinne.

"You should have found her sooner," Bronwyn sputtered. "If you'd done your job, my mother would still be alive."

Unrattled by the vitriol tossed at him, Mueller spoke calmly. "It has snowed up there ever since she was reported missing. White-out conditions. It is a treacherous area. Our team had difficulty accessing it."

"Still," Bronwyn insisted, "you had helicopters. Dogs. You should have found her."

"Bronwyn, please," Fred said, his voice hoarse. "I was up there with the team. We searched all night. They did everything they could."

"Did she die in the fall?" Bronwyn asked, fighting tears. "Or did you let her freeze to death before you got to her?"

"It's not their fault," Fred said. "Don't blame the searchers for this."

"It was an accident?" Kyle asked. "She fell off the mountain?"

"We are not sure of that." Mueller focused on each of us, studying our faces, assessing our response.

"What do you mean, *not sure*?" Luke asked. "What do you think happened?"

"We are studying the evidence," Mueller said. "And since you were all with her right before it happened, we want to talk to each of you individually, to see what you remember about the event."

"The event?" Bronwyn's voice was harsh. "This wasn't some *event*, like a fund raiser or a business meeting. This was my mother."

Mueller refused to be baited into a sharp response. "I understand how difficult this is for all of you. We will keep our questions as brief as possible." His arm sliced toward Kyle. "If you would stay in here with me, please. And if the two of you ..." he indicated Bronwyn and Holliss ... "would follow my associates. The rest of you can wait in the lobby. We will get to you as quickly as we can."

"No, you're not going to split us up like this," Bronwyn said. "You've just told us our mother is dead. We need some time together to grieve before you start digging at us with questions."

"Of course," Mueller said. "We will give Mrs. Peerland's children a few moments together. If the rest of you would please wait in the lobby?"

Fred rose slowly to his feet. "Let's let these folks do their job." Luke, Emily, Randall and I stood up to follow him.

"So now what?" Luke asked as we reached the end of the hallway. "Sit around and wait? Go for a walk? Get a drink?"

"Mueller probably doesn't want us to leave the building," Randall said. "And I don't think a drink is such a good idea, right before we're questioned by the police, but I could use some coffee. Anyone want to hang out in the restaurant?"

"Sure," Emily said, tugging at the sleeves of her jacket. "I'd like the company."

"Fred? Madeline? You want to join us?" Luke asked.

Fred shook his head. "I'd like to be by myself for a while. I can't believe this is happening."

"Understood," Luke said. "It's a nightmare for all of us. If you change your mind, come join us. Might do you good to talk."

After the others walked away, I waited a minute with Fred. "I am so sorry. I wish I could come up with the right words, but I don't know what to say."

"I don't know what to say either. Or what to do." His expression held an air of bewilderment. "When Mueller told me that they'd found her, he insisted that he be the one to break the news to the family. You saw the way they all reacted. It was horrible. I should have been the one to tell them, to do it more gently. I should never have let him take control."

"I'm not sure you had a lot of choice, Fred," I said, trying to reassure him. "Mueller seemed determined. And the news would have been as painful coming from you."

"But the way he's handling it." Fred shook his head. "Mueller's one cold-hearted cop. He's already spent hours questioning me. Now he's grilling my family one by one, to see what they remember." He rubbed his chin. "I'm going up to my room, Madeline. Let me know if anyone needs me."

"Of course." As Fred walked toward the elevators, I settled into an overstuffed chair near the lobby fireplace. Mueller was running roughshod over the family, studying the evidence, questioning us one by one. He didn't know what had happened up on that mountain, but I was pretty sure he didn't believe it was an accident. And from the suspicious way he had studied all of us in that conference room, I was sure he thought that one of us was a murderer.

Chapter 14

I WAS ON MY second coffee when the female detective came into the lobby, signaling for me to follow her. I was glad she would be the one questioning me. Despite her severe hairstyle, she had a kind face, with thin, pale eyebrows and a rosy blush that softened her cheeks. She reminded me of a kindergarten teacher, someone stern on the surface, but full of compassion and sympathy. Someone who expected you to do the right thing and tell the truth, but who realized that it was okay if you messed up a little bit every now and again.

We walked into a conference room. "If you will please wait here?" she said, gesturing to a chair. "Captain Mueller will be with you shortly."

My mouth felt dry as she left the room. She wouldn't be the one interviewing me, after all. Mueller seemed like a no-nonsense interrogator who would throw rapid-fire questions until he got the answers he wanted, probing for the weakest link. I hoped that wasn't me.

He walked in a few minutes later, his eyes stern, nodding slightly to acknowledge my presence. "Please sit down. We will record this." He pressed a button on the small machine in front of us, wasting no time on pleasantries, stating his name, my name, and the date. "You were employed by Mrs. Peerland? Please explain your job."

I spoke slowly, determined to sound professional. "I'm a public relations consultant. Mrs. Peerland was a candidate for the U.S. Senate. She hired my firm to build her brand and expand her platform. To develop a consistent message for her to deliver to potential voters."

He pulled a small notebook from his jacket pocket. "Why would she bring her public relations consultant on a family vacation?"

I was puzzled that he wanted to take notes even though he was recording our conversation, but maybe he was a belt-and-suspenders kind of guy, extra cautious in following the rules and sifting through evidence, making sure that nothing got overlooked. "It was a work vacation for Corinne and me. She wanted me to meet her family and figure out how to include them in her campaign."

"I see." He flipped through the notebook and reached for his pen. "Tell me what happened at Pilatus."

He had heard the story from the rest of the family. I was determined to make my comments as generic as possible, to make sure I didn't contradict what anyone else might have said. "It was cold. And cloudy. Disappointing, really, after we'd come all that way to see the beautiful views that the guidebooks raved about."

"I am not inquiring about the weather," he grumbled. "What happened with Mrs. Peerland?"

"Because it was cold and cloudy," I continued, refusing to let him throw me off my rhythm, "we all went into the café. The family discussed Corinne's political plans. And then she left."

"How did her family feel about her campaign?"

It was a reasonable question, but something in his tone gave me the same uneasy feeling I'd had when I talked to the security guys on the riverboat—that family members were already the primary suspects. I guess it made sense from a detective's point of view—easier to start with people close at hand, rather than throwing out a wide net. But despite his suspicions, my loyalty was to Corinne and her family. Even with their opposition to her campaign, I couldn't believe any of them would have harmed her. "They knew it was an exciting new challenge for Corinne. A chance to have a positive impact on the world."

He leaned back in his chair, his eyes skeptical. "I heard there was a big family fight. Much yelling."

I nervously grasped the edge of the table. "*Fight* is perhaps too strong a word. Her family thought it would be a difficult campaign since she was a first-time candidate with little name recognition. They worried that she'd be very disappointed if she lost."

Mueller raised a dark bushy eyebrow. One long silver hair stuck out at an awkward angle. "Perhaps they thought it was a waste of time and money?"

Kyle had said something like that at dinner. Had he repeated it to Mueller? Back at home, none of us would have talked to the police about something this serious without having an attorney by our side. Now someone was spilling out details, with no thought of the consequences.

"Politics is a tough business. Corinne knew that. But she had the support of her party. Her chances were pretty good."

He raised his eyebrow again. If I'd had tweezers in my pocket, I would have stretched across the table and yanked out that stray silver hair. He clicked his pen rapidly. "When she left the café, did anyone go with her?"

I thought back to that scene. Fred started to follow her, but Kyle convinced him she needed time to cool down. "Not that I noticed. I finished my latte, and then Wyatt and I went to the gift shop."

"Who's Wyatt?"

"Wyatt Carlton. A friend we met on the riverboat."

He wrote slowly in his notebook, taking time to carefully form the upward and downward strokes of each letter, as precise and controlled as if he were writing calligraphy. "We will want to talk to him, too. Where is he now? Still on the boat?"

"No, he's here in Lucerne, at the hotel. Came back with us because he was concerned about Corinne."

He flipped to the next page. "What did you buy in the gift shop?"

Was he trying to turn this into a pleasant chat about my shopping habits, so I would let my guard down and reveal some incriminating detail? I was tired of his endless questions. "Souvenirs."

His eyes bored into mine, as if warning me not to cross him, but he didn't press the point. If he thought it was important, he could probably pull my credit card receipts. "And then what?"

"Then I took the cable car back down the mountain. Returned to the boat."

"Were any of the family members with you on the trip down the mountain? Or this other man …" he consulted his notes. "Wyatt Carlton?"

Like most men I knew, Wyatt wasn't much of a shopper. He had wandered off as I deliberated between a silver necklace or a mixed-metal link bracelet for Lilly. By the time I made my purchase, he had disappeared. "We didn't come down together, but he was waiting for me at the bottom, so the two of us caught the bus back. I didn't see anyone else until we were all on the riverboat."

Mueller leaned forward in his chair. "Help me understand this. There was a big family fight. Your client Mrs. Peerland ran out of the café, obviously upset, but instead of following her to make sure she was all right, you casually went souvenir shopping?"

When he phrased it that way, it made me seem incredibly shallow and self-centered. But I had already agonized over my behavior—if I had stuck with her when she left the café, she'd still be alive. My only defense was that I hadn't gone to the gift shop because I was in desperate need of trinkets for my friends, or because I felt some overwhelming urge to boost the local economy. It was because Bronwyn insisted that we give her mother some time alone.

"Her family decided she needed some privacy. Time to gather her thoughts."

"So she went out on that platform all by herself. In one of the few spots that was out of range of the security cameras. How convenient." His voice was heavy with sarcasm.

I was tired of his abuse. "You sound so convinced that the family is responsible for what happened to her. But you need to focus on other things, too. The night before her death, someone broke into her safe and stole two thousand dollars of her poker winnings."

"I heard about that."

It was frustrating that he dismissed the incident so lightly. I had to make him realize that people other than Corinne's family had a motive to harm her. "Did you hear that some of the staff from the boat, including our waiter Sergey, were there yesterday? Sergey was already angry with her because she'd reprimanded him at dinner in front of his boss. Yet when I asked Sergey about it, he denied he'd been there. Obviously, he was lying. Why would he lie if he wasn't involved in her murder?"

Mueller rested his elbows on the arms of the chair. "I haven't said she was murdered."

Why was he toying with me? "But you've spent hours questioning all of us. Which makes me think you don't believe it was an accident." I tried to keep the irritation out of my voice, but he could tell I was annoyed. He probably was counting on it, thinking I would blurt out something significant.

"We are not ready to make that determination."

I sucked in my lower lip, biting down hard as I tried to bring my emotions under control. How much more of this could I take before I punched this guy? "What about Sergey? Are you going to question him?"

"We will thoroughly investigate all the evidence. And talk to all potential witnesses."

I didn't think that list of witnesses would include Sergey. Mueller was too busy trying to blame this on the family. "There's something else you need to know."

"What's that?"

"Right before we got on the riverboat, Corinne and I attended an energy conference in Basel. She had meetings with several CEOs there. When we left, people attacked us. Pretty much flattened us both." I pulled out my phone. "There's a video."

I trembled as I relived that moment ... the frenzied chants, the demonic energy that forced Corinne and me apart. I had never been in a situation like that, trapped by a rebellious throng that screamed and shattered windows, charging toward me as though I were the enemy. If Kiener's security guard hadn't forced his way through that mob, if he hadn't pulled Corinne and me back inside the hotel, we might have been killed. That same panic gripped me now, cutting off my oxygen.

"Ms. Keswick, are you all right?"

The room felt hot, the air thick with the cloying smell of stale croissants and leftover coffee. "I um ... I ..." My words wouldn't come.

"Perhaps some water?"

My voice was raspy. "Yes, please."

He tapped a message into his phone. Several minutes later, someone entered the room with two bottles of water.

Mueller gave one to me. "You were telling me about the video."

I slowly unscrewed the top and took a long drink. The cool water rinsed some of the tension from my throat. "The video ..." My voice was high-pitched and tinny, as though it came from a cheap microphone. I took another swallow of water and tried again. "If you watch the video," I said, clearing my throat, forcing my voice down into its normal register, "you'll see the guy who shoved her. He screamed at her, getting right in her face. Which was ironic since she was on the side of the protestors. She knew how much climate change was hurting all of us." I offered him my phone. "Here, see for yourself."

Mueller's expression darkened as he watched the video. Then he played it a second time. "Is that Nils Kiener in the video? Of Gurtmeyer Industries?"

"Yes. He was Corinne's last meeting of the day. We walked out with him. And then the crowd attacked. Kiener's security guy rescued us and found a car to take us to the riverboat."

Mueller slid the phone back to me and jotted something in his notebook. His writing was faster now, his pen scratching rapidly against the paper as though he had to get down all the details before he forgot anything. After a few moments he looked up, his expression grave. "I have some disturbing news."

I squeezed the water bottle. "Corinne is dead. What could be more disturbing than that?"

He paused, laying down his pen, his lips in a tight line. "Nils Kiener was killed last night. Murdered as he was leaving his office."

***

I left the hotel and walked out into the hot sunshine of late afternoon, desperate for some fresh air. I'd spent too much time in that windowless conference room.

Across the river was the train station, a modernistic building of concrete and glass, fronted by an impressive stone entrance—a classical creation of columns, arches and equestrian statues. Eager travelers scurried in all directions, seeking new adventures. A few days ago I had been like them, caught up in planning Corinne's media strategy, buzzed by the challenge of spreading her message of climate change to voters, excited about the potential new business that a successful campaign would bring to my firm. Now I wandered aimlessly along the shore, uncertain what to do next.

A café table shaded by an enormous red umbrella seemed a good place to stop. I ordered wine and quickly skimmed the menu. I hadn't eaten all day and felt ravenous. But as I waited for my order, I watched the video again of the attack in Basel. I could see Kiener at the edge of the screen, getting into his car. And now he was dead.

By the time my grilled salmon arrived, I had lost all interest in food. The entrée was probably delicious, but I could have been chewing recycled plastic. I shoved in another tasteless bite as someone called out, "Madeline."

Wyatt stepped from the sun-drenched sidewalk into the shade of the umbrella. "Glad I ran into you. I've been all over this city and haven't seen Kyle anywhere. Any news?"

I jumped up and rushed toward him. "Oh, God, Wyatt." The tears that I had kept under tight rein while I was with the family suddenly spilled out. "Corinne … she's dead."

He wrapped his arms around me, warm and solid. I hadn't been held like this since I broke up with Travis. Hadn't realized how much I'd missed it. Wyatt gently patted my back until my tears faded to sniffles. Embarrassed, I pulled away. "I'm sorry, Wyatt. I didn't mean to lose control like that."

"It's okay." He pulled out a chair beside me and we sat down. "Tell me what happened. Kyle's phone kept going to voice mail."

I reached for my wine. "They found her in a ravine. Below the viewing platform. Covered with snow." My teeth chattered as the glass neared my lips. "Without search dogs, the rescue teams never would've spotted her."

"That's horrible." He wrapped his hand over mine. "It was an accident? She slipped on that icy concrete?"

I shook my head. "The police don't seem to think it was. They've been questioning us all afternoon."

"Questioning you?" He angled his head in surprise. "About what?"

"About the argument in the café. What everyone did after Corinne left." I sipped my wine. The chardonnay, warmed in the afternoon heat, was flat and heavy on my tongue. "They want to talk to you, too."

"I don't see how I can help. I went with you to the gift shop right after Corinne left the café. I didn't see her after that."

"The thing is, the detective seems to think the family was involved in her death. That's ridiculous, of course. None of them would ever hurt her." I set down the wine and grabbed my water. "I told him there were other people who had her in their sights. Like the waiter she argued with at dinner. And the protestors in Basel."

"What did he say?"

"He didn't seem concerned about the waiter, but when I showed him the video from Basel, he got serious really quick." I took several quick swallows. "One of the CEOs she met with at that energy conference was killed last night."

Wyatt blinked at me, agitated. "He thinks her murder is tied to that one? Somebody followed her from Basel, tracked her to Pilatus and killed her? But why?"

"I don't know. Because of climate change? Because killing a Senate candidate would generate a lot of headlines?" I signaled to the waiter for my check. I wanted to get back to the hotel, to talk to Fred and Holliss, to find out what questions Mueller had thrown at them. "Who knows why people do crazy things? The person who forced her off that mountain probably wasn't the most rational thinker." I pulled some cash from my wallet. "The good thing is, I'm sure it moved the family further down Mueller's suspect list. Which is good for all of us."

"Where is everyone now?" Wyatt asked. "At the hotel?"

"Probably." The waiter returned with the bill. I gave him more than enough Swiss francs to cover my meal. He nodded his thanks and began to clear the table.

"Let's go." Wyatt stood up. "Maybe there's something we can do to help."

***

Wyatt and I were almost at the hotel when I heard screaming. Quickening to a jog, I turned the corner just as Bronwyn shoved Holliss, knocking her off balance. Fred caught Holliss's arm as she stumbled.

"Bronwyn, what are you doing?" I rushed toward them, forcing Bronwyn back. "Holliss is pregnant. You could have hurt her. Hurt the baby."

"Stay away from me." Bronwyn took short, choking gasps, her eyes wild. "It's all her fault."

Luke grabbed his wife's shoulders, twisting her away from her sister. "Stop it, Bronwyn. Holliss had nothing to do with this."

"Of course, she did." Bronwyn jerked free. "She knew this whole time, and she never said anything."

"Enough," Luke said, his voice sharp. "Let's go. Walk this off." He put his arm around Bronwyn's waist and led her away from the hotel.

"Holliss? What happened?" I asked.

She shook uncontrollably as Fred pulled her close. "It's Randall."

"Is it his stomach again? Is he sick?" I had visions of him being rushed to the hospital, writhing on a stretcher, hooked up to tubes as doctors tried desperately to figure out what was wrong.

She shook her head. "No. It was that detective. Mueller."

"Mueller? I don't understand."

"The police took Randall to the station for more questioning. They think he killed my mother."

Chapter 15

FRED WRAPPED a supporting arm around Holliss as he led her up the hotel steps to the lobby. Telling Wyatt I would talk with him later, I followed the two of them. "Can you stay with her a minute?" Fred asked, as he settled Holliss onto a sofa. "I need to make some calls. See if we can straighten this out."

"Of course." I ordered coffee. "Holliss, tell me what happened."

She shrank back into the deep cushions. When the waiter returned and set steaming mugs on the table in front of us, she grabbed one with a shaky hand. "It was the scratches on his neck."

"The scratches?" I remembered how Kyle and Luke had teased Randall about those scratches at dinner last night. "I don't understand."

"Evidently my mom struggled with someone before she fell off that platform. They think it was Randall. That she scratched him."

So much for my hope that Mueller thought Corinne's death was tied to Nils Kiener, that it had something to do with the climate change protest, that he would back off from investigating the family. Obviously, he still thought one of them was responsible. He had scrutinized our group when he told us about Corinne's death, watching our reactions, looking for a gesture, a shrug, anything to indicate who might be guilty. With that gauze bandage on his jaw and ragged scratches angling down his neck, Randall made an easy target.

Holliss held her mug in both hands, struggling to keep it level. "I waited outside the conference rooms when they were finished with me. I saw Randall go in there, to talk to that policeman. You know, the thin one? They were in there a long time. Then he rushed out of the room, went to get Mueller. A few minutes later, they walked out with Randall between them." She shuddered as she set down the mug. Brown liquid sloshed out and puddled along the table edge. "He looked terrible, Madeline. So pale, like all the blood had drained out of his face. About to collapse."

Holliss wasn't any too steady herself. "What happened then?"

"I ran up to him," she mumbled. "Asked what was going on. Randall said they thought he killed Mom. I freaked out, pulled at Randall, trying to get him away from the police. But they were too strong for me."

I could envision the perp walk, a detective on each arm as they led Randall out, past slack-jawed hotel guests trying to figure out what crime he'd committed. With his curly hair and boyish face, he hardly looked like a vicious killer. Something more cerebral … embezzlement perhaps, or insurance fraud. Maybe even a Ponzi scheme. Few would have suspected this mild-mannered economics professor of tossing a woman off a mountain. "This is a horrible mistake. Randall is one of the gentlest people that I know. There's no way he did this."

"I can't … I can't believe it, either." She swiped at her tears. "I watched them force him into that police car."

I gave her a napkin. "Thanks." She dabbed at her eyes. "Randall yelled, 'Get me a lawyer.' I called Dad right away. And then Bronwyn came outside. She had seen the whole thing. Started screaming at me."

"Randall will be all right," I assured her. "Your dad will get a lawyer and get this whole thing cleared up. There are a lot of other suspects."

"But what if he can't fix it?" Her eyes were glassy with tears. "What if they put Randall in jail?"

"We won't let that happen."

It seemed an eternity before Fred returned to the lobby. "It's all taken care of," Fred said. "My lawyer has contacted someone local to represent Randall and meet him at the police station. Randall should be back here with hours."

Holliss hugged her father. "What a relief. I had visions of him being locked away in a cell and tortured all night."

"He'll be fine," Fred reassured her. "Everything's under control."

I wasn't as convinced as the two of them that Randall's nightmare was over. Now that Mueller had Randall firmly in his sights, I didn't think he would give up easily.

***

I paced the streets of Lucerne as the hot afternoon faded into the coolness of evening, trying to figure out what to do. Corinne would have wanted me to support her family, to help them work through their grief, but that was a challenge while Mueller's suspicions turned them against each other. I needed to talk to Lilly. Maybe together we could figure out a strategy to deal with all this.

I headed to my hotel room, rolling the words over and over in my head to find a gentle way to share the horrible news, trying to come up with sentences as polished as sea glass worn smooth by tumbling waves. But when I heard Lilly's voice on the phone, any illusion of control vanished. My words rushed out, stark and unvarnished. "Corinne's dead."

"Oh, my God," she said. "What happened?"

Clutching the phone so tightly that my knuckles turned white, I told her all of it—about the recovery team, and Captain Mueller, and Randall being carted off for questioning, and Bronwyn screaming at Holliss—one sentence spilling out after another, all the kaleidoscopic details of this horrible day. When my outburst finished, I collapsed into the armchair near the window.

"What do we do now?" she asked.

I sniffed back tears. "I don't know. Everything is so messed up."

Her voice was calm. "We need to put out a news release, to manage the story before the gossip mongers put their spin on it. I'll write up a rough draft and send it to you."

"That would be terrific." Lilly knew what I needed—to focus on work, on managing Corinne's image even in the face of tragedy. "Keep it simple. And nothing about Randall."

"Of course not. I would never say anything to hurt the family."

"I'm sorry. I know that." My neck muscles were so stiff I could barely turn my head. "I can't think."

"Let me handle it," Lilly said. "For now, I'll say she was killed in an accident. But you know we can't keep the media from digging into this. A prominent U.S. citizen murdered while on holiday in Switzerland? And her son-in-law arrested?"

"It wasn't an official arrest. He was taken in for questioning. And he didn't kill Corinne."

There was the tiniest pause. "Of course not."

I would have felt better if her voice had held a bit more conviction. "Her death could be tied to the climate change protest in Basel," I said. "Mueller told me that Nils Kiener, the CEO in that video of Corinne, was murdered yesterday."

"That's horrible," she said.

"That's why I was so shocked when he took Randall to the police station. I mean, Mueller had been questioning us all afternoon, but after I showed him the video, his whole mood changed. I thought for sure he was going after the protestors."

Lilly's voice had a cautious inflection. "Madeline, are you in danger?"

"Me? Of course not. Why would you think that?" I pulled back the draperies. Down at the riverbank, tourists strolled arm-in-arm.

"Because you were in that video, too. If those people killed Corinne, are they coming after you next?"

"I hardly think so. I'm not involved in the climate change movement. I was just standing near Corinne."

"And she was just standing near Kiener. Look where that got her."

"Maybe they didn't have anything to do with this. Maybe it's tied to the theft of her poker money. But Mueller didn't seem interested in following that lead." I began to pace from one side of the room to the other, feeling trapped in the small space. "There's no way Randall is guilty. I have to figure out who did this."

"No, you don't, Madeline. Leave all of that to the police. Come home."

"I can't, not until this situation with Randall is resolved. Holliss needs me."

"Kesbolt Consulting needs you," she insisted. "Without Corinne's commissions, we won't survive six months. We need to start knocking on doors right now to find new business."

"I need a few extra days, that's all. I owe it to Corinne to make sure Holliss is okay."

"And you owe it to me to make sure our company doesn't go under." I heard a rhythmic pounding in the background. I figured that Lilly was throwing tennis balls against the wall, like she always did when she was under stress. She kept a big bowl of them on the credenza, ready for the crisis of the day: when good ideas for a project wouldn't come; when a long-courted prospect decided to sign with another firm; when a fantastic idea for a campaign was suddenly usurped by a competitor. "I risked everything to go into business with you."

"You risked everything? Are you kidding me?" Anger burned deep in my stomach. I had lost so much over the past two years. And Lilly was right at the center of it. "This is all your fault. If you had left everything alone, I would never have been fired." I flung myself down on the bed. "We could both still be working at Everett & Michaels."

"You couldn't have stayed there," she said. "Not after what happened."

"Why not? You did. You kept quiet about it."

"But I …"

I cut her off. "Let's face it, if you had told people about your *little incident*, I might never have gotten into this mess. But you were too much of a coward to tell anyone." The words vibrated along the phone lines, resentful bits of venom that grew more deadly as they bounced across the ocean.

"That is so unfair." The pain in her voice told me I'd scored a direct hit.

"There's nothing fair about any of this," I said. "Not about what happened to the two of us. Not about what happened to Corinne. But I'm not going to walk away this time. I'll stay here until I know Holliss is safe."

"You do that." The pounding of tennis balls tapered off. The silence lasted so long that I thought she had hung up on me. Then she said, her voice soft, "But realize, if you wait too long … there may not a company to come back to."

Chapter 16

OUR QUARREL LEFT me in a bad mood. I had to get out of that hotel room, to be around other people, to clear out the gloomy thoughts that clogged my mind. I headed down to the hotel lounge. Kyle sat at the polished wooden bar, one hand wrapped around his glass, the other thumping out a slow rhythm that was a beat or two behind the faint background music. There was a somberness about him, a tired melancholy that made his eyes droop. For a moment I thought of joining him, to tell him how sorry I was about his mom, but then Bronwyn brushed past me and headed for her brother. He stood up and wrapped his arms around her, the two of them forming their own private pod of grief. There was no way I would interrupt that.

Instead, I headed out and wandered through the narrow, cobbled streets of Old Town, passing ancient buildings decorated with murals of odd, distorted figures that could have been ripped from ancient fairy tales. I stopped at a busy restaurant. Six tables graced the sidewalk out front, full of young people hoisting beers and laughing as they called out to each other, their bulging backpacks shoved under their chairs. Inside were square wooden tables and a long bar that ran against the back wall.

A waitress squeezed by me as she carried out a tray of refills. "It'll be a wait for a table," she said. "Half hour. Maybe more. Or you can try the bar."

"I'll check out the bar." Music, heavy on the bass, rumbled from the speakers, blending with layers of conversation and laughter. I threaded my way back and claimed one of the few empty stools. The bartender, a bulky guy who probably could double as a bouncer in case things got rough, was serving a rowdy bunch at the end. He finally headed in my direction, wiping the bar as he stopped in front of me. The ale that I ordered was slightly bitter. I took a long swallow as I checked out the crowd.

A woman dressed all in black—short skirt, strappy sandals and a snug long-sleeved cashmere sweater—held court a few seats from me, chatting with a few folks somewhat older than the backpackers outside. Her laugh, spilling out over garbled lyrics, seemed familiar. As she turned toward the bar, gesturing for a refill, I spotted dangling earrings and a sparkling silver necklace cascading down the V-neck of her sweater. "Emily," I called out, wondering if she had to pack an extra suitcase to handle all her bling. Each day of our trip she had sported different jewelry.

Her eyebrows popped up as she recognized me. "Did he send you?" Her voice was hopeful. "To track me down?"

I shook my head. "Nobody sent me."

Her eyes swept the room. "Kyle's not here?"

"He's with Bronwyn. At the hotel."

She rolled her eyes. "No surprise there." She waved off her drinking companions and edged onto the empty stool beside me, tugging at her skirt as it rode well up her thighs. "What are you doing here?"

"Needed something to cheer me up." I hoisted my mug in a casual salute. "Rough day, you know?"

"You could say that." The bartender set a fresh mug in front of her. Foam sloshed onto the polished counter as she lifted her beer. She brushed impatiently at the amber puddle, her nails scraping against the wood. The flamingo pink polish she had been so pleased with on the riverboat had started to chip off in ragged slivers, exposing the pale underbelly of her nails.

"Manicure not working for you?" I asked.

She glanced at her nails. "They're a mess, aren't they?" She ran her thumbnail along a cuticle, scratching at the polish. "I keep picking at them. Nerves, I guess. The family's going crazy. With Corinne dead, and Randall in jail."

I quickly jumped to his defense. "He's not in jail. He was taken in for questioning. And he's innocent. It'll get straightened out soon."

"You don't think he killed Corinne?"

"Never. Randall's a good guy." I had met him back in college, when Holliss got thrown out of a campus dive near the end of her freshman year. Brandishing a fake ID, she had whined and pouted until I let her join me and my senior friends for a pub crawl. Her first beer made her silly. The second caused her to loudly chat up everyone around her. The third had her scrambling onto the bar, belting out the words to the background music as she stumbled over people's drinks.

When the bouncer tried to get her down, she let out a string of profanity focused on both his ancestry and his body parts. He escorted her to the exit, where she slammed into a skinny guy entering the bar. I grabbed her arm, ready to escort her back to her dorm.

"You can't leave," my friend Chloe protested. "There's someone I want you to meet."

"Holliss will never get home by herself," I said.

"Randall will walk her back, won't you?" She smiled at the skinny guy trying to keep Holliss upright.

He seemed innocent enough, with unruly ginger hair and a smattering of freckles, but I wasn't comfortable sending Holliss off with a stranger. "I don't know about this."

"Randall's a sophomore, in my econ class. He's fine." Chloe waved at friends gathered around a table. A dark-haired guy waved back. "I've told Dave all about you. He wants to meet you."

After a crushing week of classes, papers, and labs, I needed a distraction. Dave had wavy hair swooping low over his eyes and a very promising grin. "No funny stuff, Randall," I said, handing Holliss over to him. "She's only sixteen."

It took only two dates for me to realize that Dave wasn't the guy for me. Holliss and Randall, on the other hand, became inseparable. A few years after graduation, they got married.

I frowned at Emily over the rim of my mug. "Randall couldn't hurt anybody. Especially not Corinne. He would never do that to Holliss."

Emily shook her head, unconvinced. She leaned in close, shouting into my ear so I could hear her above the music. "He went ballistic when Corinne made that crack about Holliss's *whiny little voice*. He was certainly mad enough to toss her off that platform."

"Is that what the family thinks? That Randall killed her?" I gulped down my beer. The bartender was serving a fresh round to the boisterous guys at the end of the bar, who laughed and joked as they grabbed their refills. It reminded me of the happy-hour crowd I used to hang out with in New York, all of us eager and ambitious, moving up in our careers, ready to conquer the world. They probably still got together, but after the fiasco that Lilly and I got caught up in, it was clear that we were no longer welcome.

I held up my mug. The bartender headed my way.

"Bronwyn thinks he did it. And I think she's won Kyle over." Emily smoothed out the wrinkles in her skirt. "Kyle and I were supposed to go out to dinner tonight, the two of us. Someplace nice. I got all dressed up, and then Bronwyn called and said she had to talk to him right away. Our dinner plans were immediately canceled."

"Do you agree with them? Do you think he's guilty?" The bartender set my refill in front of me. The room grew hotter as people milled around behind us, waiting for an open seat at the bar. I quickly sucked down the cool liquid.

"Doesn't matter what I think. Bronwyn drives that boat." Emily's face was clouded with an emotion I couldn't quite figure out. Anger? Jealousy? "What about her broken finger? You think she really caught it in the cable car?"

"You don't?" I asked.

"I think Corinne would have fought back against her attacker. Whoever pushed her probably has some collateral damage. Like a broken finger."

"You think Bronwyn did it?" The second beer was slamming into my blood stream, making it difficult to reason clearly. I had believed Bronwyn's cable car story. Was it a lie? "Why would she kill her mother?"

"Money, of course. Luke was worried about his job. And with Corinne funneling all her funds to the campaign, they would be scrambling to cover college costs for Harrison."

Could Bronwyn have done this? When she lashed out at Holliss as the police took Randall for questioning, was she really trying to deflect attention from herself? Then again, Emily was hardly an impartial observer. "You and Bronwyn don't get along too well, do you?"

Emily snorted. "You've heard the way she talks to me. She thinks I'm a complete airhead. I'm sure the rest of them agree with her." She grabbed her mug. "I mean, I love Kyle and all, but his family's hard to take. You're the only one, except maybe Fred, who's been decent to me."

The music seemed louder now, its pulsating rhythm wrapping around me, rattling my beer-soaked brain cells as I mulled over Emily's theory. The bartender picked up my empty mug and offered me another.

"If anybody deserved to get tossed off that mountain, it was Bronwyn," Emily said. "She won't leave Kyle alone, calling him every day, breaking into our business meetings when we're trying to get our financing settled. I'm thankful that we're in Boston and she lives in Texas. Otherwise, I'm sure she'd be stopping by every night for dinner."

Considering that Bronwyn had a spouse and four boys living at home, that hardly seemed likely, but I overlooked Emily's hyperbole. "Holliss tells me they've always been close."

"Close doesn't begin to describe it. If she doesn't back off ..." Emily's lashes fluttered as she stared into the distance, probably plotting diabolical ways to unlock Kyle from his sister. Bronwyn was forceful and determined; Emily was ambitious and relentless. If the two of them met up with pistols at dawn, I'd be challenged to predict the winner.

"I'm sure you guys can work this out." I needed to get out of here before Emily signed me up as her second. Besides, I had guzzled that last beer way too fast. I was already lightheaded. I'd never find my way back to the hotel if I stayed here much longer. My mouth filled with a sour taste as I fought back a burp. "Good talk," I said, sliding off the bar stool, "but I need to head back." The floor was a lot farther down than I remembered. A sticky coating of spilled alcohol clung to my shoes, helping me stay upright. "Want to walk with me?"

She shook her head. "I'll hang around here a little longer. Who knows? Maybe Kyle will come looking for me."

Her poignant smile made me want to reassure her, but I had seen Bronwyn and Kyle at the hotel. There didn't seem to be any room in their grief huddle for Emily. "See you tomorrow."

I left her at the bar and stepped outside, trying to remember how to get back to the hotel. This restaurant hadn't been a straight shot. I had wandered through Old Town, haphazardly following side streets, turning one corner and then another. Now I wasn't sure which way to go. I headed left, trying to retrace my path.

None of the buildings looked familiar, and after a few blocks I stopped, trying to think through my beer buzz. There was no one around to ask for directions. The stores were closed for the night and the sidewalks deserted. It was darker now, with clouds covering the moon and mist rolling in from the river, wrapping the buildings in a soft haze. I tucked my purse more firmly under my arm. The hotel had to be around the next corner. Or maybe the next.

I crossed the street, my shoes clicking loudly on the cobblestones. Suddenly I heard footsteps behind me. It was probably another tourist, someone harmless, as lost as I was. But maybe not. Had Lilly been right? Could the same person who killed Corinne be after me?

His stride was longer than mine; soon he would catch up. The charming streets of Old Town now seemed full of menace, not my choice spot for encountering a stranger. I picked up my pace, my heart pumping faster as I walked in the middle of the street, staying away from the threatening assemblage of parked cars and shadowy sidewalks. Surely the person behind me would veer off, head for a restaurant or a hotel, and leave me alone.

But he stuck with me, relentless as a bloodhound. He was getting closer. I could almost feel his hot breath on my neck. I turned another corner, recognizing the arched doorway of a building I had passed only moments before. Was I walking in circles? I was hopelessly, irreversibly lost.

I hustled down another block and finally saw something familiar—a stone lion crouched on a tall pedestal, surrounded by gargoyles spitting out water. I had seen that fountain when we drove into the city; my hotel was only a block away. Relieved, I rushed down the street to the cobblestone courtyard, bounding up the steps of the hotel and moving through the heavy glass doors into the lobby. Once inside, I watched by the window, wondering if he would follow me.

He hesitated, standing in the courtyard under the streetlights. He was young, probably early twenties. He looked familiar, maybe part of that group at the bar? I studied his face, wanting to remember every detail so I could report my stalker to the police. The curly blond hair. The dark-framed glasses.

And then I realized where I had seen him before. In Basel. The young man with the megaphone, shouting out protests, leading chants, inciting to action.

He had targeted Kiener and Corinne. Now he was coming after me.

Not wanting to wait for the elevator, I raced up the stairs to my room, panting as I locked the door behind me. Pulling out Mueller's business card, I punched his number into my phone. As expected, my call went to voicemail. At this hour, Mueller was probably out in a bar with his cop buddies, or maybe at home with his family, having a glass of wine with his wife after putting the kids to bed— some normal, relaxing routine, while I was being chased through the streets by a murderer.

I left him a quick message. Still clutching the phone, I pondered who to call next. I needed a friendly voice to assure me that everything would be all right. Not Holliss or Fred—they had enough problems worrying about Randall. Lilly would probably say *I told you so* and pressure me again to return home. Maybe Wyatt? The operator could connect us. I picked up the handset, but then hesitated. What was I doing? I was a competent businesswoman who had managed through any number of crises. I could take care of myself. I didn't need someone to rescue me.

The door lock seemed perilously fragile. I wedged a chair against the door and tugged the nightstand in place behind it. Shivering as clammy frissons of fear ran down my spine, I flipped on every light in the room and got under the covers with my back against the headboard, knees pulled to my chest, arms clamped around my thighs. Too frightened to sleep, my eyes wide open, I listened carefully for the sound of a jiggling doorknob.

Chapter 17

I SQUINTED uncomfortably the next morning, trying to figure out why the sun was so bright even though only a few stripes of light poked through the gap in the drapes. And why my furniture was piled in front of the door. Groggy from restless dreams, I finally remembered the blond guy who had followed me home. I had left all the lights on and barricaded my door, terrified that he might try to break in.

I checked my phone for messages, but there was nothing from Mueller. Either he hadn't started his day yet or responding to me was not high on his priority list. I suspected the latter. I would call again later this morning, to tell him that the same protestor I had seen in Basel was now in Lucerne. And was following me.

Quickly dressing, I headed downstairs, checking out the lobby and the front entrance to make sure the curly haired man was nowhere in sight. Then I headed to the hotel restaurant. Bronwyn did a good job of ignoring me as I walked in. If I hadn't seen the quick roll of her eyes as she raised the coffee cup to her lips, or the subtle but tell-tale shift of her body so that Luke's broad shoulders blocked her view, I would have thought she didn't see me.

I could have let it go, but I was still mad about the way she screamed at Holliss yesterday after they loaded Randall into the police car. If seeing me first thing would spoil her day, then I was all for it.

She and Luke were out on the balcony at a corner table, seated with Kyle and Emily, the remains of a hearty breakfast spread out before them. As I walked up, Emily frowned and shook her head. I took that as a signal that I shouldn't mention anything about our evening out. Maybe Kyle never even noticed she had left the hotel. And it was a good bet that Emily had not mentioned her suspicions about his sister. I couldn't imagine the four of them calmly chomping down on pancakes and bacon if she'd shared those thoughts.

"Morning, folks," I said.

I could tell that Luke was weighing a lifetime of drilled-in manners against marital fealty to the wife who had screamed at me in Strasbourg for causing her mother's death. Manners won out as he gave me a half-hearted smile and rose to his feet. "Morning, Madeline. Would you like to join us?"

Bronwyn sniffed at his offer. If there had been room, I would have taken him up on it, to see her squirm. But their table was too small to squeeze in another chair. "Thanks, but you guys are almost finished."

Luke settled back into his chair, grateful that I'd given him an out. "The food's good. Try the buffet."

"Thanks, I may do that." I hadn't had a chance to express my sympathies. "I want you to know how sorry I am about Corinne. She was a special lady, and this is such a shock. If there's anything I can do …"

"We'll let you know." Bronwyn set her cup carefully onto its saucer. "Right now, the family wants to spend some time together. Just us. To deal with our grief."

I wondered if *just us* included Holliss. From the way Bronwyn had torn into her sister yesterday, I doubted it. I lingered a moment longer after her blunt dismissal, studying Bronwyn's body language for traces of guilt. Could Emily be on the right track? Last night in that dim, raucous tavern, with Emily and me slinging back foaming mugs of ale and my head pounding from nonstop music, her theory seemed possible. This morning, in the calm of a sunny balcony, with deferential waiters pouring coffee into Bronwyn's delicate china cup, it seemed absurd. Bronwyn could never have harmed her mother.

I headed back to the hostess stand to wait for a table. After a few minutes, Fred walked up. "Morning, Madeline."

"Morning." His face was pasty, his eyes red and puffy. "Did you get any sleep last night?"

"Not really. The lawyer brought Randall back to the hotel, and we spent a lot of time talking. Then there were countless phone calls, checking in with people back home. Everyone's shocked, of course." He squinted as he massaged his neck. "Thanks for preparing the news release. Corinne would have loved it. The perfect right mix of dignity and admiration. With your support, she would have won in a landslide."

"Thank you. My partner Lilly wrote it." There were still decisions to be made—how long to keep her online presence active so that people could express condolences, what to do with her website—but all that could wait. "It's tragic that everything got cut short. She had so many plans."

His eyes were wistful. "Senator Twisdale was heartbroken. She had already done so much … made a lot of contacts, raised visibility. Now he'll have to find someone else."

"Bronwyn said she decided to run for office because of Natalie?" I let the words hang there, determined to find out more about this mysterious woman. Corinne had only shared a sentence or two. Holliss had never met her. Maybe Fred could fill me in.

"She'd been interested in climate change discussions for a long time, but yes, Natalie's death is what put her Senate run in motion. She was her niece. Her sister Sylvia's child."

"Corinne never told me she had a sister."

"That's not a surprise. Sylvia died almost twenty years ago."

"What happened to Natalie?"

"It was tragic. Remember that hurricane we had a few years back? Lots of downed trees, power outages, flooding? Natalie went into early labor. On the way to the hospital, her car was swept off a bridge. She drowned."

"Oh, my God. And the baby?"

He shook his head. "By the time they got Natalie out of the water, it was too late."

Before I could ask more questions, the hostess walked up. "Two for breakfast?" she asked, reaching for menus.

I glanced uncertainly at Fred. "Do you want to join me?" I asked. "Or would you rather be alone? I completely understand if you'd like time to yourself."

He gave me a stiff smile. "Actually, I think I'd like the company. Holliss and Randall are on their way down. We can all sit together." He turned to the hostess. "A table for four."

She picked up additional menus. "On the balcony, or inside?"

"Are you okay with outside, Madeline?" Fred asked. "I could use some sunshine."

"That's fine."

Fred and I followed the hostess through the broad doorway to a table near the railing, several spaces over from Bronwyn and her crew. I sat down while Fred walked over to speak to his family.

It was a lovely morning, the pale blue sky feathered with wispy clouds, the river calm as it glinted under the morning sun. But it was totally out of sync with my mood. Corinne was dead. I wanted rumbling skies and swollen black clouds, with tourists racing to escape jagged streaks of lightning.

The waiter interrupted my dark musings. "Coffee?" he asked, holding up a stainless-steel pot.

"Yes, thank you."

He finished pouring as Fred returned to our table. "I'll have some of that, too." Fred gestured toward his cup. "And we're waiting for two more."

The waiter filled Fred's cup and headed back to his station.

Fred shook out his napkin as he sat down. "I told the children that I've been talking with the embassy, to make arrangements for Corinne. Bronwyn and Kyle want to send her body home, but cremation might be simpler." He picked up his coffee. "The thing is, I'm not sure what Corinne would have wanted. We never really talked about it."

"Not many people want to think about their own death," I said. "Especially when they're as active as Corinne was."

"It's crazy, isn't it?" Fred sighed. "Corinne was always such a daredevil. I mean, she went paragliding with all of you our first day in Interlaken. If something had happened that day, if she'd crashed, it would have been horrible. But at least I'd have known she was doing something she enjoyed. But this ... to be shoved off the mountain. And to have the police think Randall did it. I can't wrap my mind around that." He set his cup down and reached for the sugar. "I guess Mueller's just doing his job. A rich American was killed on his home turf. There's a lot of publicity. He wants to make sure he does it right. I get that, I really do. But I want it to be over."

"I understand."

He ripped open the packet and emptied sugar into his coffee. "I don't think I'll ever get used to this. I woke up this morning and expected her to be right there beside me, ready to start a new adventure." He vigorously stirred until a black mini whirlpool sloshed into the saucer. "Corinne's the one that's always been in charge of everything. Our family, our friends, our ties to the community. I was always working, climbing the corporate ladder, angling for the next promotion. I'd show up whenever and wherever she told me to." He tapped the spoon against the edge of the cup. "Now my career's in great shape, I'm the CFO of my company, but I'm all alone. The kids are grown. Corinne is gone. What am I going to do without her?"

"It's hard," I said. "This is a huge shock for your whole family. You guys need to talk about your memories. The good things, the bad. Have a few laughs. Let yourself cry."

He laid the spoon beside his saucer. "I'm not really the crying type. Besides, I feel it's my duty to hold things together. Although I'm not sure how to do that."

"If there's anything I can do ..."

His lips parted in a weak smile. "I may take you up on that. Corinne thought a lot of you. She felt she could depend on you. I hope I can, too."

"Of course. Whatever you need."

He spotted Holliss and Randall entering the restaurant. "Over here," he called out, waving.

Holliss lumbered toward us, her face dry and pinched, her hair flattened against her head. Randall helped her into her chair.

The waiter came with coffee. "We have a lovely buffet," he said. "Or you may order off our menu."

"Luke said the buffet was good," I said.

"Let's do four buffets, then," Fred said. "Probably more food than we need, but at least it will be quick. I have a few things to take care of this morning."

The four of us went through the buffet line, Holliss and I choosing muffins and fruit, the two men loading their plates with eggs, bacon and pastries. Back at our table, Fred turned to Randall. "I've been talking to Schelling. I don't think you have anything to worry about."

"Schelling?" I asked.

"My lawyer." Randall sipped his coffee. "The one Fred lined up for me. He met me at the police station last night. Did a good job of keeping Mueller out of my face. And getting me out of that place."

Fred kept his voice low. "Mueller didn't have enough evidence to hold you. The scratches on your neck are coincidental. Once the DNA tests come back, you should be home free."

"You let them take a DNA sample?" I asked.

"Not on purpose. We were waiting for Schelling to get there. They offered me water. And I was so thirsty that I fell for it. Once I drank out of that glass, they took it away for DNA testing."

"Can't we get the DNA thrown out?" Holliss asked. "They got it under false pretenses. It was a deceitful trick."

"It doesn't matter," Fred said, waving a dismissive hand. "It won't be a match to the scrapings they took from Corinne's fingernails. Randall will be fine."

"Schelling said those DNA tests can take a while. What if the police don't even look for another suspect while they're waiting for the results?" Randall picked at his eggs. "I feel like a fly stuck in a spiderweb, knowing something bad is coming, but not able to do anything about it."

"Schelling's bringing in his own investigative team to make sure that doesn't happen," Fred said. "I have a lot of confidence in him. My attorney back home said he was the best guy here to handle your case. Plus, I'm touch with someone at the embassy who should be able to help."

Holliss sighed. "I wish we were all at home. I've had enough of Switzerland."

"Mueller is encouraging us to stick around while he conducts his investigation," Fred said, "but as long as we're not under arrest, I don't think he can stop us from leaving. I'll stay with your mom until he releases the body, but the rest of you might want to head back to the States."

"That's not a bad idea," I agreed. "Holliss, why don't you guys go? I'll stay here with your dad."

Randall grimaced. "If I try to leave, Mueller will be convinced I'm guilty. I can see him pulling me off a plane right now, snapping on handcuffs. He would have confiscated my passport last night if Schelling hadn't talked him out of it. I don't think I have any choice but to stay here until he's had more time to process the evidence."

"I won't leave Randall," Holliss said. "If he stays, I'm staying too."

We talked quietly as we munched our breakfast. Fred was finishing his coffee when Bronwyn walked up to our table. "I need to see my mother," she demanded.

Fred rested his silverware on the side of his plate. "I don't think you want to do that."

"Yes, I do," Bronwyn insisted. "If I don't see her, if I don't see her body, I won't believe she's dead."

I realized that Bronwyn needed to hold her mother one last time, to say final goodbyes, to make sure this wasn't some horrible mistake. Otherwise, she'd be looking for Corinne the rest of her life, thinking she was the stranger caught in her peripheral vision in a packed mall, or the woman with the dark coat in the distant corner of a parking lot.

"She fell a long way," Fred said, shaking his head. "Has some broken bones. Bruises. Was out in the snow overnight." He coughed several times. "It's best if you remember her as she was."

"You've seen Mom?" Bronwyn asked.

"Yes. Yesterday. I had to identify the body."

"Then I'm going to see her, too. And Kyle's going with me."

Fred sipped his coffee. "If you're sure, I'll call Mueller and arrange it."

"Me, too," Holliss said, her voice wobbly.

"Do you really want to do that?" Randall asked. "You don't need more stress right now."

Holliss piled her silverware on her plate. "If Bronwyn and Kyle are going, I'm going, too. We're a family. We need to stick together."

Chapter 18

FRED ARRANGED for a driver to take us to view Corinne. Bronwyn wanted it to be just Fred and her siblings, but Fred insisted I join them. He seemed a bit rudderless in his new role as family leader and had already started to lean on me for support.

The hallway Fred led us down was dark, deserted and cold. We followed him to the receptionist's desk, where a heavyset woman, her graying hair arranged in tight curls around her face, sat in front of a large stack of files, entering data into her computer.

"I'm Fred Peerland," he said.

She peered at him through tortoise shell glasses, frowning at the disruption to her routine.

"Captain Mueller called to let you know we were coming. We came to see my wife, Corinne Peerland."

She sighed, putting a sticky note in the file to mark her place, and then reached for the telephone. "I will tell the attendant that you are here," she said, in heavily accented English.

We were not good at waiting. After a few minutes, Bronwyn and Kyle began to pace up and down the hallway, peering expectantly at the receptionist each time they neared her, mumbling to each other when she ignored them. Fred leaned back against the wall, his foot propped up behind him, cracking his knuckles. The sound put me on edge, so I wandered around searching for a coffee bar or a vending machine, anything to help pass the time, but there were no amenities in sight. This probably was not a place that got a lot of visitors.

Holliss was the most patient of us all. She sat on a hard wooden bench, her eyes closed, hands in her lap.

After what seemed like hours, an older man with closely cropped hair walked through the doorway. "Mr. Peerland?"

We all moved toward him. "I'm Fred Peerland. And this is my family. We're here to see my wife."

The man puckered his lips as he inspected us. "The room is very small. Perhaps two of you at a time?"

Bronwyn quickly stepped up. "We'll go first," she said, grabbing Kyle's arm.

The attendant held the door open for them.

After they left, Fred resumed his position against the wall, but thankfully left off the knuckle cracking and instead slowly rubbed his palms together. I sat beside Holliss, trying to think of something reassuring to say. I had already gone through all the traditional phrases—*sorry for your loss, let me know if I can do anything, my thoughts and prayers are with you*—and nothing new popped up in my head. It seemed best to sit in silence while we waited.

They had not been gone very long when Bronwyn burst back through the doorway, sobbing. Kyle caught up with her and put his arms around her, awkwardly rubbing her back. "Your turn," he said to Fred, nodding back toward where they held Corinne's body.

Fred grimaced. "I've already seen her. I … I don't think I can do this again." He turned toward me. "Madeline, could you go in with Holliss?"

I had hoped I would not have to go in at all. Bronwyn's wailing made it clear that seeing Corinne was a tough thing to do. But Holliss needed someone with her. "Of course." I stood as Holliss rose awkwardly from the bench.

"If you'll follow me?" the attendant said. He seemed unaffected by Bronwyn's display of emotion. I guessed he had seen enough grieving relatives over the years to learn to keep his own thoughts carefully in check.

He turned into the third doorway on the right. The room was small. A bank of metal cabinets lined one wall, while computer monitors took up most of the opposite side. The pungent smell of cleaning products almost masked the mustiness of decay.

A stretcher was positioned in the center of the room. I knew it was Corinne underneath that lumpy sheet, but part of me kept hoping that this was some terrible error, that we would see a stranger when the attendant exposed her face. But once he folded back the sheet, there was no doubt it was Corinne, even though the left side of her head was bashed in and her nose angled to the right. The unforgiving light gave her skin an odd grayish tint. Blond hair spilled in tangled clumps over the edge of the stretcher.

"Oh, my God." Holliss fumbled for my arm. "That can't be my mother."

I could understand why Fred had been so reluctant for his children to see Corinne. This image could haunt them the rest of their lives.

"Her hair," Holliss whispered as she stepped closer. "She had such beautiful hair. Was always so particular about it. And now …" Her voice trailed off as she caught a lock of Corinne's hair, slowly rubbing it between her thumb and forefinger. "It feels the same," she said. "Soft. Like I remember it."

The attendant stepped forward. "You are not allowed to touch the body."

Holliss jerked back. "Sorry." Crossing her arms over her chest, she studied Corinne's face. "When I was little," she said slowly, "I had long hair that I wore in a ponytail. At night, Mom would take it down for me, easing out the tangles. She'd use this tiny pink brush—it had a princess on the back, with long blond hair like my mother—until my hair was soft and shiny." She sniffed back tears. "And sometimes she'd let me brush her hair. She'd say we were playing beauty shop."

I put my arm around her shoulders. "That's a wonderful memory."

She held out a strand of her own hair. "I always wanted my hair to be like hers. Long and blond and silky. I thought if I held very still, if she brushed my hair long enough, that maybe she could brush out all the color, and we'd look the same. It didn't work, of course. Mine stayed dark and curly, like my dad."

"Oh, Holliss." My voice broke as I pictured that little girl wanting so much to be like her mother. "I'm so sorry."

"All these things I haven't thought about since I was a child." She blinked back a tear. "Like her hands. Mom always had such warm hands. And beautiful nails. She got a manicure every week. I remember once she took me with her, and I got a coat of pale pink polish that made me the most special girl in the second grade." She turned to the attendant. "Could we see her hands, please?"

The man turned back the edge of the sheet. Corinne's hand was discolored, several fingers bent at unnatural angles. The manicured nails had been clipped short, probably to obtain DNA evidence.

Holliss's voice was as brittle as chipped slivers of quartz. "They're not warm now, are they?" She reached toward her, then stopped as the attendant shook his head.

"Holliss, let's go," I said. "You've seen enough."

She bit down so hard on her lower lip that I was afraid she would draw blood. Then, moving quickly so the attendant couldn't interfere, she leaned down and kissed her mother very gently on the cheek. "Goodbye, Mom. I love you."

"Please, you cannot do that," the attendant said.

"It's okay. We're finished." I led Holliss out of the room.

Halfway down the hallway she stopped. "I should never have come here. I think I'm going to be sick." She leaned over and rested her hands on her thighs. "I didn't want to do this. But Bronwyn and Kyle insisted on coming. I wanted to prove I was as much of the family as they are."

"Of course, you are, Holliss." I rubbed her back. "Of course, you are. You don't have to prove that to anyone."

As Holliss and I made our way to the receptionist's desk, I heard Bronwyn's strident voice. "Where are her things?" Bronwyn demanded, leaning over the gray-haired woman.

"What things?" she asked, calmly closing the file at the top of her stack.

"Her clothes. Her purse. Her jewelry. Where are they?"

Fred grabbed her shoulder. "Bronwyn, calm down. You're worried about jewelry at a time like this?"

She whirled toward him. "You're not? What about her wedding ring? Her watch? All of that. They're mementoes of my mother. And I want them."

"You will have to talk to the police," the receptionist said. "They take care of that."

"Let's go, Bronwyn." Fred pulled out his phone. "I'll check with Mueller. Find out where her things are."

"If they haven't been stolen by now."

"Bronwyn, I know you're upset, but please try to take it down a notch." Fred guided us toward the exit. "I'm sure no one stole your mother's jewelry."

"We don't know that," Bronwyn said. "We don't know anything about what happened to her on that mountain."

***

Emily and Wyatt, waiting for us back at the hotel, quickly drew Kyle into an earnest conversation. After a quick goodbye to Bronwyn, Kyle took off with the two of them, walking toward Old Town. The rest of us squeezed into the elevator. Fred's phone buzzed as the doors opened. "It's Mueller," he said, reading the message. "He can see us at two. Let's rendezvous in the lobby and we'll ride together."

That gave me time for a quick run, to clear the stench of death from my lungs. Changing into jogging clothes, I set out along the river, inhaling deep gulps of oxygen as I ran. After a few miles I headed back toward the hotel, sweat-soaked and panting. Luke, perched on the stone wall by the river, waved at me as I approached.

"Hey, Madeline. You okay?"

I wiped my face with the hem of my shirt. "Tough morning."

"Bronwyn told me things were intense."

"That's a good word for it." My legs felt taut. I braced my foot on the wall, leaning forward to stretch out my hamstrings. "I'd never seen a dead body before. At least, not one like that."

"Neither has Bronwyn. She's pretty shaken."

"You know, I've been to visitations at funeral homes, but the dead bodies there always are kind of fake—hair and makeup all fixed up, nice clothes, satin pillows. Stiff and unreal, like a store mannequin."

"I know what you mean."

"But Corinne …" I bent down for some toe touches, hiding my face so Luke wouldn't see my watery eyes. "Corinne wasn't like that."

"Bronwyn won't talk about it."

I stood up, bending slowly from side to side, buying time until I could regain my composure. But my words still rushed out, raw and unfiltered. "Her head was bashed in. Her face bruised. Her hair stringy, like she hadn't washed it in a week." I regretted the gush of details. "I'm sorry, Luke. I shouldn't have shared all that. It's much more than you wanted to know."

"I'm glad you did. It explains why Bronwyn shut herself in the bathroom and won't come out."

"I understand how she feels. I don't think I'll ever get that image of Corinne out of my head." I sat down beside him and bounced my heels nervously. "And poor Holliss—she's devastated. Between her mother's death and Randall being taken in for questioning last night, it's more than she can handle. I'm really worried about her."

Luke shifted uneasily on the stone wall, his expression apologetic. "I feel terrible that Bronwyn screamed at Holliss yesterday. She's not usually like that. She's kind and warm ... a great mom ... totally dedicated to our boys." His eyes softened as he thought of his family. "I wish we'd never come on this trip. I didn't want to, but Bronwyn has always dreamed of a European riverboat cruise. Mingling with locals. Wandering through crumbling castles."

"Nothing wrong with that."

"Oh, yeah? I'm not interested in ruins ... our house is ruin enough. A fixer-upper we bought last year. It needs a power wash and a new paint job. Plus, the toilet in the kids' bathroom backed up last month and soaked down into the dining room. Bronwyn's been on the phone nonstop with contractors, trying to find someone to fix the ceiling."

I was glad the conversation had taken a more mundane turn. Talking about everyday disasters we could control—mildewed siding, overflowing toilets—was easier than focusing on Corinne's battered body. "Sounds like you guys have a big project ahead of you."

"I'll say. That place is bleeding us dry." He rotated his wedding ring round and round. "To be frank, we really couldn't afford this vacation, not with four kids in private school. But when Fred and Corinne said they were picking up the tab, Bronwyn kept after me until I finally agreed."

"Hard to turn down a free trip," I said.

"It's hard to turn down anything Bronwyn wants. When she looks at me with those big blue eyes ... I would do anything for her."

"Like jump off the side of a mountain?"

He tucked his head in embarrassment. "Exactly. By the way, I want to thank you again for trying to save me when we were paragliding. It was a gutsy move."

"My pilot Edgar gets all the credit. Fortunately, we were able to abort the mission at the last moment. Saved all of us some broken bones."

"Paragliding was stupid." He watched the lunchtime crowd file past us. "I don't know why I let Kyle get under my skin, pressuring me into that."

"Kyle's a persuasive guy."

"Yeah, I guess. Not my top pick for a brother-in-law. But I love Bronwyn, and Kyle's part of the package."

"Emily, too," I added. "Even though she and Bronwyn don't exactly seem to be hitting it off."

He put his palms up in a hard stop. "I'm keeping my distance from Emily. Did you watch that video she shot? Perfect focus the whole time. That camera didn't shake as she filmed me falling out of the sky."

"Yep, I saw it."

"You and a few million other people. She was probably disappointed that I got down safely. Her video would have gotten even more hits if my brains had spattered out when I hit the ground."

"Emily's intense," I admitted. "But she's smart. We've talked a lot about our companies. About the challenges of a start-up. Give her another chance. Maybe she'll grow on you."

"Like a fungus." He raked his fingernails along his arm, as if scratching an itch. "No thanks."

"You may not have a choice. Kyle seems committed to her."

"Kyle's not known for always having the best judgment. Although we've all tried to give him some slack. He's been through a lot the last couple of years."

"You're talking about his divorce?"

"Well, that," Luke said, "and the thing in Italy. That's why Kyle was desperate to stop Corinne's Senate run."

That night on the deck of the riverboat, Kyle told me that Corinne's campaign would destroy the family, which had seemed an extreme reaction to the potential loss of Luke's job. Had Kyle been talking about himself? About something that happened in Italy? "I guess she didn't realize …" I let the thought hang there, waiting for Luke to explain.

"Well, she should have." His voice was emphatic. "I can't believe she took the chance that somebody would figure it out. Especially after everything they went through to get Kyle out of jail. Some secrets need to stay buried."

Luke assumed I was familiar with the story. I needed to draw him out, to say something that would encourage him to fill in the details, to explain what Kyle did, but my brain refused to come up with anything other than a generic response. "These things happen," I muttered.

His brows slid together into a thick line. "Corinne never told you."

I tried to dance around my ignorance. "She's mentioned so many things over the past few months. It's hard to remember everything."

"Nice try, Madeline. But it's obvious you don't know." He stood up, glancing toward the river. "It's hard to forget murder."

Chapter 19

I STAYED behind while Luke walked back to the hotel, thinking about what he'd said. Kyle had been in jail. He had killed someone. And his family had jumped through a lot of hoops to keep it quiet. Kyle was handsome and charming, but that easy-going façade masked a lot of unsavory traits. He had a temper ... he had proved that when he threatened me that night on the riverboat. And he had a weird relationship with Luke ... what kind of person would pay a paragliding pilot to terrorize his brother-in-law?

Could he have killed his mother to protect his secret? Corinne had to realize that once her campaign ratcheted up, every media source would be digging into her family's background. Somebody would find out about Kyle's past. He was already struggling to lock down investors for his new company. How many would stick with him if they knew what he had done?

Corinne had always stressed the importance of family. Why would she move forward with her campaign, knowing the damage it could do to her son? Was saving the planet more important to her than protecting Kyle?

I needed to find out more. Holliss would surely have mentioned Italy if she'd known about it. There was no point in asking Bronwyn—she would never betray her brother. That left Fred, but it seemed an awkward conversation to broach with a grieving widower: *Is your son a murderer? Any chance he killed his mother so no one would find out?*

Our meeting with Mueller was in less than an hour, so I would have to wait until afterwards to catch Fred alone. I hurried to my room to change out of my jogging gear. By the time I got down to the lobby, Fred and the others were already waiting. We piled into a minivan for the ride to the police station.

A uniformed officer met the five of us at the entrance. He led us through an open area of crowded desks and ringing telephones to a small conference room. We all seemed a bit frayed. Fred and Holliss were both pale and sleep-deprived, while Bronwyn paced anxiously near the window. Kyle was the only one who seemed normal. I searched his face for a sign of nervousness or guilt or remorse, anything to indicate he might be responsible for Corinne's death, but his expression betrayed nothing. When he realized I was staring at him, he gave me a reassuring smile.

Captain Mueller joined us a few minutes later, accompanied by the same female officer who had been with him yesterday. She wasn't especially threatening—no uniform or a gun—but as Mueller walked toward us and she stationed herself in front of the closed door, I felt trapped all the same. If I stood up to leave, I knew she would stop me. Coming here was a mistake. It gave Mueller another chance to interrogate us, to drill down into our memories, to see if we would contradict what we had told him yesterday. I wondered if Fred could find lawyers for all of us. I felt we might need them.

"I am glad you are all here," he said, in the same formal tone he had used with us yesterday, pronouns and verbs carefully separated. "I have a few more questions."

Bronwyn was quick to snap back at him. "We didn't come here to answer your questions. We came here to get my mother's things."

"Yes, Mr. Peerland told me that." Mueller held up a file folder. "I have pictures of everything we found at the scene. If you will have a seat, we can go over them."

Bronwyn defiantly planted her hands on her hips. "I'm not interested in pictures. I want my mom's jewelry. Her clothing. Everything you took from her."

"I understand that. Unfortunately, we cannot release anything until we have completed our investigation. Now, I am sure you will be much more comfortable if you sit while we talk."

Bronwyn remained standing, holding her ground. Mueller stood across from her, patiently waiting.

"Bronwyn, please," Fred said. "Let's get on with this."

"Fine." She jerked back a chair and sat down. "So why can't you give us her things?"

Mueller laid the file on the table and sat down. "Because until we have finished with our forensic procedures, we will not know which items may be relevant in proving our case. At this point, as I told you yesterday, we are still examining the evidence. Various possibilities."

"Including the possibility that my brother-in-law killed her?" Bronwyn asked.

Holliss's eyes flashed with anger. "Shut up, Bronwyn."

"That is totally out of line," Fred said, his face pale. "Bronwyn, apologize to your sister."

In an unconvincing voice, Bronwyn said, "I'm sorry if I upset you, Holliss." She turned back to Mueller. "But obviously the detective thinks one of us killed Mom. He's toying with us while he tries to figure out who did it. Makes sense to focus on the most likely candidate."

"Randall is not …" Holliss began.

Fred reached out a hand to each of them. "Please, I know this is hard. But you wanted to see your mother's things. Let's do this."

Mueller pulled several pictures from the file. "You mentioned jewelry. She was wearing these rings when we found her. Are these what you remember her wearing?"

Bronwyn grabbed the top photo, a closeup of Corinne's hand. "Yes, that's it." Two diamond and platinum rings were visible on her bent finger. "Those are her wedding rings. We want to take them with us. Right now."

Mueller shook his head. "As I said, we cannot release anything until the investigation is complete."

Bronwyn's lip curled. "Why? You think someone killed her with a diamond?"

He ignored her mocking tone. "It appears that she struggled with someone while she was still on the viewing platform. There could be fibers caught in the prongs. Hair. Skin cells." He laid another picture on the table. "Here is her watch."

The gold band was still attached to Corinne's arm, but the watch crystal was shattered.

"What caused those scratches on her arm?" Kyle asked. "Are they from the fall?"

"It is possible," Mueller said. "At this point we are …"

"Still examining the evidence," Bronwyn interrupted him. "We know. We've heard you already. And let me guess, we can't take the watch with us either."

"I am sorry, no."

"Bronwyn, please," Fred pleaded. "This isn't easy for any of us. Including the detective."

Mueller continued with his presentation. "She was wearing diamond earrings." He flipped through the pictures to pull out a closeup. The blond hair that Holliss had handled so tenderly in the morgue was tucked behind Corinne's ears, revealing diamond studs. "You recognize them?"

Fred's Adam's apple bulged as he struggled to swallow. "Yes. They were her favorite earrings. She wore them all the time."

Bronwyn studied the photo and tossed it down beside the others. It pained me to see Corinne reduced to odd angles of glossy photos, a collection of puzzle pieces scattered haphazardly across the table. I reached out to gather the pictures into a neat pile.

"What about her gold necklace?" Fred asked. "She had that on yesterday." Fred turned to Bronwyn. "You remember … the one we bought on that trip to Florence?"

Mueller shuffled through the pictures. "I do not have a photograph of a necklace. She was not wearing it when we found her. Perhaps it came off in the fall. Gold chains can be very delicate."

"This was no delicate chain," Bronwyn said. "It was heavy links. Eighteen karat gold, with a diamond pendant. Worth thousands of dollars."

Mueller carefully worked through the pictures again. "We do not have it."

"You need to find it."

"It is a very isolated area," he said. "Deep ravines. Heavy snow. We searched the area as thoroughly as we could."

"You have to search again." Bronwyn insisted. "That necklace meant a lot to her. Dad bought it for her anniversary."

"Let it go, Bronwyn," Kyle said. "Dad can file an insurance claim."

"That won't fix this. It's not about the money." She was desperate to reverse this tragedy, to reset everything as it had been—before she and her siblings argued with their mother, before Corinne fell to her death.

"Bronwyn, you don't know what it was like out there," Fred said. "The cold. The snow drifts. I was with the search teams for hours. I'm thankful they found your mother as quickly as they did." He stared down at the pictures. "If the necklace is up there, it's probably under ten feet of snow. We'll never find it."

Bronwyn refused to back down. "Use a metal detector or something. I want that necklace."

Mueller gathered the pictures and tucked them into the file. "We will try."

"Is that it?" Kyle asked. "Or are there more pictures?"

"There are a few more. But I warn you, they are disturbing."

"I want to see them," Kyle insisted.

Mueller hesitated. Then he pulled out a photo and slowly slid it toward us. It was a closeup of Corinne from the shoulders up. Blood covered her face and the collar of her jacket. My stomach heaved.

"Where's her scarf?" Holliss looked as queasy as I felt. "The turquoise one I gave her for her birthday?"

"She was not wearing a scarf when we found her," Müller said.

"She had it on when she left the café," Holliss said.

I mentally replayed those last moments. Corinne had jumped to her feet, grabbed her jacket, and wrapped the silk paisley scarf around her neck.

Fred pointed to the picture. "What's that on her neck? A shadow?"

I studied the photo. Not a shadow. A discoloration. A narrow bruise that extended around her throat. I hadn't noticed it when we saw Corinne in the morgue. I had stayed behind Holliss, not wanting to examine Corinne's body too closely.

Fred ran his finger slowly along the bruise. "She was strangled, wasn't she? With her own scarf." He turned away, his face collapsing in a sudden tide of fatigue. "And then pitched off the mountain. Like yesterday's trash."

Chapter 20

MUELLER WISELY decided that this was not the best time to barrage the family with additional questions. "Perhaps we should stop now. I know this has been very painful. I will contact you later if needed."

We all waited as Fred slowly rose to his feet. He wobbled unsteadily, and Bronwyn reached for his arm. Kyle and Holliss followed slowly behind.

I turned to Mueller. "Did you get my message last night?"

"Yes. I was ready to call when Mr. Peerland requested this meeting. He said you would be joining them. I figured it would be better to talk in person."

Fred and Bronwyn were halfway to the exit. "Let me tell the others to go without me. I'll be right back."

Mueller was still in the conference room when I returned. "A man followed me to my hotel last night," I said, sitting across from him. "I recognized him. He was one of the protestors from Basel."

He pulled out a small notepad. "Your voice mail was a bit garbled. Can you tell me again what happened?"

The images came back: the dark, deserted streets, my confusion as I desperately tried to find the hotel, my pounding heart as I realized I was being followed. "I went out to a restaurant last night. When I was walking back to the hotel, he followed me. It was terrifying." My voice trembled. "There was no one else in the street but the two of us."

I expected Mueller to be sympathetic, to reassure me, to ask how I felt. Instead, he kept his eyes down as he poised the pen above his notepad, focused only on the facts. "What was the name of the restaurant?"

I could see it—the backpackers sitting outside, the harried waitress, the long bar against the back wall. "I … I don't remember the name. But I'm sure you can find it. It was several blocks from the hotel. There was outdoor seating, maybe some umbrellas out front? I sat inside at the bar."

He lifted an eyebrow. "You were drinking?"

"Well, yes," I said. "I had a beer. Maybe two." The atmosphere had been perfect for guzzling down a cold one—the music, the loud conversations, people jostling behind me as they waited for a seat. "There were some guys at the end of the bar. Noisy. Drinking a lot. He might have been with them."

"Might have been?" His thumb rapidly clicked the pen as he studied my face. "But you did not see him with this group?"

"No, not specifically. But I didn't pay that much attention to them. He may have been with them. I didn't notice."

"I see." Something in his eyes told me he expected more from me ... that anyone determined enough to call a detective late at night should have a better grasp of the details. "Anyone with you who might help us identify the restaurant? Or the man who followed you?"

"Emily Salinger was there. Kyle Peerland's fiancée."

"You went there together?"

I shook my head "No. She was already there when I arrived. We sat together at the bar."

"Did you leave together?"

"No. We talked for a while, but I left by myself."

"Then what happened?"

"I had a little trouble finding my way back. I hadn't paid attention to street names when I left the hotel. It was dark—clouds covering the moon, fog rolling in from the river—that sort of thing. I got confused."

He carefully formed the letters as he wrote. "And you thought you were being followed."

Did he not believe me? "I *was* being followed. By a protestor I saw in Basel."

He leaned back in his chair, frowning. The same silver hair I had noticed yesterday poked up from his eyebrow. Did no one help this man with his personal hygiene? "How can you be so sure it was the same man? You have said it was dark. You had been drinking. You were afraid and confused. You do not think maybe all of that clouded your judgment?"

"Not at all," I insisted. "After I ran into the hotel, he stopped in the courtyard, right under the lights. He had the same curly blond hair, the same dark-framed glasses as that protestor in Basel."

"You showed me some videos from the conference. Was this man in them?"

"No. The videos I had focused on the shoving match with Corinne. The blond guy wasn't part of that. But there's probably a video out there that includes him. He was leading chants, shouting into a megaphone."

"I see." His next questions were more generic. "Did you notice anything else about him? Age? Height? Weight?"

"He appeared to be in his early twenties. I'm not good at estimating things like height and weight. I'd say he was average."

His lips twitched. "Average height. Average weight. Blond hair. Glasses. You've described a good number of the young men living in Lucerne. Anything else?"

I was irritated by his dismissive attitude. "If you mean did he have any tattoos, or a prominent scar, or a limp, or maybe he was missing his right ear, then no, I didn't notice anything like that." I paused, trying to remember anything significant that I hadn't already mentioned. "Maybe if I worked with a sketch artist? He could draw a picture for you?"

"We use computers for that, but they generally are not that effective. Unfortunately, people's memories are not very reliable."

It was obvious he was putting my memory on the *not reliable* list. This visit was a waste of time. "Why are you fighting me on this? When I showed you that video from Basel, you told me that Kiener had been murdered. You thought the protestors might have been involved. And that whoever did it might also have killed Corinne."

"I do not remember saying that."

"You certainly gave that impression."

He laid down his pen. "I apologize if that was the case. It was not my intent."

So maybe I was making a few assumptions. He hadn't phrased it exactly like that when he interrogated me at the hotel, but that was certainly the gist. "Well, what about Kiener? Do you have any leads?"

"I am sorry. I cannot discuss an active case with you." He tucked his notepad back into his jacket pocket, signaling that our interview was over.

I dialed up my intensity. "Corinne's murder could be related to the robbery on the boat. Have you checked out that possibility? Interviewed the staff?"

"You certainly have a lot of questions."

"And perhaps you don't have enough." My voice was sharper than I intended. "I've known Randall a long time. He would never have hurt Corinne."

Tiny lines formed around his eyes. "Miss Keswick, I can assure you that we are devoting a lot of resources to this case. We are as eager to resolve this as you are. And we are investigating all possibilities." He stood up. "Thank you for stopping by."

I jumped up and grabbed his arm. "This man was stalking me," I said, speaking slowly, emphasizing each word. "I'm in danger. What are you going to do about it?"

My hand was wrapped around his forearm. "Please," he said.

I quickly pulled back. "Sorry. I shouldn't have done that. But you weren't listening to me."

"Of course, I was listening." He tugged at his sleeve and then dropped the arm by his side. "We will distribute his description to our officers. If we spot him, we will certainly bring him in for questioning." He walked toward the door. I had little choice but to follow. "And in the interim …"

"Yes?" I expected him to share a few details, maybe outline his strategy for getting to the truth.

"In the interim, I suggest you not go out after dark by yourself."

Chapter 21

I WAS STILL fuming when I got back to the hotel. Fred sat in the lobby, cradling a mug of coffee. Newspaper pages were spread out messily on a low table in front of him. I perched on a nearby chair. "That detective's a jerk, isn't he?"

Fred's eyes were so vacant that for a moment I wasn't sure he knew who I was. Then he blinked and shook his head. "I'm sorry, Madeline. What did you say?"

"Captain Mueller. I stayed after to tell him that one of the protestors from Basel followed me home last night. But I don't think he believed me."

"Followed you home? I don't understand."

I quickly filled him in. "I think they could be behind what happened to Corinne."

He struggled to follow my story. "But why? She was on their side. Trying to manage climate change."

"They didn't know that. They saw her walk out of the conference with Nils Kiener, who was the CEO of a big oil company. They probably thought she was on his side." I reached for a newspaper. "Kiener was killed the first night of the conference. And Corinne was killed the next day."

He angled his head, his eyes widening. "You think their deaths are related? That the man who followed you killed Corinne?"

"I think he was involved, yes."

He studied my face, trying to understand. "Why would he follow you? What does he want?"

I shivered as I remembered his footsteps behind me, steady and relentless. "Corinne and I were at the conference together. They saw her as the enemy. Now they're coming after me."

Fred's coffee shook. "What's Mueller doing about it? Is he providing you any protection?"

I grunted. "No. He's not taking me seriously. Treating me like a child afraid of shadows. He told me not to go wandering in the dark by myself."

He put the newspapers in a neat pile. "I can see why that upset you, but considering everything that's been happening, it's probably not bad advice."

"But don't you see, Fred, he's focused on Randall and not searching very hard for any other suspects. Like the security guy, Smithson, on the riverboat. Sticking with the easy solution—a tourist killed in a family squabble."

"Randall will be fine," Fred said, his voice firm. "We've got a legal team handling this. They'll take care of everything."

His words gave me the perfect lead-in to question him about Italy. "Like you did for Kyle?"

"Kyle? What are you talking about?"

I hesitated. "Luke mentioned that Kyle had been involved in some trouble in Italy a few years ago. He landed in jail, but you took care of it."

"Luke should have kept his mouth shut." The fierceness of Fred's gaze made me shrink back into my chair. "He doesn't know all the details."

I immediately began to backtrack. "I'm sorry, Fred. I didn't mean to upset you."

There was a cold undercurrent to his voice. "I'm disappointed that you've stooped to gossip."

I searched for words to calm him, to explain my interest. But my only justification was that I wanted to serve up Kyle as a possible suspect, so that Mueller would take his focus off Randall. Somehow, I didn't think Fred would find that comforting. I kept my eyes down and my mouth shut as I fidgeted in my chair.

After a few moments Fred spoke, more gently. "I take care of my own. I'll get my folks to keep an eye on you. To make sure you're safe."

And most likely to prevent future conversations between me and Luke. I had the feeling that a not-so-friendly heart-to-heart with his father-in-law was in Luke's near future. "In the meantime …" His jaw muscles rippled. "Stay away from Mueller. The way he treated my family today, whipping out those horrible pictures of Corinne … it was quite disturbing."

I wasn't sure that was Mueller's fault. He had shown a modicum of sensitivity by sharing only the pictures of Corinne's jewelry. It was Kyle who insisted he reveal those gruesome photos of her mangled body. Was it because Kyle pushed her? Did he want to see evidence of what he had done? "Bronwyn seemed especially upset."

"Yes. She cried all the way back to the hotel. Kyle has taken her for a walk, to calm her down." He picked up the top newspaper section with a shaky hand, glancing at Corinne's photo. "We're all devastated by this, Madeline. Corinne was an amazing woman. A wonderful wife and mother. She would have been a terrific senator."

"I agree. She had so many plans. It's a big loss for all of us." I wanted to reach out, to put my arm around him, but the grief rippling across his face stopped me. "What can I do to help?"

He ran a finger along her picture. "I'd like you to shake up these reporters. All they want to talk about is details of the death. That's not how I want her to be remembered. I need you to tell her story. What an amazing woman she was. What she was trying to accomplish. Can you do that?"

It would be easy to leverage off Corinne's website. "Yes. She had a good response to her environmental blogs. We have several queued up, waiting to be published. Are you okay if we release them?"

"Absolutely."

"What about friends and colleagues? Are there people who can give me more background, to add color to our press releases?"

"Yes. I'll give you contact information for folks who worked on her projects. They should be able to answer any of your questions." He rolled the newspaper into a tight cylinder, tapping it against his palm. "I want these reporters to know her as an accomplished woman, not a faceless victim." He stood up. "I'm depending on you, Madeline, to take care of this."

As he walked toward the elevators, I thought of following behind him, to head upstairs to catch up on emails and work projects, but the last thing I wanted was to be cooped up in my room all by myself. I needed to absorb the sights and smells of the city so I could block out those shocking pictures of Corinne's dented skull. I left the hotel and walked toward Old Town.

Chapter 22

THRONGS OF chattering tourists energized me as I wandered through the city streets, passing storefronts filled with jewelry and clothing and candy. I needed to pick up more souvenirs for friends back home, but quickly realized I wasn't in the mood to shop. Nothing caught my eye as I browsed and checked out numerous displays of kitschy keepsakes. Mugs and keychains and luggage tags with scenes of the Swiss Alps and the Reuss River didn't seem quite right for anyone on my list.

I stopped at the Lion Monument, which commemorated Swiss soldiers who died in the French Revolution. Was it only two days ago that we had stood here in the rain while our Lucerne tour guide told us the story? Now, seeing the huge sandstone carving of the dying lion, his head resting on a broken shield, the tip of a spear sticking out of a jagged wound in his back, all I could think of was Corinne's broken body. I lowered my head, fighting tears.

"It's okay to cry. She was your friend."

"Wyatt," I said, turning toward him. Yesterday I had sobbed on his shoulder as I told him about Corinne. I couldn't do that again. Fred depended on me to be calm and poised and professional. My own feelings of grief and loss had to stay locked up deep inside, not to be shared with anyone.

"Kyle told me you guys have had a hell of a day."

"It's been a little rough." Despite my best intentions, I could feel my eyes watering.

"How about we walk a bit? There's something I want to show you."

Usually when I was in a new city, I liked to zip from one spot to the next, determined to pack as many memories into a day as possible, taking innumerable photos so I wouldn't forget anything. But there was nothing I wanted to remember about this trip. I followed placidly as Wyatt led me through the winding streets.

We made our way up a steep hill. The thick medieval walls of the old city were in front of us, ancient stones stacked high, with tall watch towers looming at regular intervals. "The day we were in Lucerne, you said you wanted to come here, only we ran out of time. I figured we could try again. There's a walkway along the top with some great views of the city. You willing to tackle some steps?"

I would be willing to run a marathon if it would help me stop thinking of Corinne. "Let's do it."

We walked up quickly and joined other tourists milling along the wide walkway. On one side was a grassy field, where a bunch of guys were playing a spirited game of soccer, or football, as they called it in Europe. On the other was the river and the winding streets of the city. "You were right about the view. This is impressive."

"I thought you'd like it." Wyatt stopped at a gap in the stone parapet. "Bet this was where soldiers poured hot oil down on their enemies. Can't you hear them screaming? Their horses writhing, desperate to escape?"

I shivered. "You have such a vivid way of seeing history. Today it's hot oil and screaming soldiers. Yesterday you told me the river in Strasbourg used to be a toxic waste dump."

He pointed to a small plaque which gave details about the wall's construction. "You can read dry facts about a place. Or you can imagine stories about the people who used to live there. I think my way is more fun."

We strolled until the afternoon sun baked uncomfortably into our shoulders, and then took refuge under some leafy trees which angled low over the walkway. It was cooler here, the silver-green canopy sheltering us from the heat and giving us our own private space to talk. I broke off a small branch and began to strip the leaves, one by one, letting them fall through my fingers. Their verdant scent dissolved the medicinal smell that had stuck with me since viewing Corinne's body. "Thanks for bringing me up here." The stiff ache in my back began to ease. "The last few days have been exhausting. This is a welcome break."

"It's been hard on everybody." A squirrel dropped from a tree and scampered along the wall. Wyatt flicked a wrist to scare him away. "Emily and

I hung out together while you guys were at the police station. She's really worried about Kyle."

"Is it because of Bronwyn? That she depends on him so much?" I knew Emily was jealous of the close connection between them.

"That, too, but she's concerned about their company. She and Kyle are having a rough time getting it off the ground."

"Really? Emily told me everything was going well."

"They've hit a few bumps in the road."

I remembered when we were in the hotel lobby yesterday, waiting for Fred and Mueller, and Kyle had been glued to his phone, saying he was putting out a fire. And before that, when Kyle and Emily argued on the boat, and she said, "We can't let this deal fall apart." Maybe they were having problems. "You know, it's a funny thing about going into business for yourself. Everyone thinks you'll have freedom to make all the decisions and do things exactly as you want, but it's never that simple." I brushed off bits of shredded leaf. "It sucks up all your energy—developing a product and finding customers and keeping them happy. There's never time for anything else."

"She's worried about money."

"That's typical for new companies." Lilly and I were still struggling to build a cash cushion for our business. It was frightening to think how little we had available for emergencies.

"I've told her I might be able to help." There was a forced casualness about him, but underneath I sensed a fidgety eagerness, a secret that was too good not to share. "The athletes my company represents always want good opportunities to invest their cash."

"Wow. You have those kinds of contacts?" He'd offered tournament playoff tickets to Kyle, but finding folks ready to sink millions of dollars into a company was a different proposition altogether.

He seemed annoyed at the uncertainty in my voice. "Of course. I told you, I'm in *sports marketing*." He spoke as thought it was a concept beyond my understanding, one he needed to explain in short sentences of simple words. "I know lots of people."

So did I. But knowing people hadn't helped me transition to a new job when I got kicked out of the old one. And it hadn't produced a full stable of new clients once Lilly and I finally decided to go into business for ourselves. "It's more than knowing people. You have to find investors with a long-term focus, who share your vision and will stick with you through the rough spots."

"You don't think I can pull this off."

I busied myself with selecting another branch, giving me time to come up with a response. "I didn't say that. But I think finding big-money investors is tougher than a lot of people think."

"I've already got my buddies lined up. They'll get a good return on their money. Emily and Kyle will get the investors they need. It's a win-win."

He made it sound simple, but I was more suspicious than convinced. "And you'll get a nice finder's fee for putting the deal together."

"There's nothing wrong with a finder's fee." Sunlight filtered through the leaves at odd angles, casting bizarre shadows across his face, undulating ripples of light and dark like tangles of pulsating blood vessels popping to the surface, transforming his normal countenance into something resembling a sci-fi monster. "I can make this deal happen. Unless you interfere."

I shrank back from his disfigured appearance. "Why would I interfere? This is between you and them. It's nothing to do with me."

"That's not true. Emily thinks a lot of you. She'll never commit if you convince her it's the wrong way to go."

Emily and I shared an interest in start-up companies, but I was hardly her mentor. Her overwhelming self-confidence left little room for my opinion. Even if I wanted to give her advice, she probably wouldn't listen. "I would never do that."

"You sure?"

Our secluded canopy suddenly felt more like an interrogation room than a refuge. I backed into the sunshine, heading for the far wall, anything to put more distance between us. Below me, the soccer players had picked up an enthusiastic audience, spread out along the sidelines, cheering at every play. "I'm sorry, I'm not trying to be difficult. But I've got money problems of my own. Corinne was our biggest client. With her gone, we're really going to struggle."

He joined me at the wall, his belligerent tone softening. "Sorry. I didn't know that." In the bright sunshine his face was almost normal again, his olive complexion marked by the usual wrinkles around his eyes rather than those grotesque shadows of throbbing veins.

"Lilly, my business partner, wants me to come home right away. But Holliss has been one of my best friends since college. I can't desert her while Captain Mueller has his sights on Randall."

"Surely Lilly can understand that."

"I guess. We'll work it out somehow."

He edged closer. "I don't want you to rush home. I've enjoyed getting to know you."

I figured this was a last-chance pitch to win me over, to get me back on his side so I wouldn't screw up his deal with Kyle. I gave him a half-hearted smile and then casually maneuvered away, unpersuaded by his quick change of mood.

He moved beside me, watching the soccer game. Two players scrambled for control of the ball. The taller one wrested it free and sent it downfield with a powerful kick. There was a big roar as the ball sailed past the goalie. "Great shot," Wyatt yelled, clapping.

The players rushed onto the field, celebrating with chest bumps and high-fives. At the sidelines they sorted through the piled-up duffels. "Guess that's the end of it." I started for the exit.

Wyatt grabbed my hand. "Ready for more steps?" He pointed to the nearest watch tower. "I hear the view from the top is spectacular."

As if I wanted to spend any more time with this guy. "I've had enough for today. I want to hit the bar and enjoy a big glass of wine."

"But you'll love this. And you'll never get another chance to see it."

"I don't think so," I said, pulling free.

Deep lines circled his mouth. "I'm sorry. Those things I said about the investors, I shouldn't have dumped all that on you. Of course, you wouldn't interfere. But this is the first deal like this I've done, and I don't want it to blow up on me."

"I understand, but I really need to get back to the hotel."

He spread his arms in supplication. "Please, let's end the day with an adventure, not an argument."

A stone horseman was perched at the top of the rectangular tower, brandishing a sword in one fist and an outstretched banner in the other. I was curious, wanting to see more, knowing Wyatt would make up some interesting stories about what had happened there so long ago. "Wonder what's inside?" I asked.

He grinned, realizing he'd won me over. "Let's check it out."

We walked into the narrow space. Several flights of wooden steps stretched above us. "These steps look ancient. Are you sure they're safe?"

"I don't think they'd let us in here if it was dangerous," Wyatt said. "Most of the other towers are closed. This is one of the few that's open to tourists."

"There must be a thousand steps."

"Not quite that many, but it's not for the faint of heart. Are you up to the challenge?"

"Why not? Race you to the top."

We started at a jog up the steep steps. By the fourth landing, my thigh muscles were screaming at me. "Whose idea was this?" I yelled. "It's like climbing the Eiffel Tower. Or maybe the Washington Monument."

He laughed. "Did you miss a couple of workouts at the gym?"

I stopped at the last landing, pressing my hands against my waist. "You know, they closed off the steps of the Washington Monument because too many people were having heart attacks. I can see why."

"Quit whining. We're almost there."

I was panting by the time we reached the top. City streets stretched out below us, with postcard-perfect snow-capped mountains in the distance.

"So, what do you think?" he asked. "Was it worth the climb?"

"Absolutely." I pulled out my phone and took pictures from every angle.

He reached out to pull me close. "I'm glad we came here. The two of us. We needed some time alone." He pressed his lips against mine in a wet, sloppy kiss, forcing his tongue deep into my mouth.

What had I done to make him think it was okay to kiss me? I hadn't been slobbered on like that since Archie Devon pawed me behind the gym after the eighth-grade homecoming dance.

"What's the matter?" he asked, as I backed away from him.

I took a step toward the railing. "I'm … I'm sort of seeing someone." It was the first excuse that popped into my head. I figured he wouldn't take it too well if I told him his soul-sucking kisses were disgusting.

"You never mentioned that before. Who is it?"

I would have claimed King Kong as a boyfriend if it kept Wyatt's tongue out of my mouth. "A friend back home," I said, picturing Travis Lawson, who had been plying me with emails and phone calls during the entire trip, wanting to interview me for his big project on startup companies. "We've been dating a while, off and on."

"Why haven't you mentioned this guy?"

"I didn't think I needed to."

Wyatt's lips turned down. Not exactly a pout, but well on the way. "I thought we were having fun. Guess you weren't having as good a time as me."

"Come on, Wyatt. We've only known each other a few days." He was entertaining and attractive and a great dancer, but a big part of his appeal was that ours was a temporary relationship, no strings attached. Once I got home, I would never see him again. "We're friends. Don't mess this up."

"Friends?" He grabbed my arm, jerking me toward him, his eyes inches from mine. "I thought we were a lot more than that. Why do you think I came back to Lucerne?"

The accusing tone of his voice frightened me. Suddenly I wished we were having this conversation somewhere else, like in the hotel lobby or in a busy restaurant, surrounded by other people. Anywhere other than the two of us at the top of a very tall watch tower. "I thought you came back to Lucerne because you were poker buddies with Corinne and Kyle. You wanted to help find her."

"That was part of it. But I wanted to be with you, too. I thought you needed me." He stroked my chin, his thumb digging in under my jawbone.

"Stop that. You're hurting me." I pivoted away from him. Splinters dug into my fingers as I grabbed the railing, desperate to regain my balance on the tiny landing. The city streets sprawled below me, a long way down. "We need to go."

Indignation transformed his face into a threatening mask. For a moment I thought I could see the same pulsating, tangled veins that had frightened me before, when we were standing under the shade tree. I moved toward the door, but he blocked my way.

"We need to go," I repeated.

He glared at me, then stepped to the side, giving me a clear path to the exit. "Sure. You go ahead."

I edged carefully past him, afraid that he would try to grab me again, but he stayed behind as I started down the first flight. It was a lot easier going down than up. I developed an easy rhythm as I bounced down the steps, my pace quickening as gravity pulled me along.

About halfway down I wondered if I'd been too tough on Wyatt. After all, he did cut his vacation short—whether it was because he wanted to search for Corinne, or to line up investors for Emily and Kyle, or to spend more time with me, I wasn't sure—but maybe the stress I'd been going through had made me overreact, to see a demon where there wasn't one. Until today, we had enjoyed being together. Then I completely brushed him off because of a messy kiss and a grip that was probably a lot stronger than he realized. No wonder he was angry.

Trying to make peace between us, I called back, "Race you to the bottom?"

There was a silence, and then he yelled, "You're on," his words echoing in the rocky staircase.

My competitive streak kicked in as I heard him pounding behind me, getting closer and closer. Momentum made me fly down the steps. I spun wide at each landing as I raced down one flight to the next. Then suddenly I was out of control—unable to slow down, unable to stop—like an overturned kayak flipping wildly over a waterfall. Below me were steps and more steps, winding around the central core of the tower.

Wobbling, I reached out for the rock wall to steady myself, but my feet tangled and I lost my balance. Tumbling down the last flight, my knees scraping against the uneven wooden steps, I crashed hard on the concrete floor.

Chapter 23

I WAS SPLAYED out on my back, eyes closed, while my brain tried to process multiple sharp daggers of pain coming from various body parts. My knees. My elbows. My ankle.

"Madeline, are you all right?"

Opening my eyes, I saw Wyatt kneeling beside me, concern striping his forehead. "Man, you really did a number on your knees."

I groaned as I slowly pushed myself to a sitting position, adding my wrist to the injured list as a dull ache radiated up my arm. Below my skirt, bright lines of blood seeped past twisted strings of white skin. My knees hadn't been that banged up since I was a little kid trying out my new birthday roller skates. "Does anything else hurt?" he asked.

I sat there a moment, my senses gyrating as I processed the pain. "My left ankle."

Wyatt gently probed at it. I winced at the pressure. "Can you move it?"

I grimaced as I slowly rotated the ankle. "Sort of."

"I don't think it's broken. At least, I hope not. Probably a nasty sprain. Can you stand up?"

I grabbed his outstretched hand. "I think so."

He grunted in pain as he pulled me to my feet.

"Are you all right?" I balanced awkwardly on my uninjured ankle.

"It's my back. I wrenched it in Strasbourg. Jumping over that stupid puddle."

"Your football injury," I said, remembering. "I'm so sorry. I didn't mean to aggravate it."

"No, no, it's fine," he insisted, stifling a moan. "Give me a minute. I'll be okay."

I took a tentative step. My ankle was a lot fatter than I remembered, but at least there weren't any pieces of bone poking out, which was a good sign. "Let's get out of here."

""Here, lean on me," he said, pulling my arm over his shoulder.

"But your back. That must hurt."

"No, really, I'm good. A spasm, that's all. We can do this."

It was awkward being this close to him after our argument, but I couldn't navigate solely under my own power. Walking gingerly, I limped out of the tower and onto the walkway. He peered over the edge to the green grass below. "We've got a lot of steps still to go. Do you think you can make it to the bottom?"

The steps that I had skittered up so easily now seemed an impossible challenge. But I had to get down somehow. All those tourists who had been wandering around earlier had disappeared, so there wasn't anyone else around to help. "Sure," I said, trying to sound more confident than I felt. "As long as we take it slow."

I shuffled down the steps one by one, trying not to lean too heavily on Wyatt. Pain blurred my perspective, making the edges of the steps tuck into each like the flattening levels of a descending escalator. Distorted shapes slithered at the boundaries of my vision. Off balance, I lurched downward, threatening to send us both tumbling.

"Hey, take it easy," Wyatt said. "We've got plenty of time here. No point trying to set any Olympic records."

I clung to him, squinting to reorder the universe back into solid steps and trees and hillsides.

He waited patiently until I had relaxed my death grip. "Ready now?"

We started down again, one hop-step after another, my muscles straining to keep me upright. By the time we reached street level, I was weak with fatigue.

Wyatt maneuvered me toward the stone wall that edged the sidewalk. "You sit here. I'll go find a taxi to take us back to the hotel."

I settled on the low wall, my good leg planted with the injured ankle tucked protectively behind. Wyatt strode quickly out of sight, and for a moment I had this crazy feeling that he wasn't coming back for me, that I would be stuck on this wall for hours as payback for questioning his investment scheme and rejecting that disgusting kiss at the top of the tower. But soon a taxi pulled up and Wyatt jumped out, helping me into the back seat.

He slid in close beside me. I winced. "My wrist. It hurts."

"Sorry." He scooted toward the window, leaving a few more inches between us.

I leaned my head back against the seat. The pain distorted all sense of time, making the taxi ride last forever. I was thankful when we finally pulled into the hotel courtyard. Wyatt helped me out of the taxi, supporting me as I took a few halting steps.

The doorman spotted us and rushed down to help as I limped up the stairs to the lobby. "Can you send a doctor up to her room?" Wyatt asked as he explained what happened. "We don't think anything is broken, but she needs some medical attention all the same."

"And some painkillers," I said. "The heavy-duty kind."

Wyatt walked with me into the elevator and then down the hall to my room. I stopped outside the door, key in hand, thanking him for his help. "I can take it from here. I don't want to ruin the rest of your day."

"Don't be silly." He took the key from me and opened the door. "I'll wait with you until the doctor comes."

I hobbled to the chair. Wyatt pulled pillows off the bed and stacked them on the floor in front of me. "Elevation," he said, as he propped up my injured ankle. "Really important for a sprained ankle."

"Thanks. That's better." I waited impatiently for the doctor, closing my eyes and trying to focus on anything but the pain. Finally, there was a loud knock. Wyatt opened the door for a middle-aged man in a white coat, carrying a medical bag.

"I'm Dr. Keller," he said, spotting me and moving toward my chair. "I understand you fell down some steps."

"Yes. In the tower. The Old City."

"Interesting spot," he said. "But those steps are tricky. You're not the first one to have a problem with them." He chatted as he inspected my knees, my elbows, my wrist, sending Wyatt out for ice, wrapping my ankle in a compression bandage. "It looks worse than it is. Your ankle will be sore for a while, so keep it elevated and try not to walk around too much for the next day or so." He pulled a small package from his medical bag. "You can take these for the pain. One now, another in the morning, then every eight hours as needed. You'll feel better soon."

"Thanks. I really appreciate your coming over so quickly."

"My office has an arrangement with the hotel. We don't get many tourists in distress, but when we do, we like to give them the best care."

Wyatt walked the doctor to the door and then brought me a bottle of water from the mini bar. "Why don't you stretch out on the bed and rest a bit? I'll sit here with you. In case you need anything."

After his unwelcome groping at the tower, the last thing I wanted was the two of us alone in my hotel room. "I'm good right here, I think." I swallowed one of the pills, the water cool and refreshing on my parched tongue. "If you could give me my cell phone," I said, gesturing toward my purse, "I think I'll read for a while. A little quiet time. All by myself."

I could tell he was reluctant to leave. He bent down to fluff the pillows under my ankle and adjust the ice pack. "Are you chilly? Would you like a blanket?"

"No, I'm fine, thanks. Need some alone time for the pain pill to kick in."

He reached for my hand, but I snatched it away. "Careful with the wrist."

"Sorry." He walked slowly toward the door. "Guess I'll see you later. Maybe for dinner?"

"I don't feel like going out. I'll order something from room service."

"Okay." He twisted the door handle.

"Wyatt?" I called after him.

"Yes?"

"The room key. Can you leave it on the nightstand?"

"Oh, yes," he said, patting his pockets. "I forgot."

I watched as he set down the key. "See you later."

After he left, I placed a dinner order with room service and settled in the chair to read. I was slipping into a lovely drug-induced fog when there was a loud knock on the door. Surely Wyatt couldn't be back already? I ignored him, hoping he would think I was asleep and leave me alone. But the knocking continued.

"Madeline, are you there?"

The voice was familiar, but it wasn't Wyatt. I pushed myself to my feet and slowly made my way to the door. Through the contoured glass of the peep hole everything in the hallway was distorted, the walls bending inward and haloes streaking from the light sconces, like a mirrored fun house in a carnival. The person standing in front of the door peered back at me. His head was enormous, his eyes flashing like black diamonds.

I opened the door. "I can't believe this. Travis Lawson, what are you doing here?"

Chapter 24

TRAVIS HAD the bedraggled, jet-lagged air of someone who'd spent the last eight hours crammed into a too-small airline seat, his long legs bumping the person in front of him, futilely trying to catch a few hours of sleep while a colicky baby nearby screamed all the way across the Atlantic. A shadowy stubble coated his chin, and his dark hair fell limply toward his eyes. "I was worried about you," he said.

Travis hated flying—the loss of control, being locked up in a metal tube—totally dependent on the skills of a pilot who maybe had discovered his wife was having an affair, or had learned his teenage son got swept up in a high-school drug bust, or had dozed off in his last training class. A pilot who was perhaps irate or distracted or confused, not ready to take on the challenges of fighting gravity and speed and weather all at the same time. I knew his fears were irrational—statistics proved that pilots had much better safety records than most road warriors—but I couldn't convince him. On a trip we took a few years ago from New York to Toronto, Travis had insisted on driving, even though we could have flown in a fraction of the time.

But there were no roads from New York to Lucerne. So he had climbed into an airplane, his clenched fingers digging holes into the armrests for the entire flight, all because of me. A grand, impulsive gesture that made me feel guilty that I was still annoyed with him after all this time, that I had been ignoring his emails and calls. "Come on in. How did you know where I was?"

He grabbed his roller bag and wheeled it into the room. "Lilly."

"She told you about Corinne?"

"Yes. Lilly said that detective had been giving you a hard time. I figured you could use some help."

I'd seen this side of Travis before, a modern-day Clark Kent always ready to shift into Superman role when he needed to rescue the fair maiden. The last time he tried that, he derailed my career, throwing a punch that cost me my job.

I hadn't asked for his help then, and I didn't need it now. For him to swoop in here like I was a damsel-in-distress was insulting. Resentment pushed away the warm fuzziness I felt when I first saw him. "You thought I couldn't handle things on my own?"

"Calm down, calm down," he said, hearing the hostility in my voice. "Of course, you can handle this. But why should you? Let's face it, Madeline, you're in a foreign country, with no support system, no local contacts …"

"That's not true. Fred's been working with the U.S. Embassy."

"And what is the Embassy doing for you? Are they running interference with this detective?"

"Not exactly. But still ..."

"Come on, Madeline, we're friends." He emitted a plaintive sigh, signaling his exasperation. "We've been through a lot together. Why do I always feel like I'm beating my head against a wall when I'm talking with you?"

We *had* been through a lot together, and maybe that was the problem. He'd seen me at my most vulnerable. When I'd lost my job. When all the resumes I sent out didn't elicit a single interview. When colleagues I thought were friends didn't return my calls, in case the stigma hanging over me was contagious. My past was a festering wound that I wanted to leave alone so it could heal, but with Travis was around, it was impossible not to keep picking at it.

"Anyway, you're not the only reason I'm in town. I'm doing some interviews for my magazine."

"Really?"

"Yes. I'm focusing on entrepreneurs who are developing carbon capture systems. They're in Basel for the energy conference." He stepped toward the roller bag. "Since I was in Switzerland, I thought I'd stop by. But it seems I'm in your way. Guess I'll head out."

My ego shriveled like a withered plum past its prime. He hadn't flown here because of me, after all. I was something he had worked into his schedule while he was in Switzerland on business. I felt like an idiot, ashamed that I'd been so hostile. "Wait. You just got here. We may as well catch up a bit." I eased toward the mini bar. "Can I get you something to drink? A beer, maybe?"

"Sounds great. But what happened to your ankle? Are you all right?"

"I fell down some steps. It's not serious. The doctor said I'd feel a lot better in a few days." I pulled a green bottle from the fridge. "Stella okay?"

"Sure." He walked over to take it from me, noticing the pile of pillows by the chair. "Why don't you sit down? Prop your foot up?"

"Good idea." My ankle was beginning to throb a bit.

He settled the ice pack over the compression bandage. "How's this?"

"Perfect."

Travis popped the top off his beer and leaned back against the dresser. "So, this whole thing with Corinne. Tell me what happened."

I gave him a quick summary of the past few days. "When the detective told us they'd found her body, we all thought it was an accident. It was so foggy up there. We couldn't see from one side of the viewing platform to the other. And it was slippery … lots of icy spots. I figured Corinne left the café, maybe crying, and wasn't paying attention. Got too close to the edge."

"But the police think it was murder?"

"Because of the scratches on her arms. And broken fingernails, like she'd fought off an attacker. Captain Mueller took Randall, Corinne's son-in-law, in for questioning, because he had a lot of scratches on his neck."

"Do you think Randall's guilty?"

"No way. Holliss, his wife, said Randall cut his neck shaving, and I believe her. Randall is so mild-mannered—he's an economics professor, a quiet guy— hardly the type to push his mother-in-law off a mountain."

"What about Corinne's children? Or her husband? The people closest to the victim are generally the first suspects."

"You sound like Mueller. You should have seen him when he interviewed all of us. He seemed determined to pin this on someone in the family." The ice pack was making me cold. "Hey, can you toss me a blanket?" I asked, gesturing toward the closet. "It's chilly in here."

He wrapped the blanket around my shoulders. "That better?"

"Yes, thanks." I snuggled into the blanket as I filled him in on the family dynamics. "There was a lot of friction when Corinne told them her plans. I guess it's possible that one of them killed her, but I don't want to believe that."

He set the beer on the dresser. "I'm sure the police are under a lot of pressure to wrap this up. There's been a lot of chatter about the murder on the internet. Rich American woman. U.S. Senate candidate. It's a huge story."

"But by focusing only on the family, he's missing an important part of the case." I told him about the protesters in Basel, and the man who followed me to the hotel last night.

"And this detective isn't doing anything about that?"

"Not much. And he's not investigating what happened on the riverboat, either." I told him about Corinne's poker game and the missing money.

"Has Mueller checked out the boat?"

"I don't know. It's in Germany now, so it's out of his jurisdiction. I doubt he's arranged with the local police to question anyone on the boat or examine the evidence." The ice pack shifted, and I leaned over to push it back in place. "I want to get on the boat, interview the staff members and take another look at Corinne's cabin. But I don't know how to do that. The captain probably won't let me stroll around, asking questions and poking into corners."

"I might be able to help you there."

"How?"

"I have a local contact, a reporter here in Switzerland that I've worked with several times over the years. She's well connected. Knows everybody. If anyone can get us on that boat, it's Eva Graesser."

I wasn't that excited about having a reporter burrow into the details. "This is a family matter, Travis. We don't need reporters."

He picked up his beer. "It stopped being a family matter the moment Corinne was pushed off that mountain. The police are involved. You can't keep secrets now."

No doubt he was right. Besides, I could use some help. "You think she'd do it?"

"Let me give her a call." He pulled out his phone and walked over toward the window.

There was a sharp knock on the door. Wyatt stood there, grinning at me. "You ready for some dinner? I thought we could go to the restaurant downstairs."

"Thanks, but the ankle's still wobbly. I've ordered room service."

"Want any company while you eat?" He stepped into the room but stopped abruptly as he noticed Travis standing by the window.

"Wyatt, Travis," I said, gesturing from one to the other. "Travis is an old friend from home. Arrived in Lucerne today."

Wyatt's eyes flashed as soon as I said *old friend.* I'd used those same words when we were up on the tower. He would think Travis was the one I was in a relationship with, which wasn't exactly true, at least not anymore. But if it made Wyatt keep his distance from me, I was fine with the lie.

"We met Wyatt on the riverboat," I told Travis. "He and Kyle are friends, so he wanted to come back with us to Lucerne, to check on Corinne."

The two of them shook hands, and then backed away to eye each other suspiciously. It reminded me of one of those nature shows I'd seen on television, where two rams pawed the earth as they stood ready to battle over the same ewe, their muscles rippling, heads angled to the side. Having two men fight over me almost made me forget the pain in my ankle.

We were interrupted by a knock on the door. "Room service."

Wyatt opened the door. The waiter steered a cart into the room.

"Please put that over here," I said, gesturing toward the chair, reaching for my wallet for a tip.

"I've got it." Travis pulled some bills from his pocket. "What else can I get you?" he asked as the waiter left.

"Maybe some more water?"

Wyatt rushed to the fridge. He pulled out a bottle and unscrewed the top.

If my ankle hadn't been throbbing quite so much, I would have enjoyed watching this sparring match between two potential suitors. "Thank you both, but I'm exhausted. I'm going to eat my sandwich and crawl into bed. I'll see you tomorrow."

Travis grabbed the handle of his roller bag. "Guess that's our cue to leave," he said to Wyatt. He brushed my cheek with a quick kiss and whispered in my ear, "I left a message for Eva. I'll let you know when I hear back."

***

I nibbled at my dinner after they left, forcing down bits of arugula and chicken even though I had little appetite. Something kept nagging at me about what had happened in the tower. Wyatt's mood swings had surprised me—belligerent one moment, then trying to cover me with syrupy kisses the next. But there was something else, stubbornly stuck at the fringes of my memory. I replayed the scene—our race down the steps, my wobble as I lost my balance, the final crash to the floor—but I couldn't capture that elusive detail.

I needed to talk this over with somebody, to go through the action frame by frame, to help me figure out what was wrong. Reaching for my phone, I punched in Lilly's number. I wasn't sure she'd answer. We'd both been angry when we ended our conversation last night, each of us convinced we were right, neither willing to give in. But we'd been business partners for several years now. And friends a lot longer than that. We needed to work out a compromise.

She picked up on the first ring. "Madeline, I feel terrible for the way I talked to you yesterday," she said in a rush, instantly apologetic. "Pressuring you to come home right away. Of course, you need to be there for Holliss. Take as long as you need."

I scooped the blanket and pillows from the floor and tossed them on the bed. "You don't know how relieved I am to hear you say that. And we're still on the job for Corinne, at least for a while longer. Fred wants us to maintain her website and to interact with reporters." I settled against the headboard. "He's worried they'll gloss over her environmental work and focus only on the details of the crime."

"He's right about that. The internet is buzzing with speculation about who killed her. Crime gets more clicks than climate change any day of the week."

I spread the blanket out over my legs. "In other news, guess who showed up at my hotel?"

She didn't even pretend to be surprised. "Was it Travis? Did he finally get there?"

"None other. He said you told him where I was staying."

"Don't be mad, Madeline. He's been calling every day to see how you're doing. And with Corinne murdered, he was worried you might be in danger."

"That's silly. He's getting upset over nothing." At least nothing I planned to tell him about. Like Wyatt grabbing me at the top of the tower. Or Kyle threatening me on the deck of the riverboat. I knew it would only bring out his superhero side, and I'd been burned by that enough. "I can manage things."

"I'm sure you can, but would you try to be nice to him? Not many guys would fly all the way across the Atlantic to check up on a former girlfriend."

"He's here on a business trip, Lilly." My voice rose in exasperation. "To interview folks at that energy conference in Basel. I'm an afterthought."

"Seriously?" Pricks of annoyance wrapped around her voice. "How can you be so oblivious to all this? He could have done those interviews by telephone, or over the internet. You're the reason he's there. He would do anything for you."

I mulled over her words. She was right ... a telephone or internet call would have been a lot quicker. But I knew Travis liked to interview his subjects face to face. He always said that words could lie, but body language seldom did. "Maybe. Anyway, he's already making himself useful. He's working with a contact to get us access to the riverboat, so we can interview the staff and figure out if they were involved in Corinne's death."

"Shouldn't you leave all that to the police?"

"The police aren't looking much farther than Randall. Mueller's latched onto him like a pit bull."

She sighed. "Well, if you insist on playing detective, I'm glad Travis is there to help."

"Most of my detective work will be done on the computer," I reassured her. "I want to dig more into Kyle's background. Something happened a few years ago in Italy, right after he sold his company. Something that involved the police. Fred stepped in and got him off, but he won't talk about it. I need to find out what it was."

"Let me take care of that. I've got sources that may help."

"Like your policeman boyfriend?"

"Among others. Don't ask too many questions. Sometimes it's better if you don't know how I work my magic."

"Well, if you're so good at digging into stuff, could you tackle one more thing for me?" My back started to stiffen up. I scooted higher against the headboard.

"Sure. What do you need?"

I hesitated to put this out there, and yet I had to know. And Lilly had the skills and contacts to find the answers I needed. "Could you check out Wyatt Carlton? He's the guy we met on the riverboat ... the one who played poker with Corinne. I tried researching him myself but didn't come up with much."

Her computer keys clacked. "Carlton, you said? He's the one that arranged transportation to Lucerne for you folks, right?"

"Right." It didn't surprise me that she remembered. Her powers of recall were legendary. If I mentioned a client, she could tell me the date of our last meeting and spout out bullet points of our conversation. "He works in sports marketing, and he's offered to find some investors for Kyle's company. Says athletes always need good places to park their money."

"That's true."

I bent around to fluff my pillows. "But I wonder if he really has those kinds of connections, or if he's blowing smoke. I'm getting a strange feeling about him."

"Strange how?"

I thought back to the weird shadow that had distorted his face when we were in Old Town. At his anger when he warned me not to interfere in his plans. "It's like he's two different people. He was furious when I questioned his ability to line up investors. But a few minutes later, his mood changed and he was practically licking my face with disgusting kisses."

She snorted. "Why is your life so much more interesting than mine?"

"I'm not sure *interesting* is the word for it. Things really got weird when we were racing down the steps of a medieval tower."

"How's that?"

I closed my eyes, pulling up the scene in vivid detail. Sunlight burning through the arrow slits. A faint smell of dust. The rough texture of the stone walls. "I was almost at the bottom of the staircase when my feet got tangled up. I fell and sprained my ankle."

"Madeline, that's horrible. Are you in a lot of pain?"

"The doctor gave me some meds, so I'm coasting along right now." Maybe that was the problem. Maybe I was coasting too much, barely tethered to reality, conjuring up fictional details. "But here's the thing. Those last few steps, I know

I was going too fast, so maybe I'm imagining this. But I have this feeling ..." I kept going over it again and again in my mind. Speeding down the steps. Losing my balance. Unable to stop. "Right before I fell, I swear I felt something."

"Like what?"

I pulled at a loose thread on the blanket. "I mean, I'm not a hundred percent certain, but it seemed like ..." I paused, hoping I was wrong, not wanting to say the words.

Lilly was impatient. "Spit it out, Madeline. Seemed like what?"

I searched through my memories, sorting through the blur of those last few moments. Wyatt had raced down those steps even faster than me, getting closer and closer. I tried to speed up, to get away from him, down the steps and out of the tower. But he was right behind me, only a sliver of space between us. As I barreled down the last flight, something touched my arm. "Lilly," I said, my voice quivering, "I think Wyatt pushed me."

Chapter 25

TRAVIS'S CALL the next morning woke me from a troubled sleep. "I heard from Eva, my reporter friend. She's tracked down the riverboat. It's docked at Speyer, and she's agreed to give us a ride. Can you be downstairs in twenty?"

"I'll do my best." I pulled on jeans and a loose sweater, swept my hair into a messy bun, and dabbed on a bit of mascara. Travis was waiting for me when I got off the elevator.

A few minutes later Eva pulled onto the cobblestones in a faded blue Volkswagen, the front bumper dented, a ragged scratch branding the driver's side door. Maybe there was a code of journalistic best-practices—having the ugliest car on the street meant it would still be waiting for you when you finished an interview, even in the sketchiest parts of town. I supposed it was like the way I dressed down whenever I traveled, leaving my expensive jewelry and designer purses at home. A good friend had had his Rolex ripped from his wrist during his first hour on the streets of Buenos Aires. I had traveled all over the world, and so far, no one had shown much interest in my Timex.

She got out of her car and sauntered toward us, giving Travis a seductive look that hinted at more than a platonic relationship. She wore a form-fitting T-shirt and jeans so snug that I could almost read the label on her thong as she stretched up to give Travis a hug. Her long, dark hair framed her narrow face and spilled in carefree waves over her shoulders, shiny and bouncing like a model in a shampoo ad. As I watched her lean in for a quick two-cheek European kiss, I felt a tightening in my stomach that wasn't just hunger pangs from skipping breakfast.

After Travis introduced us, we all piled into her car, the two of them in the front while I scrunched into the back, my knees jammed against my chest. They laughed and joked as we zipped along, heads close together, voices soft. Tantalizing phrases drifted back toward me, such as *what about that time when?*

or *do you remember that tiny restaurant in Paris?* or *I never thought we'd get out of that in one piece,* the two of them celebrating a memorable past that I shared no part in. I ground my teeth and counted cows in the distant fields. I wasn't sure what bothered me more—the way Eva threw herself at him, or the fact that he seemed to be enjoying it so much.

A prickling numbness spread through my thighs as my contorted pretzel pose cut off all blood circulation. I shifted sideways, awkwardly stretching out my legs and trying to find a more comfortable position for my ankle. Eva caught my movement in her rear-view mirror. "Tell me why you think someone on the riverboat murdered Corinne Peerland."

I gave her the bullet-point version, highlighting the poker game, the stolen money, and the staff I'd spotted at Pilatus. "Corinne was in a nasty mood the night of the poker game. She lashed out at a lot of people. Our waiter Sergey, especially. Gave him a severe dressing down in front of his supervisor because her steak wasn't cooked the way she liked it."

"You think that was a motive for murder?" Eva asked.

I could hear the hesitation in her voice. "You didn't see his face," I insisted. "He would have stabbed her on the spot with a steak knife if he thought he could have gotten away with it." I gently massaged my thighs to restart the blood flow. "Corinne got him in a lot of trouble."

"You think he broke into her safe?"

"Makes sense to me. Maybe he stole the money to get even with her for making such a scene at dinner. She figured it out and confronted him. They argued and he shoved her off the mountain."

There was a long silence while Eva digested my theory. "This isn't the only robbery we've heard about," she said. "The riverboat companies want to keep it quiet so they don't scare off tourists, but my newspaper suspects there's a ring of con men who work these boats, making friends with people with money. Especially widows traveling by themselves. Corinne isn't the first woman to be robbed."

"But Corinne wasn't traveling alone," Travis said. "She was with her family."

"Right. But we've been following this story for a while now, trying to figure out who's behind the thefts. Your waiter Sergey is the first real lead we've gotten. If he *is* part of this, it could our big chance to break this wide open."

If Sergey was part of a bigger scam, then Mueller would have to back off from Randall and consider other suspects. I almost forgave Eva for her relentless flirting during our trip. "Thank you for getting us on the boat."

"Captain Becker is not thrilled about it," Eva admitted, "but we go way back, and he owes me a favor. We'll have to make it quick, though. The boat sails this afternoon, and the crew will be busy. We'll have to show a little finesse. We can't go in with both barrels aimed at the waiter."

I leaned up toward the front seat. "We should start with Werner Smithson, the security officer. He and his assistant, Jonas Lundgren, came to Corinne's cabin when she reported the theft. Lundgren was touching everything, contaminating the scene with his own prints. And the security videos were all messed up. If there's a scam, they could be in on it."

Eva picked up her phone and typed in some notes with her left thumb, her right hand still on the steering wheel. "Thanks for the heads up. We should also interview the housekeeping staff. And your buddy Sergey, of course."

"Good plan," Travis said. "We really appreciate your doing this."

"Always glad to help a friend," she said, shaking back her hair and giving Travis yet another dazzling smile.

We rode in silence for the rest of the trip. Traffic picked up as we neared the city. Eva circled around looking for a parking space. She finally squeezed into a spot a few blocks from the river, and we walked toward the water.

There was a five-boat traffic jam at the dock. Three boats were tied up end-to-end by the shoreline, and then two others were tied up parallel to the first three. "Why do they bunch the boats up like that?" I asked.

"This is a popular destination," Eva said, "so there's not enough space for every riverboat that wants to dock. Speyer has a big technology museum. Heidelberg's only a short drive away. It gets a lot of tourists because it has an important university and a famous castle."

"So it's first come, first served?"

"Whoever gets here first gets the primo spot right at shoreline. The other riverboats have to dock beside them."

It reminded me of a congested New York City street, with delivery trucks doubled-parked as their drivers unloaded merchandise onto dollies and maneuvered them across the sidewalks.

"I don't see the *Rhinelinder*," I said. "You sure we're at the right place?"

"There it is," Travis said, pointing. "First one on the second row. Beside the *Adelaide*."

"How do we get to it?" I asked.

"The same way that passengers got off," Eva said. "We walk across the *Adelaide*."

The three of us started up the ramp. A uniformed guard stopped us. "May I see your room key, please?"

Eva pulled out her ID. "I have an appointment with Captain Becker of the *Rhinelinder*."

Her smile may have won over Travis, but it wasn't having much impact on the guard. "Sorry, I can't let you on without a pass."

She pulled out her phone. "Let me call the captain."

A few minutes later a crew member appeared at the doorway of the *Adelaide*. "I'm here for Captain Becker's guests," he called out.

The guard waved us through.

There was an unsettling sense of déjà vu as I walked across the *Adelaide*. The boat was outfitted exactly like ours—the same color scheme of pale blue and brown, the same floorplan. Customer service was in the same place right inside the door, with a small gift shop opposite it. The lounge and dining room were toward the front of the boat, with guest cabins toward the back. Everything was a carbon copy of the *Rhinelinder*, even the upholstered chairs in the lobby and the granite-topped table holding a vase of fresh flowers.

Probably it was cheaper for each boat to be identical, rather than develop a unique floor plan and decorating scheme for each one. But I wondered how many passengers had wandered back late at night after a few too many drinks on shore, thinking they were on the right boat, and then struggled to fit their key into someone else's cabin door. No wonder each boat had guards on the entrance ramps.

Captain Becker met us as we crossed to the *Rhinelinder*. His stiff posture hinted at a military background, very official in navy blue pants and a double-breasted jacket adorned with gold stripes. But his youthful face and dark hair surprised me, as though someone had Photoshopped his middle school yearbook picture onto someone else's muscled torso. I had expected an older man, with gray hair and a face weathered from too many years of squinting into the sun.

Eva introduced Travis and me. "The family is distraught by the loss of Mrs. Peerland. Ms. Keswick thought if she took another tour of their cabin, if she talked with a few of your staff, that we could figure out what happened that day. Bring some closure."

Becker shook his head. "I don't see what good that would do. The police have already checked it. Besides, Mrs. Peerland's accident happened in the Alps, not here on the boat."

"The family might pick up on some details that the police missed," Eva said. "And we won't take much of your time, Heinz, I promise."

He hesitated, then pointed up the stairs toward the guest cabins. "This way."

There was a discreetly lettered "No admittance" sign posted on the Peerland's door. We followed Becker into the cabin. A few cabinet drawers were open and there was a pile of shoes dumped in front of the closet. "Who's been in the room since Mr. Peerland left?" I asked.

"Only the police," Becker answered. "The Peerlands requested that no one enter the cabin after the burglary until the local police had a chance to check for fingerprints, so housekeeping skipped it. The police checked it that first day when we were in Lucerne. Then another team came on board this morning."

Mueller must have taken my suggestions seriously after all, if he had the cabin searched a second time. That was good news.

I opened the closet. Corinne's clothes were still there, as well as some of Fred's. "Once the police are finished here, Mr. Peerland will want everything packed up and sent to him," I said to Becker. "I'll get him to send you an address."

Travis walked to the safe, now coated with fingerprint dust. He examined the door and peered inside. "I don't see any scratch marks. Whoever opened this used the combination."

"Her whole family knew it," I said. "She always used the numbers of her street address. Easy to remember."

Eva turned toward Becker. "The housekeeper is coming to talk to us?"

"Yes. She should be here shortly."

"Great," Eva said. "Travis, why don't you and Madeline wait here for her? Heinz, can you take me to the security office? I'd like to talk to Smithson and Lundgren."

A short while after Eva left, there was a timid knock at the door. A short, plump woman, her wispy blond hair pulled back by clips, stood in the hall. "Captain Becker told me to come," she said, her words halting.

"Yes, thank you." I held the door open and gestured toward a chair. "Please sit down."

She walked toward the chair but didn't sit, instead standing behind it and gripping its edge.

"You were on duty the night Mrs. Peerland's safe was broken into, right?" I asked as the door closed.

She hesitated. I wondered how well she understood English.

Travis must have had the same thought. He spoke slowly, pausing between every few words. "Did you see anyone in the hall that night? Between ten and midnight?"

Her head swiveled from Travis to me and then back to Travis again. "I bring towels."

"You brought towels to this cabin?" Travis said. "Did you see anyone come in here?"

She nervously twisted her hands. They were rough and chapped, her cuticles torn. "No."

"Are you sure?" I asked. "This is really important." Someone had entered Corinne's cabin and stolen her money. I was convinced that same person was involved in her death. "Think back to that night. If there's any detail that you can remember ..."

She glanced anxiously at the door. Was she worried that someone was out there, listening to her? "I bring towels," she repeated. "Shampoo. Soap."

I was desperate for more details. "You were here that night. You must have seen something."

Her eyes blinked rapidly. "No."

"This is important," I said, moving toward her. "The woman in this cabin was killed. We're trying to figure out who did it."

"Towels," she said.

"I don't care about the towels." Frustration dialed up my volume. She knew something. Why else would she be so nervous?

She moved toward the door, but I had more questions for her. "Wait." I blocked her exit. "Who did you see in the hall that night?"

"Madeline, that's enough," Travis said sharply, pulling me aside. He smiled at the housekeeper as he opened the door. "Thank you so much for talking with us. We appreciate your time."

Head down, she scuttled out of the cabin and vanished into the hallway.

"Why did you let her go?" I asked. "Didn't you see how nervous she was? It's obvious she knows something about what happened that night."

"That may be, but it's also obvious that she wasn't going to share it with us. Think about it. Captain Becker sent her to us. Don't you think he went over her story before he let her come here? If she values her job, she'll toe the corporate line."

"But she must have seen who came into this room. And I think she understood English a lot better than she was letting on."

"Doesn't matter. If the captain has told her to keep it quiet, she won't tell us. There's no point in berating the poor woman."

I flopped down in the chair. "But if we don't make people talk to us …"

"Madeline, I know that you are a great public relations consultant," Travis said. "If I needed that kind of help, I'd certainly hire you. But digging into a story, interviewing people, getting information—that's my thing. And I've learned that you can't *make* people talk. They have to *want* to share their news."

"But it's so frustrating not to be able to figure out what happened."

"Welcome to my world. You have to keep asking questions, digging into details, until you turn up something solid."

A few minutes later we heard voices in the hallway. "You guys find out anything useful here?" Eva asked as she and Becker entered the cabin.

I shook my head. "Not really. How about you? Did you learn anything from Smithson?"

She shrugged. "He showed me the security feeds. It was like you said, all blurry and full of static. Not very useful. And Lundgren wasn't available."

"Well, then, if you're finished here …" Becker began.

"There's still the waiter," I said. "Sergey. Can we talk to him?"

Through the sliding glass doors, we could see passengers queued up at the shoreline. "We'll have to make this quick," Becker said. "Sergey's in the lounge, getting ready for afternoon cocktails."

"Of course," I said. "This won't take long."

Becker led us down the steps to the main lobby and then forward to the lounge. It was as I remembered it—cushy chairs set up by the expansive windows, banquette sofas wrapped around low tables. On the left was the sofa where Corinne had collapsed that first night.

Sergey was standing behind the shiny granite bar when we walked up, his dark hair hanging low over his eyes. Knife in hand, he was deftly slicing lemons.

Travis, Eva and I pulled out bar stools and sat down across from him. "Sergey, we'd like to talk to you a minute," I said.

"Excuse me?" he said.

"I'm Madeline Keswick. I was at Fred and Corinne Peerland's table. You were our waiter for dinner a few nights ago."

His pale blue eyes showed no signs of recognition. "Sorry, I am not Sergey. I am Klaus."

"You're not Sergey?" He had the same pale face and dark hair that I remembered. The same sharp nose and thin lips.

"Sergey and I are cousins. Passengers get us confused all the time. They say we look a lot alike, although I do not see it." He grinned and shook back his hair. "I am much more handsome."

"I have trouble telling them apart myself," Becker said. He spoke a few words into his radio. "I've paged Sergey. He'll be here in a few minutes."

Klaus was more cheerful than the dour Sergey I remembered from dinner, but I wasn't quite convinced. "You sure you weren't our waiter that first night?"

He shook his head. "No. I was working as bartender on the upper deck."

"Do you remember Mrs. Peerland, one of the passengers?" I asked. "An older lady, early sixties, blond hair? She played poker up on the deck that night."

"Yes. She was so excited when she won all that money." He began to arrange the lemon slices on a small plate. "Captain Becker told us what happened to her, falling off the mountain. Such a tragedy."

Travis traced circles on the bar. "What can you tell us about that night? Any of the other players upset that they lost?"

"Not really. Especially when she ordered drinks for everyone to celebrate her win."

"How about when she left the game?" Travis asked. "Anyone follow her?"

"I did not notice. It was busy up there."

Another man walked up, dressed in the typical waiter uniform of black pants and a white shirt. A crate of wine glasses was hoisted on his shoulder.

"This is Sergey," Becker said. "Your waiter."

Sergey set the crate on the counter and turned toward us. He and Klaus were more like twins than cousins. The two men were the same height and weight and had the same coloring—a sallow pastiness and drooping dark hair. I had the same disorienting sense of déjà vu as when I'd walked across the *Adelaide* to get to the *Rhinelinder*, seeing two things that looked the same, but were different. Perhaps Klaus's hair was a little fuller on top? Nose a little wider, maybe?

"You're Sergey?" I asked the second man, searching for details to distinguish between the two.

"Yes."

"Do you remember me? I'm Madeline Keswick. I was at the dinner table with Corinne and Fred Peerland."

He pulled wine glasses from the crate and set them on the bar. "I see many guests. I remember food more than people."

It was hard to believe that he hadn't noticed Corinne. "Mrs. Peerland sent her steak back twice. Then she complained to your manager about how it was cooked."

"Oh." He paused. "Yes. I remember her."

"Ms. Keswick wants to ask a few questions about the excursion to Pilatus," Captain Becker said. "The day of Mrs. Peerland's accident."

"I know nothing of that," Sergey said.

"But you were there," I said. "I saw you."

He held a glass to the light, then polished it with a towel. "No. I worked that day. Here. On the boat."

"I saw you," I insisted. "You were with several staff members from the ship. Waiting in line to catch the cable car."

Sergey shook his head. "That was not me."

"I am probably the one you saw," Klaus said, hanging the glasses on the overhead rack. "I was off duty. A couple of us went up the mountain. But it was bad, no fun, with all the clouds."

"You saw Mrs. Peerland?" I asked.

Klaus started on the next row of glasses. "In the café, yes. Arguing."

"Did you see her when she left?" My questions poured out quickly. "Where she went? Who she talked to?"

"She was still in the café when we left," Klaus said. "I did not see her again."

Becker checked his watch. "We need to finish this. Our passengers will be boarding soon. Do you have any more questions?"

"Not really," I said. "How you about you guys?"

"No, I think we're finished," Travis said.

"Can I get the next tray of glasses?" Klaus asked.

"Yes." Becker watched Klaus as he walked away. "Eva, I told you these interviews would be a waste of time."

"So you did." She affectionately brushed his arm. "We were trying to nail down some details. I appreciate your help, Heinz."

"Of course. Please extend my sympathies to the family." He smoothed his jacket. "Now if you'll excuse me, I need to get back to my duties. But why don't you have a drink before you go? Sergey, can you take care of these people?"

"Certainly." Now that our interview was finished, he seemed much more cheerful. "What can I get for you?"

"A beer," Travis said. "Guinness, if you have it."

"Me, too," Eva said.

I perused the drink list. "What's your specialty?"

"I make a good bloody mary."

"Fine. I'll have that."

He picked up a glass. "You want basic, or one of variations?"

"What are the variations?"

"Bacon bloody has two strips of crispy bacon to garnish." He reached for a bottle of vodka. "Bloody bull is popular. Beef bouillon gives good flavor."

"What's your favorite?" I asked.

He unscrewed the top of the bottle. "Crabby mary. Clam juice and bits of crab."

"Sounds good. Let me try that one."

He mixed the ingredients in a blender and then poured the thick red beverage into a glass. I took a big swallow. "Water." I flapped my hands in front of my mouth as tears ran down my face. "This is really spicy."

Travis pounded my back. "You okay?"

Sergey laughed as he set the water in front of me. "Crabby has quite a kick. I should have warned you."

"I'm not sure I have any tonsils left," I said in a hoarse whisper.

"Keep drinking," Sergey said. "You get used to it."

"I guess. But it's so spicy, I can't even taste the seafood. This could have lizard guts in it and I'd never know the difference."

"Lizard guts." Sergey smiled. "New flavor. I will check it out."

I took another cautious sip of the crabby mary, hoping the second swallow wouldn't be as catastrophic as the first. Corinne had had a similar reaction to her bloody mary that first night, when she came back to the lounge after locking her poker winnings in the safe. Coughing because it was so spicy. Desperately signaling for water. At the time, I had thought it was because there was too much pepper in her drink. But now I knew the truth.

Chapter 26

I WAITED until we were in the car headed back toward Lucerne before I shared my news. "It was the crabby mary," I burst out, trying to position myself in the least painful way in Eva's cramped back seat. "That's what caused Corinne's allergy attack."

"The crabby mary?" Travis sounded surprised. "You said it was peanuts."

I stretched my legs, trying to ignore the dull throb of my sprained ankle. "The doctor mentioned peanuts. There was a bowl of them on the table, right in front of Corinne. He said they probably triggered her attack."

"But now you don't think they did?"

"No. She'd never been allergic to them before. But at the time we didn't know about the crabby mary, so we went along with the peanut story, because it seemed the most logical answer."

Travis's chin wrinkled as he considered my revelation. "How do you know hers was a crabby mary?"

"By the way she reacted. She had a serious allergy to shellfish, so her throat started to close up right away."

Eva checked her side mirror as she pulled onto the highway. "Corinne wouldn't have realized there was seafood in the drink?"

"That drink was so peppery, she never would have guessed. I certainly couldn't tell." I reached down to loosen the elastic bandage around my ankle. "I think someone gave it to her on purpose, knowing she was allergic."

Travis frowned. "Who would do that? And why?"

"Someone who knew she'd won a lot of money. And wanted to keep her out of her cabin while they stole it."

"I assume you've got someone in mind?" Eva said, changing lanes to accelerate around a blue sedan.

I grimaced as I flexed my ankle. "Isn't it obvious? Klaus was working the bar upstairs and knew she'd won the money. Probably mentioned it to his cousin

Sergey, who was still mad about the stink she made at dinner. Sergey knew she had seafood allergies; we all had to fill out information about food allergies when we first got on the boat. What better way to get revenge?"

"Slow down a minute," Travis said. "Was Sergey working as a bartender in the lounge that night?"

"We need to follow up on that," I said, "but I'll bet anything he was."

Travis pulled on his right earlobe, the way he always did when he was puzzling through the details of a story. "That seems a stretch. Even if Sergey was at the bar, how would he know the drink was for Corinne? You think the waitress was in on this, too?"

"The waitress was busy when Corinne came back, so Kyle went up to the bar and ordered for her." I gently kneaded my ankle. "Sergey would have recognized him, I'm sure. The two of them had kidded around a lot at dinner. And Kyle probably said something like, 'I need a bloody mary for my mom.'"

"I don't know about this, Madeline." Travis counted off the facts. "One, we don't know that Sergey was working in the bar. Two, we don't know if he knew that drink was meant for Corinne. And three, we don't even know for sure if her drink was a crabby mary."

There were times when I appreciated Travis's logical mind, his reluctance to jump to conclusions, his insistence on having all the facts. This was not one of them.

Eva's car slowed and gurgled as it struggled to pull the hill. "Everything all right there?" Travis asked.

"The car's temperamental. Nothing to worry about." Eva crouched over the steering wheel, her shoulders hunched. She stomped on the accelerator until we crested the hill.

"And even if you're right," Travis said, "even if Sergey did doctor her drink and rob the safe, he couldn't have killed her. He wasn't at Pilatus that day."

That was the flaw in my theory. I closed my eyes as we coasted down the other side of the hill, trying to puzzle this out, letting snippets of memory spark in my brain: Corinne arguing with Sergey at dinner; me spotting Sergey in the cable car line; Corinne stumbling out of that café, her vision clouded by the tears in her eyes. "I've got it," I said, sitting up so quickly that I bounced my head against the ceiling. "Corinne figured out that Sergey robbed her safe and confronted him. Only it wasn't Sergey; it was Klaus. They are so much alike— I couldn't tell them apart, and I bet she couldn't either. Corinne threatened to report him to Captain Becker." I grabbed the back of Travis's seat, leaning forward so my face was close to his. "I can see it now, the two of them screaming at each other. The ice was so slippery on that viewing platform. She pushed him. He pushed her back. She fell off the cliff." It was so clear what had happened. "We've got to bring Mueller in on this."

Travis rubbed his nose as though he was fighting a sneeze, another of his habits whenever he was meticulously churning through a story. "I think that's a bit premature. You're making way too many assumptions."

"You think we should let them get away with it?" My words hung in the air, frozen bits of conversation that sparkled like ice crystals in the chill of my annoyance. The atmosphere turned glacial as I waited for his response.

Eva broke the impasse. "While I agree with you that Madeline's story is a little shaky, I think Heinz was definitely hiding something."

Not exactly a vote of confidence, but better than nothing. "Don't you see?" I jumped in. "This fits your theory about rich women being targeted on these tourist boats. Maybe Klaus and Sergey have been behind that. Along with Lundgren, the security guy."

Travis was still fighting me. "And you came to that conclusion how?"

"I bet Lundgren let them into the cabin." The pieces started to click into place. "The housekeeper spotted them. They threatened to get her fired if she told anyone, which explains why she was so nervous when she talked to us." I edged forward as my voice escalated. "Lundgren corrupted the surveillance video. Then he touched everything when he and Smithson examined Corinne's cabin, so he'd have a plausible excuse in case his prints were found there."

Travis pulled on his earlobe again. At this rate, it would be stretched to his shoulders by the time we reached Lucerne. "Madeline, you're spinning an interesting story here, but there's no proof of any of this. And there's a much more likely candidate behind Corinne's allergy attack."

"Who's that?" I asked.

"The person who brought her the drink. Her son, Kyle."

Chapter 27

"YOU THINK Kyle did this?" I wrapped my arms around my knees, trying to ignore the pain in my ankle. The doctor had warned me to stay off my feet for a few days. I should have listened to him.

"Why not? You said he was incensed that she wouldn't call off her campaign. Maybe he gave her the crabby mary, thinking she'd die of anaphylaxis. That would solve everything."

"Except that it didn't," Eva said. "The doctor got there too quickly."

"Not sure I buy that," I said. "Kyle's a smart guy. If he really wanted to kill his mother, he would have come up with a better plan."

"Maybe he didn't mean to kill her," Eva said. "But to give her a warning to drop out of the campaign."

Kyle had proved he was capable of violence. He had paid the pilot to scare Luke on that paragliding ride. He had threatened me on the riverboat. He had even been in jail in Italy for murder. But dosing his mother's drink with seafood seemed much too subtle. "I don't think Corinne would have made the connection. The doctor convinced her it was the peanuts." I shifted a bit, trying to get comfortable. "You think Kyle robbed the safe, too?"

"Maybe. You said he was having problems with his investors."

I shook my head. "But there was only two thousand dollars in that safe. It wouldn't put a dent in the amount he needed."

"Didn't you say she had all her notes from the energy conference in the safe?" Travis asked. "Those documents got taken, too, right?"

"That's true."

"So maybe he was really after those, to slow down her campaign, make her spend time recreating the information. He took the money to throw everyone off track."

Those papers would have been more valuable to Kyle than cash. Maybe he thought she'd waste precious time trying to remember the details of her meetings. "Fortunately, I had my own notes."

"But he didn't know that," Travis insisted.

Eva hit the brakes as traffic in front of us suddenly slowed. Momentum threw me forward, off the seat and into the footwell. "Sorry about that, folks," she said. "Guess I was following too close."

"Are you all right?" Travis asked, twisting around, reaching for me. "Anything hurt?"

My butt was jammed down on the floor and my feet in the air. In that cramped space, I couldn't get enough leverage to push myself onto the seat. Travis grabbed my arms and hoisted me up. "Only my pride," I said.

"Buckle your seatbelt. That could have been dangerous."

The back seat was so small that there was barely enough room for me to sit up straight and put my feet on the floor, which is why I had been curled sideways. But he was right—if she had slammed the brakes a little harder, I might have knocked out a few teeth on the headrest. "Right," I said, sitting cross-legged as I reached for the seatbelt. "I'm good now."

Travis waited until I clicked it in place before he turned around to the front. "Maybe robbing the safe was a spur of the moment decision," he said. "A crime of opportunity. Kyle opened the safe while his parents were down with Dr. Maynard. You said he knew the combination."

"How would he have gotten into the room?"

It didn't take Travis long to puzzle through that one. "Fred gave you his key, right? When you went to get the EpiPen? What did you do with it?"

What had I done with the key? I remembered using it to access Corinne's cabin on that frantic dash to find the EpiPen. Then we raced back to the lounge, terrified that we would be too late, that Corinne's swelling throat would have cut off her oxygen. But Dr. Maynard had already given her a shot. Her respiration was almost normal when we saw her stretched out on the sofa.

I closed my eyes, visualizing the scene. The key was in my hand. What did I do with it? "I gave it to Bronwyn. To give back to her dad."

"Maybe she gave the key to Kyle. Or ..." Travis was thinking it through, going through a checklist of possibilities. "Maybe Kyle and Bronwyn were in on it together."

I was almost ready to believe that Kyle could have doctored her drink. But I couldn't believe the two of them had conspired to kill her. Corinne loved her family too much to have them turn on her like that. "This isn't an all-you-can-eat buffet, Travis. You can't pick up any name you want and toss it on your plate. Who are you going after next? Holliss? Fred?"

Travis stayed annoyingly calm. "You're the one who told me how tightly woven those two are. You don't think she would have given Kyle the key if he asked for it?"

I bounced my fist against the seat. "Travis, we drove all this way so you could help me figure out who on the riverboat had robbed Corinne. Instead, you're pointing the blame back at her family."

The cough of Eva's struggling engine interrupted our argument. Hopefully, we didn't have much farther to go before we reached Lucerne. I wasn't sure we would make it.

Travis leaned over to inspect the odometer. "A lot of miles, Eva."

"More miles than you think. The odometer's already rolled over."

He studied the stained upholstery and torn seat covers. "You could use a new car."

"No rush. I'm very fond of this one. We've been through a lot together."

I sulked for the rest of the ride. Bringing Travis and Eva into this investigation was a mistake. I wanted them to confirm my theories about what had happened, not generate new ones. But they weren't wrong that both Kyle and Bronwyn had solid motives to stop their mother's campaign. And the strong bond between them meant that if one of them committed to the plan, the other would also.

Finally, we pulled into the hotel courtyard. Travis and I scrambled out of the car. He walked toward the driver's side as Eva lowered her window.

"I'll check with Mueller," she said. "See what we can figure out about the staff on the boat. We've worked on a lot of cases together, so I think he'll be straight with me." She flashed a bright smile. "How about if I swing back here tonight to fill you in? We can figure out our next step?"

Did this woman ever stop flirting? It was obvious she was making an excuse to see Travis again. They could have compared notes by email, or text message, or even a phone call. There was no need for her to return to the hotel.

"I'm heading out to Basel for some meetings," he said, leaning down, his face close to hers. "I won't be back until late."

"Not a problem. You know I don't need much sleep." She shot him a mischievous grin. "Call me when you get back. Maybe we can grab a late dinner."

"Sure thing." They exchanged another of those European double-kisses and then she drove away.

Travis and I headed toward the hotel. "You two seem cozy."

"I told you, she's an old friend."

Was his defensiveness triggered by guilt? "Seemed a lot more than that." I was angry at myself as soon as the words popped out. I sounded like a possessive girlfriend.

"What's up with you, Madeline?" he asked, frowning at me. "I haven't seen Eva in years. The two of us have some catching up to do. But that doesn't mean you can't join us. Are you free for a late dinner?"

"Sorry. Fred is hosting a family dinner tonight as a tribute to Corinne, and I'm invited. You and Eva will be on your own," I said crisply.

"Madeline, wait."

"What?" I whirled around.

"Eva's not the enemy," he said. "We both are trying to help you solve Corinne's murder."

"I realize that. I appreciate what she's done. I never would have been able to get back on the riverboat without her. It's just …."

"What?"

"I didn't realize the two of you had such a past. I feel like a third wheel."

He grinned. "You're jealous.

"No, I'm not. You and I are over. You can date whoever you want."

His head snapped back as though I had slapped him. "Eva and I are not dating. We went our separate ways a long time ago."

"If you say so."

"Listen, we need Eva. There are a lot of suspects, and the quickest way to work through all this is for the three of us to split up the investigation. Eva can cover the boat staff. She knows the captain and can get access. And she's worked with Mueller before. Are you okay with that?"

"Sounds reasonable."

"Good. You can focus on the family. They had motive and opportunity."

"I don't want to believe Corinne's children could have killed her."

"Fine. Prove it. Follow up with everybody. See if any of them could have broken into her safe. Figure out where everyone was after Corinne left the café. That's fair, don't you think?"

"I guess. What about you?"

"The energy conference in Basel is wrapping up. I'm headed there to meet with some folks doing innovative things with carbon recapture."

"How will that help?"

"My contacts know everybody in the industry. I'm sure they can set up a meeting with a couple of these protestors, to get their point of view. Maybe I can find out what they know about Corinne's murder."

I reached for the railing, shifting sideways to take pressure off my ankle. "Be careful. They're getting more aggressive. You could get hurt." I'd seen Travis's temper before. He wouldn't hesitate to jump into a street brawl if provoked.

"I'm flattered that you care." His expression softened. "Don't worry. I can fend for myself."

"I mean it, Travis. They killed Nils Kiener because he represented big oil. If you start asking too many questions, if they think you're too critical of what they're doing, then they could turn on you, too."

His tone turned serious. "I'm willing to take that chance." He started down the steps, turning back for one last message. "This is important, Madeline. The protests are spreading. To Berlin. London. Paris. Amsterdam. More people are getting involved, admitting that managing climate change is a high priority. My magazine wants to be part of this. And so do I."

Chapter 28

I MULLED over the details from our riverboat excursion as I entered the hotel—trying to figure out how Sergey and his cousin Klaus fit into Corinne's murder, whether Kyle could have ordered that deadly crabby mary for his mother, what Bronwyn did with Corinne's room key after I handed it to her.

I was concentrating so hard that when I saw Bronwyn sitting in the reading room off the lobby, for a moment I wasn't sure if she was real or if I had conjured her up. She was curled up in a fat armchair, her feet tucked under her, her sandals flung carelessly on the carpet. Behind her were tall bookcases packed with haphazardly arranged volumes: aging classics with faded gold letters along their spines; well-read best sellers with tattered dust jackets; newer books with their covers encased in protective film.

An open book rested on her lap, but instead of reading it she stared off into space, chewing the ends of her hair. She was pale, even more than normal, her lids shadowed with light taupe instead of her usual smoky drama. She seemed young and lost and vulnerable, so different from the forceful woman who had blamed me for Corinne's Senate campaign.

Any illusions that this was a kinder, gentler Bronwyn were quickly dispelled, however, by her corrosive greeting. "Why are you still here? My mother hardly needs a campaign manager now."

I ignored the bite of her words as I sat down across from her. "I thought Holliss might need my help. Someone to be on her side while the police questioned Randall. You know how people can jump to conclusions in a situation like this. Deciding someone is guilty before they've seen any evidence." I shook my head. "Terrible thing, don't you think?"

She had to know I was referring to her outburst in the courtyard, when she screamed at Holliss as the police carried Randall away for questioning. But she dismissed it with a quick flick of her wrist. "Holliss and Randall will be fine. Dad has already contacted his people. He'll take care of this."

It was the perfect opening for me to dig into family history. "Like he did for Kyle, back in Italy a few years ago?"

Her vivid blue eyes scrutinized my face. "Excuse me?"

"I heard Kyle got in some trouble. Fred took care of it."

I hoped she would jump to defend Kyle, give me some details that explained what he had gotten involved in, something that might make Mueller move him up the suspect list ahead of Randall. There was the tiniest tell at her temple, an unmistakable ripple, but otherwise her expression remained annoyingly bland. "Sorry. Don't know what you're talking about." She fingered her book. "So, when are you leaving?"

The low table beside me was piled with dog-eared paperbacks. I picked up one with a medieval castle on the cover. It reminded me of the site of Corinne's announcement dinner. "Actually, your dad asked me to stay. He wants me to maintain Corinne's website and to interact with reporters, to make sure they get a true picture of everything she was trying to accomplish."

"Dad needs to let it go." She leaned her elbow on the arm of the chair, careful of her injured finger. "Mom should never have gotten involved in this ridiculous campaign."

It annoyed me that Corinne's children were so quick to dismiss her plans. "She wanted to save the world. She told me she'd always been passionate about managing climate change."

With an ugly snort, Bronwyn flipped her book closed. "Give me a break. When we were growing up, the most Mom ever did to help the environment was to keep a recycling bin in the pantry. And make sure the dishwasher was full before we ran it." She dropped her feet to the floor, her toes inching across the carpet as she felt for her sandals. "We cranked the air conditioning up in the summer and the heat in the winter. Our family drove gas-guzzling SUVs, like everybody else."

"The other night at dinner, you said she decided to run for the Senate because of Natalie." I fanned the pages of my book. "Fred told me about her accident."

Bronwyn shoved a foot into a sandal. "Mom went a little crazy after Natalie died. Said it was all her fault. Blamed herself. A few weeks later, she traded in her SUV for an electric car. Installed solar panels on the roof of the house. Switched all her newspaper and magazine subscriptions to digital."

"She and Natalie were close?"

"Not that I knew. Kyle and I used to play with Natalie when she was little. But after we moved to Connecticut, we never saw her again." Bronwyn's blond hair fell over her face as she leaned down to put on the second sandal. "This Senate campaign made no sense. Mom completely upended her life—put her career on hold and joined up with those wackos shedding tears for starving polar bears—all because of someone she hadn't seen in thirty years. She had to know how much it would hurt us. Luke's up for a big promotion at work. But do you think he would get it if his mother-in-law was in the news every day, flogging the fossil fuel companies about climate change?"

"I can see that would be a problem."

She straightened up, shaking back her hair. "A problem? It would be a disaster. And it would hurt Kyle, too. She had promised to make a big investment in his company, and she was backing out, to fund her campaign. He's been scrambling to make up that deficit." A spot of red popped out on each cheek. "Mom had a choice. To save the planet because of some puzzling sense of obligation to Natalie … or to save her children. She chose Natalie. I'll never forgive her for that." She stood up, tucking the book under her arm. "There's no point in discussing this anymore. Mom's dead. We need to go home and get on with our lives."

I followed her into the hallway. "One last thing, Bronwyn. That night on the riverboat, when you and I went to your mom's room to get her EpiPen. I gave you the room key afterwards. What did you do with it?"

"The room key? Why would you ask that?" Something in the tilt of her neck told me she knew exactly what I was probing for. "You think I went back to her room? Broke into the safe? Stole her money?"

"I'm just trying to figure out what happened."

Her mouth contorted into an ugly smile. "She had two thousand dollars in that safe. Two lousy thousand dollars. Do you have any idea how much a year at Princeton costs? That would barely cover the activity fee." She whirled around and headed for the elevators.

Chapter 29

I HOPED that Travis was having better luck with his interviews that I was. Kyle's trouble in Italy was still a mystery. Bronwyn had dodged my question about what she did with Corinne's room key. Other than a few more details about Natalie, I really hadn't learned anything new.

Frustrated, I headed to the hotel bar for happy hour. Ordering a chardonnay, I walked outside to the balcony. Holliss sat at a table near the railing, eyes closed, chin tilted toward the sky. "Enjoying the sunshine?" I asked.

She opened her eyes and smiled. "Hey, Madeline. Come join me."

I pulled back a chair. "Where's Randall?"

"I sent him out to play tourist. He's so wound up about this murder investigation that we both needed some space."

"I'm sure that Randall's lawyer will get all this cleared up soon."

"I hope so." She propped her toes against the base of the railing. "You know, I thought I wanted to stay here until Mom got shipped home, but I've changed my mind. If I could talk Randall into leaving, I'd get out of here tomorrow."

"I think everyone is anxious to hit the road."

"Kyle and Bronwyn have agreed to stay long enough to help Dad get things figured out with the embassy … you know, what to do with Mom's body and all that … but as soon as that's wrapped up, probably in another day or so, they're heading home." She stared enviously at my wine. "I'll be glad when this baby gets here. I am *so* done with sparkling water. What I wouldn't give for a few shots of tequila right now."

"At least you're well past the halfway mark."

"Good thing. I feel like I'm about to burst. The doctor assured me it wasn't twins, but I'm not convinced."

"Have you decided on a name?"

Holliss angled her chair so that she wasn't staring into the late afternoon sun. "No. We've been working on a list, but nothing final yet."

"You've got time." I sipped my chardonnay, enjoying the refreshing hint of citrus. "What's the latest from Mueller? Any DNA results?"

She sighed. "No. But Mueller was back here this morning with more questions. It's obvious Randall's at the top of his suspect list. And I'm his alibi, so Mueller is grilling me, too."

"You and Randall were together the whole time on Pilatus, right?"

"Yes. Except when I was taking potty breaks. Which seems to be happening about every thirty minutes. It's like I've got a beachball bouncing on my bladder." She caressed her baby bump. "Mueller thinks Randall could have fought with my mother while I was in the ladies room. I'm afraid he'll be locked up in a Swiss prison by the time the baby's born."

"We won't let that happen," I reassured her. "But we need to figure out what everyone did after Corinne left the café."

"I keep trying to block all that out." She frowned as she sipped her water. "Bronwyn and Kyle were in Dad's face. Bronwyn kept whining about college tuition and Luke's job. Kyle said Mom had promised to invest in his company, and it wasn't fair for her to back out. Everybody was screaming. I had to get away from all that."

"Kyle and Bronwyn were still in the café with Fred when you left?"

"Yes."

"And you didn't see your mom outside anywhere?"

"No. Randall and I went straight to the cable car and headed down."

I struggled to casually phrase my next question. "Do you think …" I spun the words around in my head, trying to soften them, make them less accusatory. But there was no easy way to ask it, so I finally blurted out, "Do you think either Bronwyn or Kyle could have been resentful enough of your mother to kill her?"

She didn't answer right away, chewing her fingernail as she stared down at the ducks swimming along the shoreline. "I've thought about that," she admitted. "Both of them have been acting weird since Mom died. Bronwyn's turned bipolar, all compassionate and loving one minute, then screaming at us and bursting into tears the next. Kyle refuses to talk about any of it."

"Kyle's been in trouble before, right? That thing in Italy, a few years ago?"

She jerked her head back, surprised. "Where did you hear that?"

I dodged the question, not wanting to implicate Luke. I was sure he had already been sufficiently chewed out by Fred for sharing the story. "Do you know what happened?"

"Nobody ever talks about it. Kyle had sold his company for a gazillion dollars, and all that money went to his head. He partied like crazy. Drinking … drugs … lots of women. His wife dumped him."

"The police got involved?"

"I never heard that. I do know that Dad talked him into a long stint in rehab. Although I don't think he would have gone if Bronwyn hadn't pressured him." She held up her glass, rotating it to catch sparkles of sun, the facets scattering rainbow slivers onto the table. "He hasn't touched drugs or alcohol since. I don't know if you've noticed, but he's only been drinking water since we've been here."

"He and Bronwyn really stick together, don't they?"

"More than you know." Holliss grew thoughtful. "I probably shouldn't tell you this, but I found out that Bronwyn invested Harrison's college money in Kyle's new company. That's why she was so upset that Mom wouldn't help out with Princeton."

"Wow. So, it's not only Luke's job that Bronwyn's worried about. She really doesn't have the money to send her son to college?"

"She can do it, but things will be tricky. Evidently Luke's been pressuring Kyle to pay him back, but Kyle said he couldn't do it until his company was on firmer footing. And with Mom backing out of her investment in the company, that wasn't likely to happen soon." Holliss downed the last of her water. "That paragliding incident in Interlaken, where Luke almost died? It was a warning from Kyle to Luke. Telling him to back off about the money."

***

After Holliss headed up to her room, I stayed out on the balcony to enjoy the sunlight, wondering how Travis and Eva were progressing on their parts of our investigation. My top suspects were Sergey and Klaus, two cousins so alike they could be twins. And I still thought the agitators from Basel could have done it, especially after one of them had stalked me here in Lucerne. But I couldn't rule out Kyle and Bronwyn. Even Holliss thought they might be involved.

I walked back inside, ready to order one last glass of wine before dinner. Kyle sat by himself at the bar, nursing a drink. I had steered clear of him since that night on the deck of the riverboat, but I needed to find out more about what he did at Pilatus, maybe even get him to talk about Italy. "Is this seat taken?" I asked, gesturing at the empty stool beside him.

He glanced up and down the bar at the empty seats and then shrugged. Not a welcoming invitation, but good enough. The bartender came for my order. "I'll have what he's having," I said, sticking out a thumb toward Kyle. I grinned as the bartender walked away. "I've always wanted to use that line."

"You may be disappointed. This is Perrier."

So Holliss was right that he had given up alcohol. "Oh. I thought it was a gin and tonic. Guess the lime fooled me."

"You want to change your order?" He signaled the bartender.

"No, it's fine. I overloaded last night and paid the price this morning. My head will thank me tomorrow for showing more restraint." After a few minutes, the bartender set my beverage in front of me. I stirred the drink with my finger, submerging the lime in bubbles, trying to figure out how to get Kyle talking. "Emily seems very excited about your new company."

"Yep."

This conversation was off to a slow start. What was it Travis had said about interviewing? That people have to want to talk to you? Surely his fiancée was a good topic. "She's really smart. We've shared marketing ideas."

"She told me." He sipped his water, content to sit in silence.

Time to try something else. "Cybersecurity, right? Your new company?"

"That's right. A huge opportunity. There are so many hackers out there, trying to break into company systems, hold them hostage. We'll be one of the good guys."

So this was the subject near and dear to his heart. "Sounds great." Fizz tickled my nose as I raised my glass. "You've done all this before, starting a company? Can you give me a couple of pointers?"

He ran a thumb along his chin, stroking the coarse hairs of his vacation beard, which was a dark auburn, an unexpected contrast to his blond hair. "Work your butt off. Focus on your customers. Hire good people."

Nothing new there. He sounded like one of my business professors back in college. "That's it?" I laughed. "Piece of cake, right?"

"Pretty much." He flashed his famous charismatic smile. "And make sure you have enough capital." He seemed different from the man who threatened me on the riverboat, more subdued, less haunted. With Corinne gone, her campaign shut down, maybe all his problems were solved.

"Ah, there's the rub. Lilly and I are in hock up to our eyeballs. Our first year in business, we barely scraped together enough money to pay the rent."

"Find some investors."

"Is that what you did?"

He nodded. "When I started, I hit friends and family for money. *Equity investments*, I called them. So that if I had to close the whole thing down, I wouldn't be on the hook to pay them back."

He must be following the same strategy this time around, since he had convinced Bronwyn to invest Harrison's college money. "Your company was a big success."

"Took us ten years, but things finally caught on. Revenues were on fire. Cash flowing in the door so fast I had trouble figuring out what to do with it."

"Lilly and I would love to have that problem." We could hire staff, move to a bigger office, have a cash cushion for emergencies. It wouldn't happen this year, or even the next. But surely sometime. "Why did you sell?"

"Typical story. A big dog in the industry made me an outrageous offer. My investors pressured me to sell, figuring they could make huge returns on their money. The proceeds would be seed money to start another company. I had spun dreams into gold once. They convinced me I could do it again."

I poked at my lime. "Guess they were right. Here you are, working on your second start-up."

"No, I shouldn't have done it."

"Why not?"

His eyes grew vague as he stared past me. "It was like selling my soul. Instead of working every day with smart people, solving problems, starting new projects, I had this big hole in my life, filled only with money. And money can make you do crazy things."

Moment of truth, I thought. He's ready to tell me what happened in Italy after he got all that money. If he really killed someone. "Like what?"

The bartender walked up, a towel slung over his shoulder. "You folks need a refill?"

"None for me thanks," Kyle said.

Annoyed at his timing, I shook my head. "No, I'm good."

The bartender walked away. I smiled at Kyle and leaned a little closer, waiting for him to pick up the narrative. "Like what?" I repeated.

He didn't answer. It was obvious that our moment of sharing was over. He stood up and tossed some bills on the bar. "It's late. I've got to go."

Chapter 30

FOR OUR FAREWELL dinner Fred had made reservations at Brassiere Julien, a popular French restaurant several blocks from our hotel. It was an elegant venue, perfect for celebrating special moments. Dark paneled walls were liberally hung with gold-framed oil landscapes. Heavily carved mahogany chairs surrounded tables outfitted with crisp white linen. Candlelight from slim tapers flickered against crystal wine glasses. Corinne would have loved it.

The hostess led us through a maze of diners to our table. Fred walked slowly behind her, his shoulders stooped as he settled himself at the head of the table. It pained me to see how diminished he was by Corinne's death, his vitality drained in only a few days, no longer the robust man he'd been at the start of our trip.

Kyle sat at the opposite end of the table, with the rest of us filling in the spaces along the sides. Emily waved Wyatt over to sit beside her.

The waiter came to our table, handing out menus, making wine recommendations. Once our glasses were filled, Fred raised his. "A toast to Corinne Peerland. A wonderful wife, mother, business executive, and visionary. Someone who wanted to make the world a better place. She was ..." He hesitated, biting hard on his lower lip. "She was the love of my life. I will hold her memory in my heart forever."

I fought back tears at the lovely tribute. Holliss blotted her eyes with the corner of her napkin. The faces of Bronwyn and Kyle showed a mix of emotions. Sorrow, to be sure, at the loss of their mother, but something else. A bit of relief, perhaps, because the campaign they had viewed as an inconvenience, an annoyance, even a threat, was over?

"I know you're all making plans to head home, so this will be our last dinner together here in Switzerland. It would mean a lot to me if each of you shared one special memory of your mom." Fred set down his glass. "Kyle, you're the oldest. Why don't you start?"

Kyle groaned. "Oh, come on, Dad, you know I'm not into all this touchy-feely stuff. I wouldn't know what to say."

"Normally, I'm not either. But nothing about this trip has been normal. We'll have a service to celebrate your mother's life when we get back in the States, but I think we need something positive now, while we're all together." Fred's stare was unrelenting. "Kyle, we're waiting."

Kyle stalled, picking up his water glass, taking a slow drink. "Okay," he said at last, "I've got one. Remember my thirteenth birthday? We had just moved to Connecticut. Mom wanted me to have a party, but I didn't think anyone would come because I was the new kid. But she was determined. She organized a paintball competition and invited my entire class. We dressed up in camouflage and ran through the woods, shooting at each other. By the end of the party, we were all great buddies."

"And I had green paint in my hair," Bronwyn said. "Took forever to wash all that out."

Fred smiled. "Thank you, Kyle. That's what we needed to start us off. How about you, Bronwyn? You have a story for us?"

"Nothing to top that one. I think I'll pass."

"This isn't a competition. We want some good memories of your mother."

Kyle gently punched her shoulder. "If I could do it, you can. Don't be such a wuss."

"Fine, fine. Give me a minute to think of something." She frowned as she concentrated. "Okay, I've got it. Mom liked to play games with us. Scrabble. Monopoly. Chinese checkers. When we were little, she'd always let us win."

"She'd let *you* win, you mean." Kyle shook his finger at his sister. "Because you were always such a crybaby when you lost."

"Not true," Bronwyn said. "As I recall, you were the one who pouted if things didn't go your way."

"You have some very selective memories there, Bronwyn. But I'll let that slide for now."

Their easy banter began to loosen the gloom that swirled around us. "Your mother would have done anything for you kids," Fred said, as the waiter returned with our salads. "I kept telling her she was spoiling you rotten."

Bronwyn sighed, chasing a bit of roasted pepper with her fork. "That was such a magical time. Why did it all change?"

"We grew up," Kyle said. "We were busy with school. Mom was super busy with her job."

"And Holliss was born," Bronwyn added, glancing at her sister. "With a screaming baby, there wasn't enough time for fun stuff anymore."

Holliss attacked her romaine, chopping it into tiny pieces. "Bronwyn, I'm so sorry I ruined your childhood."

"Don't get in one of your snits," Bronwyn said. "I didn't mean anything by it. But once you came along, the whole dynamic changed. You were the brand-new toy. Everyone doted on you, even with your poopy diapers and midnight screaming tantrums. Mom didn't have as much time for us."

I had always seen the family from Holliss's point of view, how she had felt left out because her siblings were so much older than she was. While Bronwyn was executing elaborate pirouettes in ballet class and Kyle was perfecting bicycle kicks in soccer, Holliss was barely walking. By the time she could ride a two-wheeler, they had moved on to driving the family car. Now I understood how Bronwyn and Kyle might have resented this interloper, the cute little baby who sucked up their parents' attention and relegated the two of them to the fringes of family time.

Fred glanced at the daughter who looked so much like him, so different from her mother. "Holliss, can you share a memory with us?"

She shook her head, twisting her napkin. "Dad, don't make me do that."

He smiled reassuringly. "Come on, Holliss, I know you and your mom had a few difficult years there, but you both worked to put that behind you. Your mother was proud of your accomplishments. She was looking forward to this new grandchild."

"Let's leave it there, then," Holliss said. "Mom and I had a lot of difficult years. As I got older, we tried to reconcile. And sometimes, we almost succeeded."

Bronwyn frowned at her sister. "What happened with you guys after Kyle and I went to college? You were happy enough as a little kid, although you were a bit of a nuisance, hiding under the kitchen table while Kyle and I did our homework."

"Yeah, what went wrong?" Kyle asked. "You changed from cute kid to ferocious Goth, all pierced and tattooed and dressed in black. What was up with that?"

They were pinning her down, pulling out details of her childhood that she had tamped down for years, memories she didn't want to resurrect. She glared at her siblings. "Okay, you want a mommy memory? Here's one. After you guys moved out, once it was only Mom and Dad and me in the house, everything changed. Suddenly I couldn't do anything right. Mom didn't like the way I dressed or wore my hair. She yelled at me constantly."

"That sounds like typical teenage stuff," Emily said. "I used to sneak out of the house when my mom got too bossy."

"This wasn't her being bossy. She was abusive, like she blamed me for something and was trying to get revenge." Holliss turned to her brother. "Kyle, I'm glad you had a great birthday party. You want to know what Mom did when I turned thirteen? She canceled my party after all the invitations had already gone out. A bunch of girls stood on the front steps, expecting a sleepover, and she refused to let them in."

"There must have been a reason," Bronwyn insisted. "You did something that ticked her off."

"I figured you guys wouldn't believe me. Dad didn't either, after Mom convinced him that I was lying."

Fred tried to cut her off. "Holliss, I don't think we need to get into this right now."

"Come on, Dad, you're the one that wanted a story. So let me finish."

Randall leaned closer. "Holliss, please don't."

She shook him off. "I finally figured out a way to make her leave me alone. You guys remember how terrified Mom was of spiders?"

"Yes," Kyle said. "It was a real phobia. Every time she'd spot one in the bathroom, she'd scream for me to come in there and kill it."

"Exactly. Well, when I was fifteen, my friends and I went to this scruffy place downtown to get tattoos. Had to tip the guy extra because we were all underage. They chose hearts and smiley faces, tiny little things hidden on their butts, where their parents couldn't see them. But not me. The tattoo guy had this picture of a tarantula up on his board, and that's what I picked." She pulled up her sleeve and held up her forearm. "A real piece of art, don't you think? With its hairy legs and beady little eyes. Like it could crawl right off my wrist. The next time Mom yelled at me, I stuck that arm out at her. She almost had a heart attack." Holliss speared a piece of goat cheese. "Soon after, she found a college that would accept a precocious teenager. I had already learned everything my high school could teach me, anyway, so it was time for me to move on. Best thing for everybody."

There was a moment of shocked silence.

"Interesting story," Bronwyn said. "I guess we now know which family member had the biggest motive to kill our mother. Or maybe to get her husband to do it. Looks like Mueller was on the right track about those scratches on Randall's neck."

Holliss turned a bright red. "Please note that Randall is not the only one of us with battle scars. What about Wyatt? He's had a stiff back for days. Maybe from pushing Mom over the railing?"

Wyatt startled at the accusation. "Hey, folks, I didn't have anything to do with this. My back gives out on me sometimes, but it's from an old football injury."

"And what about you, Bronwyn?" Holliss pointed at Bronwyn's broken finger. "Did you really get your finger stuck in the cable car, or did you break it when you were struggling with Mom?"

Bronwyn bristled. "That is absurd. I would never hurt my mother."

Holliss rose awkwardly to her feet. "Neither would Randall. He had nothing to do with Mom's death, and I won't sit here and listen to you try to pin it on him. We're leaving."

She rushed toward the door, almost colliding with the waiter who was bringing in our entrees. He dodged to the side as Holliss and Randall stomped out. Then, as though nothing unusual had happened, he set a dish in front of Bronwyn and said in a bright voice, "I believe you had the Veal Oscar?"

Chapter 31

WE WERE silent as the waiter distributed our entrees. He hesitated as he reached Holliss and Randall's empty chairs. "Shall I keep these warm in the kitchen?" he asked, glancing uncertainly toward Fred.

"Toss them," Kyle said. "They're not coming back."

The waiter walked off, carrying the two plates.

Bronwyn shivered, tugging her wrap around her shoulders. "I don't believe anything Holliss said. She made it all up."

"There's always been something a little weird about her," Kyle said.

"More than weird. She's a psycho. And a liar." Bronwyn's loud, stinging words sliced through the ambient hum of casual conversation, causing other diners to pause in mid-chew, their heads swiveling towards us.

Fred rested his arms heavily on the table. "You two need to lighten up on Holliss. There are things you don't know."

Bronwyn's eyebrows shot up. "So all those things she said were true? Is that what you're telling us?"

"Some of it." He spoke slowly, beginning the painful process of reconstructing the past, of sharing secrets he'd kept from his children. "When Holliss was twelve, Corinne's sister, your Aunt Sylvia, died. Corinne really took it hard. Went into a major depression—she was irritable, drinking way too much, so tired she could barely drag herself out of bed."

I had never heard this before. I stopped chewing, eager to hear the story.

"My company was doing a big acquisition back then," he said, "and I was working day and night. You guys were away at college. Holliss was the only one at home. She became an easy target for your mother's mood swings. When she says Corinne was tough on her, yes, she's telling the truth."

"Why didn't we know about this?" Bronwyn asked.

"Your mother didn't want you to know. She tried to hide it from everybody. We went through some rough years before medication and therapy finally got her back on track." He paused to sip his wine. "Meanwhile, Holliss was miserable. I had to get her out of that toxic environment. Fortunately, I found a college that would accept her."

Kyle's expression was solemn. "Guess that explains why things were always so weird between Mom and Holliss."

"And it explains why Holliss got Randall to kill Mom," Bronwyn said. "Because she hated her."

I waited for Fred to defend her, but he merely shrank back in his chair, lowering his head. I'd had enough. If no one in the family would stand up for Holliss and Randall, then I would. "No. Randall didn't do it."

They were surprised at my outburst. "Then who did?" Kyle asked.

I hadn't planned to share my theory with the family, at least not yet. But maybe talking out my ideas wasn't such a bad thing. They could help me fill in some details. "I think everything started with dinner our first night on the boat. If you remember, Corinne yelled at Sergey, our waiter. She reprimanded him in front of his boss."

"You think Sergey killed her? That skinny little guy?" Kyle shook his head as he set down his wine. "He was barely strong enough to hoist up the dinner trays. I can't see him slinging her off the mountain."

"Let me explain." I needed to convince them that someone other than Randall could have killed Corinne. "I went to the riverboat today with some friends, to interview the captain and crew. I got some insight that puts an entirely different spin on all this."

"You went to the boat?" Bronwyn asked. "Why would you do that?"

"Because Mueller seems determined to pin this murder on Randall. I don't think he's pursuing other suspects. And I don't think Randall did it."

"You think Sergey killed Corinne because she complained about her steak?" Luke asked. "That doesn't sound like much of a motive."

"I don't think he ever planned to kill her," I said. "But then his cousin Klaus got involved. And things got out of control."

"Who's Klaus?" Emily asked.

I laid out my theory, piece by piece. How Klaus and Sergey were look-alike cousins. How Sergey was angry when he was upbraided by his boss, and angrier still when he found out from Klaus that Corinne had won a lot of money playing poker, probably more money than Sergey made in a month. "He knew she had shellfish allergies. Remember, we all had to fill out those forms before we boarded the riverboat?"

"Everybody at our poker game knew Mom had shellfish allergies," Kyle said. "Some guy ordered a plate of fried oysters, and Corinne insisted on changing seats so she wouldn't be anywhere near them."

"Was Sergey working at the bar when you ordered the bloody mary?"

"Yeah," Kyle nodded. "Yeah, he was."

"Did you tell him it was for Corinne?"

'I'm not sure. We joked around a bit. I could have mentioned it was for Mom."

My theory was coming together. "Let's assume you did. Sergey wanted revenge. So he fixed her a bloody mary loaded with minced crab meat. I've tasted one. It's so thick and spicy that Corinne would never have realized what was in it. Then, after her allergy attack, when she and Fred were at the doctor's office, Sergey and Klaus had plenty of time to rob the safe."

They all frowned as they struggled to digest what I was telling them, whirling my story in their minds, comparing it against their own memories. "Even if you're right about all that," Kyle said, his voice laced with disbelief, "how does that make them guilty of murder? Were they at Pilatus?"

"Klaus was. I think Corinne figured out what had happened and confronted him, thinking he was Sergey. Klaus didn't want anyone to find out about it. He and Corinne argued. There was a struggle."

There was a long pause while everyone pondered my explanation. I waited, examining their raised eyebrows and budding sneers, fearing that they would dismiss my account as the baseless rambling of someone desperate to save her friend's husband.

"I guess it's possible." Luke brought a bite of filet to his mouth. "But how will you ever prove it? Mueller seems like a guy who wants hard evidence before he makes a move."

"That's a problem. I've got no proof. Except Klaus admitted he was there. Holliss and I spotted him, thinking he was Sergey."

Fred studied me over the top of his wine glass. "You think Corinne figured this out? That she knew what happened?"

"Yes, I do. That's the key to this whole thing."

He threw me a lifeline. "Then you need to check her journal. If Corinne puzzled out what happened with her drink, if she thought Sergey stole her money, she would have written it down. There's your proof."

I remembered that Corinne had pulled her journal from the nightstand after the security team had finished examining her safe. Would she have realized so quickly that someone had doctored her drink so they could get access to her cabin? It seemed a long shot, but worth checking out.

"She was still keeping journals after all these years?" Bronwyn picked at her veal. "There must be dozens of them by now."

"A lot more than that," Fred said. "She started a new one every year. There are boxes of them in the attic back home."

"Where is the journal now?" I asked. "Does Mueller have it?"

"He hasn't said anything to me about it."

"Then it could still be there, in her cabin," I said. This sliver of proof could exonerate Randall, or at least steer Mueller's investigation in another direction. "We need to get Mueller to look for it, to see if Corinne mentioned Sergey."

"Wait a minute." Luke threw up his hands to object. "How do we know there's not something in the journal that could incriminate one of us? We all argued with her about the Senate campaign. If she put all that in the journal, Mueller might think one of us killed her."

"He's right. The family should see the journal before the police do," Kyle said. "You've already been to the riverboat, Madeline. You need to go back and get it."

"The riverboat is probably halfway to Amsterdam by now. Besides, I don't think the captain would let me back on the boat again. He only did it as a favor to Eva, one of the people who was with me. They're old friends."

"Then tell Eva to get the journal."

Bossing people around seemed to come easily to him, doubtless honed during his CEO stints. I disappointed myself by buckling to his demands. "I mean … I guess I could ask her."

"Good. That's taken care of." Kyle casually cut off another slice of ribeye.

I wasn't ready to concede. "But I'm sure she would say that if the police don't retrieve it themselves, the chain of evidence would be broken. Which means that even if Corinne did implicate Sergey or Klaus in her journal, it might be useless in convicting them."

"I'm willing to take that chance," Luke said. "Better to let those guys off the hook than get any of us tossed in jail. What do you say, Madeline? Can you help us out?"

It was hard to hold out with all those demanding eyes staring at me. I knew it was a bad idea. Interfering with evidence that potentially fingered Sergey and Klaus would keep Randall in Mueller's crosshairs. Pointing that out, however, seemed unlikely to change anyone's mind. I laid down my fork, unable to eat another bite, eager for this dinner to be over. I didn't promise that I would retrieve the journal. But I didn't turn them down, either. I'd run this by Travis and Eva, to get their thoughts. "I'll see what I can do."

***

After dinner we all headed back to the hotel. Bronwyn walked arm-in-arm with Fred as Luke followed behind. I heard the words *college tuition* and *Harrison,* and figured she was putting the squeeze on her dad to help with her son's upcoming Princeton expenses.

Kyle and Emily argued, oblivious to the rest of us. "I've seen every church, every museum, every famous bridge in Lucerne," she said. "I've bought souvenirs for everyone I know. There's nothing more to do here. I want to go home."

"We can't leave yet. I need to help Dad arrange things for Mom."

"No, you don't. He's got that all under control. We need to focus on our company. We're wasting time here."

I slowed my pace, not wanting to be part of either of those discussions. I exaggerated a limp from my sore ankle, giving me cover to lag behind.

Wyatt matched his steps to mine. "Ankle still giving you trouble? Can I help?" He moved closer. "You're not any too steady."

I had avoided Wyatt since our confrontation in the tower. "No, I can manage," I said, pulling away from him.

"Come on, Madeline," he said, his voice pleading. "I know I acted like a real jerk yesterday. I guess I thought there was a lot more going on between us than you did. I apologize. I'm sorry if I upset you."

I was beyond upset. He had jammed his thumb so hard into my jaw that it had left a bruise. My mind still churned over details of that dash down the staircase—me racing faster and faster, Wyatt's pounding footsteps as he gained on me, something brushing against my arm. Or had it only been my own clumsiness? I tried to walk a little faster, to get away from him and catch up with the others, but they were too far ahead.

He paused at an outdoor café. "Why don't we stop here for a drink? Let you rest a minute. Give me a chance to grovel."

"Sorry, I'm tired. I need to get back." Two blocks away, the red and white Swiss flag on the roof of our hotel floated gently in the evening breeze. If I could make it that far, I would be rid of him.

"You're not being fair. We've had some good times on this trip. Just because your boyfriend's here now, that doesn't mean you have to brush me off."

"My boyfriend?"

"I saw you and Travis head out this morning on your riverboat excursion."

He was jealous, I realized. Jealous of Travis and me. I could have explained that Eva and Travis had gotten all cozy in the front seat, snuggling up together as they exchanged fond memories of days of yore, while I got tossed in the back like a sack of groceries. No doubt that would have made Wyatt feel better. But soothing his ego was far down on my priority list.

Thinking he was going to grill me more about Travis, I was surprised when he suddenly switched topics. "Tell me more about this theory of yours," Wyatt said. "About Sergey and Klaus."

"What I laid out at dinner is all I've got. If we can find Corinne's journal, that may help."

"You think it was just the two of them?" A fleck of tension underlaid the casualness of his question. Was he worried about his friends back on the boat?

"Don't know. They had to get into the room somehow. Housekeeping would have had a key. And so would security."

"Wow, you're turning this into a big conspiracy." His wavering tone indicated he didn't buy into my theory. I wasn't sure anyone else did, either.

"All I'm trying to do is raise enough suspicion so that Mueller goes after someone other than Randall. It's up to him to find the killer."

He mulled that over for a few minutes. "Randall's lucky to have you in his corner."

"I guess." Only one more block to the hotel. Once I got to the lobby, I could dump Wyatt and head up to my room.

He kept throwing questions at me, about the family, about the investigation, about Mueller. My answers were clipped ... *yes, no, maybe...* anything to discourage this guy, to indicate that I was bored and not interested in spending more time with him.

We finally arrived at the cobblestone courtyard. Wyatt stayed close behind me as I started up the steps. "I'm fine, thank you," I said, trying to shake him off. "I'm sure you have more fun things to do than stick with me. I'll see you tomorrow."

He wasn't ready to call it a night. "Let's get a drink in the lounge. I want to hear more about all this."

"There isn't any more. And it's been a long day. I'm tired." I walked toward the elevator and pressed the up button.

He stuck with me, close enough that his shoulder grazed mine. "Then how about breakfast tomorrow?"

Subtlety didn't have much impact on Wyatt. Did I have to hit the guy over the head with my purse to make him leave me alone? "I don't know. We'll have to see how things work out."

"But ..." Wyatt began. His words turned to a squeal as he was suddenly shoved backwards.

"I don't think the lady wants to talk to you," said a familiar voice.

Chapter 32

WYATT FLUSHED as he stared at Travis's face, only a few inches from his own. "The lady can make her own decisions," Wyatt spat out.

"She already has," Travis said, his voice low. "You're not listening to her."

I grabbed his arm. "Travis, stop it." A family at the check-in desk turned our way. The mother moved protectively in front of her two young boys, while the father took a cautious step toward us, unsure if he should intervene. "You're creating a scene."

The elevator doors opened. "Here's your ride," Travis said, giving Wyatt a quick thrust.

Wyatt stumbled into the empty car, glaring at Travis as he pulled his battered dignity behind him. "I'll see you tomorrow, Madeline," he said. "Good night."

Travis shook his head as the doors closed. "That guy is such an idiot." He had the smug smile of a medieval champion who had just rescued the fair maiden, ready to parade down the narrow streets of an ancient village as young girls tossed flowers in front of his prancing stallion. It was clear he expected praise, or at least a robust thank you.

But I was annoyed. "Do you always have to jump in to protect me?"

"Come on, it was obvious you wanted to get rid of that guy."

"Maybe so, but I could have taken care of it. You played the hero once before, remember, and it cost me my job." Angry, I whirled around and stomped off to the hotel lounge. It was almost deserted, only a few other guests seated at low tables. I chose a spot at the bar and ordered a chardonnay.

Travis sat beside me and ordered a beer. "This is about Bartley, isn't it?"

I kept my eyes down. "You do too much, Travis. You step in when I don't need you."

"Bartley deserved what he got. You know that."

"Both of us were at fault. Too much partying. Too much alcohol."

I would never forget that night. Three years ago Bartley, one of the senior guys at my firm, made a pass at me at a holiday party. Flattered at the attention, I followed him out of the ballroom, and soon we were groping each other in a deserted coat closet. Things progressed a lot faster than I expected. Groggy and confused, I made a weak attempt to fight him off as he shoved one hand down my top and the other up my skirt. If Lilly hadn't wandered in right then looking for her coat, the ending might have been very different. She grabbed my wrist, flung sharp words at Bartley, and pulled me outside to a taxi.

"Somebody had to hold that guy accountable," Travis said. "He spiked your drink with that date rape drug. If it hadn't been for Lilly …"

At work the next week I got sly glances and a few winks from some of the guys, which was especially infuriating because I couldn't remember much of that evening. I tried to ignore the whole thing, but when Bartley excluded me from high-visibility projects and assigned me to grunt work that a summer intern could have covered, I felt I had to do something. Lilly confessed that he had forced himself on her, too, and encouraged me to report him to human resources. My complaint quickly turned into a "he said-she said" squabble.

Soon my only projects were coffee runs for lower-level staffers. Frustrated and angry, I made the mistake of confiding in Travis. A few weeks later a bunch of us were having dinner at a nearby restaurant when Bartley and his buddies from work walked in. Travis jumped up to confront him. Bartley told him where he could shove his opinions. Soon both groups were caught up in a fist-throwing brawl of bloody noses and chipped teeth, of broken chairs and smashed glassware.

I sipped my chardonnay. "You should have stayed out of it."

"Did you really expect me to stand by and do nothing?"

"But I'm the one that paid the price. Everyone at work thought I was a liar. That I'd made up the whole thing." Bartley made sure I suffered for Travis's heroics. He embellished the details of our holiday tête-à-tête until everyone in the firm turned their backs when I walked into the room. After I left the firm, Bartley spread the word in the industry that I was a troublemaker. My only consolation was that a year later Bartley went through a very public and career-ending divorce, after his wife caught him in his office having sex with an intern.

Travis slammed down his beer, splashing a few drops onto the bar. "You're never going to forgive me for that, are you?"

For the next six months, I tried to resurrect my career, sending out countless resumes that generated no callbacks. When I finally gave up on getting another job and decided to open my own firm, I was too busy to think about Travis. He kept reaching out, texting updates about mutual friends, sending internet links to funny stories, but I didn't want to talk to him.

By the time I realized that I missed him, it felt too late to reach out. Maybe now it was time to declare a truce. "I'm working on it. I realize your intentions were good."

He grinned at me, a long, slow smile that promised better things to come. "That's a start. I'll take it."

I ran my finger around the bottom of my wine glass. "Enough about Bartley. Tell me about Basel. How did your interview go?"

"Good, it was good. These guys are doing amazing things. I've already sent a summary to my editor. He's excited about it."

"Glad that worked out."

"In fact, he now wants me to do a whole series on climate change."

"Trendy topic. Everyone's talking about it, these days. Freezing winters in Texas. Raging fires in Oregon, California, Germany, Russia. Hard to ignore."

"And yet, not a lot of action so far." The corners of his mouth turned down in frustration. "The Paris Agreement led to a lot of promises but not a lot of results. Like you said, things keep getting worse."

"At least the U.S. has rejoined the Paris Agreement," I said. "That's got to be a good thing."

"Yes, but until the big polluters—China, the U.S., India—agree to reduce their carbon emissions, there's not much the rest of the world can do. Everyone's getting frustrated. Check out this video." He pulled out his phone.

I heard loud yelling as soon as I punched the play button. Crowds shouting spirited chants swarmed the streets in front of the conference hotel, waving protest signs. Police stood shoulder to shoulder along the sidewalks to hold them back. "There are a lot more of them than when I was there."

"It was the last day of the conference," Travis said. "They wanted a show of force."

The video jerked a bit as several men advanced through the police cordon, rushing toward people exiting the conference. "You took this video? You were right there while all this was going on? That's scary."

"Isn't it? I don't think they're going to win a lot of fans with violence."

I watched the video a second time. "Hey, Travis, I've seen some of these folks before." I tapped the screen to enlarge the picture.

Travis peered over my shoulder. "Which ones?"

"The blond one with the curly hair, for sure. He's the one who followed me here in Lucerne. He was leading chants that day Corinne and I were in Basel." I studied the faces of the men beside him. "These other two. I've seen them also. Maybe that day in Basel, but somewhere else, too." Memories whirled in my brain, fragments of faces, snow covered mountains. "I can see the location, and yet I can't. Does that make any sense?"

"Sure. Be patient. It will come to you." He took a final swallow of beer. "I have a contact who's going to help me follow up on this. The climate change folks are tired of waiting. They're morphing from organizing rallies and making speeches to violence. I want to get into their heads and figure out what we can do about this."

I played the video one last time, studying the faces. Then I scrunched my eyes shut, forcing myself to remember. I could see a group of men gathered around a large table by a window. One wore a striped knitted cap. When I caught him staring at Corinne, he quickly turned away. "Oh, my God, I remember where I saw these men."

"Where was it?"

"In the café at Pilatus. The day Corinne was murdered."

Chapter 33

I PULLED out my phone. "I've got to call him."

"Call who?" Travis asked.

"Mueller, of course."

"Why?"

"To tell him that agitators from the energy conference in Basel were at Pilatus the day Corinne was killed. That they were in the café with her. Motive, means, opportunity. They've got all three."

He ran his eyes back and forth across my face, studying me as though I were an enigma that perhaps could be figured out if he put enough time into it. "I am amazed by the way your mind works. Wasn't it earlier today that you laid out that convoluted story about Sergey and Klaus confronting Corinne? Now you don't think that happened?"

"That's still a possibility," I said, ignoring his criticism, "but we always thought the protestors might be involved. Here's proof that they were there that day."

"How do you know it's the same guys?" He picked up his mug. "Memory is a tricky thing. Eyewitnesses are notorious for identifying the wrong suspects."

I could feel my face grow hot. "You sound like Mueller." I remembered his reluctance to call in a sketch artist when I wanted to describe my Lucerne stalker. "Pilatus has security cameras. These guys must be on a video." I scrolled through my contacts for Mueller's number.

"Hold on." He frowned. "I talked to Eva on my way back from Basel. Müller's not too happy that we went to the riverboat. He said we were interfering with police business. That we should leave the investigation to the professionals."

"I'm not surprised he feels that way. And if the professionals would do their jobs a little faster, I'd be happy to do that."

Travis finished his beer. "Here's a thought. Eva's coming back here tonight to fill us in on her meeting with Mueller. Let's run this by her, and then get her to call him. They've worked together on a lot of cases. She's got the guy on speed dial. Your theory will have a lot more weight coming from her."

"Fine. My last meeting with Mueller wasn't especially productive." I put the phone in my purse. "I need Eva's help on something else, too."

"What's that?"

"I told the family tonight my theory about Sergey and Klaus. Fred said if Corinne had any ideas about who robbed her safe, she would have put them in her journal. I need Eva's help to retrieve it from the riverboat."

"You don't think Mueller already has it? The police searched her cabin. And so did we. Do you remember seeing it?"

"No. But we didn't go through everything. It's possible that we missed it. And if it's still there, the family wants me to get it for them. Before the police see it."

His eyes narrowed. "Don't you see, Madeline? That proves that somebody in the group is guilty. Otherwise, why would they care what Corinne had written in her journal?"

"I don't know. This whole thing has gotten so muddled." I gave him a quick synopsis of the dinner.

"My guess is that Mueller already has the journal," Travis said. "But I'll get Eva to ask."

"I appreciate that." There was a time when I would have given him a thankful kiss. Now I casually brushed his fingertips with my own. "You've been a big help. You and Eva, both."

He gave my hand a quick squeeze. "I want you to stay safe."

"Me, too." I finished my wine and laid some cash on the counter. "It's been a long day. I'm heading upstairs." I slid off the bar stool, groaning as I put weight on my ankle.

"What's wrong?"

"The doctor told me to stay off my feet, and I didn't listen. Definitely overdid it today. My ankle is killing me."

"Let's get you up to your room. I'll get you some ice for that."

***

TRAVIS WALKED with me to the elevator and then down the hall to my room. I sat on the bed and moaned as I examined my ankle. Shades of purple were edged with swirls of green and yellow.

He grabbed the ice bucket. "Don't move while I'm gone." He came back a few moments later. "Here, this should make you feel better." He propped my foot up on a pillow and covered it with an ice-filled towel.

I stretched toward the nightstand for my pain pills. "Can you get me some water?"

"Sure." He brought a frosty bottle from the minibar. "Need anything else?"

"Maybe sit with me a minute." It had been a challenging day. I was still upset over Holliss's story. "Hearing about Corinne's depression and the horrible things she did to Holliss. I had looked up to Corinne, as a successful businesswoman, as a champion of managing climate change. Now I feel like I never knew her at all."

He pulled a chair closer to the bed. "Your heroine had feet of clay? Is that what's upsetting you?"

"Something like that."

"Those things happened a long time ago, before you met her." His voice, low and calm, was soothing. "She went through a rough spot and then came out of it. Made a good life for herself."

"I realize that. It's …" I struggled to sort out my argument. "I thought she'd believed in all this for a long time. But Bronwyn told me she only took up the cause after her niece Natalie died. And she had to know her campaign would make things difficult for the rest of her family. Why would she do that?"

"Do you think she was sincere about trying to improve the environment?"

"Definitely. She'd joined several environmental boards. Wildlife. The rain forest. Water quality. Organized lots of fundraisers."

He balanced on the arm of the chair. "Then what difference does it make why she became an advocate for managing climate change? Or how long she'd been doing it? The important thing is that she wanted to protect the planet. I admire her for that."

"You're right. Maybe I'm being too tough on her." My ankle felt numb. I reached down to pull off the icepack. "Can you toss this? I think I'm getting frostbite."

"Sure thing."

He grabbed the towel and headed for the bathroom. As I heard the cubes clink into the sink, I realized that it was time to make peace with Travis. He had traveled all the way across the Atlantic to see me. He had helped to line up the interviews on the boat. I had rejected him long enough.

When he came back, I said, "Hey, I need something out of the side pocket of my suitcase. Can you get it for me?"

"Sure." Travis zipped open the case. "Is this it?" he asked, pulling out a shopping bag.

"Yes. Would you bring it here?" I rummaged through the bag and pulled out an item wrapped in tissue paper. "This is for you."

"You got me a present?" His eyes lit up. "So you have forgiven me, after all."

"I'm working on it." He didn't need to know that I had bought that gift for my brother-in-law, and that I had only now decided to give it to him as a token of reconciliation. "But don't get all excited. It's not that special. A T-shirt."

He unwrapped it and shook it out. "A rather handsome T-shirt. With a lovely scene of a moose standing in front of the Alps. Just what I've always wanted."

"You moron, that's not a moose, it's an ibex," I said, throwing a pillow at him. "It's a type of mountain goat that lives in the Alps. A moose has thick, flat horns that stick out from the side of his head." I demonstrated by holding out my palms beside my ears. "An ibex is much more svelte. His horns are on the top of his head. They're skinny, and they curve backwards."

He caught the pillow and tossed it back on the bed. "I must admit, this is my first T-shirt of a svelte ibex. Whenever I wear it, I'll think of you." He leaned over and brushed his lips against mine.

I felt an unexpected tingle at his kiss. I hadn't dated anyone seriously since Travis and I had our big blowup. The few guys I'd been out with were nice enough—a suave Wall Street investment banker, a very intense corporate lawyer, a talkative insurance guy who seemed promising until he tried to sell me an annuity—but there had been no sparks. Nothing to warrant a second date.

Travis's kiss was tender and warm, inviting a response. All the feelings I had for him rushed back. I needed him. I wanted him. Suddenly we were tugging at each other's clothes. I shifted against the pillows, reaching out. Then a pain shot up from my ankle to my knee. "Stop."

"What is it?" Travis rolled to one side. "What's wrong?"

"My ankle. It's on fire. I feel like my leg is about to explode."

"I'm sorry." He eased another pillow under my ankle. "Is that better?"

What was I doing? I hadn't seen Travis in over two years. A casual hookup now would only set me up for more heartbreak. Maybe he had a girlfriend back in New York. Maybe he wanted to start things back up with Eva. Until we spent more time together, until we got to know each other all over again, I needed to take it slow. "Sorry. My ankle's killing me. I can't do this right now."

He studied my face. "Seriously? Is it really your ankle?"

The sharp pain had subsided, but my ankle was still throbbing. "Of course it is. You've seen it. It's as purple as an eggplant."

"Right." He sat up. "Or is it more than that? Maybe you're not ready to jump back into our relationship?"

Travis was always good at figuring out what I was thinking. I had never been able to keep a secret from him. "That's not fair."

"Isn't it? Come on, Madeline, I feel terrible about Bartley and what happened with your job. If I could change any of that, I would. I've missed you, and I want us to get back together."

I wanted to snuggle against him, to feel his slow heartbeat as I rested my head on his chest. But I needed to protect myself. "You know I'm fond of you."

Travis swung his feet to the floor. "*Fond.*" His face crinkled. "Not exactly what I hoped you'd say."

I wanted to pull him back beside me, feel his warm body close against mine. Instead, I lay against the pillows and watched him fumble with his shirt buttons. "I'm sorry. I need more time to process all this. To figure out where things stand between us."

"More time, huh? I can deal with that, I guess." He grabbed the ibex T-shirt. "But don't make me wait too long. A guy can only take so many cold showers." He paused at the door. "In case you change your mind, remember I'm one floor up. Room 406."

I stared at the ceiling after he left, cursing myself for being so stupid. Travis was a good guy. His business meetings were in Basel, an hour away, yet he was staying in Lucerne. Why would he do that unless he wanted to be close to me? What more proof did I need that he was worth a second chance?

My phone rang. I reached for it, hoping it was Travis, ready to invite him back to my room. "Travis?"

"No, it's Randall. I'm at the hospital with Holliss."

"What's wrong? Is it the baby?"

"There's some spotting. The doctors are checking her out." He sounded worried. "The hospital's not far from the hotel. Can you come here? She's asking for you."

"Of course. I'll be there right away."

Chapter 34

THE HALLWAY felt like hospitals everywhere: shiny linoleum, the stinging smell of disinfectant, glaring lights which scoured counters and corners, leaving no place for dirt or germs to hide. This late at night, the floor was almost empty. No visitors bearing flowers or chocolate. No serious doctors in white coats consulting with each other. Only a lone nurse wheeling a squeaky cart toward a distant patient.

I checked the room signs when I got off the elevator, turning right toward Holliss's room. Randall bent over her bed, gently patting her shoulder. Her face seemed almost translucent. Pale blue veins traced delicate lines in her temples. Her dark eyebrows were ragged brushstrokes against a chalky forehead.

Fred stood near the window, arms clutched, his mouth a thin line. I walked over to him and asked in a low voice, "What happened?"

He looked as drained as he had the day Mueller announced Corinne's death. "I think it was all that stress at dinner. Randall said she was exhausted when they returned to the hotel. He got her into bed, but she complained of cramping. He called an ambulance and rushed her here."

"What did the doctor say? Does he know what's wrong?"

"Not really. They're doing tests."

I clutched his arm. "But she'll be all right? The baby—it's still okay?"

"I think so. They're going to keep her overnight. Monitor her condition."

I moved closer to the bed. "Hey, kid," I said, trying to keep my voice light. "Some people will do anything to get a little attention."

She gave a weak smile. "Thanks for coming, Madeline."

"What's going on?" I asked.

She turned toward Randall. "How about you and Dad get a coffee or something? I need to talk to Madeline for a few minutes."

She waited until they left the room. "I think I panicked. You heard my family at dinner, accusing Randall of killing my mother." Tears moistened the smudges under her eyes. "Then Randall's lawyer called when we got back to the hotel. The police want to confiscate his passport, which means we won't be able to go home. The lawyer is fighting them, but I don't know if he can win this argument." She sniffed. "Everyone is convinced Randall is guilty. I know he didn't do it, but nobody believes me."

"I believe you, Holliss. We'll get through this."

"I'm not so sure. I'm scared I'm going to lose my husband. And my baby. The doctor says I'm dehydrated, that stress is causing the spotting. He told me to relax." She shifted uneasily on her pillow. "Like I can relax while my husband's being accused of murder."

I handed her a tissue. "You're not going to lose Randall or the baby. There's no evidence tying Randall to this. Once the DNA tests come back, he'll be cleared."

"But the detective said that could be weeks. What are we supposed to do in the meantime? I can't stand this anymore." She dabbed at her eyelashes. "You heard my family at dinner. They're ready to throw Randall under the bus. You've got to help me. Run interference with Mueller. Make sure Randall doesn't get arrested."

"I'll do my best. There's new evidence that Mueller needs to consider." I told her about Travis's video. "I'm sure I saw those men at Pilatus."

"That's good news, I guess."

"And there's something else. At dinner, your dad mentioned that Corinne kept a journal. We're going to track it down. If she wrote something in there about Sergey, if she felt threatened, or suspected he had broken into her safe, then Mueller will have to take a harder look at him."

"I hope you're right." She reached for her water. I raised the head of her bed and handed her the bottle. "I never remember Mom keeping a journal."

"Fred said she'd been doing it for years. That she wrote down everything. Ideas for advertising campaigns. Funny things you children did. It was her own form of therapy, to help her cope with managing a family and a high pressure job."

Holliss took several swallows of water. "Why didn't I know anything about this?"

"She started hiding them once she realized Bronwyn and Kyle were sneaking them out of her dresser. She wanted them to stay private. Fred said there are boxes of them packed in the attic."

"I've love to get my hands on them. To find out what Mom really thought of me. Why she suddenly became so nasty."

I wasn't sure that was such a good idea. Seeing Corinne's rage spelled out on the written page wasn't likely to make Holliss feel much better. "Maybe later. After the baby is born."

Trying to steer our conversation to more pleasant topics, I brought up funny stories from our college days. Holliss relaxed, her shoulders softening against the pillow as we joked about old friends and demanding professors. She was laughing by the time Randall and Fred returned to her room.

"You're much more cheerful," Randall said, setting his coffee on the nightstand. "Madeline must be good for you."

"I've been reminding her of all the crazy things we did in college."

He shook his head. "Holliss has never done anything crazy. As I recall, she spent all her time in the library studying stochastics and differential equations."

I smiled, remembering Holliss making the rounds to fraternity parties, her long hair whirling in a tangled cloud as she danced. "You keep telling yourself that."

Randall leaned down to kiss his wife. "Do you have secrets I need to know about?"

"I probably have a story or two that I could share," she said, giving him a coy smile. "With the right motivation."

"Now I know you're feeling better. And I want to hear all those stories. But not tonight. You need to get some sleep." Randall turned to Fred and me. "Which mean you guys need to get out of here. I'm staying here tonight with Holliss. I'll let you know if there's any news."

"You okay if we leave?" I asked Holliss.

She propped herself up on her elbows. "Yes. It's late. You guys need to get back to the hotel. Thank you so much for coming."

"Of course." Fred kissed her cheek. "We'll check back with you first thing tomorrow."

Randall turned toward his wife. "Holliss, let me say goodbye to Madeline and your dad. I'll be right back."

The three of us walked down the hallway toward the elevators.

"I hate seeing Holliss like this," Fred said. "That detective has got her all tied up in knots, worried about you, Randall. I'm going to get the lawyer to talk to Mueller again. Get him to speed up those DNA tests. Once they come back, you'll be in the clear and he'll have to leave you alone."

Randall absently rubbed his forearm. "Don't bother with that, Fred. It won't do any good."

"No, I'm sure the lawyer can pull some strings," Fred insisted. "And I'll call the embassy again. Holliss can't relax until we prove you're not the killer."

Randall shook his head. "The DNA won't do it, Fred."

"Of course, it will." Fred was more energized than I'd seen him in days. "Once they find out it's not your skin beneath her fingernails, you'll be off the hook."

"You don't understand, Fred." His expression was a strained mix of sadness and regret. "Once that DNA comes back, I'm a dead man. Because it's mine."

Chapter 35

"WHAT ARE you talking about?" Fred said. "How could it be your DNA?"

Randall looked around the empty hallway. "Let's find a place to talk."

We wandered through the maze of patient rooms and nurses' stations until we reached a small lounge, a soulless box of vinyl-covered sofas and chairs arranged into small seating areas, the kind of place where families could commiserate over bad news. Cancer treatments that didn't work. A fatal blood clot following surgery. A DNA test that marked Randall as a murderer.

Fred and I sat on the sofa. Randall collapsed into a chair across from us. "I haven't been truthful with you guys. Or with the police. I did talk to Corinne. After the big blowup in the café. While Holliss was in the restroom."

This couldn't be happening. He was going to confess, right now. Holliss had given such a spirited defense of Randall, denied that he had anything to do with her mother's death. This news would destroy her.

Randall stared at the floor, not looking at us. "The way Corinne's treated her all these years, always putting Kyle and Bronwyn first, making Holliss feel like an outsider. You guys have no idea how much Holliss has been haunted by her relationship with her mother." He nervously picked at his cuticles. "When Corinne insulted her in the café, it was too much. I followed her out, determined to set her straight, to let her know she couldn't talk to my wife like that."

The overhead bulbs buzzed and flickered. The light in the room yellowed, giving us all a jaundiced cast. "Corinne was standing on the overlook," he said. "It was overcast and snowing. We were the only ones out there."

I tried to picture it, the two of them on that viewing platform, slipping on the ice as they argued, thick clouds swirling around them, hiding the treacherous rocks lurking below. The rest of us had been inside, leisurely sipping lattes and wandering through the gift shop, unaware of the deadly struggle only a few yards away. If I hadn't spent so much time choosing that bracelet for Lilly, if I had passed up the chance to buy that T-shirt, would I have already been heading toward the exit? Would I have spotted them on the platform? Been able to stop this horrible disaster?

"I tried to explain to her how Holliss felt," Randall said. "How she'd felt her whole life. That with this baby, Corinne and Holliss had a chance for a new start. That it was important she take advantage of that." He paused, his eyes flittering under closed eyelids as he replayed the scene in his mind. "Then she said something that made me so angry …" He made a small sound deep in his throat, almost a whimper. "God help me, I grabbed her arms and shook her. She struggled to get loose. Slashed at my neck with her fingernails. Which means that yes, when those DNA results come back, they'll be mine."

"Does Holliss know?" I asked. "Did she make up that story about you cutting yourself shaving?"

He shook his head. "No. I wrapped my scarf around my neck so she couldn't see. When I got back to the boat, I went straight into the bathroom, and then came out a few minutes later holding a bloody towel, telling her I'd cut myself. Holliss never suspected anything." He paused. "That dinner on the riverboat was a nightmare. I didn't realize how much hassle the family would give me about those scratches. The next day I pretended to have an upset stomach, so everyone would leave me alone."

The details of his story buzzed in my brain—the struggle with Corinne, the bloody scratches, his DNA in her fingernails. Mueller had been so sure Randall was the murderer. Everyone in the family suspected him. Now he had confessed. But I still needed to hear him say the words, to get that final bit of confirmation. "You killed her?" My voice was barely above a whisper.

"No." He stood up, moving toward me. "I swear to you, when I left her, she was standing on the platform, very much alive."

I had to believe him. Not because of the evidence—Corinne must have been fighting for her life to tear into his neck like that, slicing through skin, digging deep, going for blood. Desperate to be free, he would have pushed back, hard enough to send her toppling over the guardrail and onto the rocks below.

But I had to believe him because Holliss was my friend. She loved him. He was the father of her child. She had already lost her mother. She couldn't lose her husband, too.

Fred wasn't convinced. I could tell that a heavy burden of doubt weighed on him. "It was about the safe, wasn't it?" He stroked the slick vinyl of the sofa cushion. "That's what Corinne told you?"

Randall seemed puzzled. "What safe? What are you talking about?"

"Corinne thought Holliss robbed her safe. Stole the poker money."

"That's ridiculous," Randall said. "Why would she think that?"

Fred walked toward generic landscapes of grassy fields and snowy mountains, a failing attempt to give a feeling of openness and peace to that claustrophobic room. "Because that night in the lounge, Corinne told Bronwyn she'd buy her some jewelry with the poker winnings. Holliss was jealous. The three of them had a big argument."

It made no sense to me that Holliss would steal from her mother. She held a well-paying job as an actuary for an insurance company. Randall had a steady salary as a college professor.

"The thing is," Fred said, "Holliss doesn't even like jewelry. She never wears it. Corinne knew that. But I think it was the thought that Corinne was favoring Bronwyn once again that set Holliss off." He turned toward me. "That's why Corinne wanted you to take fingerprints that night. To muddle things up in case Holliss had left any prints on the safe."

"Corinne didn't really think Holliss had stolen her money?" I asked.

"She wasn't sure. The two of them have certainly had problems in the past."

Randall's voice was low, every word slow and deliberate. "Fred, what Corinne said had nothing to do with the safe. It was much more vicious than that."

Fred's jaw was tight as a fist. He knows, I thought. Whatever Randall is getting ready to tell us, Fred already knows. It won't be a surprise.

"Corinne completely disowned Holliss. Said she wasn't her daughter. That the baby would never be her grandchild." Randall steadied himself against a chair. "I was horrified. I couldn't believe a mother could say that." His voice broke. "It would destroy Holliss if she knew."

Chapter 36

COLOR RUSHED from Fred's face, leaving him almost as pale as Holliss had been when I first walked into her hospital room. "You killed Corinne?" he said.

"No." Randall crossed his arms over his chest. "I walked away. Left her standing there on the platform all by herself, spewing in her own hate."

Suddenly the intercom squawked to life with a loud message. I couldn't understand the words, but there no mistaking the urgency. Randall jumped to his feet. "Something's wrong. Maybe it's Holliss." He ran from the room, with Fred and me following behind.

The formerly deserted hallway was now filled with medical personnel, rushing past us as they headed toward a patient room in the far corner. We heard loud demands and curt instructions.

"Stop," I said. "That's not Holliss's room."

A gray-haired woman, distraught and sobbing, staggered out into the corridor, supported by two middle-aged men whom I assumed were her sons, murmuring softly to her as the urgent drama spun out in the patient's room.

I thought of Corinne, snatched from us without warning. At least this person was surrounded by loved ones, with time for last kisses, for shared memories, for tearful goodbyes. Corinne had been denied all that. Our best hope was that she died immediately when she hit the rocks, rather than lying there alone and in pain as drifting snow covered her body. "We shouldn't be here. These people need to be alone with their grief."

"Let's go back," Fred said. "I need to tell you more about Corinne."

***

We returned to the lounge. Randall and I sat while Fred remained standing, bouncing nervously on the balls of his feet. "I have to give you some background first, so you'll understand why Corinne said those things."

He examined with great interest a bulletin board overflowing with posters in several languages. Near the bottom was a flyer with tear-off strips bearing a telephone number. Fred ripped one off and wound it around his finger, first in one direction and then in the other. Finally, he began to speak. "Corinne and I fell in love on our first date. Couldn't keep away from each other. She was already pregnant with Kyle when we got married our senior year in college. Bronwyn was born a year later." He paused. "I'll admit, those early years were tough. Two careers. Two babies. Not enough hours in the day. But eventually Corinne transformed our household into a well-oiled machine. She posted duty charts on the refrigerator each week: grocery shopping, dry cleaning, oil changes. Baseball practice, piano lessons, dentist appointments. She even scheduled sex. Every Thursday night. If we missed a Thursday, we had to wait until the next week."

"Where's this going, Fred?" Randall asked, his voice impatient. "What does it have to do with Holliss?"

"If you let me finish …"

"Maybe you could speed it up a bit?" Randall said.

Fred's eyes drifted toward the far wall. "Corinne had a sister, Sylvia. Her husband left her when their daughter Natalie was only four years old."

"Natalie?" I asked. "The woman who was killed in the flash flood?"

"Yes. A horrific tragedy. Corinne felt so guilty about that." He pulled another telephone strip from the flyer. "Sylvia couldn't cope without her husband. She kept calling us, begging for help, but Corinne had no time, so she'd send me. I'd cut the grass, hang drapery rods, paint the front railing … the kind of stuff her husband used to do. Sylvia was so grateful." Fred's eyes brightened. "It was a magical time. No duty charts. No schedules."

I started to get a bad feeling about this.

"Then Sylvia told me she was pregnant. She said she couldn't possibly cope by herself with another child. But there was no way I would leave Corinne and my two children. Sylvia decided on an abortion." Fred wound the paper strip around his finger, so tightly that the tip turned red. "Corinne and I had been going through some tough times. She'd been offered a promotion in the Connecticut office, but Kyle and Bronwyn didn't want to move. Neither did I. We'd been fighting about it for weeks. When I told her about Sylvia, Corinne stomped out of the house. Was gone for three days."

"That's the story Kyle told us, wasn't it?" I asked. "That his mother took off for a couple of days when he was a child, and the grandparents kept him and Bronwyn while you searched for her."

"Yes. And by the time Corinne came back, she had it all figured out. We would raise Sylvia's child as our own. But we would cut all ties with Sylvia once the baby was born. We would never see or speak to her again. Sylvia agreed, and Corinne gave her a big financial settlement to seal the deal."

"Surely the children figured out their mother wasn't pregnant?"

"Corinne had a plan for that. She took the promotion and we moved to Connecticut. She wore maternity clothes and strap-on baby bellies at work. We sent Kyle and Bronwyn to their grandparents for the summer, so they wouldn't be around to ask too many questions. When the baby was born, the children came home to meet their new little sister. They never suspected she wasn't their mother's child."

I could almost hear Randall's jaws grinding. "The baby was Holliss?"

"Yes."

"So when Corinne said Holliss wasn't her daughter ..." Randall said.

"She meant not her *biological* daughter," Fred said. "Which is the truth."

Randall chewed his lip. "Does Holliss know?"

"No." Fred massaged his forehead. "We thought about telling her. Even practiced the story a few times, trying to make it something a child could understand. But the time never seemed right."

"And Corinne hated Holliss?" Randall asked, his voice angry.

"No, it wasn't like that," Fred said. "Corinne tried hard to be a good mom. At first, everything seemed okay. But as Holliss got older, things got more tense. It would have helped if Holliss had been blond and blue-eyed like Kyle and Bronwyn. But she looked so much like me. And she had Sylvia's green eyes, which sent a dagger into Corinne's heart every time she saw her."

He yanked down the flyer and crumpled it into a ball. "When Holliss was thirteen or so, Sylvia called me. She had breast cancer and wanted to make peace with her sister. Corinne went to see her. But instead of bringing peace between them, it brought back all the anger Corinne had locked in for so many years. After Sylvia died, Corinne and I fought constantly. She screamed at Holliss, too, but until I heard Holliss's story tonight about her tattoo, I never realized how bad it had been."

"So you shipped Holliss off to college?" Randall said, his voice rising. "When she was only sixteen?"

"It was the best choice for all of us," Fred insisted. "Holliss had always had a tough time in school. She was a genius, so far ahead of the other kids that it was hard for her to adjust."

"And it got her out of your life. So you and Corinne didn't have to deal with her anymore. How could you do that to your own child?"

"Believe me, she fit in much better in college than in high school," Fred said. "Especially after she met you, Madeline. Corinne was always grateful for your friendship toward Holliss. That's why she hired you to spearhead her campaign, to thank you for what you'd done."

"But why did she run for the Senate in the first place?" I asked. "What did Natalie have to do with it?"

Fred's face paled. "After Sylvia died, Corinne was consumed by guilt. She tried to make it up to Natalie, sending her gifts, calling her, visiting now and again."

I was puzzled. "Bronwyn said Corinne hadn't had any contact with Natalie since you guys moved to Connecticut."

"Corinne didn't want the children to know. She was humiliated that I had cheated on her with her own sister. As long as we kept Natalie at a distance, we could keep the affair a secret." He was deep into the story now, pulling dark shards from the past into light. "When Natalie got pregnant, Corinne saw it as a second chance. She could be there for Natalie the way she never had for her own sister. She planned to stay with her when the baby was born.

"Then a hurricane hit right before Natalie's due date, a category four, stronger than anything they'd had in that part of the country. Lightning. Thunder. Falling trees. The stress started Natalie's labor, and her doctor insisted she come to the hospital right away." Fred's sentences came faster as he spooled out the story. "The rescue squads were already out on calls. Natalie couldn't wait. She started for the hospital. Through torrential rain. Winds over 140 miles per hour. Crossing a bridge, they tried their best to maintain control, but the water ... the winds ... it was impossible. The car slid into the river."

"That's horrible," I said.

"Corinne felt so guilty. I thought she was going to slip into another huge depression, like she did when Sylvia died. She went back to her therapist, went back on her medication, but it didn't seem to help."

"I don't understand," I said. "Why did Corinne feel guilty about this?"

"Because Natalie's husband was out of town. Corinne had gone down early to stay with her. When the car went off the bridge, Corinne was driving."

"Oh, my God." I could understand why Corinne felt so guilty.

"She pulled Natalie out of the car, but the current was too strong. They all got swept downriver. Corinne made it to shore. Natalie didn't. They found her body the next day." Fred's shoulders drooped. "I tried to convince Corinne that it wasn't her fault. That with a hurricane that strong, there was nothing else she could have done. But she was inconsolable." He crossed his arms over his chest. "That storm was on the news for weeks. Everybody said global warming caused it. And that things would only get worse if we couldn't figure out a way to manage climate change. That's when Corinne decided to run for the Senate. To fix the environment, so that what happened to Natalie would never happen to anyone else."

"She couldn't save Natalie, but maybe she could save the planet?" I asked.

"Exactly. It was the only way she could deal with the guilt."

Randall jumped to his feet. "But not Holliss? She didn't want to save Holliss?" Bits of froth formed at the edges of his mouth. "You were a coward, Fred. You and Corinne, both. You should have told Holliss the truth."

"You're right, we should have. But it happened so long ago. And it wouldn't have changed the way Corinne thought about Holliss."

Randall sprang toward Fred, slamming him against the wall. "But it might have changed the way Holliss felt about herself."

"Randall, stop." I grabbed his arm as he trapped Fred in a chokehold. "Let him go."

Randall slung me away. "Stay out of this."

Fred struggled to twist free, dragging Randall back toward the sofa. They collided with the coffee table, losing their balance and falling to their knees.

The door flew open. "What's going on in here?" A nurse glared at the two men thrashing on the floor. "Stop that. Get up, both of you."

Startled, Randall released his grip. Fred grabbed for the sofa as he pulled himself to his feet.

"This is a hospital," the nurse said. "Your behavior is unacceptable."

Randall took a step toward Fred. The nurse moved between them, thrusting out her arms to keep them apart. "All of you need to leave," she said. "Right now."

***

I was still shaking when I got back to the hotel. I had always thought of Randall as a mild-mannered professor, someone focused on creating esoteric theories to explain the workings of financial markets, a man of thought rather than action, content to view the world through a cerebral filter. I had been convinced that he had nothing to do with Corinne's death. But now that I knew he had struggled with Corinne, now that I'd seen him attack Fred, I wasn't so sure.

I needed to talk to Travis. It was late, a bit short of midnight, but I hoped he was still awake. I needed to get his advice and figure out our next move.

Exiting the hotel elevator, I headed for room 406. The ice dispenser at the end of the hall made a clunking sound. As I turned the corner, a young woman with long dark hair stepped into the hallway, balancing an ice bucket on her hip. She was barefoot, dressed in a gray T-shirt which barely covered her buttocks, skimming the tops of her long muscular legs.

She padded softly down the hallway. As she reached her room and held the key card against the lock, her shoulders angled toward me. On the front of her T-shirt was a silk-screened ibex, head bent slightly to the side, the ridged horns curved back. I knew that shirt. Had seen it only a few hours ago.

I hugged the wall until I heard the door click shut. She had entered a room three doors down from the ice machine. The soft carpet swallowed the sound of my steps as I checked out the room numbers. Room 402. Room 404. And then the third one, the one she had entered. Room 406. Travis's room.

Chapter 37

I STOOD there for a few minutes, staring so hard at Travis's room number that I could almost see wisps of smoke coming off it. If I touched it, I was sure it would burn my fingertips. I balled up my fist, ready to pound on the door, to see his surprised scrambling as he tried to explain why Eva was spending the night in his room. But pride won out over emotion. Rushing back down the hall, I impatiently stabbed the elevator button until the doors opened. I had believed him when he said he wanted us to get back together. That he'd give me time to think about our relationship. Time must pass differently in his world than in mine. It had been barely three hours since he'd left my room.

Right now they were having drinks together while they reminisced about past adventures, all those things they giggled about on the drive to Speyer. Would he kiss her neck the same way he did mine, his lips running from her earlobe to her shoulder? Or was there a different technique for each conquest?

My ankle hurt as I stomped off the elevator toward my room, but I welcomed the pain. It helped blur the vision of him pulling that T-shirt over her head, laughing as he tossed it to the floor. Slamming my door shut, I dug my phone from my purse, ready to call him, to tell him we needed to meet right now. I wanted to hear him squirm, stammering as he struggled to come up with a convincing lie of why this wasn't a good time for him. But then I slung my phone into the chair. Let him have his fling. I had done without him for two years. I didn't need him now.

Fumbling through the medicine bottles in my nightstand, I shook a sleeping pill into my palm and washed it down with a bit of water. Not even bothering to change out of my street clothes, I collapsed into bed.

***

Travis was already in the hotel restaurant when I went down for breakfast the next morning. "Hey, what happened to you last night?" he said, waving me over to his table. "Eva came back to update us on her conversation with Müller. I kept calling you, but you never answered."

Would he have sounded so innocent if he knew I'd seen Eva outside his room last night? "I was at the hospital. Holliss had some issues. They were worried about the baby."

He stood up and pulled out a chair for me. "Is she all right?"

"They're keeping her for observation." I shook my head at the chair. "I'm not staying, thanks."

"You haven't already eaten, have you?"

"I'm getting something to go." The thought of a leisurely breakfast with Travis held little appeal. All I could think of was Eva sauntering into his room with that ice bucket.

"Come on, at least have some coffee with me. I've got a lot to tell you." He signaled for the waiter. "Now what about Holliss? What's going on?"

Reluctantly I sat down, shaking my head as the waiter offered a menu. "I think she's all right. They're still doing tests. Randall stayed at the hospital all night." I reached for the cream. "He called this morning. He's coming back to the hotel to shower and change, but then he's going back. He'll stay with her until she's released." I stirred my coffee. "So, what did Eva tell you?"

Flaky bits of pastry cascaded down to his plate as he broke off a piece of croissant. "Mueller's frustrated. The police have interviewed everyone who was working there that day … the café staff, the gift shop people, the ticket takers … everybody. Nobody saw Corinne go off that platform. And security cameras didn't pick it up, either."

"How about tourists? Have the police talked to any of them?"

"They're trying, but it's not easy. They've been tracking down people who used credit cards, even though most of them aren't even in the country anymore. You guys would be in Germany or France right now, if you hadn't come back to Lucerne for Corinne." He popped the croissant in his mouth. "If they paid cash, there's no record of them."

That meant there were no witnesses to Randall's argument with Corinne. No evidence tying him to the murder, at least until those DNA results came back. "You're saying Mueller can't find the killer?"

"I'm saying it's more challenging than he expected. Eva called him last night and sent my videos from Basel. He's very interested in following up. In fact, he wants to see you this morning. I've got his number so you can call him." He pulled a slip of paper from his shirt pocket.

"I'm surprised." I entered the number into the contact list on my phone. The number I had for him rang through the station switchboard. This must be his direct cell. "I thought he'd brush that off as too much of a long shot."

"You're not giving Mueller enough credit. He's busting his ass to figure this out. Eva's also got him investigating the riverboat crew."

"Did she ask him about the journal? Do the police have it?"

"Yes, they've got it."

"Has Mueller read it? Did he tell Eva what it said?"

"Mueller wouldn't, but Eva's got another source, someone who works in the evidence room. She should have some details for us before too much longer."

"She's a real Wonder Woman, isn't she? What would we do without her?"

"You don't like her. What's going on? You barely know her."

"I don't dislike her. Like you said, I barely know her. Give us another couple of weeks, and I'm sure we'll be best buddies."

"There's no way this is dragging on another couple of weeks. Kyle and Bronwyn were at the front desk this morning, arranging transportation. The four of them are flying out of Zurich tomorrow, heading home." Travis reached for his coffee. "What about you? How much longer will you be here?"

"I don't know. Maybe I'll head out tomorrow, too. It's not like I'm accomplishing great things here. Besides, Lilly needs me back in the office." I stood up. "I'll give Mueller a call, see if I can get him to focus on this protestor instead of Randall."

"You sure Randall's not guilty?"

If I had met with Travis last night, I would have told him the whole story of Randall's fight with Corinne. But after he spent the night with Eva, I wasn't willing to share those secrets. "I've known Randall for years. He's quiet and unassuming. He would never hurt anyone."

Travis shrugged. "Most anyone can commit murder if someone they love is threatened. And often it's the quiet ones you need to worry about the most."

Chapter 38

THE POLICE station was almost deserted when I walked in, only a few officers sitting at their desks, checking paperwork and manning the phones. A uniformed young man escorted me to Mueller's office.

He stood up as I walked in. "Thank you for coming in so early." The lines around Mueller's eyes were carved deeper than when I had seen him last. "I understand you have some information regarding the Peerland case."

His small office, with its dingy off-white walls and battered filing cabinets, convinced me that whatever the Swiss police spent their money on, it was not interior decorating. I sat in a hard, utilitarian chair positioned across from Mueller's steel-gray metal desk. A large dent kicked into the side indicated that at least one investigation had not gone well.

"I told you before that Mrs. Peerland had been roughed up at the energy conference in Basel. I realize now that the men who attacked her were also at Pilatus the day she was killed. They should be considered murder suspects."

Mueller flipped open his notepad and reached for a pen. "Why did you not mention this previously?"

"I didn't make the connection at first. When I saw them at Pilatus, they looked familiar, but I couldn't place them. And then Travis Lawson showed me a video last night of the protests. I believe Eva Graesser sent it to you."

"Yes, I have it." He pulled up the file on his computer.

I walked behind his desk, close enough that I got a great view of a clogged pore on the side of his nose. His frown was a clear signal that invading his personal space was a serious offense. "Excuse me?" he said.

"I'm sorry, but this won't take a minute. If you will play the video?" He clicked on the screen and the video started. "The man on the bullhorn is the same one who followed me a few nights ago. With the blond hair and glasses? He was at Pilatus, only I didn't recognize him at first because he wore a baseball cap. And this one, with the narrow face and high cheekbones, wore a striped knit cap.

He was also at Pilatus. There was a group of them, sitting by the window while Corinne was in the café with her family."

Mueller enlarged the picture. "Did they talk with her? Follow her out of the café?"

"No, I didn't see anything like that. But they were definitely staring at her."

He stopped the video. "Staring is not a crime."

"But murder is. They saw her talking with Kiener at the conference and figured she was on the side of big oil. They followed her to Pilatus after they killed him."

"We don't know yet who killed Kiener."

"Then you don't know that these guys didn't do it."

Mueller tapped a rapid staccato with his pen. "A lot of these people are college students. They are very emotional about climate change, taking to the streets all over Switzerland. Did you know that our country is warming at twice the global rate?"

"No. I didn't realize that." Was he willing to give these guys a pass because they were young and emotional, anxious to protect their country?

Mueller's chair squeaked loudly as he leaned back. "Climate warming is serious business for us, Ms. Keswick. Glaciers are melting everywhere."

I was as concerned as the next person about melting glaciers and warming oceans and rising sea levels. But even more than that, I wanted to protect Holliss and Randall. "Mrs. Peerland was very aware of the dangers of climate change. Her Senate campaign focused on finding a global solution. That's why she went to the energy conference. To learn cutting-edge solutions to this problem." I rapped my fingers on his desk. "Do you think you can find these men? Bring them in for questioning?"

There was a smugness in his tone. "The Basel police have them in custody."

"That's wonderful news. So now you'll leave Randall Epperly alone? Give him back his passport?"

"I will not comment on the status of Mr. Epperly's passport."

"How much longer are you going to focus on him as a suspect? Did you know that Randall's wife Holliss is in the hospital right now, at risk of losing her baby, because of your constant questions, the stress you're putting them under?"

"I did not know that. I am very sorry."

"Sorry is not good enough. You need to find this killer."

He colored at my attack. "And you need to stop interfering in police business. Going back to the riverboat, questioning suspects."

"I wouldn't do that if you could move this process a little faster. I don't understand what's taking so long. Have you finished interviewing the riverboat staff? How about Corinne's gold necklace … have you found it yet? And when are you going to interrogate the protestors?" The questions spilled out, one after another. I knew better than to attack him like that, but my emotions had banished all logic from my brain, causing venomous words to pour out on autopilot. "Holliss Epperly has been a good friend for many years. I will do whatever it takes to protect her and her husband."

He stood up, spinning his chair backwards. "Our department is following all leads and examining all the evidence. When we have enough proof, we will make an arrest. I understand that you are a friend of the family. That you want to help them. But you can help the most by staying out of our way." He walked around me and opened the office door, gesturing toward a uniformed woman standing in the hallway. "Officer Pulfer, will you please escort Ms. Keswick to the exit."

I stormed away from the police station, frustrated that Mueller wouldn't listen to me. But even more frustrated with myself, for fumbling that interview. Public relations was my job. Usually, I was good at dealing with people. Figuring out what they wanted. Writing persuasive copy to bring them around to my point of view. But that skill went up in smoke when I was around Mueller. Why did he bring out the absolute worst in me?

My phone chirped with an incoming text. I fished it from my purse, squinting as the glare of the sun obscured the screen, and moved to the shade of a nearby building for a clearer view.

The message was from Travis. *Eva has a copy of Corinne's journal. Meet us at Andre's Café.*

I typed the name into my phone. It showed that Andre's was within walking of the police station. "On my way," I texted back.

Chapter 39

I FOLLOWED the maze-like map on my screen, turning corner after corner until I finally spotted the green awning of Andre's Café. Eva and Travis sat at a table near the window, their heads chummily close as they stared down at their phones. Today her hair was pulled back and secured with a giant clip. Dark tendrils curled down in front of silver hoop earrings. A disadvantage of an impromptu night with a boyfriend, I guessed—no supplies on hand to recreate her typical flowing hairstyle.

Signaling to the waiter for coffee, I pulled out a chair beside Travis. "Where's the journal?"

"Morning, Madeline." Eva smiled, totally without remorse. But then, why should she feel guilt for their midnight rendezvous? She didn't know the history between Travis and me. She was rekindling a relationship with an old boyfriend, same as I was. It was Travis who was the bad guy here, trying to double dip. "My guy in the evidence room didn't give me a lot of time with the journal, but I was able to take screen shots of everything Corinne wrote in the past month." She poised her thumbs over the keyboard. "What's your email? I'll send them to you."

My phone dinged and I opened the files, turning the phone sideways for a larger view. "You two have already read this? What did Corinne say? Anything about Sergey?"

Travis shook his head. "We just started. It's a real info dump—lots about climate change and her plans for the campaign. Sounds like she was really pleased with the work you were doing."

"Good to hear." I had been so excited to work on my first Senate campaign, anticipating all the doors it would open for Lilly and me, convinced it would bring in much-needed business to our firm. That was all over now. We'd have to come up with a new plan to replace those lost commissions. If we kept our expenses low, then maybe …

I mentally smacked myself as I realized what I was doing. The woman had been my friend, my mentor. She had been dead only a few days, and already I was writing her off as merely a failed business venture. Worse than that, I was ready to dig into her journal, exposing her most private thoughts. "Guys, are you sure we should be doing this? I mean, maybe we should leave this up to the family."

"Hey, you're the one who told us about the journal," Travis said. "That it might expose Sergey or Klaus as a murderer. We're following your lead. What's with the cold feet?"

"Having flashbacks to my teenage years, I guess. Thinking of that horrible time my mom read my diary and found out what I was really doing all those weekends when I told her I was at sleepovers at a girlfriend's house. I got grounded for a month."

"You quit writing in your diary?" Eva asked.

"No, but after that, I started writing everything in code. She couldn't figure out what I was talking about."

"Fortunately for us," Eva said, "Corinne was very straightforward—no code here."

"Great." The waiter brought my coffee. I reached for a sugar packet. "What's our strategy? It's a lot to get through."

"Let's break it into thirds," Travis suggested. "Eva, you take the first section. I'll pick up the middle. Madeline, check out the final ten pages. Share anything you think is important."

"Sounds good." I thumbed through the screens to find my section.

After a few minutes of focused reading, Eva said, "She really was committed to this climate change stuff. She talks about Japan, how they shut down all their nuclear plants a couple of years ago after that tsunami. They switched to coal, but that made air pollution worse. She planned to reach out to them to discuss alternative energy sources."

"She talks about climate change in my section, too," Travis said. "Did you know that the Great Barrier Reef has had three catastrophic coral bleaching events in the last few years, due to rising ocean temperatures? And that several states back home are in danger of losing their state birds due to higher temperatures? Songbirds fly greater distances to find cooler weather. To compensate, their bodies are getting smaller and their wings longer."

"How in the world did she know all this stuff?' Eva asked. "She's like a climate-change guru."

"She was passionate about it," I said. "Did a lot of research. Talked to people in the field. Even managed to get herself on the boards of some environmental non-profits."

"You're okay that she only took up the cause a few years ago?" Travis asked.

I picked up my coffee, stalling for time as I figured out how to explain my change of heart. "Last night at the hospital, Fred told me a lot of things about Corinne that I didn't know." I remembered his face, pale and tortured as he confessed his infidelity and the tragic events that followed. Corinne had felt guilty for disowning her sister and locking Natalie out of her life. Running for office and trying to save the planet were her attempts to set things right, even if it put her other children at risk. "I can't share all that with you guys—Fred hasn't even told everything to the family yet—but I'm convinced that Corinne was sincere about improving the environment."

Eva spoke up. "Hey, guys, listen to this: *Not sure Emily will ever fit in with our family. Smart. Ambitious. But does she love Kyle, or only his new company?*"

"I agree with Corinne on that one," I said. "Emily will stick with Kyle as long as she's learning from him. But once she has this entrepreneurship thing all figured out, I wouldn't be surprised if she went out on her own."

"You ambitious women are heartless," Travis said. "We guys don't have much of a chance against you."

"Men have controlled the world for too long." Eva's smile was seductive. "It's about time you shared the power."

Being around these two lovebirds was about to make me barf. I chugged down some coffee to distract myself, which triggered a coughing jag as it went down the wrong way.

"You okay?" Travis asked, slapping my back.

"Fine," I mumbled.

"This woman had issues," Eva said. "She should have been seeing a therapist. But then, I guess the journal was her therapy. I can see why she hid it from everyone." She held up her phone and began to read. "*I've tried to love Holliss, but all I feel is anger and guilt. I don't deserve a grandchild.*"

Travis winced. "That hurts. Maybe Mueller's right about Randall. With vibes like that between Corinne and Holliss, he could have easily been persuaded to get rid of Corinne."

Eva skimmed through the pages and read another passage. "*Bronwyn was a fool to give Kyle the Princeton money. Her problem, not mine.*" She reached for her coffee. "What's that about?"

"Bronwyn invested her son's college fund in Kyle's company," I said. "He won't give it back until the company goes public."

"Nice family." Travis held up his phone. "Here's another one: *What if my campaign to save the planet destroys my family? They are all so upset with me. Kyle's afraid the media scrutiny will unearth those secrets we so carefully buried, making his investors run for the exits.*" His eyes focused on mine. "What secrets does Kyle have?"

"Not sure," I said. "Something happened in Italy, right after he sold his company, but I haven't been able to figure out what it was. Lilly is digging into it for me."

"Wow," Travis said. "I was already suspicious of Kyle. And what about Bronwyn? You said she got a manicure right after she sprained her finger. Who does that unless you have a dead woman's DNA under your fingernails, and you want to make sure all the evidence gets scraped out?"

"Women always hang out at the spa when they're on a cruise. I got a manicure, too. So did Emily. It doesn't mean either of us killed Corinne." I went back to my screen. "Here's something."

"What is it?" Eva asked.

"*Allergy attack tonight. Someone stole my poker money,*" I read. "The word *someone* was underlined three times."

"Sounds like she knew who stole the money. Did she say who it was?"

I shook my head. "No. And that's the last entry."

"I guess we'll never know who she suspected," Travis said.

"I guess not." I was thankful that she hadn't mentioned Holliss by name. Holliss obviously wasn't physically capable of hoisting her mother over that guardrail, but could she have convinced Randall to do it? Had she waited all these years to get even with her mother, and finally saw the opportunity? Was I wrong to defend him?

"Well," Eva said, "Madeline, I know you want to think the riverboat guys killed her, or the climate people, but it seems to me there's plenty of motive right here in the family. And Mueller thinks so, too, even though he's still checking into all those other leads."

"He's convinced Randall did it."

"Not necessarily. He's got his eye on everyone."

"I have to agree," Travis said. "I think someone in the family did this. And I'd put my money on Kyle. Maybe with help from Bronwyn. But how are we going to prove it?"

Eva suddenly snapped her fingers. "I've got an idea of how we can know for sure if the family's involved. But I'll need Mueller's help to pull it off. Let me go talk to him, and I'll get back with you guys as soon as I can. In the meantime, don't say anything to the family about any of this. Agreed?"

"Agreed," Travis said.

"Madeline?"

I wanted to warn Holliss. To tell her and Randall to get out of Switzerland, to leave this nightmare behind. But I wanted to be fair to Corinne, too. As much as I cared for Holliss, if Randall had killed Corinne, could I let him escape?

Travis noticed my hesitation. "The family's getting on a plane tomorrow. Once they've left Switzerland, it will be harder for Mueller to bring them to justice. Corinne was your client. Your friend. If one of them did kill her, do you really want them to get away with it?"

"No. Of course not. Okay. Not a word to anyone. But what's the plan?"

Eva tucked her phone into her pocket. "You said the family was worried about what might be in the journal, right?"

"Yes. They wanted to see it before the police did."

She grinned. "Let's make that happen. And make the killer show his hand."

Chapter 40

AFTER EVA left to meet with Mueller, Travis and I headed back to the hotel. "What's this grand plan that Eva's cooked up?" I asked him.

"No idea. But she's pretty creative. Whatever she comes up with, it might break this case open. Can you deal with that? I know you've gotten close to the family in the last couple of days."

"Her plan might prove the family is innocent."

"Yeah. Maybe."

My phone buzzed as we neared the corner.

"That can't be Eva," Travis said. "She can't have wrapped up her meeting with Müller already."

"It's Holliss." I put the phone to my ear. "How are you feeling?"

"Much better." Her voice sounded strong. "I'm back at the hotel."

"The hotel? Shouldn't you still be in the hospital?"

"The doctor thinks I'll be fine if I stay off my I feet for a few days. He said it was stress and dehydration." She paused. "I'm so embarrassed that I dragged you out of bed last night. I apologize."

"Don't worry about that. I'm glad I could be there." A passerby brushed against me. I backed up against a building to get out of pedestrian traffic. "Is there anything I can get you? I'm on my way to the hotel right now."

"You don't need to do that. Randall is falling all over himself to take care of me. He makes me feel like some fragile porcelain doll, ready to break at any moment."

"Are you sure? I can be there in ten, maybe twenty minutes, tops."

"I don't need anything, but there is something I want you to do."

"Name it."

"Dad told me the rest of the family is heading home tomorrow. I want you to go with them. You've been away from your job long enough. Time to get back to work. Mom would want that."

I wanted to go home, but I didn't want to leave Holliss behind. "What about you? Are you leaving tomorrow?"

"No, the doctor doesn't want me to fly yet. Besides, the police have Randall's passport, so he can't leave, and I won't go without him. But dad will still be here with us, at least for a few more days. He's finalizing all the arrangements for Mom. And he's working with Randall's lawyer to get him cleared of these ridiculous charges."

"Fred's with you?" Fred and Randall must not have told her the truth about her mother. She sounded much too calm to have gotten news like that.

"Yes. He felt terrible when he heard my story last night about the tattoo. He admitted that he'd neglected me back then. We've been having a lot of good conversations, trying to make up for lost time."

"Good to hear." I wondered how long it would take him to tell her the truth.

"Anyway, I wanted to let you know where I was," Holliss said. "We're getting lunch, and then I'm going to my room for a nap. I'll see you later this afternoon."

"Take care."

"What did she say?" Travis asked as I hung up.

"She's out of the hospital, but she needs to stay off her feet for a few days. Considering how weak she was last night, I'm amazed." I dropped my phone into my purse. "Holliss wants me to go home tomorrow with the rest of the family."

"She's leaving tomorrow?" Travis sounded surprised.

"No. She and Randall will stay her until her doctor clears her to fly. And Fred's staying with them. But she's hopeful they can leave soon."

Travis raised an eyebrow. "You think Mueller will agree to that?"

Not if he gets those DNA results, I thought. "Holliss thinks their lawyer can straighten everything out. She doesn't expect a problem."

"So everything's fixed?" Travis asked.

"That's what she thinks. I hope she's right."

***

Eva called us a few hours later. The three of us rendezvoused at a café near the hotel. "What the hell did you say to Mueller this morning?" Eva asked as she approached our table, her eyes flashing.

I wriggled out of my jacket. "What do you mean?"

Her chair scraped loudly as she pulled it toward her. "I figured out a fantastic plan to flush out the killer, using Corinne's journal. Mueller was interested until he found out it involved you. Then he turned me down flat."

"Why was that?"

"He doesn't like you. He doesn't trust you. Doesn't want you to be part of this." She sat down, scooting her chair slightly closer to Travis, claiming her territory.

"Let's say we have different points of view on how he should proceed with his investigation. He's ignoring some suspects."

"That's not true," she said. "Everyone is still in the mix, but his instincts tell him someone in the family is the murderer. He was apoplectic when I told him they were leaving town tomorrow. Once they are back across the Atlantic, his job becomes much harder. Unless he's ready to confiscate everyone's passport, which doesn't seem to be the case, he needs to make a bold move to close this thing. So he finally agreed to my plan."

"Which is?" I asked.

"There's a big concert tonight at the Jesuit cathedral, that big one across the river. A group from Germany is performing the Brandenburg Concertos."

"The Brandenburg Concertos?" Travis asked.

"You know, by Bach? It's famous. Everybody loves it." She hummed a few lines.

He nodded. "Oh, yes, I recognize that."

"Madeline, you tell the family that I went to the riverboat today and found Corinne's journal. Tell them I'm meeting you at the concert to hand it over. Then you'll bring it back to the hotel so everyone can check it out before we give it to the police."

"I don't get it," Travis said. "How will that identify the murderer?"

She seemed frustrated that he had missed the obvious. "Don't you see, whoever is guilty won't want to take the chance that Corinne fingered him in her journal. He'll try to grab it from Madeline, before she takes it back to the hotel."

I thought about that for a few minutes. I guess it made sense. "You figure if no one shows up at the cathedral, it proves that it's not a family member that killed Corinne?"

"That's my thought," Eva said.

"And Mueller bought into this?" Travis asked. "That's a flimsy plan. If no one shows up for a sneak peek at the journal, that doesn't mean they're innocent. Maybe they don't think Corinne would have suspected them. After all, we didn't find anything in the journal that implicated anyone."

"Travis, don't throw cold water on this," Eva cautioned. "It wasn't easy to persuade Müller. I'm convinced this will work, and he's willing to give it a try. Besides, can you think of anything better?"

"Well, no, but …"

"Let me get this straight," I said. "If no one shows up at the cathedral for the handoff, Mueller will back off from the family? Focus instead on Sergey and Klaus? And the guys from Basel?"

"Well, I can't promise that," Eva said. "But it would be my assumption."

"What do I need to do?"

Eva pulled a folded paper from her jacket and smoothed it out on the table. "Here's a floor plan of the cathedral. The musicians will be upstairs in the balcony. Madeline, you sit here, near the back. I'll come in with the journal near the end of the concert. Mueller will have the place packed with plainclothes officers. If somebody shows up to claim the journal, they'll grab him."

"Mueller's giving you the journal?" Travis asked.

"Of course not," Eva said. "He's having a dummy copy made right now. Same size. Same cover. Even a bunch of pages which forge Corinne's handwriting."

Travis put a finger on the floor plan and pulled it closer. After studying it a few minutes, he said, "I don't like this. It's too dangerous."

"What's dangerous about it?" Eva asked. "We'll be surrounded by policemen."

He leaned back in his chair. "Let's say you're right—someone in the family is the killer, and he shows up to grab the journal. He's going to be nervous, suspicious, desperate to get away. He won't give up easily when the police close in. It sounds so simple, but there are a hundred ways it could go wrong. And both of you will be in the crosshairs."

It was nice to think that Travis was worried about me. Of course, he was worried about Eva, too. How charming that he didn't want either of his love interests to get hurt.

"I'm willing to take that chance," I said firmly. "We need to resolve this, so all of us can get out of here and head home."

"Why doesn't he send in a policewoman to do this?" Travis asked. "Why does it have to be you?"

"Because I told him the family knew me," Eva said. "If someone else tried to deliver the book, they'd realize something was wrong."

"That's a lie," I said. "They've never met you."

"But Mueller doesn't know that. And I'm not taking the chance that someone else gets to this story before I do. This plan is my idea."

"I still don't like it," Travis said. "This isn't some kind of lark, like running with the bulls in Pamplona." Several years ago he and I had channeled our inner Hemingway in that Spanish city, scampering aside as pounding hooves claimed center real estate in the narrow cobblestone streets. One young man, fueled by an overpowering mix of sangria and testosterone, vaulted to the broad back of a stampeding bull. The frenzied animal tossed him to the street, lowering its head to run a curved horn along the back of his thigh. The man staggered to his feet, bleeding but triumphant, as his buddies cheered. "This is serious. You're squaring off with a murderer."

"Come on, guys. Mueller thinks this is worth a shot." Eva worked to persuade us. "He'll have plenty of backup at the cathedral."

I was ready to take action, tired of being on the sidelines. "So how do we set this up? Should I call everybody and tell them I'll be at the cathedral tonight?"

Eva pulled a paper from her pocket and slid it toward me. "Mueller wants you to send them a group text. So everyone gets exactly the same message, at exactly the same time."

"He doesn't want me to tell them in person?" I asked, surprised. "What if someone doesn't check their messages? That would screw this up."

Eva hesitated. "Can't be helped. Mueller doesn't trust you. Thinks you'll tip off the murderer if you deliver the news in person."

"I wouldn't do that," I said indignantly.

"Maybe not intentionally. But it would all too easy to let something slip, an expression, a tone of voice ... to let them know something's up. And that would spoil the whole thing."

She was right. Holliss would know I was hiding something. And she would be sure to tell Randall. "I understand." I reached for the paper and unfolded it. The message was short and concise, laying out the basics of the plan. It didn't say, *Be at the cathedral if you want to snare the journal before the police see it*, but it came pretty darn close. It wouldn't take a rocket scientist to figure this out. I began to type Mueller's text into my phone. "Let's do this."

Chapter 41

THE DISCORDANT squawks of tuning instruments drifted down from the balcony as I entered the cathedral later that evening. Eva had been right about the Brandenberg Concertos being popular. Most of the cavernous nave was already filled, with people jamming the aisles as they searched for seats. I found an empty spot about six rows from the back, the wooden pew creaking as I sat down. Pretending to study the concert program, I peeked out at the audience, trying to spot Mueller's undercover policemen.

I ruled out all the elderly couples, neatly dressed for an evening of culture. Many of the jeans-clad millennials scattered throughout the church seemed likely candidates, including the woman sitting several rows in front of me. With her hair pulled back in a ponytail, sunglasses perched on top of her head and a map of Lucerne poking out of her backpack, she seemed to be trying a little too hard to play tourist.

I didn't see anyone from the family. I hoped they were all innocent and this whole exercise was a big waste of time. But they could be hiding in the wings somewhere, or up in the balcony, waiting for the end of the concert. Ready to grab the journal.

Nervous, I tried to clear my mind, to let the beauty of the cathedral calm me. Soaring white arches framed the elaborate gold-tipped altar and rimmed the delicately painted ceiling. Fading sunlight filtered weakly through the stained-glass windows, the duskiness offset by strategically placed chandeliers.

The musty smell of well-worn hymnals and burning candles reminded me of the church I had attended as a child. My sister and I would reluctantly follow our parents down the aisle toward my mother's favorite pew—on the left, ten rows from the front—close enough for the priest to keep an eye on me. Mom would pinch me if I squirmed too much or fell asleep during the sermon. Back then the routine of church had been reassuring, even if I understood little of the prayers and homilies. That reassurance was broken when my dad died unexpectedly in his mid-thirties, around the same age I was now. I hadn't been back to church since.

The audience gradually settled into their seats. The priest made his way to the front to welcome everyone and give us some background on Bach and the concertos. A few minutes later the concert started. The spirited opening made me think of a Renaissance ballroom, with elegant women in long dresses being spun around the floor by noblemen wearing form-fitting knee pants and white stockings.

Listening carefully, I could pick out the high notes of the recorders and the smooth melody of the violins, even though I wasn't an expert on orchestral music. Did the low notes come from a cello, perhaps? A bass?

My mind drifted as I tried to follow the music, checking to see if any family members had shown up. So far, I hadn't spotted any familiar faces.

The concert progressed to the adagio movement, mournful and mystical. Across the aisle from me, a white-haired elderly woman struggled to stay awake. She nodded once, twice, three times as her eyes closed. When her head dropped to the side, she jerked abruptly upright, fumbling for her program. But the soothing music was too much for her. A few minutes later she succumbed to sleep, her chin drifting down until it touched her chest.

The musicians played over the next hour. I followed the program as the orchestra transitioned through the first several movements, but then I closed my eyes and let the notes wash over me. Much sooner than I expected, the orchestra finished. The priest returned to the front, leading the audience in rousing applause.

Everyone slowly filed out, clogging the aisles. Eva would be making her way toward me now. Would anyone show up to snatch the journal?

Suddenly the chandeliers were switched off, plunging the nave into darkness. Around me, people shifted anxiously, trying to figure out what was happening, waiting for someone to turn the lights back on. Then a woman screamed, "Help! He's got a gun."

Everyone panicked, stampeding toward the exits, stumbling in the dark. People shouted as they tried to figure out what was happening, to understand the threat. Was it a terrorist? A suicide bomber? They rushed to get out of the church, away from danger. The white-haired elderly woman stepped into the aisle, where she was broadsided by a fleeing backpacker. I grabbed her arm as she fell to her knees, and then eased her back into the pew.

The map-toting woman seated in front of me ran toward the confusion. I raced behind her, searching for Eva, trying to see what was happening. Travis was bent over in the back row.

"Travis, what happened?" I called out. "Are you all right?"

As I got closer, I could see a woman was sprawled out on the pew, eyes closed. Travis pressed his hands against the bloody wound in her stomach. "It's Eva. She's been stabbed."

Chapter 42

"OH, MY GOD," I said, leaning over the pew. "Did you see who did this?"

Travis shook his head. "No. He was too quick for me. And he got the journal."

The map-toting woman stood beside him, summoning help on her cell phone. I hurried to the front exit. A lone figure dressed in black sweatpants and a black hoodie bounded down the sidewalk, chased by muscular men that I figured were part of Mueller's undercover crew.

The figure had a good lead over his pursuers. I tried to figure out who it was. Please don't be Randall, I thought. Holliss would never survive if she lost him. He was her anchor, the person who'd helped her through all the wildness of her college years.

My ankle wobbled as I skipped down the cathedral steps, and I grabbed the railing to maintain my balance. The runner was thin and fast. Could it be Kyle? He had told me how miserable he was after he sold his first company. Could he have killed his mother to prevent his new company from going under?

The runner seemed too short to be Kyle, although it was difficult to be sure at this distance. Could it possibly be a woman? Could Bronwyn have done this? Pushed her mother off the mountain to protect Harrison's college dreams?

He pounded alongside the river in long strides, too long for a woman. Not Bronwyn. Not Emily.

I didn't want it to be Luke. He was the kindest of all of them, the one who shielded the rest of us from Bronwyn's wrath. And yet, he would do anything for his wife. What was it Travis had said? That anyone could become a murderer with the right motivation?

The hooded figure was fast, yards ahead of the charging policemen. I followed them, struggling to keep up. Tourists gathered along the edges of the sidewalk, uncertain what was happening, but determined to video it. An overly zealous photographer stepped out in my path. My foot caught on his shoe. His camera skittered across the sidewalk as we both sprawled to the ground. He screamed at me, but there was no time for long apologies. "Sorry," I yelled. Ignoring the fresh ache in my ankle, I bounced to my feet to continue the chase.

The runner hesitated as he neared one of the wooden bridges that spanned the river, debating whether to cross to the other side. He turned slightly and I caught his profile. The hoodie angled enough so I could see a dark streak along his chin. Was it a shadow? A beard?

My lungs were exploding as I fought to get closer. But he took off, keeping the river on his right as he approached the dam which controlled the water level in the Reuss River.

The river roared louder and louder as we neared the floodgates. The scene was chaotic—everyone screaming, cheering, yelling out encouragement—as though this were part of some medal-qualifying footrace.

The policemen were close to him now, one a few lengths ahead of the rest, stretching out to grab the runner's hoodie. Desperate to escape, the runner threw one leg over the concrete wall of the floodgates, ready to plunge into the churning river below. The policeman lunged forward, pulling him away from the river, turning him back toward me.

I caught a glimpse of his face. "It's not Randall, it's not Randall, it's not Randall," I said over and over, sucking in precious air as I slowed to a walk.

The runner struggled to get free, but the policemen swarmed around him, throwing him to the ground, yanking his arms behind him as they secured his wrists with handcuffs. Pulling him to his feet, they shoved him roughly past me toward the flashing lights of the police cars gathered in front of the church.

"I didn't do it, Madeline," he called out as they passed. "Please, you've got to help me."

My heart pounded so hard I thought my chest would burst, as I watched them load Wyatt into the back seat of a waiting police cruiser.

Chapter 43

TRAVIS AND I waited anxiously at the hospital while the doctors worked on Eva.

He crouched in a hard plastic chair, elbows planted on his knees, gripping his coffee so tightly that I thought his fingers would puncture the paper cup. Any skepticism I had that he and Eva had rekindled their relationship was erased by the anguish in his eyes.

"Travis, here, take this." I offered a fresh coffee.

"What?"

"Your coffee is cold. Take this one." I eased the crumpled cup from his hand.

"We shouldn't have done this. I knew that setup at the cathedral was too dangerous." He pulled off the lid and sipped the hot liquid. "You can't poke a bear in the eye and not expect him to strike back."

"This isn't your fault. Eva and I knew what we were getting into."

"Did you?" His look was accusing. "Eva thought her buddy Mueller had everything under control. Do you think she really would have signed up for this if she thought she'd get stabbed?"

I sat down beside him. "Eva's a seasoned reporter. This can't be the first time she's been in a challenging situation."

"This was more than a challenging situation. It was a disaster. I should have stopped her."

"How would you have done that? This whole thing was Eva's idea. She thought it was an acceptable risk. So did I."

"Well, you were both were wrong." His voice broke. "My God, Madeline, how will I live with myself if she dies?"

"She won't die, Travis. This is a good hospital. She's getting excellent care." I spoke with conviction. "I know how much she means to you."

"We've been friends for a long time." His eyes were bright with unshed tears.

"Friends," I said slowly. "It's more than that, isn't it?"

"What?" he mumbled.

"I saw her last night, going into your room." I regretted the words as soon as they spilled out. Travis was guilty and grieving, blaming himself for Eva's injuries. It was petty to make this all about me.

"Last night? When?" He rubbed his shirt sleeve across his eyes.

"Around midnight."

He thought for a moment. "Oh, I get it. That's why you acted so weird this morning. You think we slept together. You're jealous."

"I am *not* jealous," I said indignantly. "I'm disappointed. You said you wanted us to get back together. But a few hours later, you were sleeping with her."

He shook his head. "We didn't sleep together."

"Right." His betrayal stung. Lying about it made it worse. "What was it, Travis?" I remembered their front-seat murmurings on the way to Speyer. "You couldn't resist those old memories of the two of you in Paris? Or staying at that quaint little hotel in Calais?"

"What are you talking about?" He stood up abruptly, sloshing coffee. "You want to stay in that fantasy world of yours, or do you want to hear the truth?"

"Try me." My voice was angry. "What is the truth?"

"You knew she was coming here last night, to tell us about her conversation with Müller. We tried to get in touch with you, but you weren't answering your cell."

"I was at the hospital. With Holliss."

"We didn't know that. We went out for dinner while we waited for you to show up. We hashed over the case, going back over everything we knew about all the people involved."

"Your cozy little dinner was just business, right?"

"That's right. Just business." He stepped away from me, putting more space between us. "We decided to call it a night. I walked Eva to her car."

"Such a gentleman."

He ignored my sarcasm. "You know what a trashy clunker she drives. On the way back from Speyer, I thought it would never pull those hills. Sure enough, when she tried to start the engine, it made a couple of wheezy noises and then died. It was too late to call a mechanic. A hired car would have cost a fortune. So she stayed in my room."

My irritation increased as I played back the scene of her with the ice bucket. "I saw her in the hall, wearing the T-shirt I gave you. And not much else."

"She didn't have anything else," he said, his voice rising. "Only the clothes on her back. It's not like she was planning to spend the night."

I raised a defiant eyebrow.

"Hey, nothing happened. She got the bed. I got the chair."

"Sure." I knew my behavior was despicable. Eva was in surgery. We didn't know if she would live or die. And here I was, acting like a petty teenager, sullen because her boyfriend had hooked up with another girl. But I couldn't keep that hateful tone out of my voice. Travis had once meant a lot to me. Last night in my hotel room, I thought we finally had a chance to get back together.

"Believe what you want," he said. "I can't deal with this right now."

We glared at each other, neither willing to back down. My phone rang. Grateful for the interruption, I fished it from my purse. "Hello? What?" I walked toward the windows. "I'm sorry, this is a terrible connection." I pressed my palm against my ear. "Who is this?"

I listened carefully. "I don't think so. I'm at the hospital right now. The woman he stabbed is in surgery." I could see Travis's reflection in the window. He was slumped in the chair, his face buried in his hands. "I can't help him. I won't."

My caller was insistent. I listened for a few more minutes. "Fine. I'll come." I walked back toward Travis. "That was Wyatt's lawyer. They're at the police station. Wyatt wants to talk to me."

"About what?"

"Wyatt says this whole thing is a big mistake. That he didn't stab Eva."

Travis snorted. "Yeah, right. You know he did it. You were right there with the police, chasing after him. You know he's guilty."

"The lawyer says Wyatt has important information about Corinne. That he won't share it with anyone but me." I shoved the phone back into my purse. "I think I need to hear him out. You want to go with me? Get his explanation firsthand?"

"Are you kidding? The only thing I want to see is that guy strapped to a gurney, with somebody shooting poison up his veins."

"I don't think they have capital punishment in Switzerland."

"Maybe they should rethink that."

I reached for my jacket. "I've been searching for answers about what happened to Corinne. This is my chance to find out. I need to see him."

"Go ahead," Travis said, frowning. "I'm staying here with Eva. But be careful. That creep can't be trusted."

"I think I'll be safe enough in a police station."

Travis stood up. "Make sure the lawyer stays in the room. You don't want to be by yourself with that guy."

***

The police station was noisy, so different from the quiet of this morning. A uniformed officer grappled with a belligerent fat drunk who reeked of vomit, his faded burgundy T-shirt stretched over his beer gut. A young mother, stringy hair barely concealing her bruised jaw and black eye, balanced a toddler on her hip as she screamed at the man trailing behind her.

The overwhelmed clerk at reception cradled a telephone receiver against his left shoulder while he pecked at his computer keyboard. It took a few minutes to catch his attention. "Hi," I said. "I need to talk to Captain Mueller."

"You'll have to wait." He rummaged through the paperwork in front of him. "He's busy right now."

"Tell him it's Madeline Keswick. I'm here about Wyatt Carlton. He was arrested tonight."

"I'll give it a try." The clerk punched some buttons on the telephone keypad. After a brief conversation, he hung up and gestured toward a bench near the door. "Wait over there."

Mueller walked into the reception area a few minutes later. "Hell of a night, eh?" he said, leading me back through the hallway.

"Wyatt Carlton's lawyer called me."

Mueller rolled his eyes. "Yeah, Carlton must have that guy on speed dial. Got him in here right away."

"Has Wyatt confessed? Did he have the journal?" I asked.

"Nope. And he didn't have the knife on him, either. Probably tossed them both while he was running. But we'll find them." He stopped in front of a closed door. "We're not ready to make this public yet, so it has to stay off the record. But considering the role you played in this, I figure you have a right to know. We took his prints. Ran them through our databases. They matched the prints lifted from Mrs. Peerland's riverboat safe."

"So he's the one who robbed her?"

"Most likely."

"You think he killed her?"

"Don't know." He reached for the doorknob. "He won't talk to anyone but you. See what you can get out of him."

***

Wyatt and his lawyer were seated at a narrow table in a small conference room. The lawyer, with a face as rough and cracked as a dry riverbed, stood up when I walked in. He was bald except for a few white wisps above his ears. "Otto Bachman. Thank you for coming. Please, sit down."

"Thank God you're here," Wyatt said. "This has been a nightmare."

I sat down across from him. It was hard to believe that the man who had whirled me so gracefully around the dance floor could be a murderer. But I had seen his violent side. The bruise on my jaw had faded, but my ankle was still tender from my fall down the tower steps. "Why did you call me?"

Bachman put on glasses and opened a folder in front of him. "My client thinks you have information that will help him in this police inquiry."

"He stabbed Eva, stole the journal and took off running. What more is there to say?"

Wyatt's eyes widened at my comments. "I didn't do it. I didn't stab Eva."

"Not a word," Bachman said to Wyatt, warning him to remain silent. He turned to me. "Tell me what happened tonight. Did you see my client in the cathedral?"

"No. But I saw what he did." I shuddered. "Blood was everywhere."

Bachman angled his head, peering at me over the top of his glasses. "But you did not see my client do it? You did not witness the actual stabbing?"

"No. The lights went out and somebody yelled, *'He's got a gun.'* Everyone started screaming, running for the exits. When I got to the back of the church, Eva had already been stabbed."

Bachman scratched some quick notes in the file. "If you didn't see him stab her, why do you think Mr. Carlton did this?"

"Are you kidding?" I knew that lawyers dug into every detail of a crime, manipulating witness statements and forensic evidence like the brightly colored squares of a Rubik's cube, convinced that the solution could be uncovered if only they worked at it long enough. But this case was so obvious that no line of questioning could make Wyatt seem innocent. "He ran out of the church. When the police caught him, he was covered in her blood."

"It's because I tried to help her." Wyatt's forehead wrinkled. "She was sprawled out on the back pew, blood gushing everywhere. I couldn't let her bleed to death. I pressed down hard to stop the blood. It got all over me."

Did he really expect me to believe that he was a good Samaritan who had jumped in to aid a dying victim? "What did you do with the journal, Wyatt? And the knife?"

"I never got the journal. It wasn't with Eva when I saw her." He chewed nervously on his fingernail. "And I didn't have a knife. I didn't stab her."

"If you didn't do it, why did you run?"

He blinked rapidly. "Are you kidding me? Who's going to stick around when people are yelling *there's a gun*? And when some crazy guy is in there stabbing people? Everybody was running. I followed them outside. Next thing I know, the police are chasing me."

"Mr. Carlton, please," Bachman said, annoyed. "Let me handle this interview."

Wyatt sat back, his elbows snug against his sides.

"I understand that you were at the cathedral to receive a journal from Eva Graesser," Bachman said, angling his pen toward me. "Can you tell me more about that?"

"Corinne Peerland kept a detailed daily journal," I said. "We thought there might be clues in there about her murderer, things she'd written down during the riverboat cruise. I told everyone that I'd get it from Eva at the concert and then bring it back to the hotel, so they could read it before we handed it over to the police. We figured whoever killed Corinne would want to grab it before the rest of the family saw it."

Bachman pursed his lips. "You thought someone in your travel group killed her. A family member?"

"Captain Mueller thought it might be a family member," I clarified. "We hoped that if no one showed up for the journal, he'd back off the family and focus on other suspects. But if somebody showed up, we'd have our killer. And obviously we do."

"I didn't kill Corinne," Wyatt said.

"Quiet." Bachman glared at Wyatt. He turned to me, arranging his mouth in something that was a parody of a smile. "This was a sting that you and the detective set up." There was an odd lilt to Bachman's voice. I could almost hear the word *entrapment* spinning in his brain.

I wasn't worried. We hadn't lied to Wyatt or forced him to do anything. He came to the cathedral because he thought the journal implicated him. If he'd been innocent, he would have stayed away. "I know you did it, Wyatt. You robbed her safe to get back your poker money. When Corinne figured it out and confronted you, you killed her. Then you came after the journal to make sure she hadn't written anything that would connect you to the crime."

Wyatt leaned in for a whispered consultation with Bachman. I think he was beginning to realize how much trouble he was in. Stabbing Eva was bad enough. Killing Corinne was something else altogether. Wyatt's eyes darted back and forth between Bachman and me like an animal in a trap, desperate enough to chew off his own foot if that's what it took to escape. "I'll admit I robbed the safe. Usually I win at poker, but Corinne made some big bets and had a run of good luck. Suddenly I was out a lot of money. Money I couldn't afford to lose."

"You killed her for two thousand dollars?" My voice was heavy with disgust.

"Two thousand may not seem like much to someone in your tax bracket, but me, I've got expenses. I had to get it back."

"Pretty convenient for you that she had that allergy attack. You had plenty to time to break into the safe while she and Fred were down with the doctor. It was the crabby mary, right?"

He seemed surprised that I knew. "She told everybody at the poker game that she had seafood allergies. So in the lounge, when she asked Kyle to get her a bloody mary, I saw my chance. I ordered two crabby marys and slipped one to her."

"You're despicable," I said. "She could have died."

"Not likely. Doc Maynard's pretty good. Passengers have allergic reactions all the time. I knew he kept EpiPens around."

"Was the doctor in on it, too?"

"No. He didn't have anything to do with it."

I leaned toward him. "But Corinne figured it out, didn't she? Confronted you on that viewing platform. And you pushed her over." I shivered, remembering the biting cold and the heavy clouds that masked the steep drop below.

"No. I was with you the whole time." He had the look of a condemned man desperate to prove his innocence. "That's why I called you. You're my alibi."

"Good luck with that." I tapped my fingernails on the pressed wood of the table. "You disappeared while I was still in the gift shop. When I finished my shopping, you weren't anywhere around."

"I took a bathroom break. Ten minutes max. And I was waiting for you at the exit, remember?"

"I don't know how long you were gone. Seemed like much more than ten minutes. Definitely enough time to kill her."

"You know I'd never do that."

"I have no idea what you're capable of. You've been lying ever since we met." Coming here had been a big waste of time. I had hoped Wyatt would tell me what happened up on the mountain, provide the details that would exonerate Randall and remove suspicion from the rest of the family. But all he wanted to do was protect himself, to use me to wriggle out of this damning situation. "Tell me this—why did you come back with us to Lucerne? If you'd stayed on the boat, no one would have suspected you."

He hesitated. "I follow the money."

"What does that mean?" I asked.

"I convinced Kyle I could find investors for his new company. I needed to collect my finder's fee."

"He believed you?" My tone was skeptical.

"Not sure about Kyle, but Emily sure did," Wyatt said. "She would have danced with the devil to get that company off the ground."

"Let me guess ... once you had collected, you would disappear. And so would all those mythical investors."

"Hey, a guy's got to make a living."

"I've got a question for you. That day in the tower, when we were running down the steps. You were right behind me. Did you make me stumble?"

A vein in his temple throbbed as he searched for an answer. First one, then another, rising to the surface, distorting his face. Not the full-blown man-to-monster transition that I'd seen when we were under that tree by the castle wall, but enough to convince me of his guilt.

"Of course not. You were going too fast. Lost your balance." His words were coated with defensiveness. "Hey, I'll admit I stole the money from Corinne's safe. But I didn't kill her. And I didn't stab Eva. You've got to help me prove it."

"I don't have to help you do anything."

"Madeline, please. I need you to back me up on this."

I had no sympathy for him. He showed remorse only because he'd gotten caught. "Sorry, Wyatt." I stood up, nodding to his lawyer as I moved to the exit. "I don't think there's anything I can do."

Chapter 44

AFTER I LEFT the police station, I sent a quick text to Travis. He responded that he was still at the hospital with Eva.

I caught up with him in the waiting room. "She's out of surgery. Still in recovery, so I can't see her yet. But she's going to be okay." He bounced slightly as we hugged.

"How much coffee have you had?" I asked.

"No idea. Lost track after the fourth cup."

"You'll never get to sleep tonight."

"I wouldn't sleep anyway. I'm too wired up. She was almost killed, Madeline. Over a stupid book. And to think that slimy Wyatt was the one who did this to her. I never thought he had the balls for something like this."

"Me, either." I filled him in on everything Wyatt had told me. "He says he didn't stab Eva. Or kill Corinne. Although he admits to robbing the safe."

"And you believe that little weasel?"

"I don't know. Like you said, he doesn't seem brave enough to pull all this off on his own. I can see him sneaking around to give Corinne a crabby mary, bringing on that allergy attack so he could break into her safe. But pushing Corinne off a mountain when all of us were only a few feet away? And stabbing Eva in front of all those people? I'm not convinced he has the guts for that."

"You were there in the cathedral, Madeline. You saw what he did to her." His eyes skimmed over my face. "I heard you flew down that sidewalk like a woman possessed. You almost caught Wyatt yourself."

I shook my head, remembering the pointed questions of Wyatt's lawyer. "I didn't actually see him do it. I only saw him running away. And the police haven't found the knife or the journal. Müller's still searching for them."

"He could have tossed those in the river."

"I don't think so. I had my eye on him from the moment he left the cathedral. I didn't see him do anything like that."

"I can't believe you're taking his side in this."

"I'm not taking his side. But I want to make sure the police have the right guy." I walked toward the sofa. "Let's sit a minute." He sank down on the cushions, leaving plenty of space between us. "I'm leaving for home early tomorrow, so I may not see you again. I wanted to thank you for your help in all this. It meant …" I could feel my eyes watering. "It meant a lot to me to have you here. I hope when we're both back in New York, that maybe we can get together, go out for a drink, maybe catch a movie." I missed him—his curiosity, his adventurous spirit, his ability to make me laugh. I wanted the relationship we used to have. Before all the craziness with that stupid senior partner at my former firm. Before Travis's superman heroics cost me my job. Before I blamed Travis for everything.

"Sure. That would be great."

Any hope that we could be more than casual buddies quickly fizzled at his casual attitude. In the past he'd shown more enthusiasm over which takeout we should order for dinner. Last night in my hotel room, we seemed so close to recapturing the magic we once had. But I squelched our romantic moment, driving him toward Eva. "I think it's wonderful that you and Eva have gotten back together again. You guys have a great history."

"We're friends, Madeline. Good friends. That's all."

"Oh, come on, Travis. I've seen the way you look at her. I know it's more than friendship."

He slapped his palms against his knees. "That's priceless. You've known me for years, but you don't believe me when I tell you I didn't sleep with Eva. But you believe Wyatt, a guy you met only a couple of days ago, when he says he didn't stab Eva, even though he was covered in her blood when the police caught up with him?"

It did sound stupid when he put it that way. "It's been a confusing week. I don't know what to believe."

"Well, think about this. If Wyatt didn't stab Eva or kill Corinne, then we're right back to the original list of suspects. Which includes Corinne's family. Especially your buddy Randall."

Chapter 45

I LEFT the hospital in the dark hours of early morning and headed back to the hotel. Setting my alarm, I tried to get a few hours of sleep, but my brain refused to shut down, flinging up an inescapable slideshow of all the terrifying details of the day—Eva collapsed on the back pew of the cathedral, Wyatt running from the police, Travis in the emergency room as he paced during Eva's surgery.

After checking my clock for the third time in twenty minutes, I gave up on sleep and decided to call Lilly. She answered on the second ring. In the background I heard the loud pounding of her favorite heavy metal band. "Lilly, it's Madeline."

"What?" she asked, her voice loud. "Who is this?"

"It's Madeline," I yelled.

"Madeline, hold on." I heard laughter as she called out, "Hey, turn that down, will you?"

"Is this a bad time?" I had been so focused on the tragedies swirling around me that it was a shock to realize other people were leading normal lives, partying and listening to rock music. "I'm sorry. I can call later."

"No. No, it's fine. I've got a couple of people here, but I can talk. In fact, I've got some news for you. Hold on a minute." I heard a door close, and the music faded to a rhythmic thumping. "You still there?"

"Yes, I'm here." I pulled out my suitcase to pack for the trip home.

Her voice was clearer now that the background noise was muted. "First of all, I couldn't find out much about Wyatt. It's weird that someone in sports marketing has such a low profile."

"Weirder than you think. He's been arrested for stabbing Eva Graesser, Travis's reporter friend. And the police think he killed Corinne."

"Are you kidding me? What happened?"

I described the events at the cathedral. "Wyatt insists he's not guilty, but I think he'll have a hard time convincing Captain Mueller of that."

"How's Travis dealing with this? He's known Eva a long time, right?"

"He's pretty much wiped out by the whole thing. He keeps insisting she's a friend, but it's obvious he's in love with her. He won't leave the hospital until they let him see her."

Lilly sighed. "Even if he is a little bit in love with her, long distance relationships are hard. Once he's back in New York and she's still in Switzerland, you guys will have another chance to get back together."

"It's a nice thought, but I don't see it happening." I emptied the closet contents onto the bed.

"Don't give up so easy. You guys were good together."

I gave a noncommittal grunt. "So, were you able to find out anything about Kyle?"

"Yes. It's quite a story. After he sold his company, Kyle created a glamorous life for himself, partying with the rich and famous."

"No surprise there. He told me he made a lot of money on the sale."

"*A lot* is an understatement. He bought a mansion in Tuscany, a couple of racehorses, and even a yacht."

"Sounds nice." I laid a pair of too-snug jeans on my *arrivederci* pile, for clothes that were good enough for travel but not loved enough to bring back home, a strategy which freed up more space for souvenirs. The jeans joined a navy sweater with a pulled thread and a T-shirt in an odd shade of green that never went with the rest of my wardrobe.

"At first, yes. But things started to unravel when his wife caught him in bed with another woman. After they divorced, he kind of turned up the volume. More parties. More alcohol. Got in with a rough bunch."

"He told me that selling his company was like losing his soul. That it left a huge hole in his life."

"Maybe that explains why everything went downhill so fast. One night there was a big brawl in a high-stakes poker game. Kyle was accused of cheating. He threw a couple of punches, and then everybody piled into the fight. When the cops finally got it all sorted, there was a dead guy at the bottom of the pile. Everything pointed to Kyle."

"That's horrible. He killed somebody?"

"Who knows?" Lilly said. "Kyle's family hired a lot of high-powered lawyers. Made large donations to some influential people. Politicians. Judges. Media types. Got the whole thing hushed up. Spun it as one more dustup among some criminal lowlifes that nobody cared much about anyway." The music suddenly got louder. "Shut the door, guys," Lilly yelled. "I'll be out in a minute."

"Are you sure this isn't a bad time?"

"It's fine. Somebody's desperate to use the bathroom, but they'll have to hold it. Anyway, it must have been a turning point for Kyle. Seems he's walked the straight and narrow ever since."

"But it's the kind of thing you wouldn't want your investors to know." I headed to the bathroom to gather my cosmetics. "They might have balked at putting their money with a murderer."

"Yes. And with the media digging into Corinne's background, the story would have turned up sooner or later."

I squatted to rescue a pair of flats that had gotten shoved under the chair. "If Wyatt is telling the truth and he didn't kill Corinne, could Kyle have done it, to keep a lid on his past?"

"Better Kyle than Randall, I guess," she said. "How's Holliss?"

"Out of the hospital. Taking it easy here at the hotel."

"Give her my best."

"Sure thing." I gathered my dirty laundry and stuffed it into a plastic bag. "Anyway, I'm leaving Lucerne today and catching a flight out of Zurich." I gave her my flight number. "I'll see you tomorrow."

"I'm glad you're coming back," she said, "but don't even think of coming to the office. Go home and crash for as long as it takes to get your head together. You've been through a lot. I can get along a few more days without you."

"But if I focus on work, then I don't have to think about everything that's happened here." I closed and zipped the suitcase. "I'd do most anything to block this week out of my mind."

***

I gathered up my things and headed toward the elevator. Down at lobby level, I checked out of the hotel and wrestled my roller bag down the steps. The sun poked through gray skies of thinning darkness. The streets were deserted, tourists still in bed, locals enjoying a quiet breakfast before the morning rush. Bronwyn and Luke were in the courtyard, waiting for the van that would take us to the train station to start our trip home.

"Here comes the hero," Luke said as I clattered across the cobblestones. "Dad told us what you did last night at the cathedral. We owe you a big thanks for finding our mother's murderer."

I didn't feel like a hero. There was nothing brave or inspiring or noble about seeing blood gush from Eva's stomach, or Travis's despair as he waited for news of her surgery, or even Wyatt begging for my help to escape a charge of murder. Nothing that happened last night could bring back Corinne. Nothing could erase the painful memories of Holliss reaching out to touch her mother's hair as she lay on that narrow stretcher. Instead, I felt an overwhelming sense of loss.

"How's your friend?" he asked. "I can't believe Wyatt stabbed her. Is she all right?"

If there was a hero in all this, it was Eva. She was the one who had figured out how to trap the killer. If she identified Wyatt as her attacker, there would be little his lawyer could do to save him. "She's still in the hospital, but hopefully will be released soon."

Luke zipped up his jacket against the morning chill. "I'm surprised that Wyatt was behind all this. He seemed like an okay guy."

"Surprised me, too," I said. "He hasn't confessed to murder, so this isn't all wrapped up yet. And you know Mueller—he's very careful, and he'll take his time *examining all the evidence*," I said, putting his words in air quotes. "But Wyatt did admit he stole the poker money. After he gave Corinne the crabmeat-infused bloody mary, to bring on an allergy attack."

"You thought I stole that money, didn't you?" Bronwyn chomped down so hard on her lip that I expected to see teeth marks. "All those questions about what I did with mom's room key."

I never thought she was guilty of robbing the safe, but I was still suspicious of her broken finger. Maybe Bronwyn had caught it in the cable car door, like she said. Maybe she had hurt it fighting with Corinne, as Holliss and Emily had suggested. Maybe Travis was right, that Kyle and Bronwyn had conspired together to kill their mother. Most likely, we'd never know the truth. Mueller would try to pin the crime on Wyatt. If that failed, he would go after Randall. But Kyle and Bronwyn, once safely back in the U.S., faced little chance of being charged. No witnesses. No evidence. The perfect crime.

"Bronwyn, we talked about this," Luke scolded her. "Madeline's done a lot for our family. You need to take it down a couple of notches."

"What do you want me to say?"

"You could apologize."

Bronwyn's nose flared as she faced me. "Fine. I was wrong to accuse you of goading Mom into this campaign. She was a strong-willed woman who did exactly what she wanted. No one could have talked her out of it, although all of us certainly tried."

It wasn't the warmest apology I'd ever heard, but better than nothing. "Thank you."

"I mean," she said, waving her Velcro-splinted finger in front of my face, "I still think this whole climate change thing was misguided. The world needs oil. Sun and wind can't provide all the power we need."

"There's no easy solution," I said. "But we need to start thinking of alternatives. That's what Corinne was trying to do."

"Her campaign was a slap in the face to Luke," she insisted, her voice sharp. "He's worked in the industry for years, and our family depends on his income."

"Bronwyn, that's enough," Luke said, tugging at her sleeve. "Stop."

A black van pulled into the courtyard, providing a welcome distraction. "Bronwyn Fisher?" the driver asked, lowering his window.

"Yes," Bronwyn said. "Glad you're here. We've got a train to catch."

Luke began to wheel the luggage toward the back of the van. "Where's that brother of yours?" he asked Bronwyn. "He's always late."

"It's not Kyle, it's Emily. It takes her forever to get ready for anything. She's probably getting her nails done again." Bronwyn paced, glancing at her watch several times as the minutes passed. "Maybe we should call them?" She pulled out her phone.

"No, wait. Here they come."

Emily came through the revolving doors first, holding her carry-on as she navigated the steps in her high-heeled ankle boots. Luke helped Kyle bring down the rest of their luggage, grunting as he lifted a large leopard-spotted suitcase. "Careful with that one," Emily cautioned him.

The wheels caught on the cobblestones as Luke rolled the heavy suitcase toward the driver. "Did you pack rocks in here?" Luke asked.

"Souvenirs," Emily said. "But maybe I bought a little too much stuff."

"You think?" Kyle wrestled Emily's suitcase into the van. "You should see this woman with a credit card," he said. "She's deadly."

He picked up my roller bag and stowed it beside Emily's. "I understand we have you to thank for catching our mother's killer."

"Holliss is one of my best friends. I couldn't let her husband be charged with murder."

"There's a lot to be said for loyalty." He shifted the luggage to make a spot for his duffel bag. "Anyway, we've all been a little rough on you, and I'm sorry for that. But Mom's campaign caught us all off guard. I still don't know why she did it. Bronwyn thinks it had something to do with Natalie, but that seems a long shot to me."

Obviously, Fred had not yet shared the truth with his family. I wondered if he ever would. "I'm sorry she didn't get a chance to explain it to you. But I know the campaign was important to her."

"Yeah. Enough that she was willing to sacrifice the rest of us."

"I don't think she saw it that way, Kyle. She was so proud of all of you. Thought you would land on your feet no matter what happened with the campaign."

"Maybe." He didn't sound convinced.

We all climbed into the van and headed for the train station. Inside, it was crowded: businesspeople toted coffee cups and briefcases, holding ear-bud conversations as they walked with purpose toward their trains; tourists congregated around the departure boards, fumbling with water bottles and adjusting their backpacks as they tried to figure out where they were supposed to go. Luke scrambled through the throng to study the board. "This way," he said, pointing to the right. "We're on track 14."

As we maneuvered through the station, I noticed a bookstore. "I want to pick up a paperback for the ride. I'll catch up with you guys in a minute."

"Keep an eye on the time," Luke cautioned. "Swiss trains are almost always right on schedule. You don't want to miss it."

"Right." I quickly browsed through the paperback racks, picking out a best seller. The checkout line took longer than I expected. By the time I started for the tracks, I had only a few minutes to reach my train. I walked quickly, pulling my roller bag behind me, sidestepping a boisterous group of teenagers, carefully wheeling around a young mom with a baby stroller.

Luke stood outside the first-class car, waving. "It's packed. We couldn't get seats together."

"That's fine." He hoisted my luggage up the narrow steps, and I claimed the first empty seat. "Thanks," I said, as he lifted my bag onto the overhead racks.

"No problem. We're about ten rows up, if you need anything."

The last whistle sounded, and the train pulled slowly away from the station. Settling into my seat, I watched until the last of Lucerne's buildings disappeared. Then I pulled out my paperback, a thriller by a favorite author. The opening scene was graphic, a detailed description of a taxi driver being garroted by someone hiding in the back seat. I had had enough of violence. The description reminded me too much of the strangulation bruise on Corinne's neck. I should have chosen a cozy romance, one of those gentle stories about small towns and cupcake shops and winter festivals.

Our early departure meant I had rushed out of the hotel with only a large to-go coffee, and my stomach was rumbling. I headed for the dining car, adapting my stride to the swaying rhythm of the moving train. Ordering an apple danish, I picked up a newspaper from the counter and settled into a nearby booth, skimming through articles as I sipped my coffee. A headline caught my eye: *Melting Glacier Triggers Rockslides; Five Dead.* The accompanying photo showed several cars at odd angles on a narrow mountain roadway, crushed by large boulders. Corinne would have been devastated to see this. It was exactly the type of tragedy she hoped to prevent.

Kyle walked in as the waiter set the warm pastry in front of me. "Anything interesting in there?" he asked, gesturing toward the paper.

"Same old, same old. Trade wars, natural disasters, a couple of bombings here and there." I folded up the paper and offered it to him. "You interested?"

"After that rousing recommendation, are you kidding me? The last thing I need is more bad news."

"Right." I slid the paper to the edge of the table. "Hey, have you got a minute? There's something I wanted to tell you."

"Sure. I've got no place to go until we reach Zurich." He sat down across from me. "What's up?"

"It's about Wyatt."

He glanced out the window, the scenery blurring as we sped past. "I don't want to think about him. This whole thing was my fault. If Mom and I hadn't joined his poker game, she would still be alive."

"You can't blame yourself. Wyatt was on the prowl for victims. In fact, you were his next target."

"Me? How do you figure that?"

"He told you he could get investors for your company, right?

"He mentioned that, but as far as I was concerned, it was a non-starter. I mean, the guy talked a good game, but I never took him seriously. There was something a little off about him."

"Good call on your part. I'm glad you didn't get suckered in." Stray chunks of sugar glaze fell to my plate as I took a bite of pastry. "That's why he came back with us to Lucerne. He figured he could get referral fees from you, by promising to match you up with wealthy athletes interested in good investments. But it was a scam."

"You mean he killed my mom and then came back to Lucerne so he could steal from me? What kind of a psychopath is this guy?"

"Not a nice character. But we don't know for sure that he killed Corinne. He hasn't confessed yet, although Mueller is pretty sure he's guilty."

He reached for the newspaper and skimmed the front page. "This whole thing has really upset Emily. She trusted Wyatt. Was convinced that he was the answer to all our investor problems. In fact, we had a huge blowup about him back on the riverboat."

I scooped up loose sugar glaze with my fork. "She's committed to your company."

"That's for sure. Maybe too committed." He ran his knuckles along his beard. "She was furious with my mom about her Senate campaign. Thought it would dig up a lot of ancient history. Scare off our investors."

"Ancient history?" I sipped my coffee, now unappealingly tepid. "You're talking about the incident in Italy?"

"You know about that?"

"I know your dad paid a lot of money to save you from a murder charge."

"He told you?"

"No. But the story is out there, if you dig hard enough."

He didn't seem surprised. "Hard to hide anything these days, isn't it? I finally came clean with my investors. Thought it was better if they heard the whole story from me, rather than in bits and pieces as my mom's campaign heated up."

I wondered how he had explained it. An altercation? A horrible accident? Surely, he didn't confess to murder. "How did they take it?"

"I admit I lost a few. But some folks that I'd been working on for a long time finally committed, so it's all good." He stood, turning toward the counter. "I'd better go. I promised Emily I would bring her a coffee. She'll be wondering what happened to me."

Chapter 46

WHEN WE pulled into Zurich, I jerked my roller bag off the overhead rack and joined up with the rest of our group. Trains and planes both shared this same building, so we didn't have far to go to catch our flight home. Balancing luggage on the moving steps, we rode the escalators up through a cavernous expanse of glass and steel toward the airplane check-in level.

"Good thing we're here in plenty of time," Luke said as we neared the counter for our flight. "It will take forever to get through that line."

A host of weary travelers, their expressions glazed and fatigued, snaked their way through multiple rows of belted stanchions. We entered the queue, pushing our luggage up a few feet, stopping to wait as the next person in line got processed, and then scooting it up a bit more. Emily bounced nervously in front of me. "Why can't this line move any faster? I want to get out of here. To get home."

"I knew I shouldn't have given you all that coffee," Kyle said, brushing his lips against her hair. "It won't be long now."

Almost thirty minutes later we reached the front of the line. Bronwyn and Luke gave their passports to the attendant, who keyed their information into the computer. After Luke loaded their luggage onto the scale, the attendant strapped on tracking tags and heaved the bags to the conveyor belt behind him.

Kyle and Emily were called up next. Kyle handed over their passports and set Emily's leopard-print bag on the scale. The attendant frowned. "This bag is overweight."

"I knew it would be," Kyle said. He turned to Emily. "I told you not to buy all those souvenirs."

"There will be a surcharge," the attendant said.

"That's fine," Kyle agreed.

"No, we don't need to do that." Emily grabbed her suitcase. "I'll pull some things out of my checked bag and put them in my carry-on."

"Emily, we'll pay the fee," Kyle said. "Put your bag back up here."

"It's stupid to pay a fee when we don't have to. Let me rearrange some things. This will only take a minute." She unzipped the suitcase and pulled out several items: a pair of knee-high leather boots, a set of carved brass bookends, a bubble-wrapped eight-inch statue of the mythical dragon of Pilatus, and a large coffee table book with a dramatic cover scene of the Swiss Alps.

"Good Lord, Emily," Kyle said. "No wonder your bag is overweight. Here, give me some of that. I've got extra room in my suitcase."

"No, I've got this. I'm fine." She shoved the dragon into the carry-on and reached for the bookends.

"All that stuff will never fit," Kyle said.

"Of course, it will," Emily insisted. "Give me a minute." She shifted her makeup bag to the side.

"Come on, you're holding up the line. Let me take something." Kyle grabbed a boot by the instep. As the top of the boot rotated downward, a small plastic bag fell out.

"Here, you dropped something," Bronwyn said, bending down to scoop up the bag. She fingered the contents through the clear plastic. "Emily, what is this?" she asked, her voice suspicious.

Emily shook her hair back over her shoulder. "Give me that." She stepped closer to Bronwyn. "It's some jewelry I picked up in Lucerne."

"A necklace?" Bronwyn opened the bag and shook out a chain of thick golden links into her palm.

"Yes. I bought it in a cute little shop in Old Town, right down the street from the candy store we liked so much. You know, the one with the chocolate waterfall?"

Bronwyn held the necklace by its clasp, letting it swing free. A diamond pendant dangled from the center link. "Oh, my God. This is my mother's necklace."

"No, it isn't. It's a lot like hers, of course. That's why I bought it. Because I liked hers so much. You guys all know how much I love jewelry." Emily babbled, her words tumbling out as she struggled to explain. "But hers was solid gold, 18 karats. This one is gold-filled, only 12 karats. And that isn't a diamond. It's cubic zirconia."

Bronwyn stepped closer, almost nose to nose with Emily. "You're a liar. My dad gave this to Mom at their thirtieth anniversary party. We were all there when he fastened it around her neck. I would know it anywhere."

Emily's face reddened. "No, you're mistaken. It's fake. Costume jewelry. It's not Corinne's necklace." She tried to snatch it from Bronwyn. "Give it back."

Bronwyn whirled toward Kyle. "Mom was wearing this the day she died."

He frowned, glancing from Bronwyn to Emily. "Let me see it."

"She was wearing it in the café," Bronwyn said. "This is the one the police couldn't find. The one they thought was lost in the snow."

"No, Kyle, she's wrong," Emily insisted. "I would never take your mother's necklace. Why would I do that?"

Kyle draped the necklace across his fingers, the buttery links gleaming in the light. "Mom's necklace has her initials on it, right up by the clasp." His eyes constricted to pinpoints as he studied the tiny writing. His voice was grim. "Where did you get the necklace, Emily?"

"I … I …" She struggled for an answer.

"Her initials are right here. This is my mom's necklace." Kyle stepped toward her. "My God, Emily, what have you done?"

The passengers were getting restless. "Hey, buddy," a portly man called out, thrusting his passport into the air, "can you and your wife settle this later? Some of us have a plane to catch."

Kyle ignored him, grabbing Emily's wrist and pulling her close.

Her words came in labored puffs. "It was an accident, Kyle." Her sleeve rode up as she tried to pull away from him, revealing long scratches along the inside of her arm.

Bronwyn moved in closer. "How did you get those scratches, Emily? Fighting with my mother?"

"I never meant …" Emily began.

"You killed my mother," Kyle said, his voice fading to a whisper. "You killed her."

Bronwyn slapped Emily, leaving a red palmprint on her cheek. "You monster. How could you?"

The slap jolted Emily from panic into defiance. "It's all your fault, Kyle." She jerked her arm free. "If you'd had the balls to stand up to your mother, this never would have happened."

"How do you figure that?" he asked.

"You knew publicity from her campaign would put your family under a microscope. Once our investors found out you'd been arrested for murder, how long do you think they'd have stuck around? And when they pulled out, the company would go under. Everything we'd worked so hard for would disappear."

Bronwyn's voice spiraled upward. "You killed my mother over a stupid company?"

"Come on, Bronwyn," Emily said. "You wanted her to drop this campaign as much as I did. You were the one who kept saying Luke would lose his job. I tried to explain to her how much her campaign would hurt the family, but she wouldn't listen. That day on the platform, we argued. She dug her fingernails into my arm. I had to defend myself."

"All those scratches she had, the bruises … you did that?" Bronwyn asked.

"It wasn't my fault."

Kyle jumped in. "You choked her with her own scarf? And stole her necklace?"

"I didn't mean to choke her," Emily said, frantic to explain her case, to make what she had done sound reasonable. "I was trying to get away from her, but she wouldn't let go. I never meant for her to fall. The necklace got caught on my hand when I was trying to save her, to pull her back."

A couple near the middle of the line jostled against a stanchion, knocking it to the ground. "What's going on up there?" a woman yelled. "We're gonna miss our flight. Get out of the way."

"You folks need to move to the side," the airport clerk said to Kyle. "You're tying up the line. We have lots of people waiting."

Bronwyn ignored him, her eyes only on Emily. "Nobody's going to believe that story. You didn't do this to protect the family. You did it for yourself. For your own greed."

"Maybe she deserved to die." Emily's lip curled. "After all, she cared a lot more about melting glaciers and stupid polar bears than she did about the two of you."

"Are you insane?" Bronwyn jumped at Emily, knocking her to the floor.

"Kyle, get her off of me," Emily yelled.

The attendant picked up his microphone, repeating his message in several languages. "Security needed at Counter Six. Security needed at Counter Six."

Emily thrust her fist into Bronwyn's stomach and sprinted off, shoving people out of her path as she headed toward the escalator. Kyle followed close behind, jumping over roller bags to keep up. I circled around, coming to the escalator from the opposite direction, hoping to cut off her escape. But Emily beat us both, grabbing the escalator handrails to vault around an elderly couple as she headed down.

"Excuse me," I mumbled, apologizing as I maneuvered around them.

Kyle raced after her. She bounded down three steps at a time, shoving people aside. She was almost on the main landing, heading toward the exit. Once she reached the sidewalk outside, it would be a lot easier for her to disappear. "Hurry, Kyle," I screamed. "She's getting away."

Kyle had been a decent athlete in his college days, but now he struggled to keep up with his young fiancée. She barreled recklessly through the crowd, knocking down anyone who got in her way, increasing the distance between them. She was almost at the exit. Only a few more feet and she would be gone.

Jumping off the escalator, I ignored my screaming ankle and put on a last burst of speed, trying to catch her as she neared the door. Right before she reached freedom, two men with *Polizei* in big letters on the backs of their jackets blocked the exit. Kyle and I watched, both of us panting, as the policemen wrenched her arms behind her back and forced her to her knees.

Chapter 47

SUNLIGHT PEAKED through the curtains, pulling me into that drowsy, end-of-night battlefield where waning sleep struggles to fend off emerging consciousness. I lay very still, trying to coax myself back into a doze, but it didn't work.

It had been almost three months since that horrible scene in the Zurich airport, but pictures still flashed in my head each morning like snippets from a crime show trailer: Bronwyn grabbing Corinne's gold necklace as it fell from Emily's boot, Kyle's shock as he realized that his fiancée was a murderer, and Emily's mad dash through the airport as Kyle and I chased behind her.

Giving up on sleep, I got out of bed and pulled on my running gear, determined to jog a quick two miles before work. New York had experienced overcast skies and swirling rain all week, a harbinger of the late summer hurricane that was slowly making its way up the East Coast. This morning's sunshine was a welcome respite, but I knew it wouldn't last. A new wave of storms was forecast for midday.

The August morning was hot and muggy, with scattered puddles from yesterday's rain steaming on the sidewalks. By the end of the first mile, salty sweat stung my eyes. I pressed on, eager to get back into the morning routine that had been put on hold by intermittent downpours. The sidewalks were jammed—strolling pedestrians, energetic dogwalkers and the occasional skateboarder—all eager to soak in their own bit of sun.

Lilly beat me to the office. "Hey, check out the headlines," she said, sipping coffee as she focused on her computer screen. "Big news today."

I peered over her shoulder. An unflattering picture of Emily, her hair disheveled, her expression somber, stared back. "You think that's her mug shot?"

"She sure wouldn't have taken a selfie looking like that." Lilly skimmed the news article. "Says here that her lawyer insists Corinne's death was an accident. You believe that?"

I plopped down in my chair and switched on my computer. "In her defense, I don't think Emily planned to kill Corinne when she followed her onto that viewing platform. She was probably as surprised as the rest of us when she realized what she'd done."

Lilly sniffed. "You're too softhearted. I'll bet she knew exactly what she was doing. You don't strangle someone and toss them off a mountain on a whim." She slowly swiveled her chair from side to side. "She'll never get away with it. The article said there's DNA evidence. Emily's skin cells were found under Corinne's fingernails."

I nodded. "She got a manicure to cover the damage from their fight. You wouldn't believe how calm she was at dinner that night, showing off her flamingo-pink polish."

"You guys never suspected her?"

"No. She sat there with her iPhone, skimming through her emails while the family ignored her. I even felt sorry for her, that she was being left out of the conversation. But looking back, I don't think she was as steady as she seemed. By the next morning, when we were ready to start our Strasbourg tour, she was already starting to chip away at her nail polish."

Lilly reached for her coffee. "How could a smart woman like Emily do something so stupid?"

"She wanted to create a powerhouse company. We know what that feels like. But Corinne threatened her dream, and Kyle wasn't doing anything to stop her. Emily felt she had to fight back."

"How's Kyle doing?"

"It was no surprise when he broke off the engagement. Now he's totally focused on his company. It's off to a great start."

"And Emily will miss it all." Lilly turned back to the article. "They've also charged her with stabbing Eva Graesser."

"Yes. We were all sure that Wyatt did it, until Eva came out of the anesthesia and identified Emily as her attacker."

"Her lawyer can't say *that* was an accident," Lilly said. "Why would she bring a knife to the cathedral, if she didn't plan to use it?"

I opened my email and quickly skimmed through the messages. "As it turns out, it was a souvenir for her nephew. One of those medieval dagger things she picked up at a gift shop. A toy, really, but strong enough to do big damage to Eva."

"This says the police found the knife in a dumpster."

"Yes. Not very clever on her part. If she'd tossed the knife and the journal in that muddy river, they might never have found them. She must have thought Corinne had written some damaging information about her." I deleted a string of emails. "The thing is, if she hadn't stolen the necklace, if it hadn't fallen out of her luggage in the airport, no one would have suspected that she was the murderer. But Emily had a thing for gorgeous jewelry. She grabbed it as Corinne was falling off the platform. And she couldn't bear to get rid of it."

A low rumble of thunder rattled the windows as the sun disappeared behind a thick bank of clouds. "I'm getting so tired of this weather," Lilly said, as raindrops ferociously attacked the building. "The humidity absolutely destroys my hair." Lilly fished around in her desk drawer for a hair clip. "The one I feel sorry for is Holliss. She was totally innocent in all this. She didn't deserve a psycho mother."

"That's true. At least Fred finally explained about Sylvia. Holliss hasn't forgiven Corinne for the way she treated her, but now she understands why." I opened the project file for one of my new clients. "All she cares about right now is her baby. It's due any day. Thankfully, Randall will be with her for the big event."

A jagged streak of lightning split the sky. My watch beeped with a weather alert. "They're issuing flood warnings."

"Terrific. I don't want to stay downtown until we need a boat to rescue us. How about we knock off early today? Work from home?"

"Good idea. I had a client coming in after lunch, but I'm going to reschedule."

The office door began to open. "You expecting anyone?" Lilly asked.

"Not me."

We both watched as Travis walked in. I hadn't seen him since I left Lucerne. He'd stayed behind to keep an eye on Eva as she recuperated from her stab wounds. He sent an occasional email, cheerful and chatty, but impersonal enough that he could have shared it with everyone on his contact list.

"Travis," Lilly squealed, rushing to give him a hug. "It's so good to see you."

"Careful." He stepped back from her. "I'm really wet." His sodden hair, styled by wind and rain, stuck out in all directions. He fingered the front of his rain jacket. "Any place I can put this? I don't want to drip all over everything."

She reached out. "Here, I'll take it."

I edged out from behind my desk and walked slowly toward him. What was the appropriate greeting for a former lover? A handshake? A hug? "Good to see you, Travis," I mumbled.

"And you," he said.

Lilly played the gracious hostess. "Have a seat." She gestured toward what we whimsically called our reception area. The entire office wasn't much larger than the master bedroom closets of my suburban friends, but we had somehow managed to carve out a seating area for clients, a triangle of two consignment-shop upholstered chairs and a faded overstuffed love seat, close against the wall so no one could see the ripped fabric in the back.

Travis relaxed on the loveseat, stretching an arm along the top edge. Other than the wet-dog hairstyle, he looked good. I sat across from him, waiting for him to explain why he was there.

"Look at that rain," Lilly said, crossing to the window. "It's a mess outside. I think I'll knock off for the day." She grabbed her umbrella and headed for the door. "Madeline, you can lock up when you're done, right?"

She wouldn't win any awards for subtlety. It was obvious she wanted us to have some time alone. "Sure. Be careful on the way home."

A suffocating silence wrapped around Travis and me after she left. In the past we had comfortably babbled about friends and news of the day and sporting events. Now we were as taciturn as two strangers on a train. I finally broke the silence. "I've seen some of your energy articles. Good stuff."

"Thanks."

More silence. This was as awkward as a blind date with someone who looked nothing like his online picture. "And the posts you did about Corinne. Very powerful."

He crossed an ankle over the opposite knee. "My editor wants me to turn all that into a book."

"A book about Corinne? You're not going to talk about why she was driven to save the planet, are you? Her guilt over Sylvia and Holliss and Natalie?"

"Of course not. But it will include interviews with the environmentalists she supported. And I'll work in a lot of information about new energy technology, innovations that show a lot of promise in managing climate change. It's a complicated topic, with no easy answers. No matter how the world ends up dealing with this, there will be winners and losers all down the line. But we need to start the discussions, to find some middle ground."

"I'm sorry Corinne won't be here to participate in that. What does her family think about the book? Are they okay with it?"

"Bronwyn's not totally on board—still worried that any scrutiny of fossil fuels will be a negative for Luke's job. But Kyle and Hollis are good with it. And Fred's very much in favor. In fact, we're going to work on it together."

"That's terrific. I look forward to reading it."

He tugged on his earlobe, the way he always did when he was puzzling through a problem. "By the way, I interviewed the men you saw at Pilatus. They weren't there because of Corinne. As it turns out, they had set up monitoring equipment all over Switzerland, to track temperature and precipitation levels and wind speeds. Collecting data, to convince policy makers that they need to protect the environment."

"Oh, come on, Travis. Those guys weren't some passive scientists. I saw them in Basel, shoving people, breaking windows. And they killed Kiener."

"They protested," he admitted, "but they didn't kill Kiener. Another more militant faction has claimed responsibility."

"What about the man that followed me in Lucerne? The blond with the glasses? You're telling me he's one of the good guys?"

"He thought the militant group had killed Corinne, and that you might be next on their list. He was trying to warn you."

I had been so scared that night, with the fog, the confusing streets, the persistent footsteps behind me. "He had a weird way of showing it. I was terrified."

"He's sorry he scared you. He asked me to apologize on his behalf."

"Yeah, right." My watched beeped with another weather alert. Pounded by rain and buffeting winds, the office tower swayed in a gentle two-step. I wanted to get home, to the safety of my apartment, before the subway flooded. But there was one more question I had to ask. "How's Eva?"

"Doing well. Recovered from her stab wounds."

"Good to hear. Is she working on the book, too?"

He tugged at his pants leg, shaking out the dampness. "No. She's got a book deal of her own. About the riverboat swindlers. You remember she told us about them the day we drove down to Speyer."

How could I forget? I had been uncomfortably squashed into the tiny back seat of Eva's car while the two of them giggled up front, reminiscing about their past adventures.

"It turns out that Wyatt was part of it. Mueller cut him a deal if he would give up everyone else in his network. Lundgren, the assistant security guy, was high up in the food chain. When it all comes out, there will be a huge scandal. Eva has negotiated exclusive access to Wyatt's story. Her agent loves it. Thinks it might get made into a movie."

"That's wonderful," I said. "Maybe you and Eva can do a joint book tour."

"Not very likely. Eva's too busy to have time for me. She got a lot of sympathy from being stabbed in the cathedral. Made the round of talk shows. Now she's a celebrity."

"That's too bad. You two seemed really good together."

There was a long pause. "I told you before, Madeline. We're just friends."

I scrutinized his face, taking in every detail. The angle of his eyes. The thin line of his lips. The slight twitch of his jaw. Looking for evidence that he was telling the truth. Or that he was lying to me. And trying to decide if I cared.

"I still want to do a feature on Kesbolt Consulting. You and Lilly have done a fantastic job building this business. Even without Corinne, you've brought in a lot of new accounts."

We had worked hard all summer to replace Corinne's lost revenue. Lilly's vacation resort client had been so pleased with her work that he'd signed her up to manage a winter holiday promotion. I had reached out to some of Corinne's former "save the bay" associates along the East Coast to create videos and podcasts about the environment that were generating a lot of buzz. "I don't want to jinx us with too much publicity. Give us a year or two to prove this isn't all a fluke."

"You've got enough of a track record for me." He tilted his head, giving a persuasive grin. "How about we get a drink and talk all this over?"

"Talk over your article on Kesbolt Consulting?"

"Well, that, and other things. It would be good to catch up."

Catch up on what? We'd already covered his book deal, the protestors, and the riverboat swindlers. He'd tossed out the *just friends* line yet again in connection with Eva. What did that leave us to talk about?

He noticed my puzzlement. "I'm a big believer in new beginnings."

"New beginnings?"

"Yes. New beginnings. Second chances. Those kinds of things."

Was he talking about us? A *just friends* label seemed the safest thing for us, too, even though when he walked into the office, my stomach had lurched as though I'd plunged down the steep drop of a roller coaster. "It's a little early for a drink."

"A coffee, then."

"There's a hurricane barreling down on us. Everything will be closed."

"This is New York. The city that never sleeps. Something will be open. A bar. A diner. Something."

"I don't know."

"Come on, Madeline. I screwed up. I admit it. We need to talk."

Part of me wanted to watch him get all misty eyed while he pleaded for us to get back together, so I could tell him I wasn't interested. But was that really what I wanted? Or was I as eager for a second chance as he was? There was only one way to find out.

Rain sheeted down as we stepped outside. In a few minutes my shirt clung to my chest. "Bad day to forget my umbrella. I'm getting soaked."

"Sorry." He pulled off his jacket and wrapped it around me. "Maybe this wasn't such a good idea after all."

I pointed to a lone sidewalk vendor in the next block, standing under a sagging tarp whipped by the wind. "I'll bet he has umbrellas."

Only a few umbrellas were left, arranged in a small bucket. I picked up one that could have been a castoff from a long-ago yard sale, with a bent rib and several missing plastic tips. "This won't work. One gust of wind will flip it inside out." I pointed toward the table. "Are those rain ponchos? I'll take one."

The vendor was eager to make a sale. "Something else for you today? A designer purse? A necklace?"

A gust of wind whipped my hair across my face. "I don't think so. Just the poncho."

"Special hurricane prices." His dark eyes were pleading.

Generally, I passed sidewalk vendors without noticing them, but maybe Travis's talk of second chances had softened me up. The man had to be desperate for sales to be out here in this weather. There were numerous items on display. Sunglasses. Books. T-shirts. A pink one had "New York" spelled out in silver sequins. Another had cartoon characters. Several had sports logos. Nothing that appealed to me. Then I saw one in dark gray with the outline of the Empire State Building silkscreened on the front, the least gaudy of anything he had in stock. I could stick it in my dresser drawer, ready as a last-minute gift for a visiting friend. "That one." I pulled cash from my pocket.

"Let me get your change."

"I don't need any change. Consider it a hurricane bonus."

He smiled gratefully as he pocketed the money.

"You made his day," Travis said as I stuffed the T-shirt in my purse.

"He needed the money more than I did." I slipped on the poncho and pulled the hood up over my wet hair. "There's a coffee shop in the next block. Let's hope it's open." We sloshed through inches-deep water. "Corinne was right about rising sea levels. Manhattan will flood once the hurricane gets here. We need to be out of here before that happens."

The coffee shop was packed with customers. I maneuvered toward one of the few empty tables. "You get the coffee. A flat white for me. I'll hold our spot."

I pulled off my poncho and draped it on the back of a chair. Travis returned with the coffees. "It's good to be back. I've been out of the country too long." He eased the lid off his cup. "I wanted to have this discussion over a quiet dinner, with a bottle of good wine. But I was afraid if I didn't get in touch with you now, if I had to wait any longer, I might lose my nerve."

I studied him over the top of my coffee, waiting for him to deliver his pitch.

"The thing is, I feel terrible about everything that's happened between us." He dropped the coffee lid to the table, where it bounced and then rolled to a stop. "I was trying to protect you when I punched your boss, but that turned out all wrong, and it cost you your job. I hoped we could straighten everything out in Switzerland, but then Eva got involved, and it got more complicated." He struggled to pull his words together. "I guess what I'm trying to say is, I've missed you. Is there … is there any way we can start over?"

Was he only interested in me because Eva was thousands of miles away? Because he was lonely, and I was convenient? I wasn't sure I could trust him. "That isn't a good idea. I don't think …"

"You could help me on the book," he said quickly, ignoring my objections. "Give me insight on Corinne."

"You don't need me. You've already signed up Fred. He knows more about her than I do."

"You would have a different perspective." He tried hard to convince me. "Come on, Madeline, you share Corinne's commitment to the environment. You're already working with all those 'save the bay' folks. The book would be so much better if you were part of it."

Did I really want Travis to complicate my life? I could shut this down right now, walk away, never see him again. Or I could give it some time, to see if there was still anything special between us. "What did you do with the T-shirt? The one I gave you in Switzerland?"

"The T-shirt with the ibex? I've still got it."

I set down my coffee. "Get rid of it."

"What?"

"Toss it. Burn it. I don't care."

"Okay," he said slowly. "But why?"

If we were going to do this, I somehow had to get that vision of Eva and her long, bare legs out of my head. To replace it with something more positive, something tied to the city that both Travis and I loved. I pulled the dark gray T-shirt out of my purse. "Take this instead."

He shook it out. "The Empire State building. I like it. Even more than the svelte ibex."

He would probably never wear it—it was more a tourist token than a wardrobe staple for a resident New Yorker. But maybe, on a lazy Sunday morning after an unexpected sleepover, I might get a chance to wear it myself. "Just be careful who you share it with."

He smiled, his dark eyes locked on mine. "No one but you."

The End

ABOUT THE AUTHOR

Frances Aylor is an avid traveler who has paraglided in Switzerland, climbed the Great Wall of China, gone white-water rafting in Costa Rica, and fished for piranha in the Amazon. She likes to incorporate her adventures into her writing.

After an investment career, during which she earned the Chartered Financial Analyst (CFA) designation, she turned her hand to writing mysteries and won the IngramSpark Rising Star Award for her financial thriller, *Money Grab*.

Choosing Guilt, her second novel, was first runner-up for the 2021 Claymore Award. Her short stories appear in *Deadly Southern Charm*, *Malice Domestic: Mystery Most Theatrical*, *Murder by the Glass*, and *Virginia is for Mysteries, vol iii*.

She is a member of Sisters in Crime and International Thriller Writers.

To join her newsletter for travel and financial tips, as well as information about her latest releases, email her at fjaylor@hastingsbaycapital.com.

Website: www.francesaylor.com
Facebook: www.facebook.com/FrancesAylorAuthor
Amazon Author Page: www.amazon.com/Frances-Aylor/e/B071CX9HQ8/
Instagram: www.instagram.com/francesaylorauthor/